A SHARED FIRE - PART I
©2021 ROY KLABIN

ISBN 978-1-66780-107-0

In gratitude to my magnificent wife, loving family,
and all those who most made me who I am…

"At the birth of existence, the Raya awoke as one seed
in which all creation's bounties were held.
Asha, first of the Primals, bound and entwined
fledgling souls into a dark slumber of silence.
All were born, dreamt, and vanished, within the serene
vastness of the Void's black garden.
It was Koba, Birthmother of Chaos, who bloomed
the first fires and illuminated the restful.
Her abundance of new wonders lifted souls from the shadow,
and bathed them in unending light.
This discord between the two Primals tore at the Raya,
manifesting the turmoil which followed.
Shura, Father of Control, was born from the disharmony,
and bore witness to its devastations.
Shura imbued every soul with a shared awareness,
and bonded them in common understanding.
These Primal Forces are woven into the fabric
of the Raya, and all who dwell within it.
The Void, Chaos, and Control."

- Translated Runes from the Ayanakol,
Excerpt of 'Origins of the Raya', Maije Library

PROLOGUE

Of all the sensations Queen Siranna could have noticed, as the dagger pierced her belly, it was the blade's frostiness that first seized her awareness. The cold bite lingered in her thoughts for a faint moment; before her blood warmed the knife and awoke her to the searing agony of its intent.

Siranna was born with the gift of sensing time's colors; yet this assault had come as a complete surprise. Her mouth hung agape in silence. She couldn't yet give breath to her anguish. Her tear-filled gaze followed the hand which madly gripped the blood-drenched handle. Her shattered voice croaked in stunned confusion.

Her brother.

Duke Marash's expression was soaked in a wild cruelty. Siranna couldn't recall ever seeing his eyes so vacant of their familiar kindness. She had noticed a difference in his manner of late. A heavy emptiness surrounded him ever since he returned from his journey to the Raya's furthest reaches. Whatever Marash had brought back with him, a lingering hidden passenger, was now fully unleashed.

No one in the crowd of reveling onlookers or clusters of guards seemed to notice the violence befalling Siranna. They were all mesmerized by the fire puppets above, who enthralled the masses with their delicate entwined sky dances. Even the royal family, who applauded as enthusiastically as anyone, seemed unaware of Siranna's suffering. Her loving husband and five beautiful children. She had to keep them safe.

Siranna raised her trembling hand to her brother's face. She gently pressed her pale white fingers against the thick red hairs of his bearded cheek. She needed to bring him back from whatever chasm was consuming his mind. Marash's eyes flickered with the smallest fragments of hesitation as he met his

2

sister's gaze. There was still some of him left. Siranna struggled to draw breath and form words to reawaken their ancestral bond.

"Brothe…AAAHHHHHH." Siranna shrieked in sudden agony as the Duke wrenched the serrated blade out of her, and with it all her hope. She fell to her knees, weak from the outpouring of her wound. She watched in absolute horror as Marash made quick work of her husband and youngest child.

The crowd erupted into chaotic scatterings of screaming panic. Their frenzied footfalls crashed heavily on the courtyard's icy surface. The royal guards ran up to the Duke, weapons drawn. Marash held another of Siranna's children in his grasp, knife pressed to their frail little throat. The guards hesitated, unsure of their duty amid the dreadfully surreal circumstances.

Siranna collapsed forward, her fingers sinking into the frost. She barely had strength left to look up and witness what was happening. She noticed her blood pooling on the snow. Its vividness slowly turning dark as it thickened in the cold. So much of it. A nearby puddle of blood spread towards hers. She dreaded to consider who it belonged to. The edges of lost life nearly touched, seemingly reaching out to one another in strained hope.

Siranna saw her eldest son, Sal'Haf, kneel in terror before his uncle. Her precious first born. A darkness washed over his expression. His eyes filled with fear and a strange growing vacancy. Siranna had but one last opportunity to save what remained of her family. She drew the balance of her strength and crystalized her thoughts. She recalled a sacred ritual; a wild spell taught to her by the priestesses of her childhood temple. The death whisper. She would hurl her urgent message across the Raya, towards an old friend she hoped would make it here in time. Her fading mind could only form two words: "Save them."

#

3

Wynn wiped the rich honey wine from his lips and let a playful dance pour into the patter of his stride. The bottlers had been ambitious with this season's fermentation, and he was certainly feeling their intended effects. Wynn neared the imposing doors of his King's chambers. He coughed lightly, dispersing the remnant sweetness from his throat. He straightened the most visible creases on his pale robes, and made a semi-sincere attempt to adjust his unkempt mane of vivid orange hair.

Wynn eased the doors open. As always, he was struck by the exquisite beauty of the room's palatial windows; three large ovals were carved out of the thick marble wall which separated the King's chambers from the vast balcony he was so fond of spending his evenings upon. The long terrace overlooked the city of Maije below; a view which offered the King great comfort whenever he chose to survey the tranquility of his realm.

Wynn let his eyes roam over the details of the room. Intricately woven carpets warmed the stone floors. Large cushions and carved chairs lingered with the memories of cherished friends. The King's modest bed was surrounded by pillars of stacked books, seemingly too precious to be forgotten on distant shelves. Wynn explored various pieces of art from faraway lands, their arrangements and form always yielding new discovered details. The King's chambers were meticulous, yet full of life.

A movement caught Wynn's eye. He spotted his King on the far side of the balcony, swaying in a slow rhythmic trance. King Kai's powerful arms moved across the many wooden limbs of his ancient Borosa'am – a complex harp of cross-woven strings and elegantly curved timber. The King applied gentle pressure on various sections of the instrument's frame, curving the soothing sounds beautifully as the moonlight washed over his dark blue skin and black braided hair. He explored the instrument's denser bass strings, for a moment, forming a deep humming crescendo. King Kai tilted his head ever so slightly, methodically working his way along the instrument's three separate spines to pluck at the higher pitched harmony strings.

An array of small vibrant lights floated around King Kai in synchronicity with his song. They formed dancing coils and shifting geometric shapes which orbited his serene concert. The small congregation of luminescent orbs and swirling lines encircled his form, growing brighter as they ebbed and flowed in agreement with his improvised melody. Wynn was momentarily hypnotized by the feast of sensory beauty before him.

Rama, ever present and watching over her King, stood in the center of his balcony. She focused her gaze entirely on his musical ministrations. Wynn stealthily advanced on her from behind. He hoped the soaring notes would conceal the sound of his soft-footed approach. Rama's lower two arms were folded neatly behind her back, each hand firmly gripping the opposing wrist. Her upper two arms crossed over her chest in a tense, restive state. All four limbs rippled with devastatingly dense muscle.

Wynn drew closer, and noticed how much her dark grey skin resembled a refined stone statue: polished and poised. Rama Commanded King Kai's Regal Guard. Her pristine armor and immaculately braided lilac hair belied the countless times she had endured bloodshed and agony in defense of her kingdom. She stood stoically; exuding a dedicated patience.

"Rama..." Wynn thought to himself, "...you have the dignity of an anvil."

He tried to close the gap between them, sneakily floating one furred foot in front of the other. As he got to within a stride of her, Wynn prepared to flick Rama's ear.

"You're welcome to try it, you furry sarkaf." Rama's heavy voice rumbled over her shoulder. "You're overdue for a disciplining."

Wynn's shoulders slumped, dejected by the lost promise of mischief.

"The parade is leaving the city." Wynn informed his formidable friend.

He followed Rama as she strode to the balcony's edge to watch the last of the Moon Festival procession dance and sing their way through the city gates. As mesmerizing as their King's melodies were, there was nothing quite as stunning as the view of Maije's shimmering landscape – especially from their current elevation. The city's brightly painted domes, lush gardens, intricate courtyards, and countless temple fires radiated with harmonious energy. Maije was bathed in a generous layer of moonlight, and it suited her well. Wynn could see Rama exhale the slightest hint of relief as she watched the last cluster of revelers leave her city.

A rare night without incident.

Now that the festival was pouring into the night fields, the real mayhem would no doubt begin. Wynn frowned slightly thinking of the animal dances and firework rides he would miss. But duty demanded his presence here.

"Tea?" Wynn offered halfheartedly, as he walked back into Kai's chambers.

"No, gratitudes." Rama replied, her gaze vigilantly focused on the souls still lingering near Maije's gateway.

"Make her a cup, Wynn," Kai's voice commanded from the balcony, "and one for me."

Rama faced her King and saw he was still in the flow of his ballad. His eyes were closed in deep focus. As Wynn prepared their drinks, Rama's gaze turned to the curtains billowing across the balcony. They were made of Hunter Silk. Layers of hidden enchanted chainmail were stitched into the soft material - capable of sensing and ensnaring any would-be assassins. But in lieu of their normal state of restive diligence, the curtains floated along to Kai's decadent melody. Their protective duties lost in the serenity of song.

"Let them all dance." Rama sighed softly.

Wynn mixed various dried herbs and powders into three ornate cups. He swayed in an overly animated fashion, purposely out of rhythm with Kai's ballad. Laid out before him, the King's collection of containers, bowls, and spoons rested in their reliably ordered arrangement. Wynn rolled his eyes at the intricate precision. He couldn't resist temptation and knocked over a statuette. A sly grin slid across his beard. A single dusting of chaos to feel alive.

As Wynn poured the dense brew, he observed the reflection of his King in the mirror. Kai wore his usual contemplative expression, his thoughts undoubtedly considering the homes below, the endless terrain beyond the city walls, and the depths of his own mind.

Wynn studied Kai's deep cobalt skin. The color reminded him of those final brave moments, before daylight succumbed to the night's devouring darkness. A myriad of bright silver markings were adorned across Kai's arms, chest, and back. Each symbol had been painted onto his body by one of the King's most honored guests or cherished friends. The shimmering ink was forever bonded to his flesh by sacred ritual. The enchanted symbols moved fluidly around each other, a pulsating river of beliefs and blessings swimming across his form. Wynn still found pride in having gifted Kai the only marking to ever make him blush.

"Your tea is ready, *Your Majesty!*" Wynn yelled over his shoulder.

Kai brought his music to an abrupt halt and opened his bright azure eyes. He met Rama's exasperated gaze. She could protect him from any danger, except Wynn's imprudence. King Kai smiled at her warmly. He turned to look at Wynn, who still continued to dance and sway despite the absence of music.

7

Wynn stirred the last of the tea's ingredients with his usual impish manner.

Kai wondered how much longer he would have to endure being teased with that title. Your Majesty. When uttered by Wynn, the slight had two intended targets: Rama's fiercely loyal dedication to protocol, and the reluctance with which Kai had accepted his current mantle.

"In times of war we need men of wisdom; in times of peace we need men of vision."

Kai thought back to his predecessor's words. The burden of their unspoken duty weighed heavily on his mind. He beckoned for Rama to join him and they walked back into his chambers.

"How was the honey wine this season?" Kai inquired of Wynn's back.

Wynn hid a ripple of guilty tension poorly, before resuming an air of confident calm.

"I'll let you know if I get a chance to try some." Wynn's tone was a masterful display of feigned ambiguity.

"I'd be surprised if there's any left..." Rama teased. "...this late in the evening."

Wynn handed them their drinks, his expression never hinting at anything but playful conviction. He flashed Rama a wry toothy grin as they waited for their King to offer his words. They all raised their cups, and gently pressed the three rims together. The trio closed their eyes. Kai allowed a few silent moments to pass before he spoke.

"To Maije, birthmother of souls. She is a lightgiver and rare jewel in our perilous Raya, which too often falls victim to turmoil and darkness. May countless generations know her warmth, and keep her splendor sacred."

"To Maije!" Wynn and Rama cheered in unison.

They drank the hot brew, and felt it move through them. The sinews of their bodies coursed with invigorated sensations.

"So, what do you plan to do with the rest of your evening, Your Majesty?" Wynn asked, as he plucked the cups, cleaned them, and returned them to their place. "Some heavy reading?"

"Aren't monks meant to shave their head?" Kai replied, seated in his heaviest chair.

"Oh, I'm afraid my kind rely on our hair for balance." Wynn chuckled. "You wouldn't want to risk diminishing my agile dexterity." Wynn pirouetted for emphasis.

"Any more than the honey wine already does…" Rama murmured loudly.

"I would, of course, be quite happy to shave my magnificent mane, for you." Wynn taunted. "You need only admit you are filled with a jealous rage, whenever you set eyes upon its indescribable beauty. For we both know, it is only a covetous king who would have a bald and clumsy servant blending their teas."

"Do you want me to beat him, Your Majesty?" Rama offered, as Kai closed his eyes.

"You can both go. I'll take my meditations and rest for the night." Kai said.

"As you please." Rama bowed.

She grabbed Wynn by the arm and dragged him through the door with her. Once outside, she shoved Wynn against the wall before making her way down the corridor.

"I'll be training new guards in the courtyard." Rama chastised him over her shoulder. "Try not to find too much trouble, y'pest!"

"Oh, I'm done for the night. I'll be in my chambers being just as boring as our King." Wynn assured Rama as she strode away. He rubbed his arm where she had gripped him, wondering what foul godling had gifted her such unreasonable strength.

Kai surveyed his bedchambers one more time in preparation for his contemplations. The smooth dark stones of his floor were lightly frosted by the night air. Thick moonbeams danced into the room through his vast windows, and bathed every surface in milky light. Curious winds slithered in from the balcony, fluttering the silk curtains in with them.

Kai closed his eyes. The ebb and flow of his breathing slowed. Eventually, his stillness was absolute. On various surfaces, small flames struggled to escape the remnants of old candles. The unruly fires tugged in one direction, then another, frantic for release from the anchor of their wicks. Desperate to burn the world. But the shackles of their wax prisons were unforgiving. Ultimately, the rebellious flames and pitiless candles consumed each other. Their memories rose in faint wisps of grey smolder.

Kai sat in the darkness, his mind searching the immeasurable. A sudden series of spasms seized his body. His brow furrowed. His inhalations came in sharp and swift. The symbols on his shoulders and arms grew still, sensing a disturbance. One rune in particular began to shake violently. Fragmented words bubbled from the King's lips between hasted inhalations.

Kai's eyes flew open. He yelled out in unbearable anguish. He collapsed to the floor, clutching at his chest. The silver markings flurried around his body in panic. All but one. He heard the crescendo of rapid footsteps approach his chambers. Wynn burst through the door; alarm strewn across his features.

"What happened? Are you hurt?" Wynn asked, approaching Kai.

"Get Rama!" King Kai heaved, choking through his pain. "NOW!"

Wynn's momentary shock quickly washed away as his orders sank in. He ran to the balcony and peered over the edge.

Seven floors below, he could see Rama berating her new recruits in the courtyard.

"RAMA!" Wynn roared, with all the urgency he could muster.

Before he could construct any further explanation, Rama whirled to look up at him. Without a moment's pause she commanded her guards to ascend the staircase to their King's chambers. Instead of following them, Rama vaulted directly onto the palatial walls, climbing up the flat stone by hand at a staggering pace.

Wynn turned and saw Kai rising to stand unsteadily. He ran to help his King, and heard the heavy thud of Rama arriving on the balcony behind him. Kai reached for his wall-mounted war spear, an ancient powerful weapon. The implications made Wynn waver in his stride. Rama slowed behind him as well.

"My King, what…" Rama's confusion was cut short, as she noticed the wild look of dread melting Kai's features.

"Tell the Elders to prepare the Eye for passage. We have to get to the Kahltam Kingdom. The royal family…they…" Kai's voice wavered and trailed off. "Rama, gather your finest fighters! Now!" The King's abrupt tenor was strained with a hollowing fear.

Neither Wynn nor Rama had ever heard their composed ruler use such a tone. The naked panic washed over his face deeply unnerved them. Rama nodded and ran to fetch her warriors. Wynn watched Kai struggle to take slow labored breaths, while leaning against his silver spear. His voice sounded ragged.

"Go, Wynn! We don't have time."

#

Wynn panted as he matched strides with Kai, Rama, and her seven elite guards. The warriors varied in size and form.

Their bodies were covered in a polished blue armor, adorned in ageless runes. Whatever damage these fighters could do with their claws, fangs, or crushing strength was overshadowed by the weapons they carried: fire bows, orb-hammers, fist cannons, and several blades with fiercely sharp edges. Their weapons glowed with the enchanted fire that was infused into the metalwork.

The group ascended an isolated hill overlooking the city. Rama spared a quick glance at the banquet of shimmering lights below. She felt a pang of vulnerability whenever she left Maije. It was the only home she had ever known. But defending the city against threats often meant traveling to faraway realms – where many enemies lurked. She absorbed Maije's beauty. The spherical stone houses, tree-temples, and moving statues looked serene in the moonlight. Rama had done terrible things to keep this jewel, and the souls within it, forever safe.

She regretted none of them.

As they plateaued the hill's crest, the sacred gateway revealed itself. An orb of brilliant blue fire hovered atop a stone courtyard. Its surface rippled with cords of cascading energy. The Sacred Eye. Robed elders circled the holy star, chanting in perfect unison. As Kai's group approached, the fiery storm on the sphere's surface surged with increased intensity.

Kai, Rama, and her guards all raised their right arm, revealing wrists wrapped in ornate silver bracelets. The Eye hummed loudly and spat out cords of energy, which connected to gemstones on each warrior's wristband. The metal cuffs glowed as the Eye's storm simmered back to a calm vibration, radiating a soft cobalt hue. Each bracelet's gemstone burned with a similar brilliance to the Eye's tranquil sea of sapphire light. King Kai turned to Wynn, and forced his features into the assurance he knew his friend longed to see.

"We'll be right back." The King announced loudly. Without hesitation, Kai and his followers strode into the Eye…

...a moment later, an orb of blinding blue light exploded in the snows of a distant land.

King Kai and his guards materialized in place of the fading burst of energy. Their eyes adjusted to the vast frozen wasteland before them.

Immense shards of dark stone pierced the landscape, like shattered mountains erupted in a long-forgotten cataclysm. Violent winds moved rivers of sleet through the air. A frail sun lay obscured behind the thick white veil of an endless storm. The group began their hurried trudge forward through dense snow. Distant haunting wales and pained screams drifted through the howling gales that engulfed them. Rama and her guards formed a protective circle around their King, whose maddening pace was becoming difficult to match.

A sudden respite in the winds cleared the mists ahead of them, revealing the great city of Kahltam. It sat at the base of a vast black mountain; a sophisticated citadel of unflinching ancient towers. The city's flag whipped in the wind above the main gates; a bone white canvas with a shadowy serpent coiled beneath a black star. The group saw several aberrant pillars of smoke rising from various parts of the kingdom.

"The city..." Rama uttered; her lilac eyes filled with horror. "...Kahltam is on fire."

As they approached the city gates, shrieks of agony filled the air around them. Rama could smell burning wood, clothing...and flesh. A small swarm of citizens fled the city and poured out into the wild terrain. Kai grabbed the first one to cross his path, a young woman with bone white skin, crimson hair, and black eyes brimming with panic.

"What happened?" Kai demanded of the bewildered youngling.

"Queen Siranna's brother...the Duke...he slaughtered the royal family. In the courtyard." She stammered, slipping from Kai's loosened grip and running into the howling storm.

Rama and her guards vaulted ahead, sprinting towards Kahltam's central castle. They flew through the streets, passing fleeing civilians and frenzied beasts of burden. Many of the houses were aflame. Out of the corner of her eye, Rama glimpsed a streak of black smoke moving sideways. It slid between the buildings unnaturally. She shook it from her mind, as they approached Kahltam's palace. Kai was the first to arrive. The carnage revealed before them was unspeakable.

The castle's courtyard was a frozen deep lake whose waters had not thawed in centuries. Kai saw dozens of bodies torn asunder, still ablaze, and littered across the icy surface. The corpses were mutilated and bent, as if twisted by hundreds of opposing forces. Some of their faces bore distorted maddening grins and silent howls of terror, which stretched their features until the skin cracked at the edges. Their eyes were open, unmoving, staring off at distant unknown horrors. In the center of the lake, Kai could see the Queen's brother, Duke Marash, encircled by the carcasses of his sister, her husband, and several of their children.

All but one.

The eldest prince knelt before his uncle, his back to Kai and the approaching guards. They stepped towards the scene cautiously. As they neared, Kai saw Marash's face more clearly. It was a mask of rage. His frothing mouth drenched his thick red beard. In his hands he held bloodied knives, warm gore still slithering down their blades. Most alarmingly, Marash floated above the ground - suspended and unable to move. A clear tension gripped his limbs; he groaned as he attempted to free himself from the invisible bondage. Kai gazed down at the kneeling boy.

Prince Sal'Haf. He was only a few seasons shy of adulthood. His youthful face was awash in the blood of his family. The slain bodies of Sal'Haf's siblings and parents formed a crumpled barrier, separating him from his hovering uncle. Even in death, they sought to protect him.

Sal'Haf seemed to stare through them. His breath came in short gasps. His disheveled maroon hair was strewn across his face. Kai looked at the youngling's expression. Sal'Haf's eyes were black stones soaked in tragedy, their gaze flickered across the bloody mayhem.

Kai noticed strange shadows slither across the youngling's trembling skin. Some sank into the ground around him. They formed cracks and tremors in the deep ice, causing the vast lake to moan with movements it hadn't felt in generations. Kai began to understand what had happened. Marash's blades may have killed the royal family, but the sphere of destruction that followed came from the prince. This was beyond any power Kai had seen before.

"You did this..." Kai whispered, staring at all the twisted bodies scattered across the ice.

Marash mumbled gruffly, dropping his knives and desperately trying to reach forward. Not towards Sal'Haf, who held him in suspension, but towards the crown which had rolled from the butchered King's head. Kai looked at the intricately designed coronet resting in the snow. It was a ring of interwoven black marble vines, holding a central white gem in a crest of thorns.

Kai's guards approached Sal'Haf watchfully. They couldn't understand how the youngling held his uncle afloat. A pulsing vibration radiated from Sal'Haf's body. The hum undulated into the air loudly. Rama signaled her guards with a flick of her eyes. They raised their weapons.

"Marash, what have you done?" Kai demanded, in as measured a tone as he could muster.

Kai's eyes lingered on his old friend, Queen Siranna, whose cold hands were outstretched in an unmoving reach for her children. Despite the surrounding slaughter, and the power his nephew seemed to hold over him, Marash's face remained utterly consumed with a wild hunger for the crown. It lay so close to his frantic grasp. The Duke addressed Kai, his mouth bubbling with vile foam and murky blood.

"I have seen the black star!" Marash rasped. "The final embrace is upon us."

Before Kai could respond, he saw Sal'Haf raise his young hand. The Prince appeared unaware of Kai and his guards. He pointed his frail fingers at his uncle. Marash's body began to shudder in dense pulsations. The duke gasped and bared his blood-soaked teeth in agony. His body shook, as wispy black tendrils emerged from his skin. Both Marash and Sal'Haf's emitted a mirrored booming hum, which soon grew deafening. The frozen ground trembled and cracked. Marash gargled, facing Kai with a crooked expression.

"St...stop." Kai urged the youngling. "Please, Prince Sal'Haf. Release him!"

Marash continued to bleed rivers of densely dark smolder. His screams became shrill as the skin on his face fell apart. The Prince's arm was fully extended towards his uncle now, small fingers forming a claw that puppeteered unseen forces. Marash turned his demolished face towards his nephew and smiled savagely.

Before Kai could form any words to calm the Prince, Marash exploded. His shredded limbs fell to the ground. Where the Duke had once stood, a sphere of glowering darkness now pulsed. Kai had never seen anything like it. The black cloud moved differently; at its core darker than any shadow he could imagine, but also absorbing and cloaking itself with the surrounding light. It formed a shimmering layer of energy that enveloped the growing black jewel.

Kai turned to give Rama instructions, but the dark orb surged forward and collided with Sal'Haf's small form. It slithering into the prince's flesh and lifted him into the air.

Sal'Haf's eyes grew wide with awe, anger, and unholy power as the darkness filled him.

Kai saw similar black mists rise from all the ruined bodies around them. Each tendril gleamed with hints of light being consumed on their surface. Rama saw Kahltam's crown rise from the snow, lifted by another snaking dark vine. The currents of shadow all crawled towards Sal'Haf, who began to float above them. A storm of clouds formed to greet the ascending prince.

"Your Majesty..." Rama yelled, not sure what they should be doing.

Kai gripped his spear in one hand, but raised his other gently towards Sal'Haf. He tried to focus, to sense the powers at play. He attempted to insinuate his will into the growing cloud. Prince Sal'Haf spun to face King Kai, sensing his invasive efforts. The youngling's face was a calm mask, white skin and jet-black eyes unflinching. All the shadows rose to join Sal'Haf's violent cyclone of darkness.

Kai met the Prince's gaze. In the chasm of his bottomless expression, Kai felt the foundations of his soul fracture. Something horrifying swam within the youngling's eyes. Thoughts began to splinter in Kai's mind. The silver markings on his body sizzled and burned. The frozen lake cracked with thunderous groans. The storm surrounding Sal'Haf grew vast, a petrifying hurricane that shuddered the ground.

Rama shook the terror from her mind as she saw her King groan in pain.

"Bring him down! Kill the Prince!" She yelled, snapping her guards out of bewilderment.

They raised their weapons and charged before Kai could stop them. The Prince turned to face the threat, a mask of rage contorting his features. His arms pointed down at the guards. Fuming black bolts rained down from the clouds. They crashed into the ice in deafening cracks.

As soon as one touched a guard, it would lift them into the air. The warriors screamed in frenzied pain, as their bodies were violently shaken. In rapid succession, each fighter burst into black smogs; the twig-like remnants of their shriveled carcasses flung back to ground. The tempest continued to grow, feeding into the Prince. Rama could not believe what she was witnessing. The air was filled with screeches of wind and agony. Kai raised his spear.

"No, Kai!" Rama insisted. "You must return to Maije."

He knew she had no intention of joining him; that she would see this battle through. Rama fired her beam cannon at the Prince. The thick mist shrouding Sal'Haf's body absorbed her blasts. He sent several black pillars crashing down around her. Rama dodged them deftly and vaulted around the ice as it began to fragment.

Kai aided her by blasting ferocious arcs of light from his spear. The searing energy cut through the Prince's armor. But this only angered him further. Sal'Haf's vicious gaze returned to Kai once more. Kai heard Rama shriek somewhere in the distance. He looked up and saw her body hurled to the ground. A scream of despair and anguish erupted from Kai's throat. A purity of pain he hadn't felt since childhood.

The lake's thick ice shattered in thunderous cracks, spewing cold waters up in surges. King Kai stumbled, dropping his spear into the depths. The skies were a violent canvas. Sal'Haf floated in a vortex of foul darkness and crackling energy. Kai clung to a bed of jagged ice, and swayed wildly in the churning waters. He saw the Prince's cold eyes focus down on him. They were filled with an unfathomable craving. Depths that knew no limit. The Prince slowly raised a pointed finger and shrieking black swirls descended down on Kai.

The King of Maije had but a moment to press the glowing gemstone on his bracelet, before he closed his eyes and awaited his fate…

ACT I - ENTER THE DREAM

1 – HOME

Mark Pierson sprinted through the frozen forest. His panicked breath matched the stumbling pace of his footfalls. As he pushed through thick unyielding foliage, gnarled branches clawed at his shoulder and twisted him into a tumble. Mark threw his hands forward to stave his fall, but they landed in the slime of a snow-covered puddle. Frosty sludge ensnared his fingers.

"You can't hide forever, Pierson!" Sebastian Martin's voice rang through the tree trunks.

Too close.

Mark picked himself up, wiping the dirty water off his face with his sleeve. He could hear the other boys give chase, dry leaves and thin ice crushed under their boots. The dog barked again, even closer now. Mark quickened his pace. He ducked repeatedly, trying to avoid the storm of dark twigs relentlessly scratching his face and clothes. Mark's blue eyes glistened in pain. He spotted a solitary tree ahead and ran towards it. Mark crouched down behind the wide trunk, gulping for air. Hid in the tree's substantial shadow, he lost the sound of the other boys. Perhaps they had run in the wrong direction?

Mark pictured Sebastian's cruel face; his cold expression always hungered for violence. Sebastian was only a year older than Mark, but abnormally large for a fourteen-year-old. He often enjoyed shoving Mark in the school's corridors or calling him names. But as Sebastian's crowd of sniggering followers grew, so did his sadism. Mark could no longer anticipate what his tormentor was capable of, and he was terrified of finding out.

Mark heard a rustling above him and spotted a grey owl on the tree's biggest branch. She looked down and met Mark's gaze. Her fiery orange eyes seemed filled with disdain for the pitiful creature below her. Mark lowered his head in shame. He hated his circumstances, but he truly loathed himself for being such a coward.

"I'm going to kill you, Jewboy!" Sebastian's distant taunts resounded through the icy air.

Mark closed his eyes. He desperately wished anyone would save him from this misery. He imagined the forest protecting him. He pictured the trees transforming into giant wooden warriors. He thought of beautiful and outlandish creatures emerging from the undergrowth, powerful guardian spirits from distant worlds appearing before him. He longed for a circus army of odd beasts and magical champions to safeguard their boy king.

But he was alone.

That realization, more than anything, fueled his last burst forward. He sprinted as fast as he could for a path to safety. His dread amplified when he heard the footsteps chase behind him. Mark ran faster, and so did they. An intoxicating dizziness soaked his mind. He was watching life happen, almost removed from the terror which engulfed him.

Ahead, Mark could see a sturdy black fence slicing through the tree line. It was his father's fence, and beyond it lay his family's home. Normally, Mark would have enjoyed the final portion of his stroll through the woods by following the tall fence all the way around to the property's main gates. But the dire situation gave him cause to be more ambitious.

Summoning the last of his strength, Mark vaulted as high as he could and crashed against the metallic barrier. He collided about halfway up its imposing height. Mark felt his small fingers slip into the gaps between the cold rods. He clambered upwards in a sloppy panic, dragging his body, backpack, and suffocating fears with him.

Sebastian's dog was the first to arrive at the fence. The vicious mushroom-colored mutt had a wide jaw and wild fur. It reminded Mark of the hyenas he'd seen on television. The beast launched its paws against the metalwork, snarling its slobber-filled mouth. Mark almost lost his frail grip as the partition shook. Mark only had a small section left to climb before he could drop over the other side. He glanced over his shoulder quickly, and saw Sebastian arrive with his cohorts.

Sebastian's jet-black hair framed a chubby face, drenched in sweat from running. His bright hazel eyes locked onto Mark with a predatory craving. The other boys began hurling small rocks, ice balls, and branches at Mark.

"You're such a coward, Pierson!" Sebastian yelled, glaring as Mark slid his body over the fence's peak. He viciously hurled a fist-sized stone that collided against Mark's shoulder. The force of the blow sent Mark hurtling off the railing. He landed on the other side in a heavy thud. The boys all laughed as Mark groaned in pain.

With taunts of "Pyro", "Coward", and "Kike" yelled behind him, Mark slowly rose to his feet. He felt a searing tightness in his lungs as he struggled to recover from the wind being knocked out of him. The wet leaves he landed on hadn't absorbed much of the impact.

"See you soon, chickenshit!" Sebastian shouted at Mark's back.

Mark couldn't muster the courage to look back at their laughing faces, he just wanted to put another day behind him. He began to walk home in a slight limp.

Mark trudged through the last of the forestry, revealing a beautiful clearing of manicured frost-tipped lawns. The estate's flower gardens stood bare; perennial roots and bulbs hidden under dark soils, waiting for warmer seasons to bloom. Sporadic polished statues were littered across the grounds, their sculpted bodies posed against the chilled air.

Ahead of him, Mark saw a lavish and imposing home. It was a three-storied mansion of resilient stone, colossal pillars, and ornate windows. After two years of construction, it had been a great source of pride for Mark's father. But for all the envy it elicited in so many of his classmates, Mark had only ever felt embarrassed by it.

Mark wanted to avoid being seen until he could clean himself up. He walked around to the south-facing side of the manor, hoping to sneak in through his father's office. He looked out onto the grounds of the Pierson estate – forty acres of private woodlands with a small lake in the middle. The property line connected to the public forest Mark walked through from school every afternoon. A forest divided by the metal fence he had just scrambled over.

The barrier supposedly protected him, and yet was no doubt the source of many people's anger towards his family. Mark was embarrassed by the overstated security measures, and how they defiled the surrounding nature with their industrialized precision. But his father had insisted they be installed, and Arthur Pierson was rarely known to change his mind. *They keep us safe*. Mark heard his father's adamant voice echo in his mind. But the fence had only ever made Mark feel trapped, and terribly alone.

Lost in his reflective daze, Mark turned a corner and came face to face with his grief. Two elegantly carved marble gravestones rested side by side, in a small enclosed garden. They were surrounded by evergreen plants and adorned with glass candle holders. The faces of both headstones were engraved with stars of David. Beneath the symbols, Mark read the names of his mother, Alice, and his younger sister, Isabelle.

It had been over a year since their deaths. The absence still tore at his insides with unwavering sorrow. After all, it was his fault they were gone. Mark remembered his mother's voice on the phone. She had always been an anxious driver. But on that day, she was especially nervous. He could still hear her urgent promise. She was coming. On her way, to save him.

Mark pushed the memory from his mind. It was too much. He couldn't feel all of it again, not today. He sighed heavily, and tried to think of more pleasant recollections. He looked at the neglected glass conservatory, where his mother had housed her most precious flowers. He remembered Isabelle running around inside, playfully screaming at the top of her lungs as she sprinted between the rows of blooming petals. Mark's mother would pretend not to notice her chestnut haired daughter shrieking for attention. It was their mischievous dance, pitting loving patience against enthusiastic mayhem. They had the same hair, same eyes, same playful smile.

A cold gust of wind sliced across Mark's wet features, mixing his tears with the muddy water stains. The warm recollection faded from his thoughts. He looked at the conservatory entrance, and read the sign that hung above the glass doors.

"The dream is the seed. The work is the water."

Mark's mother had always been fond of incorporating newfound wisdoms and maxims into the home's décor: statuettes with quotes carved into their base, black and white photographs of sage street graffiti mottos, small pillows embroidered with rhyming adages, and an ever-amassing collection of dog-eared books filled with highlighter fluid drenched pages. Mark still hoped he would find new discoveries of her quote collection. Knowledgeable whispers that had once pleased his mother's imagination, hidden in the house somewhere.

Mark moved cautiously as he approached the outer doors of his father's office. He turned the handle and pulled the glass partition open, slipping in on the soiled tips of his muddy shoes. It was only once he was inside that he realized several other people were in the room as well.

Mr. Pierson's vast office was a stadium of refinement. Each polished detail exuded an air of focused consideration. The carved marble fireplace, the towering crescent balcony of meticulous book shelves, and Persian carpets lingering with the faint aromas of their homeland, all served to aggrandize anyone who stood within the space.

Mark saw four men of varying ages fill the two large leather sofas in the room's center. Their immaculate suits spoke to their influential stature in the community. They had all turned to face Mark as he made his entrance, and stared curiously at the wide-eyed disheveled boy. Mark scanned the room, drowning in trepidation. Eventually he met his father's gaze.

Arthur Pierson leaned against his oak desk, facing the other men. He held a piece of paper he had clearly been reading before the interruption. Mr. Pierson's black suit was much finer than the men in his company, though its neglected winkles were painfully apparent. His wire rimmed glasses encircled a pair of vivid green eyes which moved with a hawk's precision; though they were undeniably drenched with heavy sorrow.

"Is this the son we've heard so much about, Arthur?" A portly man inquired cheerfully, his eyebrows raised and his voice soaked in sympathy.

Mr. Pierson's eyes fell in disappointment at seeing his only child covered in mud, scratches, and sweat. He looked like he was about to introduce him, but Mark hurriedly strode towards the exit.

"I'm sorry, please excuse my interruption." Mark mumbled, as he walked across the room, pulled open the door, and eased it shut behind him.

As he climbed the stairs to his room, Mark overheard his father continue his meeting.

"I apologize for my son. As I was saying, this city has lost half its labor force due to recent closures. Perhaps if we pour our resources into a diverse development opportunity, we can capitalize on this devastated econo…"

Mark closed his door.

Before he came down to dinner, Mark spent a while in the bathroom scrubbing the mud and memories off his body. He wasn't going to lie about his day, he only hoped his father wouldn't ask. He could barely stomach the feeling of disappointing him anymore. There was a heavy twisting discomfort that seemed to always live in Mark's belly. He could feel the heaviness surrounding his father's mood, trapping them both in a prison of sorrow.

As he made his way down the corridor, he heard voices from the dining room below. Mark approached the crest of the staircase, and crouched low to get a discrete view. He saw that his father was joined by Rabbi Levin, from their former synagogue. From Mark's vantage point, he could see their faces and hear their discussion. But they would have to crane their necks upwards to notice him.

Rabbi Levin was a short man, with a square jaw and kind eyes. His silver beard was neatly trimmed, and always glittered with flecks of reflected light. Mr. Pierson's hair, which had always been so methodically combed over the years, had rough trenches formed by his constantly agitated fingers. The coloration grew increasingly salt and pepper, with new streaks of grey gaining territory each month. Mark could see the Rabbi's posture adjust as he exhaled in thoughtful patience.

"Arthur, I want to thank you for your generous contribution to the synagogue." Rabbi Levin began, his tone measured and warm. "I can't tell you how much it means to us. But if I may be presumptuous…you need only ask, if you ever just want to talk."

Mr. Pierson smiled weakly. He appreciated the candor and consideration.

"I'm not sure I can maintain the focus and motivation I need to succeed anymore, Rabbi." Mr. Pierson's voice was dry, and heavy. "I've got a lot of people relying on the next few decisions I make, but my head just isn't…there."

Rabbi Levin let the weight of the moment fade through the air before responding.

"If I can ask something directly, Arthur…at this point, how would you define success?"

Arthur's brow furrowed at the question, annoyed by its rhetorical nature.

"You are a wildly accomplished man." Rabbi Levin continued. "You've built an empire, and you haven't lifted your foot off the accelerator for even a moment. It's barely been a year since Alice and Isabelle passed. Perhaps work shouldn't be your priority right now?"

"Work is all I have…" Mr. Pierson responded curtly. An awkward coldness cut through the room. Mr. Pierson's features softened in contrition. "…to distract me from the memories. I can't sit in this pain all day, Rabbi. It's breaking me."

"We cannot run from our pains, Arthur. Only feel them, and grow around them." Rabbi Levin saw he wasn't swaying his friend's temperament. "Perhaps you can find strength in your role as a father?"

Mr. Pierson's face barely registered a reaction, beyond the soft raising of his eyebrows.

"Your community could also benefit from your presence, in ways beyond your industrial talents. Your colleagues revere you, I doubt any of them would fault you taking some time to yourself, to connect with your neighbors and friends. Even our shul would welcome your presence, if you chose to share some of your life within our walls. You could sit in the back row, and listen to my boring sermons!" Rabbi Levin offered with a genuine smile.

"She was the love of my life, Rabbi." Mr. Pierson said, raising his eyes to meet the Rabbi's gaze. "Do you know what it's like to share your life with someone so completely?"

27

"Twenty-seven years," Rabbi Levin nodded, placing his hand on Arthur's in heartfelt sympathy. "and each day is a blessing. I cannot fathom your loss."

"And Isabelle..." Mr. Pierson's voice cracked slightly. "...she was pure light."

A heavy silence drowned them.

"I know you weren't as bonded to your faith as Alice..." Rabbi Levin ventured.

"I always appreciated what the synagogue meant to her, Rabbi. I really did." Mr. Pierson interjected. "Your lectures brought her a great deal of serenity."

"But *you* never felt the word of your creator in my words." Rabbi Levin smiled, waving a finger skywards. "It's ok, my ego is not so fragile. Yet, despite your lack of faith...here I am."

"Your presence, it...helps me remember her." Mr. Pierson sighed. "All the things she loved in life. If I'm honest, I never knew God before meeting her. She was as close as I've come to seeing the beauty of creation. Every moment with her was precious. And our children."

"All the more reason to find comfort in your connection with Mark. This is a pain you both share. A loss you both feel." Rabbi Levin said firmly, pushing through Arthur's thoughts.

A ripple of conflicting emotions fought across Arthur's features. Flashes of bitterness, the fragility of grief, and heavy guilt.

"He's being bullied at school again, getting pushed around like he was at Berrington." Mr. Pierson said. "He needs to learn to stand up for himself. To take responsibility."

"Give him time, Arthur." Rabbi Levin insisted gently. "These are formative years, hard enough to find ourselves and nurture our bonds when we're that young – even without such heavy loss clouding our hearts."

Mark didn't want to hear what his father might say next. He descended the stairs, noisily. Rabbi Levin turned to face Mark, and offered a cheerful greeting.

"Hi, Mark. Your father invited me to join you for dinner today. How have you been?"

"Nice to see you, Rabbi." Mark smiled softly.

Mr. Pierson stared at the food on his plate. He cut a precise measure of carrot, then took a restrained breath instead of raising the food to his mouth. The rabbi noticed his sigh, and intercepted the moment.

"How's life at school treating you, Mark? How are your friends, Elise and Bobby?"

"The school asked them to show a new girl around," Mark explained, not raising his eyes from his food. "Her name is Naiyana. She's from Thailand originally. Seems really nice."

"That's lovely." Rabbi Levin said, tilting his head and trying to establish eye contact with Mark. "Always a mitzvah to make an outsider feel welcome."

As he was listening to the Rabbi, Mark dared a glance at his father's face. He could see the anxiety layered under his expression. His lips moved ever so slightly, rehearsing words that were forming in his mind. Mark knew his father was concerned about the ongoing conflicts with Sebastian. First the accident, now this. He felt terrible guilt for causing his father more distress.

"Mark, we need to talk about today." Mr. Pierson stated impatiently.

"I'm sorry I interrupted your meeting, Dad." Mark said flatly, trying to meet his father's gaze. He noticed Rabbi Levin sigh across the table.

"No son, that's not it." Mr. Pierson continued, undeterred by the fog of tension filling the room. "Why do you keep allowing these boys to torment you? We talked about this."

Mr. Pierson's voice drifted with his last sentence, the weight of the memories draining his strength.

Mark breathed slowly, trying to calm his anxiety. He could see the conversation ahead of him unfold in his mind. He didn't want to cry.

"Sebastian had five friends with him today. And a dog." Mark explained.

"A dog!" Rabbi Levin exclaimed. "Maybe this is a matter for the school administration?"

"No," Mark mumbled dejectedly. "please, don't do that."

"That won't make his life easier, Rabbi. Mark has to resolve this!" Mr. Pierson asserted.

"Well..." Rabbi Levin treaded softly. "...there is certainly a virtue in being righteous and brave. And we mustn't allow ourselves to suffer injustices. But six boys and a dog? That just seems a little barbaric."

"He'll only have to confront the leader. It's the way of the world." Mr. Pierson stated decisively. "Mark has to learn to stand up for himself. To be his own man."

"Perhaps. But *Vengeance is mine, sayeth the lord.*" Rabbi Levin offered cautiously.

"Is there no righteousness in defending ourselves, Rabbi? Must we always be victims?" Mr. Pierson asked curtly. "Is that what God has chosen us for? To suffer while he watches?"

Mark saw the pain in his father's eyes, and felt his own features wince in shame. Mark's familiar detachment engulfed his senses. He watched the conversation unfold before him. His father's stern concerns, the Rabbi's tender assurances. Words seeped out of their mouths, filled with strange currents that flowed through the room. The hidden forces hunted their way across the dining table, searching for Mark's body. Perhaps if he just sat still, they would glide over him. Mark could feel the weight of the day. The food in his mouth had no flavor.

"You need to show this Sebastian that he can't push you around." Mr. Pierson said, addressing Mark directly. "Fight back. That's the only language bullies understand. They pick on people they see as weak, because they're weak themselves."

Mr. Pierson suddenly noticed the rigid deference in Mark and Rabbi Levin's expressions, as they absorbed his anger. They had no intention of challenging his pain. The overt display of pity embarrassed him. Mr. Pierson's eyes simmered with tears.

"I won't always be here, Mark." Mr. Pierson finally said, before he occupied his mouth with the remainder of his meal.

Mark felt the coldness of his father's thoughts. The bitterness. He sensed the specter of death that loomed over them, swimming in the room, and clawing at their hearts. Even though he had never said it, Mark was sure his father blamed him for the accident. Why wouldn't he? And now Mark's inability to face his circumstances was giving his father something else to fret about.

Mark wanted to take care of his father, more than anything. To heal his wounds. To give him the assurances he needed. But in a chilling realization, Mark recognized he would always be the source of his father's pain. Mark's thoughts crystalized onto a brittle conclusion. Maybe he should just do what his father asked. Maybe he if fought Sebastian, he'd bring his father a slight semblance of pride again. The gesture would be a small price to pay, if it gave his father hope.

Rabbi Levin stared at Mark's crestfallen face. He took a measured breath.

"This is your house, Arthur. So perhaps it's not my place to say. But in my opinion violence only begets more violence. Who's to say this Sebastian boy hasn't suffered some sort of abuse himself? Perhaps he's lashing out. I don't see how punching him is going to fix anything." Rabbi Levin turned to Mark with a gentle tone. "Have you tried talking to him?"

31

Mark smiled weakly. He had tried talking to Sebastian on several occasions, but hadn't yet managed to find the right words to avoid a beating. Whatever storm of thoughts had consumed Mr. Pierson's mind, had become too much for him to bear in the company of others. He exhaled as much of the weight out of his chest as he could, wiped his mouth with his napkin, and gently placed it on the table.

"I'm sorry," Mr. Pierson said flatly, after he composed himself. "I think it's best I go to my office for a while. I didn't mean to upset anyone. Please enjoy the rest of your dinner."

Arthur stood, and left before anyone could respond.

Mark had stopped eating. He could feel the Rabbi observing him.

"I'm sorry, Mark." Rabbi Levin said heavily. "These are difficult times for both of you. You know, your mother and I were very close. She often spoke about how much she loved you."

Mark smiled weakly.

"Between you and me, I don't think you're to blame for what happened at Berrington. Those boys coerced you. You couldn't have fully appreciated the consequences at the time. Or what happened after…"

Mark looked up at the Rabbi. His eyes were filled with tears, his jaw clenched in a desperate attempt to keep his misery buried in his chest.

"The pain we're given is the pain we pass on…" Rabbi Levin continued, easing himself into a spiritualist's soft tenor. "…unless we find a way to heal, we only flow our anguish onwards. A river of misery. Your father doesn't mean to lash out at you." Rabbi Levin assured. "You're both suffering so much. It's hard to connect with one another when we're in pain. Even though that's when we need each other most!"

Mark's thoughts drifted to the police report he had read on his father's desk one night. It hadn't concluded definitively whether his mother was to blame for the accident, or if it was the other driver. But Mark knew the truth.

"It was my fault, Rabbi Levin." Mark said, barely containing his tears. "I'm the reason he's so sad. I'm the reason my mom and sister..."

"No, you're not." Rabbi Levin insisted. "None of this is your fault, Mark. Don't ever think that. It was an accident."

Mark wasn't really listening. His thoughts poured out of him.

"I don't blame him for being angry. He should be." Mark stumbled through his words. "It's only me left now, and I keep causing more...I owe him some..."

"Mark..." Rabbi Levin's voice was drenched in pity. "...that's not how family works. Whatever your dad is feeling, deep down he only wants you to be happy. He is afraid, like you, that he'll lose you. In some way or another, you're both afraid of more loss. More pain. Because of how much you miss your mother and sister. They were both such incredible beacons of light." Rabbi Levin paused on a series of fond recollections. "The void that their deaths have left in you...Mark, absence can be a form of presence. Do you understand? That sadness, that longing...it's a contrast to the light that should fill our hearts."

Rabbi Levin could see Mark considering his words.

"This fear and anguish you're both bearing, it's clouding your minds. It makes you forget that you still have each other. That you should cherish each other. You're both going to have to work through this, in your own ways, so you can find each other again. To make a bridge between your two islands."

Mark calmed his breathing, taking in the sweet man's well-intentioned advice. The words were introspective and philosophical, but they didn't really offer any specific guidance on an approach. Mark's thoughts returned to the same cold conclusion he had earlier.

"How do I do that, Rabbi?" Mark asked. "How do I show him that I love him, and want to do better? That he can trust me? Should I fight Sebastian?"

The weight of the conversation shifted Rabbi Levin's body into an uneasy posture. He had encroached onto ground he had hoped to avoid. He held his tongue for a pensive moment, then offered his measured thoughts.

"I don't ever recommend violence, Mark. Simply because it's not in my nature, and I believe that anyone can be reached with the light of our Creator's glory. But Jews have often suffered as a result of their hope and optimism. My parents had memories from their time in the camps that were never spoken aloud in our home. Pains that haunted them till their last days, and lingered behind every smile they tried to form."

Rabbi Levin let the conflicted thoughts uncoil in his mind.

"Whether you fight Sebastian or not is up to you. But don't do it thinking it will fix things between you and your father. That's not what he truly wants. He's just worried about you, and he wants to be able to quell that concern. He wants to see you as your own person, capable of making your own decisions. You could do such great things, Mark. You're a very bright boy. You could change the world...but not if you let others define you, and push you around. No one will live this precious life of yours, but you. That includes your father. What you do will shape the man you grow up to be. If you find your courage, that quality will stay in your heart for the rest of your life. But if you keep running away, those are the moments that will haunt you. We have to learn to face life's cruelty and hardship, without becoming cruel ourselves. We have to face our fears, or they'll always rule over us. Do you understand, Mark?"

Mark had listened to the Rabbi's words politely, and finally felt a silence fill the room again. There was a clarity in the emptiness. He looked up at Rabbi Levin's face. Mark thanked him for his patient guidance, then excused himself and went back upstairs. He saw the Rabbi make his way to his father's office, hoping to offer more advice before his departure.

Mark closed his door behind him. He took in the details of his room. His mother had chosen the elegantly designed bed and furniture, and the windows looked out onto his father's vast estate. The only things that truly felt his own, were the many books strewn across every available surface. He picked up one he had borrowed from the school library, and plopped himself down in bed.

The book's cover displayed an illustration of a small group of silver owls. They were surrounded by, and fighting against, a threatening horde of menacing red bats. Below them, a fantastical kingdom sat in the middle of a dense lush forest. Mark's expression softened and glowed as he scanned the pages. A weak smile crept across his face. A determined flicker shone in his eyes as he followed along in the adventures. He felt a serene sense of presence wash over him, as he pictured himself soaring through the air alongside his winged heroes.

A memory of his mother reading to him and his sister drifted into his awareness. They were all huddled on this very same bed. He couldn't recall which novel she had in her hands at the time, but he remembered noticing her own book resting on his bed side table. Something she was hoping to return to after Isabelle and him fell asleep. Mark interrupted his mother to make a curious inquiry.

"What's your book about?" Mark had asked, gesturing at her novel.

The question had immediately sparked Isabelle's curiosity too, and she lifted herself out of her embrace with Mark to dramatically peek at the cover.

"Yeah, what's yours about?" Isabelle added, her theatrical pout was laced with far too much mischief for a ten-year-old.

Alice looked at her children with a smile, "Might be a bit boring for you two."

They both stiffened with a surge of intrigue. Without speaking, Mark and Isabelle firmed their features into a playfully defiant '*try me*' impression. Alice picked up her book, opened it on her folded page, and resumed where she had left off. She read aloud in her lyrical voice:

"It is a rare thing to find your personal truths within mountaintop monasteries. Yet despite the odds, countless swarms of wide-eyed wanderers ascend the great ancient slopes every year. I wonder, how often will the musings of a meditating monk truly unearth something relevant to their story? For those seeking to gain the esoteric knowledge that our universe is grand, that our lives are fleeting rarities, and that being present is the key to serenity…one might consider simply cracking open a fortune cookie instead. The coils which tether each of our soul's turmoil are rooted deeper, in the dark soils of our personal histories. You could listen to preachers panhandle their parishes for meager donations, while pontificating recycled verses. You could listen to politicians bluster moral platitudes at people they have no intention of ever truly leading. Or, you can listen to those around you. Your truest tribe. Those who've lived their lives besides you, who've shared in your joys and your pains. The people who've breathed from the same air, drank from the same rivers, and aspired to the same hopes. Those who helped cultivate the branches of your complexity, and share the closest roots in the hidden depths of our celestial consciousness. With them, you'll find your inner truths. It is only ever with them that you will discover your most relevant wisdoms, spiritual salvations, and firmest paths in life."

Alice placed the book down on the bedside table and mimicked her children's defiant gaze, eyebrows raised and waiting to hear their thoughts.

"Boring!" Isabelle giggled with a dismissive sigh, as she collapsed back on the bed.

But something within the words had captured Mark's attention.

"So, it's saying…you should always come home?" Mark proposed, semi-confidently.

Alice chuckled adoringly, her eyes glistening with pride.

"Yes." She said, gently kissing Mark on his forehead. "And don't ever forget it!"

Mark's mind was still drifting between his own book and the warm memories, when he heard his father's footsteps in the corridor outside. He spun to his side so his back was facing the door. Mr. Pierson knocked twice and entered the room without waiting for a response. He saw his son pretending to be asleep and furrowed his brow. He walked over to the bed, sat down on the mattress, and placed a gentle hand on Mark's shoulder.

"I…I don't know what to say, Son. Things will get better in time." Arthur offered, the fatigue of a heavy day weighing him down. "I'm sorry I push you too hard. I'm trying to show you…well, that you're responsible for the person you're going to be. You have to be strong, and wise, and determined if you want to become your best self."

Seeing no visible response from Mark, Mr. Pierson turned and looked at the bedside table. He saw the cover of Mark's book. His eyes squinted at the overly lavish illustrations.

"At some point we all have to grow up, Mark. Maybe it's time to focus more on reality and less on fantasies?" Mr. Pierson cloaked the scrutiny of his suggestion with a semi-light tone.

His son's stillness seemed as much of a response as he was going to get this evening. He sighed and rose to leave. As he reached the door he heard Mark speak, his back still turned.

"I'm sorry, Dad. I've been…" Mark spoke softly, his lower lip trembling slightly. "…weak. I promise, I'm going to stand up to Sebastian. Tomorrow."

Arthur felt a cold rush of guilt wash over him. He thought of running to his son, comforting him and assuring him he loved him. But he considered how these years would lay a foundation for the man Mark would become. He swallowed a dry throat and chose to press on.

"Goodnight, Mark." Mr. Pierson said tenderly. He turned off the room's main lights, left Mark under the glow of his bedside lamp, and closed the door behind him. "Sleep well."

Mark stared at the wall and thought about his life. He had been feeling increasingly trapped, by his circumstances and his shortcomings. He wished he was braver, like the characters in his books. As he lost himself in thought, Mark's breathing began to slow. He felt the tension leave his body, helping to forget the day it had endured. A slow calm crept into his sore muscles, giving him a glimmer of hope that he might sleep soundly tonight. The peace was shattered by an intrusive vibration from his bedside. He turned to see a text on his phone from his friend Elise:

"Finished the owl book yet? Good as you hoped? Tell me tomorrow. G'night bird boy."

Mark smiled softly. Elise was an expert at having conversations with herself. He didn't need to reply. He closed his eyes and felt the stillness of a restful sleep begin to cradle him.

Elise Mokette giggled to herself as she saw the text "read" confirmation pop up on her screen. Her self-congratulating laughter was interrupted by a sudden burp that vaulted itself through her gullet. She took another sip from the soda can beside her bed and let her vibrant emerald eyes dance across her room looking for a new distraction.

Elise admired the chaos of her space: posters of various bands, a large collection of small pets roaming their terrariums and cages, half-finished drawings on scraps of paper littering the floor, and explosions of clothes forming their own color fountains in every corner.

Elise jumped off her bed to make her feeding rounds, sprinkling some pellets for the gerbils, throwing crickets in for the lizards, and a few dry flakes for the fish. An errant cricket bounced around the room and caught her eye. Elise turned to face it with a mock predatory glare. The hunt was on. She crouched down low, ready to leap at the first opportunity, when her older sister came barging into the room.

"Holy crap, Elise. This place is a pigsty!" Sara exclaimed in genuine disgust.

The contrast between the two sisters couldn't be more apparent. Sara's refined form-fitting clothing, chic French twist hairdo, and stylish make up was a defiant polished presence in Elise's frenzied abode. Elise turned to face her sister, angry at having lost sight of her bouncy prey. Her thick unruly red curls hung like a wild mop around her shoulders, her baggy jeans and hoodie draped off her body, proudly airing a two-day old odor.

"Maybe if you cleaned up once in a while, you wouldn't stink so bad all the time." Sara remarked in a snide sugary voice.

"Maybe if you weren't such a bitch people wouldn't talk about you behind your back all the time!" Elise retorted, without blinking an eye.

The comment clearly struck a nerve, but before Sara could utter another word Elise hissed at her in her best impression of an alley cat. To add absurdity to insult, Elise made a face that looked like she was trying to bite her own ear and stuck her tongue out mockingly.

"You're such a stupid weirdo." Sara said, rolling her eyes and turning around. "Mom said come down for dinner. Now!" She added over her shoulder, before slamming the door shut.

Elise smiled victoriously, before realizing her room was now sealed and the anxiety of being clustered into a closed space began to percolate through her mind. She hurriedly skipped to the door, and pried it open until a decent gap left it comfortably ajar. For all her mother's beliefs in mysticism, spirituality, and horrid tasting teas, nothing had ever managed to reduce Elise's fear of small spaces.

Elise sauntered over to her desk, and plopped herself down in a chair. She resumed a detailed sketch of a dragon she'd been working on for some time. She dragged the pencil across the page in deft and erratic strokes alike, adding muscle, claws, and expansive wings. Elise's obsessions with dragons was likely the only facet of her personality she didn't broadcast loudly. Kids at school were familiar with her favorite dragon print hoodie. But no one would guess she had matching dragon themed pillow cases, or that her walls were adorned with fantasy posters of dragons fighting mid-flight and billowing carpets of fire over helpless terrains.

As Elise finalized the details on her mythical beast, she imagined what potential career would allow her to explore the lore of these powerful creatures. Maybe she'd be a paleontologist, who specialized in looking for large dragon bones deep in the ground of faraway lands. She would be known as the *Dragon Queen* in her field, while all the other nerds searched for their boring dinosaurs. Elise smiled at her stream of fantastical thoughts. She decided to finish her sketch later, and folded the paper into her biology book. She was eager for tomorrow's class; certain she would learn about new exotic species. Classes…that reminded her. Elise jumped on her bed to construct her next abusive text.

"Bobby! Grab Naiyana after class tomorrow for lunch. Don't be a flakey dick :)"

Bobby Kendell looked at his phone and sighed. He replied "K" just to ensure he didn't get five more messages from his annoying friend. He resumed looking in the bathroom mirror, and a familiar sense of displacement washed over him. A girl in class had told him she liked the color of his "caramel skin." The compliment had confused him. The initial indignation at being reduced to his race brought up old wounds and echoed taunts. But the unfamiliar gesture of affection from a pretty girl added a fledgling voice in the chorus of his mind that made him question his initial gut reaction.

Bobby tilted his jaw in his reflection, as he examined the skin on his face and hands. The distinctive chestnut tone was a reminder of his uniqueness, even within his own home. His father and brother Ethan both shared a rich umber coloration, originating from Mr. Kendell's Nigerian heritage. Meanwhile, Bobby's mother and his oldest brother Kauri both displayed the Polynesian complexions of Mrs. Kendell's Māori lineage. Bobby's singular composition had increasingly become the focal point of his burgeoning angst.

Bobby didn't feel like he fit in anywhere. Everyone else seemed so certain about their life. About their identity, choices, dreams, and sense of belonging. Or at least they were all very good at pretending. To Bobby, everyone's smiling confidence and cheer felt nauseatingly insincere. He wondered how people found the energy to care so much. He sighed as he turned off the lights and walked out.

Bobby heard strange noises from the living room, and sauntered that way. He peered around the corner, and saw his brother Kauri practicing a traditional New Zealand Haka – a war dance which called upon ancient ancestors for strength and courage. Bobby's mother Maia and his Uncle Nikau smiled in admiration as they watched Kauri yell and stomp his way through the ancient ritual.

Kauri planned on performing the Haka at his next track meet, to both surge his confidence and shake his competitors' poise. Kauri wore a mask of absolute determination, his large muscles bulged and carved through the air in agile swings. He finished the routine with a powerful exhalation, his eyes bulged and tongue stuck out.

Bobby couldn't help but snort at his brother's exaggerated features. As if their ancestors would be watching this lame display. Bobby realized his snort was a little louder than intended. His mother, uncle, and brother all stared at him.

"Why you spying on us, little weirdo?" Kauri taunted, between heavy breaths.

"Be nice to your brother, Kauri." Mrs. Kendell mediated half-heartedly. "And Bobby, please don't ever disrespect the Haka. Your brother is doing a great job honoring our ancestors."

"Maybe you could try learning our history sometime!" Uncle Nikau added.

"Sure, some day." Bobby replied in a sullen tone, as he turned to leave.

He felt his family shake their heads in disappointment. But Bobby didn't know how to fake enthusiasm. He genuinely didn't want to trudge and scream in a language he barely understood, to impress dead relatives he didn't even believe were watching him. Wasn't it better to just be honest?

Bobby made his way outside to get some air. He flipped his hoodie over his head to block the night's chill. He noticed errant sparks and noises coming from the open garage door. He went to investigate. Bobby strode to the edge of the entrance and peered in. He could see his other brother Ethan and his father leaning over a complex robotics project. They were welding two segments of metal together. Even though they both wore heavy safety masks, Bobby could tell his father was beaming with pride.

Bobby heard a yelp from beside him and saw the family's new puppy Shane stare up at him. He scooped up the young mutt and brought him to the warmth of his chest. Ethan stopped soldering as soon as he saw his young brother. Ronnie Kendell lifted his mask up to greet Bobby.

"Hey Son, did you need help with something?" Mr. Kendell asked.

He quickly realized the implication of his question from Bobby's annoyed look, and made a stumbling attempt at recovery. "Wanna help us with this? You could hold one of the limbs while Ethan solders?"

Bobby pretended not to hear the contrition in his father's tone.

"No that's ok, Dad, you guys do your thing. I'm gonna take Shane for a quick ride around the block." Bobby said, lifting the puppy and turning his back on the conversation. "Don't worry, I'll flip all the bike lights on."

Bobby could hear his father sigh as he got on his bike. He placed Shane inside his hoodie, and zipped it closed – leaving enough space for the puppy to wiggle his head through a snug opening near Bobby's neck. Bobby pedaled fast and cycled up the incline of his quiet street. He was going to explore until he found something that grabbed his attention, or helped him forget his frustrations. His mother and father were clearly too busy with the warrior athlete and robotics nerd to deal with him. On some level Bobby knew they were just encouraging his brothers' interests, but he couldn't help feel neglected by his parents just because he hadn't found his own passion yet.

Shane panted happily as he stared out at the world in front of them. Bobby could feel the puppy's hot breath on his chin, as he turned down various narrow streets of the suburban neighborhood. Bobby slowed down to look through the windows of people's houses, peering at the families going about their evenings. He felt like a ghost, gliding through the streets and observing the world's inhabitants. He judged the lazy fathers passed out on their living room sofas, ignoring their kids. He tried to see what one cheerful mother was cooking through a large set of kitchen windows. He made up a story about the kids who had a two-level treehouse, imaging they grew up in a forest and hadn't gotten used to regular human homes yet.

Eventually, he got to Naiyana's block and cycled up to her house. Bobby picked up a few pebbles, and started pelting them against the window. Naiyana opened it after the third hit. She wore a calm inquisitive expression.

"Meet us in the cafeteria after 3rd period!" Bobby whispered loudly. "We'll eat with Elise and Mark."

"Okay." Naiyana replied, adding a slight head nod.

Bobby got back on his bike and cycled home.

Naiyana Tanaka closed her window and returned to her desk. She only needed ten more minutes to finish her homework. Describing her home life in essay form had initially been an elusive task; she hadn't known which details to focus on. But she found that sticking to the facts alone gave her enough structure to flesh out two pages. She reviewed what she'd written so far: her father was Japanese and worked for a large tech company, which required him to travel a lot. That was how he had met Naiyana's mother, who lived in Thailand at the time. Naiyana's mother used to be a prominent chef in Bangkok with a renowned restaurant. It was very hard for her to leave Thailand, but Naiyana's father had a big work opportunity in America, so they agreed to make the move. Naiyana had now lived in America for almost two years, and moved houses a total of three times. Her parents promised this house would be their home for a while.

Naiyana stopped reading her essay. She thought about it, and realized nothing quite felt like home to her yet. The town, the house, the kids at school…everything was still too new. She shrugged and kept reading her summary: Naiyana's mother had recently started working with some local farms to open a new restaurant in town. It made her happy, but also very busy. With Naiyana's father still traveling for work, she was mostly being raised by her grandmother, Buppha. Her grandmother regularly talked about their Thai heritage and traditions, constantly trying to remind Naiyana about the homeland they had left behind for this American "dream".

Rereading her words, Naiyana realized she had repeated a mistake her teachers frequently criticized her about. There was no mention of how any of this made her feel. But she wasn't sure that she felt anything she could genuinely add. This was her life, and she accepted it. If she did feel anything now, it was…hunger.

Naiyana walked downstairs and saw her grandmother cooking in the kitchen. Buppha's tiny body moved with a playful animation as she rearranged fire scorched pans and stirred a fragrant soup. She was singing an old song from her childhood and kept tucking a fork back into her hair bun whenever she wasn't using it to stir. Naiyana sneaked around her swaying form, and tried to pinch delicious morsels that were already plated. Buppha swatted her hands away and berated her in Thai. Naiyana resigned herself to the living room to watch TV and wait for dinner.

A few minutes later, her grandmother brought out the food and placed it front of her. Buppha half-muttered something about the "rude Japanese half of you" in her typical teasing reprimands. As she sat, Buppha pressed her palms together and closed her eyes to pray. Naiyana didn't know how she felt about her Buddhism now that she was in America. None of the other kids seemed to practice it, or any religion for that matter. But she knew better than to upset grandma. She closed her eyes and joined her in prayer. Soon enough they were laughing and enjoying the warm meal together. Naiyana loved Buppha. Maybe she'd add that to the essay.

Back in her room, Naiyana looked for a fitting reward to celebrate having concluded her schoolwork an hour before bed time. Books in various languages were stacked neatly on her desk. Scientific textbooks, fantasy sagas, Buddhist teachings…none of the topics seemed to draw her tonight. Naiyana chose to play a video game instead; she wanted to get to the last level and see if the robot demons in the game got any scarier.

Naiyana thought about her new friends at school: Bobby, Elise, and Mark. She liked them, though she didn't feel like she was genuinely a part of their group yet. She'd worked hard to study English when her family first moved to America, and she was still figuring out the cultural nuances. Her parents said studies were important, but that she should also try to fit in.

Naiyana found most kids her age to be...weird. She couldn't really say she was all that interested in understanding them. Suddenly, a massive demon appeared on screen and all her focus was required to defeat it. Naiyana adapted in bursts of creative strategy, using a jetpack, freeze ray gun, and lighting grenades as she bounced around the screen. The warm glow of the television's light gave the room a silver hue, which she found incredibly soothing.

#

Mark awoke to an unfamiliar sensation. He felt a terrible discomfort consume his mind. He realized he was standing beside his own bed in the darkness, but he wasn't in his body. When he looked down, he saw himself lying there deep in sleep. Fear gripped him like a cold claw. He felt like he was being attacked, but he had no body that could endure the assault. He was frozen in absolute dread.

Gradually, he noticed a particularly dark corner of his room and sensed something stare back at him. Mark could see ripples in the darkness. It looked like a boiling cauldron, only the bubbles were black, the steam was black...everything in the corner seemed to get impossibly darker.

Mark felt a presence within the shadow, somehow female, but not at all human. He could barely understand how he even knew these things, but he was sure the entity was looking at him. She stared with eyes he couldn't see. Mark sensed pure hatred in her furious gaze. He had never felt so terrified in his life. The entity wanted to kill him, she desperately needed him to die. Mark was sure of it. The drumming terror in his mind hammered at his psyche and he felt himself struggle to think. He tried to close the eyes he no longer had, to shut out the room around him. To shake away the rush of terror that filled every fiber of his soul.

He wanted to scream.

Just as swiftly as the nightmare had began, Mark suddenly found himself back in bed. His eyes were open and staring at the same corner. His real eyes. His real body. He couldn't move though; his muscles were still frozen in tense shock and drenched in a cold sweat. He wondered if this was still part of the same petrifying hallucination. The shadows in the corner seemed lighter, more familiar. They moved, and Mark realized they were coming from the tree branches outside his window. When he turned his gaze to the dark twigs, they seemed to retreat away from him in the wind. He doubted he could get back to sleep.

Tomorrow was going to be a long day.

2 – SCHOOL

As the morning light bathed Mark's face, he heard a stir of sounds dance around him: clattering pans in the kitchen, winter chirps of half-frozen birds, and a high-pitched breeze whistling through the gap in his window. As his eyes adjusted, Mark noticed his room had a bizarre glow to it. The surface of everything pulsed with an oddly vibrant gleam; a distinctly silver light radiated off his table, books, and floor. Mark assumed his brain was still acclimating to reality and shook the vision from his mind. He headed to his shower to wash the fatigue off his body, and got dressed in a rush so he could grab some breakfast before school.

Mark waited outside for his father's driver, Eddy, to bring the car around. He saw Victor, the family's gardener, approach with a wheelbarrow full of recently trimmed plants. Victor had a half-halo shock of silver hair crowning the dark leathery skin on his smiling face.

"Morning, Marko." Victor said, removing his gloves to shake the boy's hand. "How you feeling today?"

"Doing okay thanks, Victor. How's your day going?" Mark replied.

"No complaints for me. Just cleared some dead bushes near the lake. Making room for the bloom to come…"

Mark could hear Victor's pleasant voice carry on in his mind, but his attention drifted. He noticed a tattoo on Victor's exposed wrist he'd never seen before. It read: "*Mors Est A Porta*". The font was graceful and there were thorny vines swirling between the letters. Mark wondered what it meant, but thought it was rude to ask. Victor caught the boy's distracted preoccupation.

48

"You sure you're okay, little man?" Victor inquired warmly. "You seem…" Victor tapped the side of his wrinkled temple. "…a little in your head."

Something about his tender tone broke a wall in Mark. He looked up at the old man's kind face and unburdened himself.

"I have to fight a boy at school. He's much bigger. I'm a little scared." Mark's voice wavered as he heard his inner thoughts materialize.

Victor sighed with heavy empathy. He knelt down to meet Mark's eye.

"These things happen at your age, Marko." Victor began, before he interrupted his own speech with a sudden idea. "Wait, come here. I wanna show you something."

Victor led Mark down one of the estate's many woodland paths, ducking under branches and crunching dead leaves underfoot. They arrived at a vast apple tree that stood in a circular clearing. The tree's branches soared upwards in twisted contortions.

"Remember a couple years back, when this tree got hit by lighting?" Victor said, smiling at the tree with pride. "You can see the scar right there. Everyone said she was a goner. But I knew she still had a lot of life left in her. Look closely." Victor encouraged Mark to lean in. "See how the wood grew around the fracture, made a stronger foundation for these branches up here." Victor turned to Mark, his eyes full of kindness. "That's the key to surviving, Mark. Grow around our pains, and beyond them. Become larger than them. Or we get consumed by them."

Mark absorbed Victor's words silently.

"Let's get you back for Eddy." Victor said cheerfully, patting Mark on the shoulder.

As they strolled back, Victor saw Mark's mind was still heavy in thought.

"About this boy at school. Violence is often a reflection of pain. He may not show it, but that boy is probably suffering too." Victor explained. "Unfortunately, cruel people don't realize the pain they cause others. Until someone punches them back."

Victor's tone was reassuring, but he saw Mark was still doubtful. He looked around to make sure they were alone. Victor puffed up his chest and squinted with a newfound vigor. He began to move Mark's body around illustrating his instructions.

"If you have to hit him, ball your fist up like this, with your fingers rolled into your palm. Hit him with these two knuckles, right here." Victor said. "The power of a punch comes from the back foot. From down here, all the way up to here. See how the energy flows through your body? You gotta smash him square on the jaw, or even better right on the nose. Be strong and follow through till the end. A punch must be certain!"

Mark was surprisingly amused by the absurdity of the lesson, as well as Victor's vigor. He formed firm fists to match what the old man was keenly demonstrating. He imitated the motions, ducking and moving as instructed. As Victor described aspects of timing, countering, and maintaining focus, Mark began to imagine his punch actually striking Sebastian's face. It stewed a mixture of conflicted feelings.

Eddy pulled up and playfully honked his horn three times, winking at the boxing duo. Victor mussed Mark's hair and wished him luck. Somehow, Mark felt readier to face the day.

As he pulled up to his school, Mark noticed he was very early. Only a handful of children were unenthusiastically plodding their way through the snow and into the bland grey building. There was fresh graffiti scrawled on the side of the colossal cement walls. It read: *"Don't let school get in the way of a good education."*

Mark peered through countless rows of semi-opaque windows and saw the squares of monotony in which he'd soon be spending most of his day. He realized he had enough time to run to the library and return his book before class began. Mark hadn't expected to finish the novel so soon, but he had found it nearly impossible to fall back asleep after his terrifying nightmare. The courageous owls and their adventures had offered Mark a welcome reprieve from the shadows in the room; carrying him into the early morning light.

Mark pushed open the library doors and tapped the snow off his boots. He approached the reception desk and saw the librarian, Mrs. Habib, sorting through a pile of books. Her silver hair shimmered beautifully, like thousands of lush cobwebs weaved into elaborately thick braids. A few resistant strands always stuck out from the side of her head; unruly twigs refusing to adhere to the design forced upon their neighbors.

Mrs. Habib's library shelves, and the books that slept on them, were all old and faded. But she kept the place clean and orderly; forever eager to share the magic of one of her stories with a young mind.

"That was fast, Mark." Mrs. Habib stated in a honey sweet voice without looking up. "I'm impressed you still read these paperbacks. Most kids your age seem lost in a stream of stupidities on their shiny screens."

"I actually really liked this one, Mrs. Habib." Mark said, deftly avoiding one of her lectures on the downfalls of civilization.

He placed the book on her counter. Mrs. Habib met Mark's gaze and smiled warmly. Her face glowed with uninhibited warmth, but there was also a familiar sorrow in her expression that made Mark feel uncomfortable. Another pair of sad eyes on a happy face, concealing a portion of their story.

"Who was your favorite character?" She asked, blinking through an unspoken thought.

"I actually really liked the teacher." Mark answered, after some consideration. "He was a little mean to everyone, but I think he helped them more than anyone else did."

"That's what I like about this series." Mrs. Habib said, nodding her head. "It really captures the difference between a lecturer and a teacher. You see, a lecturer tells you how the world works, but a teacher helps you discover it in your own way."

"Which one are you?" Mark asked teasingly.

"I'm a librarian. I just make sure no good truths are lost." Mrs. Habib arched her eyebrow, while holding her hand out for Mark to give her the book back. "Would you like to read the sequel?"

"Is it any good?" Mark asked in genuine curiosity, as she pulled the book out of a pile.

"Well…I could tell you what happens, but that would likely affect the choice you make." Mrs. Habib suggested, leaning in to whisper. "Even worse, it would deprive you of the chance to experience the adventure yourself." She added in a theatrical hush, waving the sequel playfully.

Mark examined the book's cover. There were far fewer owls on this one, and they were surrounded by new ghoulish green beasts. He gently took it from Mrs. Habib's wrinkled hand and endured her overly dramatic wink.

"Thanks, Mrs. Habib." Mark smiled sheepishly.

"Let me know what you think, when you're done." She said, returning to her tasks as Mark turned to leave. "I'm sure you'll find the journey particularly captivating."

#

Mark walked into his history class and slid into a stiff chair. His whole body felt sore and tired. Most of the kids around him were sneaking glances at their phones, watching silent videos or sifting through streams while ignoring their teacher's enthusiastic lecture. Mr. Gati drew battle lines of an ancient war on the blackboard, reciting the events over his shoulder. Mark heard fragmented words glide passed him as his mind drifted.

Something about overly confident Roman forces falling into a trap set by Hannibal's rebellion.

Mark thought of the countless wars which had plagued human history; all that violence and suffering. He thought of the other ongoing miseries he saw whenever he watched the news: crime, corruption, mass-shootings, refugees, disease, poverty. It all seemed so hopeless. A cloud of dread permeated everyday life. A vision of the future only filled with fear. He desperately wished he could fix it all; but he felt so small and insignificant.

Mark noticed a small potted tree, close to the windows. Uprooted from its natural habitat, enclosed in an artificial room, straining to grow towards a light that only touched it through glass barriers. The plant stood, surrounded by the indifferent children of an alien species. Mark felt sorry for the tree. It seemed feeble compared to the potential undoubtedly lingering in its limbs.

Mark floated through the rest of his morning classes. He occasionally thought about his dad, his new book, seeing his friends later, and even that awful nightmare. He wondered why it had left such a strange feeling in him, how real it had all felt. Perhaps it had something to do with Sebastian. Mark felt himself dozing off a bit. The sleep he was deprived of last night weighed down on him. Thankfully, it was nearly lunchtime. He'd rest a little after he ate.

Mark walked through the corridors, avoiding bumping into any other kids. They moved in unruly swarms around each other: rolling on skateboards, diving in between clusters of friends, gliding in torpedoed paths without looking up from their devices, throwing paper airplanes, and generally creating a cacophony of yells, laughter, and noises.

A group of girls gathered around their friend's tablet and shrieked in dramatic envy at a photo of some celebrity. A faction of boys laughed at a video on one of their phones showing drunk people falling over. On the fringes of these clusters, isolated outcasts stared at the floor with looks of forlorn loneliness. Everyone seemed to share the same space, but existed very much in their own worlds.

The noise and frenzied movements felt like a blanket enveloping Mark's senses. He calmed his breathing. He was nearly at the lunch hall entrance. Mark raised his gaze, and saw Sebastian standing with his vicious group a few paces ahead of him. Mark sighed heavily, but continued to march forward. Sebastian noticed Mark approach and narrowed a venomous squint at his favorite target. There were teachers nearby, so Mark knew Sebastian wouldn't do anything too outrageous. But his tormentor rarely missed an opportunity to make Mark feel his loathing.

Mark decided to look up and meet Sebastian's stare. He felt a fluttering of familiar fear as he looked into his bully's eyes. So full of cold festering rage. Mark wavered slightly in his step. Sebastian shoved his friends aside so he could move towards Mark's advance.

Mark remembered what Victor had told him. He tried to maintain a look of calm defiance as he walked by the group of larger boys. He manifested a righteous confidence in his stride. Mark studied Sebastian's face as he neared him. He imagined punching it, actually smashing his knuckles against the boy's chubby cheek. The longer Mark stared, the madder Sebastian got.

A shrill bell rang above them, reminding everyone to go eat. As Mark passed by, he heard Sebastian spit. Mark felt the gob strike his shoulder and heard the other boys chuckle. Mark refused to turn around. He wouldn't give them the satisfaction of seeing his eyes. He took a deep breath, blinked away the tears, and walked towards his friends.

"Later, Pierson…" Sebastian uttered menacingly, watching Mark walk away.

Mark ambled into the cafeteria. He saw his friends sitting in the far corner by the windows. He plated a short stack of reheated sludge and hurried his way over to them. Elise was the first to spot Mark and beckoned him over with an overly theatrical wave of both her arms. Mark increased his stride, worried she might add some loud animal calls for her own amusement. He saw Bobby sitting beside Elise watching something on his phone, and the new girl Naiyana across from them with a neatly stacked pile of books by her elbow.

"Hey guys." Mark said, sliding his tray down and taking a seat next to Naiyana.

"Hey man." Bobby responded, almost looking up from his screen.

"Very nice to see you again, Mark." Naiyana declared, noticeably sustaining eye contact.

"Holy crap, Mark. You look tired as shit." Elise chortled, while wolfing down an overly-fried potato remnant. "I hope my hilarious texts didn't keep you up all night laughing." She ran her fingers through a thick lion's mane of red curls and revealed her beaming excessive grin.

"Thanks." Mark sighed, raising a forkful of questionable slime up to his face. He thought better of it and pushed his tray forward. "How can they serve this to children?"

"I love it." Elise smiled widely, as she scooped a heavy spoonful into her mouth.

"I've had worse." Bobby muttered.

"It's salted too heavily." Naiyana added. "But it's okay."

"Same recipe, four opinions. Can't please everyone." Elise mumbled through a mouth full of semi-chewed starches.

"What you watching, Bobby?" Mark asked, trying to change the subject.

"Some movie about a loner cowboy being moody as shit." Elise teased.

"It's almost over, get off my ass." Bobby groaned, clicking the volume up on his headphones and watching the cowboy slump over his horse as it sauntered towards a fiery sunset.

Naiyana studied the exchanges between the other children and wondered whether this was one of those playful bantering moments or an actual argument. She decided to remain silent and keep observing. Mark noticed Naiyana's flickering eyes and offered her an assuring smile.

"Ugh." Elise grunted loudly looking across the cafeteria. She was watching a cluster of pretty girls with near uniform outfits and generous layers of make-up. "Looks like Trish found her way into the pink clique. Another brain gone plastic."

Bobby rolled his eyes and Mark looked out the window. They knew better than to delve into this topic with Elise. Naiyana tried to interpret what Elise was focusing on; to understand why she suddenly seemed so hostile. She noticed Elise's clothing was significantly different than those other girls. They wore pink tones and revealed their shoulders and arms, While Elise seemed comfortable in a baggy dark hoodie with a dragon illustrated on its front. She thought a compliment might demonstrate her understanding.

"I like your hoodie, Elise." Naiyana said, in an overly enthusiastic tone.

Elise turned to her with a confused expression. "I wear this thing like every day, Dingus. Don't be weird."

"Leave her alone you monster." Mark said with a smile. He knew the difference between Elise's genuine rage and her mischievous posturing.

"I'm just teasing, Naiy. This hoodie is rad as fuck." Elise said, her eyes comically wide.

"I wish you'd shower as often as you cuss." Bobby muttered, barely under his breath.

"Pardon my reach..." Elise replied, leaning her armpits over Bobby's face to grab a book.

"Ugh, you're so nasty." Bobby groaned, turning his phone off and looking up at the group. "Can we throw her in a pool or something?"

"Oh man!" Elise interrupted. "That reminds me. We should totally go to Echo Lake later. It's frozen as hell. We could run across it, slide on our asses, look at the fat fish under the ice."

"What's with you and Mark freaking out over animals?" Bobby asked, gesturing to Elise's book and the bizarre creatures plastered on its cover.

"Well, mine's an actual biology book about exotic species from around the world." Elise replied, in a mock explanatory tone. "And Mark's is a children's book about stupid Owls that fight demons or something."

Naiyana looked at her own pile of books and wondered why no one had mentioned her reading material. She stared at Elise as the fiery redhead continued to taunt the group. Elise's eyes were so vibrant and full of life. Constantly evolving expressions cascaded across her animated face, as the thick curls of her ginger hair flung all around her. Naiyana was enchanted by her confidence. She felt herself drawn to Elise, and hoped they would grow close.

Mark noticed Naiyana offer a rehearsed smile, as she withdrew into the depths of her mind. He wondered if Naiyana tended to get too lost in observing people and trying to understand them. Maybe it was creating a distance that limited her presence in the moment.

It occurred to Mark that he might be guilty of the same quality. Even now he was escaping into the safety of his watchful mind. It made him wonder about his place in the group. Did his friends really like him? Or were they just being tolerant and kind. His school life would be unbearable if they ever grew tired of him.

"Hey, why do you guys hang out with me?" Mark asked, an unbidden sadness in his tone.

"Because you're not a dickhead." Elise offered quizzically.

"And your dad can buy us good grades!" Bobby added, his even tone hiding the sarcasm.

"You can purchase better grades?" Naiyana asked, genuinely surprised.

The other kids grinned guiltily.

"No Naiyana, you just have to headbutt these books into your face repeatedly." Bobby said, with a far more demonstrative smile.

Naiyana caught on to the humor this time and grinned back at the group.

"Why do you ask, Mark?" Elise probed, noticing the cloud of gloom in his eyes.

Mark took a second to respond. "Sebastian's turning more people against me." Mark sighed. "It's like they want to watch him beat me up."

A quiet fell over the group. This was a familiar topic, and they had witnessed much of Mark's abuse. Sebastian liked to pick on all of them in different ways, but Mark was unquestionably his favorite target. They usually preferred not to discuss the subject too often. The group's collective friendship was a haven away from their unspoken troubles.

"I think…" Mark tried to formulate the words. "…it's time I did something about it."

"You're gonna try to punch that brick wall he calls a face?" Bobby asked.

"Sebastian is larger than you, Mark. The odds don't favor you in a fight." Naiyana said.

Naiyana's perpetually blunt observations were not unexpected, but another awkward silence fell over the group as they considered how an altercation between the boys would actually play out.

"It might help if I just stood up to him once." Mark said, in an uncomfortable echo of his father's sentiments. "Show him I'm not such an easy target."

"Yeah, he might realize it's not worth the effort if you like... scratch his nose or something." Bobby teased.

"How much worse of a beating could he give me?" Mark asked listlessly.

"Facts." Bobby agreed, adjusting to a more penitent manner.

"Mark, I hate what that dickhead does to you." Elise interjected in a conciliatory tone. "But Sebastian comes from a messed-up home, dude. I heard rumors it was his dad that broke his knee last year. Even though Seb told everyone it was a skateboarding accident. He still walks weird on that thing. How is punching him gonna fix anything? That guy has so much hate and anger scabbed over his messed-up brain already."

"Seb can't get a free pass to beat Mark up just because his dad is a jerk." Bobby retorted.

"You're right Bobby, kicking him in the shins will fix everything." Elise chided.

"I can't change who he is, Elise." Mark said, finding more confidence. "But maybe he'll stop picking on me if I fight back. He might see how much he's hurting me."

"He'll likely just find someone weaker to pick on instead." Naiyana said.

"Well that would solve our problem." Bobby proclaimed cheerfully. Everyone else stared at him disapprovingly. "I could ask my brother for advice on how to fight." Bobby suggested, in an attempt to be helpful. "But Seb is huge. And much stronger than you. And way angrier!"

"You're a real cheerleader, Bobby." Mark said.

"I dunno man, I guess you gotta get in his head or something." Bobby said.

"That dude's head is the last place I'd wanna be." Elise shuddered.

"Yeah, Sebastian's soul is like a…clown cemetery." Bobby agreed.

"You can hit certain parts of the body that hurt much more than others." Naiyana offered.

Everyone looked at her curiously, waiting for Naiyana to elaborate further.

"Like his balls." She stated, matter-of-factly.

The group burst out into laughter. They quieted down when they noticed other kids nearby staring at them.

"He called me a '*Sped*' yesterday." Naiyana recollected, her face furrowed in confusion. "What does that mean?"

Another awkward silence hovered over the group.

"It means Special-Education." Elise said softly. "He's trying to make fun of you because you're on the spectrum, Naiy."

Naiyana was suddenly awash in confusing emotions. A wave of shame soaked her features. She opened her mouth to reply, but wasn't sure what to say.

"Don't worry, Naiy." Elise assured her with a grin. "All the most interesting people are."

Naiyana saw her three new friends smiling at her warmly. It melted her anxieties in a sudden swell of acceptance.

"Whenever he sees me, he usually just says something like '*hurt yourself, loser*'" Bobby added, doing his best impression of Sebastian's grimy voice. "Or, *die in a hole.*"

"He called me *Lezbo Barbie* once, but it didn't really bother me." Elise said. "I kinda wish I was into girls. It'd be less of a headache than dealing with you dickhead boys."

As Elise reached for her book Bobby noticed her beaded bracelet.

"When'd you get that, ya dirty hippie?" Bobby asked.

"Ugh, my mom went to India for like…two weeks. Now she wants me to do yoga and wear this spiritual stuff for my energy balance or some wacko shit." Elise groaned. "She thinks this will keep me protected from evil spirits. Anything to keep her precious girl safe forever."

"It's so unlike people in your family to be flaky about their interests..." Bobby goaded.

"Hey Dickface, I take care of a small zoo in my room." Elise huffed, getting into a confrontational posture. "You know how much commitment it takes to keep eight different animals alive for two years? You've had your puppy for what…a week?"

"You have way too many pets." Bobby retorted. "How many is enough animals?"

"I'd be satisfied with one dragon." Elise stated matter-of-factly. "Can you get me a baby dragon, Bobby?"

"You're stupid." Bobby mumbled.

"Yeah, that's what I thought. So, shut the fuck up." Elise taunted playfully.

Mark absorbed the conversation with a smile. He saw Elise ready to pounce on Bobby. He heard the clattering of dishes and cutlery all around him, the undulating soundwaves of other children talking in the distance. He caught Bobby's condescending eye roll dismissing Elise. He watched Naiyana arrange her textbooks so their spines were perfectly aligned. It was a suffocating surge of details, yet Mark couldn't help catalog it all. Understanding the forms and shapes of his surroundings gave him an odd sense of comforting control.

"The principal offered me the role of hall monitor." Naiyana announced suddenly. "He told me it was a great responsibility to help the school maintain the rules."

"No, Naiyana." Bobby said, in a categorical deadpan. "Hard pass. That's a definite no."

"Yeah Naiy, you don't want to be part of the system."
Elise said with a slight look of disdain. "That's a quick way to
get people to hate you. Which reminds me! Let's break some
rules and run on Echo Lake later."

"I'm down. It's getting boring playing video games all
the time anyway." Bobby said.

"The lake is probably a good place to avoid Mark's
bullies." Naiyana added.

"If Sebastian comes, at least I can get this fight over
with." Mark said reluctantly.

#

Mr. Alderson leaned on his cane, scrawling on the chalk
board as he lectured the class over his shoulder.

"There is a rich symbolic wisdom in the fates of Greek
mythologies. In Atlas, for instance, we see someone who is
punished for choosing the wrong side of a war. He is burdened
with holding up the celestial heavens on his shoulders...realms
where those who defeated him now reside." Mr. Alderson's
voice croaked, in his strained and petty British lilt.

"In another example, we have Sisyphus: one of the most
fabled residents of Hades. He was a vainglorious King
who yearned for notoriety. Now he pushes a boulder up a hill for
all eternity. You see, unlike the Hell of modern religions, Hades
is where everyone went regardless of their sins or virtues. But
the shades of our spirits which occupy Hades, are only an echo
of our purest selves...the remnant of our soul's greatest
yearnings. In turn, the poetry of their suffering reflected the
nature of their life on earth. And so, Sisyphus' soul pushes the
impossible upwards, in hope of glory. The irony, of course,
being that all shades in Hades have no actual connection to the
living. If one of you were to go to Hades to visit your ancestors,
according to Greek myths, you'd have to feed them blood first to

make them aware of your presence or even recognize you. Such is the futility of glory!"

He turned to face his students and was surprised to find so few sneaking glances at their devices. He squinted through his wire rim glasses and raised his furry caterpillar eyebrows. Rows of neutral meek expressions stared back at him. They knew to not appear too vulnerable, too confident, or even too indifferent.

Mr. Alderson enjoyed making examples of his students. It was an auxiliary form of learning which complimented the coursework. At least that's how he justified his sadism. He spotted Sebastian staring out the window, utterly oblivious to his surroundings. Mr. Alderson sighed in faux disappointment, and then smiled.

"Daydreaming are we, Sebastian?" The Teacher asked loudly, startling the boy.

"No." Sebastian said in a shrug, adjusting his gaze back to the chalk board.

"No doubt lost in thought as you consider my existential quandary." Mr. Alderson said, gearing up to shred his target. "A child's imagination can often be a powerful anesthetic to boredom or responsibilities - but in this case I'm sure you were keeping a vigilant eye on the subject matter, weren't you?"

"Yeah." Sebastian said flatly.

"Of course." Mr. Alderson replied, his eyebrows crawling up even further on his wrinkled forehead. "Perhaps you'd be so kind as to share what your keen mind absorbed? Let's start off simply: who is Sisyphus?"

Sebastian stared at his tormentor, his eyes narrowing with barely veiled disdain. He hated being humiliated, especially by this crusty old prick.

"The guy who flew too close to the sun." Sebastian said, feigning an air of certainty.

"Hmm. Often wrong but never in doubt, eh young Seb?" Mr. Alderson chuckled, turning to face the rest of the room.

"Anyone else?" Mr. Alderson asked, waiting longer than necessary. "No one at all? Your generation would struggle to pour water out of a boot with the instructions on the heel." He sighed, before turning back to face the chalkboard and continuing his lecture.

Sebastian felt a vibration in his pocket and pulled out his phone. His friend Ricky had texted: "Mark talked about you in cafeteria! Said he'd beat you up at Echo Lake after school."

Sebastian felt shivers of rage wash over his body. A familiar hunger formed in his belly. He was going to absolutely pummel that rich little shit.

3 – LAKE

The cold dread of facing Sebastian gnawed at Mark's thoughts. He felt a brewing disquiet in his mind, looming like a storm. Mark sat on Echo Lake's frozen surface; arms wrapped around his knees. The canvas of wintered forestry offered a calm contrast to his tightly coiled concerns. Mark's eyes roamed the serene landscape hoping to absorb the tranquility. Light saltings of snow drifted across an otherwise motionless background. Clusters of evergreen trees congregated around the lakeshore, huddling together in the chilled crisp air.

Mark imagined fighting Sebastian. He wondered if he'd find his courage in the moment. Would he live up to his father's expectations? Would his friends be proud of him if he stood his ground? Would Sebastian finally leave him alone?

More than anything, Mark felt a longing to just be left alone.

He lay down and let his back come flat against the ice. He spread his arms and legs wide, trying to flatten himself against the lake. He imagined the hidden body of water beneath him, and the creatures that still inhabited its chilly depths. He thought of the massive amounts of earth even further below, the entire planet he was laid upon. A giant orb hurtling through space, spinning around a vast burning star. But no imagined insignificance could diminish his anxiety.

Mark heard a heavy thud, and saw that Elise had jumped up and stomped down on the thick ice, trying to startle the fish below.

"Stop doing that you fucking idiot!" Bobby yelled at her, unable to hide his exacerbation. Elise's eyes were wide in glee, her pursed mouth barely contained a delirious chortle. She had all but transformed into a troublemaking chimpanzee. Mark knew she was far from done amusing herself.

"I thought you hated deep lakes and oceans." Bobby added. "Don't you have waterphobia or something like that?"

"I have claustrophobia, you idiot." Elise laughed, waving her arms all around her. "Does this look like a small confined space?"

Mark rose and pressed his foot down on the ice. It looked thick enough, but its heaviness felt oddly fragile...as if the water below still had the power to tilt and sway the world above ever so slightly. Mark moved some of the surface powder aside with his boot tip. He saw slithers of fish sliding through the seemingly bottomless lake. To his right, Bobby was teaching Naiyana how to take running slides across the ice. They both sprinted and slipped onto their backs to see how far they could carry the momentum. Naiyana seemed focused and determined to master the technique, while Bobby wore a mask of feigned casual indifference. Elise chased the dim glimpses of fish at her feet, imitating their movements in a freeform dance. Naiyana strolled over to join Mark.

"Look at that one." Naiyana said, pointing at a vibrantly colored fish swimming by itself. "He looks so different compared to the silver ones. I wonder what his life is like."

"Probably same as the others." Mark said flatly. He could feel Naiyana studying him.

"Hey Mark," Naiyana began. "why do the other kids at school call you *Pyro*?"

Mark smiled weakly. The subject was a specter which loomed over him. But he could see Naiyana's curiosity was innocent.

"I was at a different school before. A place called Berrington Academy." Mark said, feeling the memories resurface in his mind. "Some of the other kids didn't like me very much, but I really wanted to fit in. One day they bought some fireworks in town. They convinced me to help them set some off, aiming them near the teacher's lounge. One broke through the window and the whole room caught on fire. It caused a lot of damage. When the principal asked us about it, I didn't say anything. But the others all blamed me. They said it was my idea, that I bought the fireworks, and I was the one that lit them. So, I got expelled."

Mark paused for a moment, trying to steady his emotions.

"They think it's the nickname that bothers me. But it's not that I got blamed for the fire, or that I got kicked out of Berrington." Mark's voice wavered. "That's the day that my mother and sister died. I called my mom, and cried on the phone, and she got so worried...because that's what she always did." Mark lingered on a memory. "She rushed over to come get me from school. Isabelle was with her in the car. They got in an accident on the way, crashed into another car at an intersection. The cops said it wasn't clear whose fault it was. But that doesn't matter. It all happened because of me. Because I couldn't say no, to people making me do something I knew was wrong. People who weren't even my friends."

Naiyana didn't respond right away, which oddly comforted Mark. They stared down at the ice together, playing the story out in their minds for a moment.

"I'm very sorry, Mark." She said softly. "I don't think the accident was your fault. I don't think your mom would blame you."

Mark nodded slightly, making an earnest effort to believe her.

"I know what it's like to try to fit in." Naiyana added. "My family moved many times, even before we came to America. I feel like I see a lot, but I'm never sure about anything. People always seem to know something I don't. Like a hidden language I can't speak. I'm not seeing all the details, so it becomes frustrating."

"Curse of the outsider." Mark nodded, and smiled at her assuringly.

"Well, as hard as it is to understand the other kids sometimes, you guys have made me feel very welcome. I'm very glad we're all…friends." Naiyana's gaze followed the lone colorful fish. "I'm happy you and I are in the same school, Mark."

Mark looked up and offered Naiyana a grateful smile. "Me too, Naiyana."

The ice suddenly groaned in a shifting echo that creeped across the lake's surface. The children turned around and saw Sebastian stomping towards them with seven of his friends.

"Shit." Mark muttered softly.

"Heard you were talking shit about me, Pierson." Sebastian seethed, increasing the pace of his strides. "Told everyone at school you were gonna beat me up, right?"

Sebastian's friends were snickering behind him. All the older boys had a glean of violence in their eye. Mark tried to focus on Sebastian alone, but the large entourage added an ominous presence.

"Look, they added the autist Asian to their crew." Sebastian sneered, gesturing to Naiyana. "Now it's a full set of losers!"

Naiyana bristled at the name-calling. Elise put a supportive arm around her shoulder and glared at Sebastian. Bobby stood next to Mark and clenched his jaw.

"Here I am, Marky." Sebastian said. He slowed as he closed the distance between them. "You gonna fight me like a man this time, or run away to daddy's house again?"

Mark considered how far away home actually was. The distance between him and his father's stern disappointment. He heard echoes of the resigned sighs his father thought went unnoticed. Mark remembered countless clumsy attempts at reassurance sliding out of his father's mouth, in a half-hearted malaise. The fog of grief awaiting him brought Mark no comfort.

Despite the distance and frozen ground between them, Mark felt very much pressed between his father and Sebastian. He noticed a growing pressure reverberating in his mind. It made him feel faint with anger.

"Why are you always such a dick, Seb?" Elise chastised loudly.

"Shut up, Lezzie." Sebastian barked, his fiery eyes roaming over her. "You look enough like a boy for me to be cool beating your ass too."

Another round of sniggers from his cronies.

"You like being his cheerleaders?" Bobby taunted the boys behind Sebastian.

"Yeah, we get to beat up pussies like you." A straggly blond boy replied.

"Let's go, Marky." Sebastian said, his cold eyes filled with hate. "You think you're better than us, rich boy?" Sebastian's features cracked into wild shivering rage as he ranted. "Half the town loses their jobs, and your daddy buys up five plots of land to build that stupid fucking house! You stupid clueless Jews. Don't you get it? You aren't welcome!"

Something in Sebastian's tone sounded mimicked, like he regurgitated a learned venom. Mark sensed an unexpected clarity quiet his mind. He knew what he had to do, and he didn't want his friends to get hurt.

"I don't want to fight you, Seb. But I'm not running away this time." Mark stated calmly. "If you really want to do this, it should be just you and me."

"Or do you need all your friends to help you?" Bobby added.

Sebastian stared daggers at Bobby and spat out an enraged retort.

"Pretty sure I can pummel this Kike all by myself, thanks Blacky!" Sebastian yelled.

Bobby felt a familiar rage wash over him and took a stride towards Sebastian. Mark turned and stopped his friend, pressing a hand on his chest. He looked Bobby in the eye, and shook his head. Not worth it.

"You're fucking foul, Sebastian." Elise gawked, aghast at the older boy's overt racism.

"Tell your girlfriend to put a tampon in, Mark." Sebastian sneered. "Or she'll get hurt."

Mark felt a deep rippling of anxiety as he met Sebastian's sadistic gaze. But the longer he stared the more he noticed small flickers of uncertainty in the older boy's expression. This was the first time Mark had stood up to him and there was an undeniable hint of doubt in those menacing brown eyes. It was only a drop, but it was a fear Mark recognized. It gave him hope.

Mark thought back to Victor's advice and balled his fists, rolling his fingers tightly into the palm of his hands. He raised them up to either side of his jaw and placed one of his feet behind him in his best impression of a fighting stance. Sebastian's friends laughed openly and stepped back to form a circle around the two combatants. The ice creaked and groaned slightly under the shifting weight of the bigger crowd. Mark's friends whispered words of encouragement and stepped back, apprehensive hope strewn across their faces.

A cold fear filled the pit of Mark's stomach. He watched Sebastian form his own fists and raise them at a mockingly slow speed. All those times Mark had fled through the woods, all those desperate evasive paths, had all still led him here. He tried to focus on Victor's techniques and the encouragement of his friends. He tried to picture colliding his fist against Sebastian's arrogant mouth with all his strength. He desperately tried to stay calm.

"Be certain." Victor's gentle voice echoed in his mind.

Sebastian vaulted forward, and Mark's thoughts crystalized into a sudden surge of panic. Heavy thuds cascaded across the ice as Sebastian stomped headlong and raised a fist behind him. Mark clenched his jaw and charged forward too. His eyes almost squinted shut as he threw his small fist upwards. The uppercut crashed into Sebastian's jaw with a loud crack. Both boys stumbled back in genuine surprise.

"Yeah!" Bobby roared in unbridled astonishment. "Kick his ass, Mark."

Sebastian held a hand to the side of his face, and focused his vicious eyes on Mark. Whatever fleeting confidence Mark had felt evaporated as Sebastian charged and tackled him onto the ice. They both fell in a dense crash. Before Mark could think, Sebastian was seated on top of his torso, raining wild punches down on his head. Mark raised both his arms to shield his face. Sebastian's heavy painful blows thudded Mark's head against the ice.

Mark was overwhelmed by the battering. His bones felt sore. He went numb. Mark became aware of Sebastian's true cruelty. Not in his vicious strikes, but as an aspect radiating off his body. It was strewn across his face. Mark felt the cloud of fury grow and infect him. It filled his nostrils. He absorbed it, hardened it in his core as he suffered each savage impact. It overcame him.

Mark yelled out in sudden rage. He lunged out with both hands, gripped Sebastian's jacket and pulled him forward. As the larger boy was pulled down, Mark slammed his forehead directly into Sebastian's nose. The impact caused a sickening crunch and splattered blood on both their faces.

Sebastian howled out in pain and covered his face with his hands. In a blind rage, Sebastian stood up so he could stomp Mark's belly. As he raised his foot, Mark saw an opportunity and punched upwards, powerfully striking Sebastian in the crotch. The older boy groaned in nauseated agony and fell backwards.

The reactions from Mark and Sebastian's friends grew animated as they moved around the fight. They cheered and shoved each other in a condensed circle. Mark jumped on top of Sebastian and started raining frantic strikes down onto his face. Sebastian punched back clumsily, hitting Mark's ribs and chest. Both boys were in pain, slipping across the bloody ice, and surging with adrenaline.

The noise of the cheering, the ache of the blows, the determination to keep going, it was all a hazy blur to Mark. But in the frenzied speed of it all, he caught a slow lingering glimpse of Sebastian's face. Mark saw that his efforts had surprised Sebastian, and the flickering of fear had now filled his eyes completely. He could see this wasn't the first time Sebastian had felt dread. It had a familiar hold over the deepest parts of his mind.

Mark suddenly felt empty. His fear had hollowed him out, and he had allowed Sebastian's brutality to fill the void. He tried so hard to be what was expected of him today, but now he felt sick to his stomach. Mark thought about his father. He wished he could hug him right now, to feel his loving embrace and take both of their pain away. He lowered his fists.

Sebastian took the opportunity and hurled Mark off of him. They rose to their feet, panting heavily. Mark's nose was bleeding too now. Sebastian had a vicious cut on his brow. Sebastian buried his doubt and fright, and renewed a mask of determined malice.

Mark realized he had to end this fight. To snap Sebastian out of his sadistic haze. Mark noticed Sebastian was limping on his right leg, where he had broken his knee last year. Mark focused on it and mustered all his resolve. Sebastian rushed forward. Mark leapt towards him, kicking both his feet squarely onto Sebastian's kneecap in a devastating collision. Sebastian buckled in agony.

"I'm going to fucking kill you." Sebastian yelled, rising on a shaky leg.

"You can stop, Sebastian." Mark pleaded between ragged breaths. "Please. Let's stop."

Sebastian sensed the judgmental stares of his friends. He quickly buried his hesitations. He looked at Mark and saw that the boy didn't have much fight left. Sebastian smiled viciously and rampaged forward with a ferocious promise of cruelty. Mark felt drained and terrified as he watched Sebastian advance. His small fists unfolded and his fingers pointed outwards, as if trying to hold back the situation. He closed his eyes in anticipation of the collision. Just as Sebastian reached Mark, the children heard a loud terrifying shatter fracture the ice.

Everyone froze as a bottomless yawning groan spread across the lake. Before they could react, the ground erupted into massive shards of ice and bitter black water. Mark heard screams as he slipped backwards on an immense inversion of ice. Whatever fears he had felt earlier turned to shrieking utter terror as the dark waters enveloped his body and dragged him below.

The cold was unfathomable. Mark felt it soak his clothes and fill his bones. He opened his eyes and saw all the other children thrash around trying to find their way out. They were all screaming. The sound of it moved slowly, like dull fogs of fear drifting through the water. The outside light struggled to break through the abyss, giving the skies above them a faint ghostly glow. Mark kicked wildly, forcing his body through a small opening. He got his head to the surface and gasped for some desperately needed air.

Mark could see adults in the distance running down the hill towards them. He wondered if they could make it in time. His ears filled with wild screams but he couldn't tell if they were coming from below the water or outside it. He felt himself slipping down again, his hands sliding off the frozen segment.

Underwater, Mark heard the murmured yells of his friends. He saw Bobby floating upside down, his knees trapped between two large sections of ice. He was twisting around violently trying to free himself. Elise tugged on Bobby's shoulders like a wild animal. Naiyana smashed her small fists against the unmoving ice blocks, trying to make an opening. Mark swam towards them, passing the floating still bodies of Sebastian and his friends.

Everything moved slower. Sounds grew dense. Mark couldn't feel a difference between the cold around him and his own body. The more he swam towards his friends, the further away they seemed to drift. It was getting darker. Mark was losing the sensation of his own thoughts. A deafening shaking hum filled his mind. He was suddenly certain that this was the end. He was going to die. And yet, somehow the sensation felt remarkably familiar. The lake around him grew still, the boundaries of it spreading out into infinity. Mark heard a voice enter his mind.

It told him to let go.

4 - DREAM

Mark found himself inside of a memory.

He had closed his eyes in a desperate attempt to shut out the cold terror soaking his mind. There was a gentle moment where he felt the sadness and fear leave his body, and then quite suddenly he had no body. Mark faintly recalled the frightening rumbling. The deafening crescendo had filled his thoughts and shook him out of existence. Fragments of his life scattered away from him: his parents smiling at him, running through the woods with his sister, playing with his friends, the faded echo of a song he had once loved, old memories and secret fears alike, all drifted into nothingness.

A thunderous call pulled unrelentingly on the fibers of Mark's being, demanding his full awareness. He was hurtled violently towards something he knew, and yet couldn't see. He was pulled backwards, and upwards, and with each flickering moment lost more of everything he once knew to be true.

Mark hung in the open enormity. Unbound from a world he no longer remembered leaving behind. Untethered by time. Mark swam in a vast frozen moment, which enveloped every moment that would ever yearn to be. He was beyond the boy he had been a mere memory ago. No more recollections, or world, or form, or countless other familiarities.

He was pure.

Mark drifted towards an eternal truth hidden just beyond him. He felt himself preparing to face it. To be open to it. To see himself without eyes. He realized there were others there too: entities that were apart from him, aware of him, and yet somehow connected to a shared oneness. The certainty swelled throughout the reaches of his consciousness.

The others invited Mark to recognize their shared unity; urging the everlasting all to know itself once more. To see the truth fully. The darkness faded away and Mark saw before him an endless bounty of light. He realized that he wasn't seeing it, because he no longer had eyes. He was the light. Every layer of it permeating the entirety of existence. Mark was a miniscule leaf on a tree of immeasurable awareness, branching off into infinity. He was everything.

He was home.

In an instant, Mark knew that he could wholly accept the serenity before him. It was waiting on the other side of a simple choice. It offered him a warm embrace of boundless love which would erase all the woes he had ever known. To float peacefully in a sea of light which spanned the entirety of existence. But a sliver of his mind clung to an old fear. He heard the faint voice of a lost understanding longing to be heard once more; a singular story not yet fully told.

Mark felt the conflict fester within him. The wild hum of discorded voices tore at his thoughts. The disharmony formed a deep chasm which drained every other consideration. The valley of light surrounding him began to tremble. Immense fissures of shadow scarred the waning luminescence. Everything was coming apart, wildly undulating and cracking into colossal storms. Bright geometric shapes flurried past his vision and morphed the reality around him. The once boundless field of light condescend into vibrant manic orbs; frantic and furious stars shrinking ever-smaller. They revealed the endless void of darkness beyond them. It was a cold black ocean waiting to consume everything it touched.

Mark saw the foundations of the cosmos. The boundless celestial mechanics of a galaxy unfolded before him. Majestic fields of vibrant stars pulled away from each other, swirling in slow gargantuan cyclones through the black silence. Entire eons of creation were swallowed into bottomless pits. Their desperate fading light drifted into black holes of oblivion. Each star sung its own tragic song. The grand collective chorus of their requiem radiated across the stillness. Long lost siblings of a singular brightness desperately reaching out to one another across gaping maws of emptiness.

As the darkness consumed the last flickers of light, Mark saw the unfathomable defeat of it all. Felt an unknowable loss. The black stillness rejoiced in its terrible tranquility. Mark heard the feeble whispers of countless souls suffocated into dark silence.

Mark's fears turned to anger. He wanted to resist the inevitable. He wanted to go back. He felt a flurry of wild hope and chaotic desires flourish in his mind. Each thought frantic to be surged into rebirth. Storming possibilities tore at each other for his full recognition. The hysterical dissonance blossomed into a deafening explosion in his mind. His awareness shattered into fragments.

Mark desperately sought clarity; to attain a singular sense of self above all the cacophony. Through the very act of seeking the island of his identity, Mark calmed his mind. Everything he knew had almost been obliterated in the tide of a new reality, but Mark had bundled his once familiar awareness into an orb that could no longer be corrupted. He felt the roots of his lost inner voice spread once more. It blossomed into a full understanding.

Mark was floating in nothingness, but he was without a doubt...himself. Awash in his newfound lucidity, Mark gradually became sullen and filled with despair. He realized he had no idea what to do now, how he could get home, or what this state of existence even was. He missed the memories of his friends. He desperately wanted to find Elise, Bobby, and Naiyana. He longed to get back home to his dad. He couldn't imagine the pain his father would endure if he lost Mark too.

Mark suddenly became acutely aware of another presence approaching his consciousness. And then another. Two distinct variances of existence. Vast conscious entities with minds wholly separate from his own. They watched him, with profound curiosity. Their thoughts entered his, discussing him in voices that were felt rather than heard. It was a timeless form of knowing.

One of the hidden voices was colossal in presence, commanding and powerful. It filled Mark with its judgment, questioning an important choice that had to be made. The second voice felt gentle, observant and full of wonder. Its thoughts smiled on Mark's awareness, assuring the other entity that all would end well. After some deliberation they formed an agreement, and exhaled Mark into the beyond. A surge of silver light enveloped him, as a new reverberation roared through his mind. Eventually, the thunderous rumble faded away. Mark became aware of a sensation he thought he had lost forever.

He was awake.

Mark sat upright, eyes wide in alarm. He had eyes! They struggled under the sudden onslaught of light, but their soreness brought a delirious elation to Mark's heart. He was in his body; blinking and smiling. Mark drew heaving breaths. He felt his lungs fill with a warm and strangely scented air. His limbs were terribly sore. He brought his hands up to his face and rubbed his eyes, trying to adjust his vision to the blurry landscape before him.

In a confused haze, Mark realized he was seated in a pristine white desert. The expanse was endless, with faint hints of dark mountains in the distance. Mark ran his fingers through the sand. Fine as powder. Mark saw it was nighttime, but there was a peculiar glow in the sky. Lustrous streaks of azure and violet clouds danced across an implausible canvas of exquisite stars. Mark saw the moon. It appeared oddly close. Then he saw a second moon further away. And a third even further.

"Wha…" Mark uttered, before being startled by a movement behind him.

Mark looked over his shoulder and saw a flurry of white feathers altogether too close to his body. He spun around and rose to his feet. The storm of feathers spun with him, wrapping itself around him and slicing the air near his ear in sharp wisps. Mark yelled, and spun away in twists, desperate to escape the attack. It was only when he fell to his knees and wrapped his arms around his head that he realized the large feathered creature had grown still. Mark peaked cautiously over his shoulder.

With a profound sense of disbelief, Mark realized the feathers were connected to a large set of wings, and that those wings were attached to his back. Mark rose to his feet sluggishly. His head dizzy in confusion. He could barely breath anymore. He reached out with trembling fingers to touch the wings. Mark felt the touch from both ends. He tugged on a large feather and pulled it out. A pang of pain shoot through him. The wings took a rooted presence in Mark's mind. He thought about controlling them. He tilted one and was amazed by the rapid response. Cautiously, Mark yawned them open to stretch out their fullest form.

He noticed a smaller set of wings tucked under the larger ones, lower down his back. The feathers on the second set were charcoal black. The wings collectively formed a large X across Mark's back. He ran his hand under his shirt, and touched the base of one of the wings with his fingers. The feathers and leathered skin seemed to spread across most of his upper back.

Mark wondered if he was dreaming; or perhaps something worse. He remembered the cold waters, his friends screaming in terror, and the darkness. Mark faintly recollected the surreal visions that had followed. But how had he gotten here?

Mark heard a murmur. He saw several bodies lying in the sand nearby. He ran towards them, but stopped abruptly when he noticed a shimmering puddle on the ground where had gotten up moments ago. The small pool glittered with pulsing lights, radiating a hypnotic vibrancy on its surface. Mark approached it cautiously. He looked down into the liquid and saw a surreal image. It was as if he was at the bottom of a dark lake, looking up at a distant sky obscured by large segments of ice. In a flash of understanding, Mark recognized Echo Lake.

He pressed his fingers to the waters, hoping to touch his lost world. But as his flesh connected to the liquid it pushed back. It refused entry to even the smallest part of his hand. After several frustrating attempts, Mark heard the murmurs again and looked up to see one of the other bodies strewn across the ground stirring.

As Mark approached, he recognized the other children. He saw there were pools of glowing water beneath all their heads, creating a thin halo of light. More alarmingly, Mark noticed they each had their own unique physical abnormalities.

One of Sebastian's friends had three large green horns protruding from his skull. Another one was covered in slimy red vines that pulsed and moved around him. All of their skin appeared to be pale and grey, with sizable black scars and murky festering wounds. Mark's eyes fell on Sebastian. He had four large emerald appendages jutting outwards from under him. They looked like coarse scorpion tails with menacing barbs. Sebastian's fists were covered in rough looking grey stone. Even in his restive state, Sebastian's face was twisted into a cruel grimace.

Mark moved towards the stirring body and realized it was Bobby. White sand covered both his legs and one of his arms. His face was partially obscured under a cowboy hat that rested on his head, but his skin looked normal and free of any scars. Mark leaned down, brushed away some of the sand and gently tried to wake him. Bobby opened his eyes suddenly and gasped for air. Mark was kneeling beside him and tried to steady his frenzied rise.

"Wha...What...Mark. Wh..." Bobby muttered incoherently.

"Bobby, calm down." Mark urged, placing a gentle hand on his friend's chest. "Bobby!"

Bobby's breathing slowed to a milder panic. He looked up at Mark in confusion, then down at his body and the sand still covering half his form. It took him a moment to realize it wasn't snow.

"What the hell..." Bobby said, trying to rise.

Both boys heard a noise below the sand. It was the undeniable whirring of machinery. Mark and Bobby froze and stared down in confusion. Bobby lifted one of his legs. As the powdery earth fell away, it revealed a shiny metallic limb. Segments of glowing blue light emerged from the joints of the complex metalwork. Bobby vaulted backwards in confused fear, his other leg revealing itself to be made of the same material. It reminded Mark of advanced robots he'd seen in films.

"My legs!" Bobby screamed as he scurried back. "Where are my legs? What the hell?"

Bobby's legs moved at blindingly efficient speeds. They steadied his stumbling retreat and bounced to counter his imbalances. They held him in a solid composed posture. Bobby froze in astonishment. His legs had intuitively helped him, reacting with incredible swiftness to his movements. He reached down and cautiously tapped them.

"My legs are...metal." Bobby murmured in confusion, before looking up at Mark. "You have wings?" Mark saw the baffled look on Bobby's face. "Mark..." Bobby's voice was faint, "...we drowned."

All Mark could do was nod his head. The situation was beyond any measure of understanding that his mind could grasp. He felt a dense confusion dull his thoughts.

"Elise!" Mark said, in a sudden realization. "Naiyana!"

He moved to scan the remaining bodies spread all around them, trying to find his friends. Bobby moved his legs in hesitant increments, staring down in disbelief.

"Help me, Bobby." Mark yelled, as he found Elise.

Bobby went to join him and was surprised at how rapidly he arrived. He had sprinted to Mark with extraordinary speed, and come to a smooth halt.

"Woah." Bobby said, in near admiration of the advanced technology attached to his body.

Mark gently shook Elise's shoulders. He saw her take a few short inhalations before her eyes shot open. She sucked in a huge strained gasp, filling her lungs as she blinked in wild panic.

"Whaa...the frackin shit!" Elise yelled, heaving between vulgarities. "Holy fuck! Mark?"

Elise looked up to see her friend's familiar face, then noticed Bobby standing beside him. It only took her a moment to absorb the rest of the picture.

"Why the hell do you have wings? And why are you made of metal?" Elise asked, her tone surprisingly flat.

"No idea." Bobby mumbled. "You look pretty normal...for you!"

Elise looked down at her body. She was wearing weird clothes: purple silk pants with bizarre gold symbols, and an intricate layered black top wrapped around her torso. She looked at Bobby, and saw he was wearing a white dress shirt with a dusty brown vest. His cowboy hat seemed to be made of the same brown fabric. Mark wore tattered black pants and a simple dark blue shirt. Beyond her odd fashion, everything else seemed normal enough on Elise's body.

"Seriously guys, what the hell is happe-RRAAHHH..." Elise's sentence was cut short as an enormous growl erupted from her throat. Her teeth morphed into large fangs that deformed her mouth and jaw. Elise leapt up in surprise and saw that portions of her arms were covered in green reptilian scales. She screeched, and it sounded like a crazed baboon.

"Holy shit." Bobby yelled.

Mark watched various parts of Elise's body transform for fleeting moments into patches of feather and fur, claws and tentacles appearing quickly, before shrinking away entirely.

"Elise! Try to stay calm." Mark suggested, in an uncertain urgency.

"You fucking stay calm!" Elise screamed back as she watched her body go through chaotic alterations. She shuddered and moaned in frustration as the changes washed over her. Elise took deep slow breaths. She looked down at her body. Everything looked normal. She looked up at her friends.

"Well," Elise said, smiling half-heartedly. "guess you two aren't the only freaks."

"Guys." a soft voice nearby startled the group.

They looked over and saw Naiyana sitting upright in the sand. She was dressed in a bizarre monastic garb and holding her arm up in front of her face. It was encased in a thick layer of ice. The frozen glove changed and grew with the movement of her fingers, forming sharp blades and long spikes. Naiyana shook her arm wildly from side to side in confusion. The ice fell apart all around her. She looked at her friends with a concerned gaze.

"What's happening?" Naiyana asked.

"Where are we?" Elise added, looking around her.

"I have no idea." Mark murmured, staring into the vastness for clues. "Those puddles we were all lying on. I think that's the bottom of Echo Lake. I tried to get back into mine, but I couldn't push through."

The other three children looked at the puddle Naiyana just rose from. Bobby pressed one of his metallic feet against it. He couldn't advance passed the surface. He stomped down harder, repeatedly slamming his foot against the unyielding barrier. He yelled out in frustration as his strong robotic legs crashed loudly against the wet portal with heavy deafening thuds.

"Stop, Bobby." Elise shouted, annoyed by her throbbing headache.

She knelt down to look at the strange water. As she peered into the puddle, she saw the image of Echo Lake begin to vanish. The children watched as the ethereal glowing waters drained into the white sand. After a moment, there wasn't any trace of its existence left.

"Nooooooo!" Bobby yelled loudly, as he scrambled down and started pawing at the sand. "What did you do, Elise?"

"I didn't do anything, asshole." Elise barked back indignantly. "I just looked at it."

"That…" Bobby mumbled despondently. "…that was our way home."

"What do we do now?" Naiyana asked, fearfully looking to her friends for guidance.

Before anyone could answer, the children heard a deafening noise fill the air. They looked up, and stared in astonishment as a flock of colossal fish swam across the skies above. Each one of the gargantuan creatures was covered in vibrantly colorful scales. Their eyes were white and glowing; enormous orbs lighting the path ahead. The immense fish soared through the night as if swimming in an invisible ocean. They moaned deep cavernous songs at each other; paying no mind to the tiny children below as they continued their journey towards the horizon. Bobby watched the outlandish creatures fade into the distance, then turned to his friends.

"Where the fuck are we?" Bobby asked, a look of deep concern engulfing his face.

"I don't know." Mark replied softly, as he moved his wings to examine them. He felt a growing sense of normalcy unfold in his mind, despite the unexpected circumstances and surroundings. His body felt…natural.

"Hey!" Elise blurted out abruptly. "Do you think we sank so deep in the lake, that we broke through into some kind of underwater world?"

"Are you serious?" Bobby asked, staring at her incredulously.

"I dunno, look around man." Elise replied defiantly.

"You can't be that stupid." Bobby huffed.

"Well how do you explain the giant fucking fish floating above our heads, genius?" Elise yelled back.

"This isn't water." Bobby screamed at her, waving his hands through the breeze in front of them. "It's air!"

"It doesn't explain Mark's wings or Bobby's legs." Naiyana assessed in an agitated tone. "Are we on another planet?" She asked, noticing the three oddly colored moons.

"Maybe. But how did we get to another planet?" Mark asked in genuine curiosity. "We drowned."

The memory stilled all their minds, as they thought about their last moments in the lake.

"Do you think…" Elise shivered in a somber tone. "…did we die?"

"I can remember swallowing water." Naiyana said, her features trembling.

"The water was so cold." Bobby recalled softly. "But I don't feel dead." He blurted out in sudden defiance of the mood. "And if we died, what is this supposed to be? Heaven?"

"I mean, I don't know what being dead feels like, but this seems…normal." Elise began, before noticing everyone's confused stare. "You know what I mean. The place is weird, but I feel the same. Kinda." She moved her fingers and wobbled her limbs.

"These aren't our regular bodies." Mark said. "But they do feel natural."

"I guess." Bobby agreed, as he bounced lightly on his new metallic legs.

"Maybe this is heaven!" Elise exclaimed, and looked around her. "It's definitely not Earth. Mark even kinda looks like a weird angel with four wings. Do any of us even know what heaven is supposed to look like?"

"Depends which book you're reading." Bobby moaned. "If this is the afterlife, where's everyone else? Why are we the only ones here? Except for the giant sky fish. And those guys…"

The children looked at Sebastian and his friends. None of them were stirring.

"They don't seem to be waking up." Mark noted.

"Do you really want them to?" Bobby asked skeptically.

The children examined the bodies of the boys on the ground. Their physical deformities seemed terribly menacing. Their pallid wound-covered skin gave them a uniformly grotesque presence, even in their slumber.

"We can probably wait to wake them for a bit." Elise offered.

"I'm not sure they'd know any more than we do." Naiyana added warily.

"Or that they'd even want to help us." Bobby said. "They were jerks before. And now they have horns, and look like gross zombies." He strolled over to one of the boys, and gently tilted their head searching for another puddle. But they were all gone. Bobby backed away in frustration, trying not to stir any of the others.

"We have to do something. None of this makes sense." Mark said.

"Maybe it's all a dream." Bobby suggested glibly, an absurdly hopeful chirp in his tone.

"That we're all in together?" Mark asked.

"I mean, well…maybe this is my dream and you guys aren't really here." Bobby adapted.

"You would say that, jerk." Elise scoffed, as she kicked his metal leg. "I'm real!"

86

"Then why the hell do I have robot legs?" Bobby yelled in exasperation, shaking a leg for emphasis. "Why is Naiyana some kind of ice witch that can make frozen blades on her hands? You can grow goddamn animal parts, and Mark has four wings sticking out his back!"

"Calm down Bobby, you're being hysterical." Elise said, rolling her eyes.

Bobby stomped over to Mark and plucked out a clump of feathers from his wing.

"Ow! Stop that, you dick." Mark shouted, pushing Bobby back.

"Feels pretty real." Bobby said in surprise, as he let the feathers fall to the ground.

"We're probably not dreaming then!" Mark yelled angrily, rubbing his sore wing.

"This place seems weirdly familiar." Elise said, looking around with a vague squint. "Have any of you guys ever been here before?"

The others stared at her blankly.

"Let's find some other people. Adults!" Mark suggested. "There's gotta be someone that knows what's going on. Maybe they can help us get back. Or at least explain where we are."

"Might be a better idea than waiting for the next giant sky monster to float by." Elise said. "Or for those jerks to wake up."

Everyone looked at Sebastian and his friends. They lay unmoving. Their stillness took on an unnerving quality. They weren't breathing. A somber silence fell over the group.

"Should we try harder to wake them?" Naiyana asked timidly.

"Ugh, I mean it's probably the right thing to do." Elise groaned. "But maybe they...didn't make it? I mean, look at all of their skin. It's a weird grey color. And they're covered in gross black scabs. We look normal enough. Maybe these guys aren't ever waking up."

"We have to try." Mark stated softly. "I'm sure they want to go back home too."

"They wanted to torture us before we got to this crazy place." Bobby declared angrily. "Can you imagine what they're gonna do now that they have claws, and horns, and…spikes."

The group contemplated the likely outcomes. But the decision was obvious.

"Fine." Bobby groaned. "But if they start trying to rip off parts of us, I'm running!"

The children crouched down over one of the boys, and tried to shake them, slap them, or jolt them awake. Bobby seemed particularly enthusiastic about vigorously striking one of the boys across the face.

"No luck." He said, hints of a grin dancing across his mouth. "Guess they'd rather sleep."

"Mark, they're not waking up." Elise moaned pointedly. "Let's just focus on finding some help for now. Then we can come back for these assholes, or send someone to get them."

"Maybe we can leave a trail of clues and notes telling them which way we went!" Naiyana added. "So they can catch up."

"I'm not sure they'd do the same, but that works for me." Bobby agreed.

Mark's gaze lingered on Sebastian for a moment.

"Okay." He sighed. "But we still need to figure out where the hell we're gonna go."

The group looked in all directions, hoping for hints of a path onwards. Mark strode ahead, and stared at the horizon. Bobby joined him, squinting as he took in their environment. After a while, he turned to Mark. Bobby rolled his eyes in a sudden realization.

"Hey, Moron." Bobby exclaimed. "You've got wings. Fly up and get a better view."

"I don't know how these things work." Mark said defensively.

"Flap." Bobby offered nonchalantly, mimicking the movement with his arms. "Hard."

Mark folded his wings, trying to tuck them behind his body.

"I don't think you're hiding those things from anyone any time soon, man." Bobby observed. "And now it looks more like you have a dorky feather cape."

"You're one to talk." Elise shouted over. "You think you look cool in that hat?"

"Don't be jealous just because you're not bad ass enough to be a cowboy." Bobby yelled.

Mark looked over at the girls. Elise was trying to control the transformations on one of her hands, making her nails grow into claws and changing the skin on her arm to reptilian scales.

"Dude! I can do different animals if I think really hard about one!" She said excitedly, looking over to Naiyana.

Naiyana was seated on the ground, creating increasingly complex ice statuettes in the sand. She looked up and offered a polite smile, but her face soon returned to a despondent look of frustration. The ice figures weren't entirely conforming to her intended design.

"Those are so cool." Elise encouraged, as she admired the sculptures. "Can you make something over there?" She asked eagerly, pointing a bear-like claw just ahead of them.

Naiyana looked at the empty space. She raised her arms and focused. After a moment a slow swirl of frost formed and solidified into a rough block of ice.

"Hmm, even harder to make precise shapes at a distance." Naiyana observed.

"See, the girls are figuring their stuff out." Bobby said. "So, you gonna fly or what?"

"Why don't you sprint a couple miles that way, Speedy!" Mark retorted. "Let us know if you find something."

Mark took a deep resigned breath and spread his wings. In full outstretched form they took up an impressively wide span. Bobby backed off and watched Mark attempt to control his new feathered limbs. Mark flapped them once, kicking up a small storm of white sand. He repeated the movement, harder. It raised him off the ground and immediately turned him sideways. Mark crashed down in a twisted tumble. He looked up at Bobby.

"Don't say it!" Mark said sternly. "I still have to figure out the balance."

"Hey man, you got this." Bobby replied, backing away a little further.

Mark began the process again, bending his knees slightly to better anchor himself. His larger wings rose and fell in heavy arcs, while the smaller wings flapped lightly to stabilize his ascent. Mark rose off the ground.

"Woah." Bobby and Mark uttered in shared awe.

Mark soared above his friends. Each downward thrust of his wings surged him higher. It frightened him somewhat, but it also felt natural. A rush of excitement washed him. The view was beautiful. Mark was intoxicated by an unfamiliar sense of freedom.

Bobby watched Mark hover in the air. His legs made a whirring hum, and he looked down to inspect them. The mechanisms, joints, blue lights, and metal all seemed to radiate a powerful vibration. A newfound curiosity washed over him. Bobby bent his knees and felt a swell of potential build up in his body.

"Screw it." he whispered.

Bobby leapt upwards, and was immediately amazed by how high he could launch. Mark saw Bobby rising towards him at an impressive speed. Bobby was wearing a competitive smirk. As he came face to face with Mark, he tipped the rim of his cowboy hat. Mark pointed down to the sand below.

"You still gotta make it back down." He said, matter-of-factly.

Bobby's face fell as he began to drop back to ground.

"Oh shiiiiiiit." Bobby screamed, as he plummeted. His arms flew forward to protect himself from the looming crash. As soon as he hit the ground, his legs smoothly absorbed the impact in a graceful knee bend. Bobby stood up warily, amazed by his new abilities.

"Did you see that?!?" He yelled at Mark. "I'm stupid fast, *and* I can jump really high!"

Mark smiled at his friend. He began gliding down in circular arcs. Each movement made him feel more connected to his wings, more in control. He rose, and he fell. He spun and turned tight corners. He decided to see how high he could go.

Mark beat the air around him, ascending upwards. The rapid wind caused his eyes to tear up. But his heart pounded in pure euphoria. Mark came to a stop and hovered in the sky. He could barely make out his friends anymore. After some time in the open enormity, he began to search for a good route they could take. To the left there was nothing but barren mountains. Turning to his right, Mark could only see more desert. Behind him, in the distance, Mark saw a vast forest stretching out into the horizon. Just beyond the trees, on the other side of the woodland, Mark saw hints of what he thought could be smoke trails from small fires.

"Villages?" Mark wondered. "There might be people there."

A large purple cloud floated in front of him, obscuring his view. Mark's wings continued to flap, holding him in place as he tried to peer through the mist. Without realizing, Mark raised his arm and pointed his fingers at the fog. It slowed to a stop. Mark felt a surge of energy course through him, clarifying his mind. He could sense the cloud: the intricate arrangement of water droplets that gave it structure, the weight of the wind flowing through it. Countless impressions and details set root in his awareness, blossoming in a surge of understanding.

Mark heard the faint murmur of an ethereal whisper ripple through the air around him. The words were disjointed and indiscernible. The sounds slid around him in a rushed torrent. Mark wasn't sure if he was hearing it with his ears…or within his thoughts. Mark noticed small cracklings of silver light ripple across his fingers. The sparks snapped as they grew and wrapped around his arm fully.

The cloud started to dissipate as Mark felt his connection to it become more potent. He panicked as the streams of silver energy on his arm flourished. Mark pulled his hand back and shook it frantically. The current disappeared, and so did the cloud. Mark sailed back down to his friends, landing softly in the sand. He didn't know what had happened up there. He felt a peculiar shame, urging him to keep it secret.

"There's a forest that way." Mark said to the others. "Maybe some towns on the other side of it. I saw what looked like smoke from fires. Seems like the best way for us to go."

His friends nodded, and continued to drag the heels of their feet in the sand. Mark realized they were putting the final touches on a large message they had engraved into the ground. It read:

HEY JERKS! WE WENT THAT WAY

Elise added an arrow pointing towards the forest. She smiled at Mark.

"In case they wake up." Elise shrugged.

5 – RUIN

It was every monarch's worst fear.

King Hematen watched his civilization collapse into frenzied destruction and death. He stared from his balcony as the invading horde ravaged his once glorious realm. While the enemy lay waste to his city, his people ran in screaming terror. Wherever they turned, more monstrous grotesqueries awaited them.

The vicious conquering creatures had ferocious claws, terrifying fangs, and colossal bodies full of rage. They were drenched in a foul slime which trailed behind them as they charged through the streets. The unholy liquid seeped out of them, blending into the endless rivers of blood left in their wake.

Where had they come from? How had they swarmed his city so rapidly? Hematen knew he had to quell the despair that filled his heart. He had to act with great resolve if there was any hope of escaping this devastation. Behind him, thirty of his fiercest knights yelled at each other. Their words felt dull and faint in his mind.

"My King!" Basvoh's heavy voice rose above the clamor. "We must help the remaining people flee. There are too many of those…beasts."

Hematen listlessly turned his back on the wreckage of his realm and looked at his knights. They stood in his hall, breathing heavily and clutching swords that would bring them no salvation. Fear flickered and flourished in all of their eyes as unnatural shrieks rose from the homes below. Hematen looked utterly defeated.

"My King, please." Basvoh's tone was kinder now, though full of resignation.

Hematen approached, gaze downcast, and placed a hand on his old friend's vast shoulder.

"You are right, Basvoh." Hematen said, the timber of his voice waning. "We must act."

King Hematen sighed in deep sorrow, then raised his chin and looked up at his faithful knights. Loyal and stalwart, every one of them.

"Order the remaining guard to hold the horde back as long as they can. Set the barricades ablaze. The creatures seem to avoid the flames. Perhaps that will slow them." King Hematen spoke with an air of certainty. "Gather the remaining civilians and get them to the tunnels below the keep. Once you've sealed the doors, create as large a blockade as..."

The King's voice trailed off as he noticed three of his men smile. Their grins widened beyond the natural limits of their face. Their eyes rolled upwards. A wild madness spread across their distorted features. Two of the men wailed loudly, their faces full of pitiful despair. They fell to the ground, convulsing and howling shrilly. The last smiling knight turned his head with a sudden twist and ran screaming towards a wall. He collided against the unforgiving surface and fell to the ground. He scrambled back up to kneel, and repeatedly slammed his face against the stone.

King Hematen and his remaining men could only stare in bewildered confusion. The deranged knight's face was a bloody ruin. He stood and turned to his former friends. He laughed manically, through the gargled deformity of his mouth. He made a move to suddenly draw his sword, but before anyone could react his body burst into a violent plume of black powder. As the sediments fell to the ground in clumps, the men could see they were made of small arachnids which scurried across the floor.

No one spoke. The men sensed an arresting chill fill the room. They felt bled of their thoughts as an emptying dread engulfed them. A spine-chilling moan reverberated off the walls and crept its way around the hall. It brought desolation to their faint hearts. Candles snuffed themselves out. The sudden sound of shattering ice cracked from a dark corner.

The knights turned to face a growing pillar of thick black smoke rise from the floor's foundations. Tendrils of darkness seeped out of every nearby crack and fracture in the walls. The tentacles trailed an ooze behind them as they crept. Despite their bewildered terror, the remaining knights gathered around their King, forming a protective barrier and raising their swords.

As they looked on, a small form emerged from the dark cloud. It was a youngling, with skin as pale as bone. He seemed to be floating midair. His crimson hair hung loosely around his forehead, nearly obscuring the blackest eyes Hematen had ever seen. Save for his head, the youngling's entire body was encased in jagged black stones which moved and morphed around him. They glinted with razor sharp edges. The youngling floated down to the floor. A halo of frost formed around each foot; the stone beneath them shattered.

The nearest cluster of knights vaulted forward in immediate attack. The swirling storm of shadows surrounding the youngling reacted swiftly. Ferocious shards of black rock flew forward, and impaled four of the knights. The stone easily pierced their armor, pulverizing the organs incased within.

One of the knights nearly closed the gap, his sword raised above him ready to slice. Three apparitions appeared before him, screaming in wild rage. They all bore his face, only distorted with lunacy. The knight hesitated upon seeing his own visage in the floating distortions. The specters descended on him to viciously shred the skin off his body with their claws.

Another knight prepared to hurl his axe, when he suddenly saw his own three children run towards him from the other side of the room. They were covered in blood, their skin pallid and grey. Their mouths hung open in haunting howls; eyes wide in shrill terror. The knight fell to his knees in incomprehensible shock. He didn't see the stone daggers in his deformed children's hands. His mind barely comprehended his fate as their teeth tore his throat.

"Stop!" King Hematen commanded loudly, before more of his warriors hurled themselves into the onslaught.

His knights held back, panting in fear and confusion. They all looked at their imposing invader. His face a mask of cold rage. His eyes stared at Hematen's crown. The morphing pulsing shadow that danced around him throbbed with heavy sounds and groaning appetite. It stirred a captivating fear in the knights, calling them to stride towards their own oblivion.

A dozen small black orbs emerged from within the shroud. They floated forward, surfaces shimmering with distorted flickers of lights. Hematen thought they looked like small oval clouds, containing fierce storms within. The black hovering orbs circled their master. The knights tensed up, prepared to defend against an attack. Years of battle had hardened their unity and awoken a shared bond of unspoken instincts. But their king would allow no more bloodshed.

"Hold…" King Hematen's voice was soft, but commanding. He stepped in front of his knights, holding his ancestral war hammer. The weapon was adorned in precious gems.

"Our realm does not seek war…" Hematen pleaded. "…please allow me to surrender on behalf of my people, and spare them any more suffering."

Hematen knelt before his conqueror, bowed his crowned head, and raised his hammer in offering. He noticed an unrelenting silence soak the room. Hematen could barely sense the presence of his men or even the nearby walls. He was in a chasm, only aware of his own mind and the fear that drenched it.

Hematen slowly looked up, and was met with a frozen stare. There was something unholy in those dark eyes; they hungered to defile. Hematen could see fleeting flickers of white light sail across the dark orbs, only to be snuffed out in the unending abyss of their depths.

"I offer a peacefu..." Hematen began again, before he was interrupted.

"You are distortions and noise." The youngling hissed through a clenched jaw. His haunting cavernous whisper soaked the room. "We will return to the serenity."

Hematen was certain he had heard two voices fused into one; the gentle frail speech of a youngling, and the unnatural vastness of a commanding power flowing through him. Hematen tried to think of a response, but felt the air drift out of his body. He grew weak. He dropped his hammer in a crash.

Hematen looked up at the youngling's unforgiving eyes and saw his doom call him. The skin on Hematen's face cracked open and seeped with foul liquids. He croaked and sputtered, unable to form words. His hands turned to ash, falling apart before his terrified eyes.

"Protect your king!" Basvoh bellowed, charging ahead with his sword raised.

Several other knights vaulted forward. The floating black orbs flew at each of them and crashed into their bodies with a shattering force. All the knights fell to the ground howling in agony as the orbs spread a cold gliding liquid across their chest and limbs. The fluid crushed their armor, twisted and snapped their frail bones, and contorted them into crumpled piles. The slime crawled into their open whimpering mouths, turned their skin to charcoal leather, and emptied their eyes of all light.

The remaining knights watched as their king joined the bravest of his warriors on the floor, a devastated husk of his former glory. They looked up and saw the youngling stare at them.

All of them.

Their conqueror raised his arms. A rift of black energy formed between his small hands. The widening void pulsed and expanded into a vortex from which light seemed incapable of escape. The slaughtered bodies rose into the air and were hurled into the pit of darkness; disappearing from existence entirely. The abyss shrunk down to form one of the many orbs which still floated around the room. Their surfaces crackled with hints of a long-lost light.

The remaining knights dropped their weapons. They fell to their knees, begged for mercy, swore their loyalty, and rambled in incoherent terror. The youngling opened the palm of one white hand. A cloud of dark mist formed above it. The quivering knights watched as the cloud expanded. At its center a clear sphere took shape; a looking glass into another world. Four distinct shapes materialized within the sphere. Younglings. They walked on endless white sands. One of them had four wings.

"Hunt..." their conqueror commanded.

Before the knights could respond, their bodies engorged with grotesque distortions. Their armor and clothing fell away in torn fragments. Their eyes bulged with agonized frenzy. Anguished screams erupted from their throats. Dark slime spewed out of their ears, noses, and mouths. Spikes of hardened bone erupted from the skin of their twisting bodies. Layers of thick fangs filled their monstrous maws. Their hands contorted into bleeding clawed hoofs. Dripping tar seeped from their sore covered muscles.

Prince Sal'Haf watched his hunters be reborn. They galloped out of their former King's hall. They ran to different paths, but with shared purpose. They would scour the wilderness between the realms, find the four wandering younglings, and slaughter them.

Sal'Haf strode to the balcony and overlooked the final moments of another decimated realm. The fires snuffed out, the screaming ceased, the veil of nightfall darkened the streets. Sal'Haf felt the voice deep within him sigh in relief. Finally...there was silence.

6 – FOREST

The children stood in front of a vast collection of strange trees, illuminated by the early morning light. They struggled to fully comprehend what they were seeing. Each tree was adorned in uniquely outlandish and exotic bark. One was covered in glittering black scales, another had feathery red fur, a cluster of skinny stems seemed encased in cold green marble, and the largest of all the trunks was wrapped in thick interwoven yellow cords that slithered around each other.

Some of the trees pulsed, others vibrated occasionally. Those that didn't have leaves, wafted plumes of indigo powders from cracks in their branches. Others dripped lingering streaks of purple slime or burst with occasional flutterings of bizarre bugs.

"This fucking place." Elise muttered in awe.

"Yeah, do we really think it's a good idea to walk into *that*?" Bobby asked skeptically.

"Well, we can't go back into a big empty desert." Naiyana replied matter-of-factly.

Mark looked above them. Multiple suns arced across the sky in different directions. Waves of unusual colors shifted through the thin blanket of clouds.

"It's getting hotter. If we need to find water, food, cover, or anything else our best bet is probably in there." Mark asserted. "And we need to find help."

"In *there*?" Bobby reiterated incredulously.

Mark looked ahead. There was a narrow clearing between the trees, a path with several slivers of light. He felt a surge of certainty grasp him. Something within the forest urged him forward. The pull was unrelenting. Mark started walking.

"Let's go." He said abruptly.

Elise was quick to follow. The others shuffled in behind her. Mark waded through a thick layer of foliage. He pushed through, revealing a lush garden of vibrant plants. The children stepped into the clearing and examined the unfamiliar world, utterly awestruck.

Elise wondered if she had ever seen the colors surrounding her. Naiyana noticed that neighboring branches swayed around each other. Petals and fragments of fruit floated from tree to tree. Bobby heard a concert of sounds sailing overhead: the rhythmic shuffling of leaves, the chirping of unseen insects, and the soaring music of peculiar birds offering imitations of each other's music.

Mark sensed a current in his chest and fingertips. His body pulsed with a curiosity to connect to the environment. His friends were distracted exploring the area, and seemed not to notice the faint hum emerging from Mark. He tried not to panic, to breathe through whatever was happening.

Every time he inhaled, Mark felt more connected to the lifeforms around him. The trees nearby, the small creatures hiding from view…all took root in his awareness. He absorbed their presence in a new and stirring way. Something inside him could feel the world, rather than see it. A wave of calm washed over Mark.

He stared directly at one stunning tree in particular. It reminded him of the weeping willows near his home, only the bark was covered in shimmering clear crystals. The tree's absurdly long branches stretched outwards, swirling in striking spirals. Draping vines of varying color swayed from the tree's limbs. They were covered in sparkling crystals. Mark felt every aspect of the tree, the details of its lustrous structure formed in his understanding.

Mark began to see a gleaming layer of silver light radiate from the bark. Small rivulets of the luminescence floated off the trunk, sailing off in different directions. The countless vines all dripped their own floating droplets of the same light, gradually splashing out a fragmented fog of radiance.

The light seemed to pull ahead of the tree's actual swaying movements. Mark saw the light build up and precede each swung arc. He realized he was somehow witnessing the tree's potential. The light's movement anticipated where the vines or branches would move, sailing forward in a heralding path that the tree's segments soon followed.

"*Remember.*" An otherworldly voice whispered to Mark.

It was the same voice which had spoken to Mark when he flew among the clouds. It was clearer now, manifesting in his thoughts. Mark felt a surge of presence wash over him. Despite the peculiarity of his circumstances, his nearby wandering friends, and the alarm of not knowing what was happening…Mark was overcome with lucidity. Nothing else seemed to matter, but the connection he felt to the moving elements of the iridescent swaying tree.

Mark reached out his hand. His fingers pointed at the illuminated branches. He imagined them growing still. He focused on the thought. He sensed every aspect of the enveloping light. At first, Mark was met with resistance from the tree. It wished to repel his will, sever the bond.

Mark furrowed his brow, and pushed harder with his mind. The tree suddenly grew still. The vines stopped moving altogether. Mark didn't know what to do next. His curiosity felt like an unwelcome stranger. He looked at the tree and noticed the silver light begin to fade from it completely. Leaves dropped off the vines at an alarming rate. Mark lowered his arm. He felt a swell of anxious panic.

What was happening to him? What was that voice? Was he going crazy? Did he really stop that tree from moving…with his mind? He checked to see if anyone noticed.

With hands cupped around her mouth, Elise screeched her attempt to emulate distant bird calls. Bobby gently tapped his metallic leg against a tree made of coarse blue stone. Naiyana observed him with a curious gaze. Bobby swung his leg back and kicked the tree powerfully. The impact shattered a section of the trunk's foundation with a loud crack. Bobby turned to face his friends, with a look of guilty surprise.

"Did you feel that?" Naiyana asked, pointing to the remnants of stone on Bobby's foot.

"Not really." Bobby replied. "I mean, it didn't hurt or anything. But I can feel the leg in general, like when it touches stuff. Which is kinda weird, actually."

Mark sighed in relief. He didn't understand what was happening here, but he didn't want to worry his friends. He turned his head and noticed that the forest had divergent paths winding off in various directions. He hadn't seen it before, but each path was covered in a blanket of distinctly colored leaves.

"Look at the ground." Mark said. "Each way has a different colored path."

The children examined the trails. Broad velvety lilac leaves covered the route on the left, crisp small dried up blue leaves covered the path to the right, and long caterpillar-like furry red leaves covered the way straight ahead.

"Anyone have a favorite color?" Bobby asked.

"Oh, we should absolutely take the purple one!" Elise exclaimed excitedly.

"I don't even want to know how you picked." Bobby sighed.

"How big is the forest, Mark?" Naiyana asked, trying to see where the blue path led.

"I don't really know. It was far away when I saw the whole thing." Mark replied. "But if we keep going straight through from where we came in, that should be where I saw the fires."

"Looks like red's the winner then." Elise sighed in disappointment.

"Cool, so we just have to walk through this entire weird forest, filled with who knows what, towards a fire you might have seen, and hope some friendly people are there to help us?" Bobby asked dubiously.

"Got a better plan, robo-legs? Or you just gonna whine?" Elise taunted, trotting ahead.

"Only you could be having a good time right now." Bobby gritted in frustration.

"Dude, look around us." Elise said, twirling and staring above. "I have no idea where we are or how we got here, but it's beautiful. We have super powers, basically. Our clothes are weird. We have absolutely no clue where we're going. What can you do but smile?"

"I'm not sure I understand your logic." Naiyana said softly.

"That's because she wasn't born with any." Bobby chortled.

"Logic this!" Elise muttered, revealing a large furry grey paw with a middle finger raised. The hefty black claw nestled within the pelt of her finger looked formidably sharp. It occurred to Mark that dangerous creatures might live in these woods.

"Guys, I think we should get ready for...I don't know. We might come across trouble, or like wild animals or something." Mark stated, cautiously looking around.

"You mean other than Eli..." Bobby started.

"Shut the fuck up, Bobby." Elise cut him off, raising both fists. They transformed into hulking purple crab-like claws. She snapped them in thunderous claps. "I'll be ready, Mark."

"Gross." Bobby grimaced in utter revulsion. "Crab hands? That's what you chose?"

Naiyana explored how she could weaponize her abilities. Thick layers of ice formed all around her torso and limbs. She raised her hands, and sprouted dense frozen swords. She examined her work, admiring the clumsy imitation of a knight's armor.

"What do you think?" Naiyana asked bashfully.

103

"Doesn't that make you cold?" Mark wondered aloud.

"I don't really feel the temperature." Naiyana replied.

The kids shuffled close together on the red path, planning out imagined defenses. Elise jumped ahead describing all the ways she would clamp her claws down on theoretical enemies. Naiyana sliced her swords through the air, practicing wide arcs and short jabs.

Mark wondered how many of them he could carry if he needed to fly them out. He looked up at the canopy of trees and realized the thick branches would make it hard to get any elevation. Hints of the silver light drifted off of the leaves as they swayed in the wind.

"Well if something happens, I sure hope you guys can run as fast as me." Bobby smiled, before turning to Mark in a hushed tone. "Why did the girls get all the cool weapon powers?"

"Don't worry boys," Elise chimed in, eavesdropping on Bobby's concerns with a new pair of bat ears. "if something happens just run and fly away. Leave it to us ladies to…"

The children froze as they heard the unmistakable sound of other people's voices ahead. The mutterings were faint, and hidden by the thick tree line, but two distinct voices argued with each other in the distance. Mark looked at his friends. He gestured to silently suggest approaching the unseen people. The group exchanged a few hesitant stares, but eventually nodded in agreement.

Elise widened her claws and raised them in preparation. Naiyana held her swords up and took a few calming deep breaths. Mark and Bobby eyed each other, and slowly lifted their fists in support. The group pushed through the leaves and cautiously marched ahead.

As the thick foliage parted, the children saw a vast and stunning oasis. The crystal-clear lagoon sat nestled within the surrounding flora. Unspeakably beautiful waters shimmered reflections of light in every direction. It took a moment for the mesmerized children to realize the voices had stopped talking. Across the water, two men stared at them.

One of them sat on a large boulder. He had a thick main of long orange hair and a heavy beard, framing his beige fur-covered face. His implausibly large green eyes blinked at the children in a curious gaze. He wore blue monastic robes hung loosely from his furry body, tied around the waist with a silver sash.

The other man stood beside him, and looked far more menacing. His muscular bulk was encased in a dark green metallic chest plate, which connected to an assortment of tubes and pipes protruding from - and returning to - his abdomen and head. His skin was stone grey, but his forehead had a lustrous green circle painted on it. His two red eyes squinted at the children. His hair was as white as the fangs he now displayed at the unwelcome intruders.

Before the children could say anything, the larger man disappeared in a puff of green smoke and reappeared behind them holding two long black blades.

"Who are you?" He barked at the startled children. "Who sent you?"

"Woah, woah, wait a second." Mark blurted out in a fluster, moving himself between the menacing grey man and his friends. "We didn't mean to surprise you. We're just lost. We're trying to get home."

The large man stood firm, staring down at them with swords raised. The children heard weird sounds behind them, and turned to see the other man walking across the water. His arms were raised in front of him, palms facing the sky. An assortment of large rocks hovered towards him and placed themselves at his feet, making a solid path across the lagoon for him to walk on.

Mark saw hints of silver light surround each rock. The vibrant layer poured forward in the direction the stones soon followed. Mark looked at the man's face as he neared. There was worry and uncertainty in his expression, but his feline eyes were also filled with kindness.

"I won't ask you again!" Grey Man growled, pointing his blades closer.

Flurries of steam and bizarre vapors hissed from the pipes of his armor. Elise snapped one of her claws at the hulking brute.

"Listen man." She huffed. "We don't want to mess you up. We just wanna get home."

"Are we speaking English?" Naiyana asked her friends. "How do they understand us?"

The question took the group by surprise, and even the grey man squinted in confusion. Mark caught Naiyana's gaze and gestured with his eye towards her swords.

"Naiy…" He muttered under his breath. "…focus."

"Fyzo." The Furry Man said, emerging from the water. "Leave the bambas alone. They're clearly too young for your blades, or our concern."

The large man scrutinized them a while longer, before reluctantly sheathing his swords.

"That one has swords too!" Fyzo stated pointedly, gesturing towards Naiyana. He pulled an iridescent jade powder from a small satchel at his waist and proceeded to snort it into his four nostrils one at a time. "So much for meeting in secret, old friend."

Fyzo raised his wrist and revealed a large glowing emerald nestled within his armguard. He went to press the crystal, but the other man grabbed his arm to stop him.

"The council..." The Furry Man said. "…Mokko must attend. This is no time for pride."

"I heard the first time, you hairy sarkaf." Fyzo muttered reluctantly. "May fate find us."

"May fate find us." The Furry Man replied with a weary smile.

Fyzo turned to face the children once more, before sticking his two tongues out at them. The duo of yellow appendages flailed and flickered like writhing slugs. He pressed the jewel on his arm, and vanished in a burst of emerald light. Mark felt a pull towards the light as it faded.

"Please forgive my ill-mannered friend." The Furry Man said, staring at the confused group. "His mother fed him escartaf serpents as a youngling."

He took a moment to look over the strangers and examine their unique physical traits. Naiyana allowed her ice armor and weapons to fall to the ground, and Elise transformed her body back to its regular form.

"Bless the Watchers and their endless creativity, you certainly are an odd bunch of wonders." He continued. "My name is Wynn. Who might I have the pleasure of speaking with?"

Not having any inclination as to what else they should do, the children all mumbled their names and introduced themselves politely.

"Very nice to meet you all." Wynn proceeded in an infectious cheer.

He examined Mark very closely. A look of awed fascination spread across his face.

"You have wings! I've never seen a youngling with wings! What a rare gift! When you fly, is it quite fun?" Wynn asked enthusiastically.

"Uhh…" Mark hesitated.

From the confused looks on their faces, Wynn understood the children weren't in the most conversational of moods.

"So, if I heard correctly, you are trying to find your way back home." Wynn adapted. "Tell me where that is, and I will happily offer my assistance in returning you there."

The children stared at the friendly creature. His beaming green eyes, his fur covered skin, his lustrous mane of orange hair adorned with small braids, his unique clothes, and the fact that he was speaking to them in such a clear manner - it was all too weird to fully comprehend.

"Sir...what's happening to us?" Mark finally asked, in a timid tone.

"I'm not sure I follow your meaning." Wynn replied.

"Where are we?" Bobby asked.

"You're in the Moriae Forest." Wynn responded, amused by the question. "Where did you think you were?"

"No, not just the forest man..." Bobby groaned. "...like, the whole thing." Bobby motioned wide with both arms.

"Are we in Heaven?" Elise asked, examining their new feline friend with a curious smile.

"I've never heard of...Hehvahn." Wynn replied, swatting away Elise's outreached hand with his tail.

"Are we dead?" Naiyana asked.

"How could you be dead? You're standing here talking with me." Wynn chuckled. "What an odd bunch of bambas you are."

"What did you call us?" Bobby bristled.

"What...bamba?" Wynn asked, perplexed. "It means little one. A youngling. Someone who is not fully formed." Wynn squinted his large eyes. "Where are you from?"

Mark watched Wynn throughout the exchange. He sensed Wynn's intention and knew he was being sincere. Much like the tree, Wynn's presence filled a secret part of Mark's mind. A version of the man's nature was seeded in Mark's awareness. Wynn felt Mark's absorbing gaze and turned to lock eyes with him.

"Strange bambas indeed." Wynn muttered, with a knowing smile.

"We're from Earth. Do you know how we can get back?" Naiyana said, taking charge.

"Can't say I've heard of that realm either. Is it near the Hehvan place you mentioned?" Wynn asked. He saw the look of frustration on their faces and pressed on. "Do you know where it's located within the Raya? How did you even get here?"

"We fell in a lake." Elise said, trying to simplify the situation as best as she could.

"You fell into a lake...and appeared in a forest?" Wynn asked, his face reflecting his growing puzzlement.

"No man." Bobby groaned.

"What's a Raya?" Naiyana asked.

Wynn allowed a burst of true bewilderment to erupt across his features.

"What's a Raya...I..." He stuttered. "...I honestly don't even know how to answer that. You're standing on the Raya. The Raya is everything around you. All the realms and kingdoms put together. Every far away land and unexplored territory. The collective everything." Wynn waved around grandly. "The ever-changing landscape on which the three Primals play out their timeless game." He turned to face them. "How could you be here and not know where you are?"

"Holy shit dude, that's what we're trying to ask you!" Bobby yelled in frustration.

"What's a Primal?" Elise muttered in quiet confusion.

"Do you know someone who could answer our questions?" Naiyana asked. "Or that can help us get back?"

"We just want to go home." Mark said, trying to instill calm in the situation.

"I honestly don't know where your home is, that's what we've been discus...never mind." Wynn said, resisting the urge to fall in a loop with these strangelings. "You have too many questions. Your home must be somewhere within the Raya. Perhaps you all hit your heads when you fell in the lake and simply forgot. We just have to find the shortest way back there."

An idea sparked into Mark's mind.

"Your friend..." Mark inquired. "...the guy with the grey skin and the swords. How did he disappear like that? He pressed something on his arm."

"That was a token. It's bonded to his Eye." Wynn answered, matter-of-factly. He saw the blank looks on their faces and elaborated. "Sacred Eyes are powerful gateways. They allow travel from one place to another. They are rare, ancient, and powerful relics."

"Can we use one? To get back home? Can we get tokens?" Mark asked in cautious hope.

"Tokens are only given to the guardians of each Sacred Eye." Wynn explained calmly, raising his wrist to show a silver bracelet adorned with a glowing blue jewel. "They aren't customarily used to send misplaced bambas across the Raya." Wynn caught their crestfallen faces. "Though I suppose if you are particularly lost, and can't remember how you got here, it might be best to get you home before the war descends on us."

"What war?" Elise asked.

"Elise, stop." Bobby urged firmly. "It's none of our business, let's just get out of here."

"Where's the nearest Eye?" Mark interjected.

Wynn stared at the group, slightly suspicious for the first time.

"It's in the Kingdom of Maije. Where I'm from. One of the realm scholars will probably have heard of your *Uerth* village, and know how to get you back there."

"What the fu..." Bobby muttered.

"I have to go meet a few other people so I can't take you there myself, but if you mean to head to Maije, follow the blue leaf path until it hits the High River, you can take one of the boats downstream. You'll see the city soon enough. But stay on the river to guide you, because the look of everything else can change later in the day." Wynn said, as he looked up at the sky. "Especially if the Storm-Bats start playing with the clouds again."

"What…" Bobby asked, a horrified look on his face. "…the hell are Storm-Bats?"

A rustling sound in the leaves distracted the group, and they turned to see a spiral of small birds erupt from the tree line. The creatures fluttered around each other, and flew towards Wynn. He grinned and raised one of his large paws. The birds were colored in vibrant purples and oranges. Instead of beaks they had small tusks protruding from their mouths, and proboscis noses that drooped down to their bellies. They danced around Wynn's arm, hovering mid-air on six layered wings while chirping cheerfully.

One of the birds dove down to nestle within the fur of Wynn's paw. The peculiar bird rolled its body around, revealing four small legs that twitched and kicked in joy. The fluttering birds emitted a chorus of frisky chirps. The one in Wynn's paw flipped back onto its feet, leapt into the air, and joined the others in a swirl of playful squawks.

"I love birds." Wynn said cheerfully, watching them fly away. "Freer than most of us."

He looked to Mark, and smiled in admiration of his wings.

"Thank you, Mister Wynn. We appreciate all your help." Mark said, reaching out his hand to shake Wynn's paw.

Wynn looked at the boy's outreached hand, and in confusion gently grazed his claws across Mark's palm. Wynn arched an eyebrow to see if he had read the intention correctly.

"Close enough." Bobby said, marching ahead towards the blue-leafed path.

7 - RIVER

Blue leaves crunched beneath the children's feet, floating into the air in fine azure powders. Mark watched as his friends explored their surroundings. The mysterious aura of perception was manifesting in his awareness more often. With each emergence, Mark felt his resistance diminish. While Bobby, Elise, and Naiyana discussed the exotic foliage around them, Mark trailed behind and explored the newfound sensation.

He watched as the increasingly familiar hints of silver light glowed around his friends' movements. It draped off their limbs and slid ahead of their reach. Mark saw smaller droplets of it cascade and pull the sway of branches overhead. A full current of potential surged in a swirling silver river that flowed through everything around him.

Mark noticed a corner of his mind yearn to control the moving elements. While his curiosity simply wanted to understand the various components of his environment, Mark couldn't deny a strong desire to change so much of it. He wished he could rearrange and improve the flaws he perceived.

Mark resisted the urge. His previous influences on the cloud and tree still felt like a shameful secret. He couldn't quite explain what had happened, and he felt too uncomfortable adding more mystery to a world his friends were already struggling to comprehend.

Mark's attention was drawn to Naiyana. Something in her movements had changed. Swirling silver cords swam around her temple. Her breathing fluttered in short shallow gasps. Naiyana stumbled in her stride and fell slightly behind Bobby and Elise's pace.

"Hey Naiy," Mark said, rushing over and placing a hand on her shoulder. "you okay?"

Naiyana was startled by the touch, and seemed embarrassed by the state she was in.

"Ah, I…" She began, in a haze of confusion. "…I don't know, what's happening."

Mark realized that ever since they arrived in this place, Naiyana had displayed a constant façade of stoic calm. But her tense expression and disjointed movements now seemed highly panicked.

"Where are we?" Naiyana asked, looking at Mark with a fearful gaze. "What is this place?" Her voice rose by a significant octave. "That furry man in the woods. He didn't know about Earth. He had no idea what we were talking about." She gulped inhalations between each sentence. "What if we're stuck here? Are we never gonna see our families again?"

"Calm down, Naiyana!" Bobby urged in agitation, absorbing her distress.

"Don't be such a jerk." Elise barked, shoving Bobby.

"What?" Bobby yelled. "We don't have time for this, we need to get to out of here."

Naiyana fell to her knees, gasping for air and clutching her chest.

"Ahh, I…I can't breathe!" She wheezed in a strained whimper.

"Is she having an allergic reaction?" Mark asked in alarm.

"Did you eat something Naiyana? Did you touch one of the plants?" Bobby yelled, kneeling down close to Naiyana's face.

Naiyana bent lower. Her trembling hands shook as she tried to hold onto the ground. Tears streamed down her face. She wheezed. The grass between her fingers frosted and cracked under the widening ovals of ice forming around her hands.

"My…lungs…are…freezing." She rasped.

"Guys, we have to help her." Mark yelled.

"Are her ice powers messing with her body?" Bobby rambled in a flood of concern. "I'm sorry I freaked you out, Naiy! Should I carry her the rest of the way?"

"Shut up guys. Just give her some room." Elise insisted, clearing the boys away from Naiyana and kneeling down to comfort her.

"Hey Naiy, sit back. Sit down on the ground here. Shhhh, it's ok. Come, sit with me. Breathe. Slowly, just breathe. Listen…" Elise said calmly. "…I think you're having a panic attack. It's alright. I get them sometimes when I'm in a small space."

Naiyana tried to breathe, but it felt like she was drawing air through a stone. She looked up and saw Elise's kind eyes. They brimmed with tenderness. Elise smiled, and guided Naiyana through her gasps. Elise placed a hand on Naiyana's chest, and encouraged her to inhale deliberately. Naiyana felt warmed under Elise's touch.

Eventually, they began to share a breathing rhythm and a calm washed over Naiyana. She exhaled heavily, releasing the tension from her body. Naiyana blushed at Elise awkwardly, and hesitantly placed a hand on her shoulder in gratitude.

"I'm sorry." Naiyana spoke softly. "I, uh, I was just thinking about my family. I suddenly realized how much I miss them. This place makes me forget home a little. I looked around, at all the strangeness and at you guys. And I felt…" Naiyana trailed off. "…I like you guys. But you don't really know me. I'm new to the group. I just felt very alone."

"Naiyana, we're all scared." Mark said, kneeling to meet her eye. "None of us have any idea what this place is, or how we're gonna get home. But we're in this together. New or old, you're one of us. You're our friend. We'll figure this out. If there's a way to get home in that Maije place, we're gonna take it. I promise." Mark rubbed Naiyana's back.

Elise noticed that Naiyana's attention was wholly focused on her. There was a lingering warmth in Naiyana's eyes that made Elise feel slightly awkward.

"And in the meantime, look at how beautiful this place is." Elise said, rising in a swirl of excitement. A wild realization spread across her features. "Bobby!" She blurted out. "Can you run ahead and see how far till we hit the river?"

Bobby hesitated. He liked the idea of exploring the speed potential of his legs, but doing anything at Elise's bidding didn't sit well with him.

"Alright." Bobby replied nonchalantly. "I'll see if I feel like coming back for you."

The group watched as Bobby tore ahead at extraordinary speed. A short moment later he reappeared in front of them, coming to a smooth abrupt stop. Bobby touched the tip of his cowboy hat and flashed a smirk.

"It's not too far. There's a couple of turns ahead. Then a short downhill part. After that you can see the shore of the riverbank in a big clearing." Bobby said, a surprisingly optimistic chipper in his voice. "Like ten to fifteen more minutes, at your slow ass walking speed."

"Oh man, can we go explore outside the path for a little then?" Elise asked in a rush. "Please, please, please? I smelled something amazing back there coming from the tree line. And I've been hearing these really beautiful bird songs…"

"No way!" Bobby said with firm frustration. "Are you trying to get lost?"

"How the hell would we get lost? I'm talking about a couple of steps into the jungle."

"Elise, just stop!" Bobby groaned. "We're so close to the river."

"Exactly dude." Elise replied theatrically. "You said we're just ten minutes away. What's a little fun gonna hurt?"

Elise did her best impression of a pout while bouncing in uncontained excitement.

"Are you that bored?" Bobby asked. "You need a crazy adventure, even in this weird place?"

"Bobby..." Elise composed herself. "...this jungle is fucking magic, dude. I don't know what to tell you. I'm not weirded out by everything like you are. I wanna see as much of this as I can. Who knows if we're ever gonna get another chance to be here again. Especially if we're getting sent right back home soon as we get to Maije. We could be the first humans to explore this place."

"Can you help me here?" Bobby turned to Mark.

Mark struggled to focus on the conversation. As his friends argued, the streams of light drifted off their bodies in oscillating directions and shifting sizes. Uncertainty was adding chaos to their currents.

"Look Bobby, I know you can be kind of a chicken." Elise goaded. "So, if you agree to do this, I promise not to make fun of you for the rest of the way."

"I think we should stay on the path." Mark attempted to mediate. "We don't know anything about this place."

"Of course *you'd* say that." Elise moaned. "I'm not talking about running off into the wild without a plan, I just want to see a little bit of this world, then come right back!"

"Hey guys." Naiyana interrupted, hoping to quell the debate with pragmaticism. "Why don't we go down the path until we pass all the turns Bobby talked about, and when there's only the downhill part left, we can explore some of the jungle. Elise can enjoy herself, and we'll still be very close to the final part of the path, so it'll be easier to find our way back."

"Thank you!" Elise yelled, and hugged Naiyana enthusiastically.

Naiyana's cheeks flushed through a shy smile.

"Elise, you have to promise to keep it to five minutes." Mark added, in a hopeful negotiation.

"No problem." Elise grinned. "See, we can all agree on stuff if we try."

"Does no one else remember that Wynn guy talking about the whole forest changing?" Bobby asked in alarm. "Something about big ass sky-bats. Is this place making you two just as crazy as she is?"

"Let's just get it over with, it's not worth the headache." Mark sighed in resignation.

"Well I'm not running to save her if she does something stupid!" Bobby shouted.

"By the way, the majority overruled you and you never actually agreed, so technically I still get to make fun of you, Dickface." Elise laughed as she sauntered ahead.

"I hate you..." Bobby gritted. "...so much."

Soon enough, they arrived at the crest of a downhill slope. Bobby, Naiyana, and Mark all turned to Elise to see which direction she'd choose to explore in the dense surrounding foliage. She beamed an unabashed smirk and roamed around theatrically.

"Oh, look over here." Elise said, pointing the group towards her chosen trail. "You see these weird flowers? The ones that look like yellow tarantulas. I don't see them anywhere else on the tree line. And they kinda form a straight line into the woods. So, if we follow them in, we should be able to follow them right back out easily enough." She declared confidently.

The others stared back at her with flat expressions.

"Look, I promise not to go deeper than like...fifty steps." Elise offered.

Elise dove into the thick branches ahead of her. The group sighed in resignation and followed her lead. She transformed her arms into heavily furred bear paws so she could part the vines and broad leaves. After a few moments of pushing their way through, the group emerged in a clearing. All four children were instantly mesmerized.

"Holy shit." Bobby uttered, in complete awe.

The small meadow before them was alive with vibrant movement. Flowers of kaleidoscopic colors littered the terrain. Their petals floated gracefully into the breeze, forming vivid clusters that danced into the sky. Occasionally, one of the petals was snapped out of the air by small jumping animals or swooping birds. As the children strolled into the valley, the warm grass welcomed their feet in soft embraces. The playful winds caressed their hair and pulled them onwards.

Naiyana noticed a group of yellow lizard-like creatures with big blue eyes hopping across the landscape on their hind legs. They reached out for small bugs or flower fragments with their six arms, and chirped in laughter as they shoved them into their hungry mouths. Elise saw plumes of fuchsia and lilac mists form fogs that shimmered and glided across the vale.

Bobby spotted what appeared to be a large blue upturned turtle shell, with several holes in its sides. Various long appendages emerged from the openings. They reminded Bobby of elephant trunks, only they were sapphire in coloration and the ends had fat bulbous spheres. The trunks swayed and sprinkled an indigo powder on the surrounding area. It caused the plants below to shine with a brilliant luminosity.

Mark could barely process the concert of moving lights in front of him. Every single creature and blade of grass spouted a silver hue that collided against neighboring streaks. It was overwhelming, and intoxicating. Mark felt dizzy, alarmed, and yet alive in a way he had never known possible.

He closed his eyes and breathed calmly. He concentrated on diminishing the perception's presence in his mind. The sensation resisted at first, but Mark found a way to calibrate his sensitivity to it. When he opened his eyes the silvery glean still shone off everything, but its saturation had lessened significantly.

The banquet of light was no longer blinding, only sharp silver edges hinted at the flowing river Mark knew was there.

"This place is beautiful." Naiyana said in reverence.

"Elise…" Bobby said. "…I hate to admit it. But man, you were…"

"I know." Elise interjected softly. "This is so much better than I expected."

Elise smiled; her eyes full of worship. She was utterly enchanted by the splendor. The children wandered into the valley. They drank in the sights, smells, and pretty sounds. It felt like they were absorbed into their surroundings. Mark noticed a large cluster of turquoise insects flying above him in a perfect grid. They moved in symmetrical rows and changed direction in flawless unity.

Naiyana listened to the bird chirps above. She couldn't see the creatures hidden in their treetop sanctuaries, but the music they offered in each response had a common rhythm. She realized they were having a conversation in shared song. Bobby came across a single large flower with fat white petals. Its central floret was jet black, and covered in a dark syrup. A small galaxy of sparkling red gnats swirled around the flower. One delved too close to the dark core, and landed in the slime. The ooze absorbed the bright bug, erasing it from existence.

Mark saw Elise by the tree line on the far side of the valley. She approached the floating pink mist clouds, and danced around them as they moved closer to inspect her. Mark noticed the small fogs changed the shades of their coloration, and shivered in reaction to Elise's twirls. As the purple clouds encircled around her, Mark realized he could no longer see any hint of silver on Elise's body. The playful mists were obscuring it completely.

The absence of light around Elise added a creeping alarm to Mark's mind. He increased his sensitivity to the light, just to be sure. Everything else in the valley radiated brightly. But Elise's form remained completely void of silver.

Before Mark could think about what it meant, a deafening bestial roar rolled over the air. The sound was monstrous, but had clearly come from a decent distance away. The kids turned to each other in fear. Mark saw Elise step back cautiously, nearing the trees behind her. The clouds around her parted abruptly and flew away. Mark saw the silver light envelope her once more. It formed a large current that plunged downwards behind her. Mark could barely issue a warning before Elise tumbled backwards and fell off a cliff, hidden just beyond the shrubbery. Her shriek of fear grew faint as it followed her over the edge.

"Elise!" Mark yelled, vaulting forward.

His four wings beat the air around him ferociously as he flew to the precipice. Naiyana gave chase; she barely noticed Bobby sprint ahead of her. He reached the edge first and looked over in wild panic.

Elise was a short distance down, groaning in a strained effort to cling to the cliff face. Her transformed claws desperately dug into the sheer rock, clutching the smallest protrusions. She wouldn't last much longer. Bobby spotted the waters of a lagoon far below her. He didn't think she could survive the fall. He looked up and saw Mark fly above him, and swiftly pivot to dive down towards Elise. Naiyana finally made it to the edge. Bobby turned to face her.

"I'm gonna get some vine. Be right back." He said, before sprinting off.

Naiyana knelt down to peer over the edge. She saw Mark hover beside Elise.

"Stop, Mark!" Elise shrieked over gusts of wind caused by his wings. "You're gonna blow me off the fucking cliff."

"I'm trying to catch you!" Mark yelled back, hovering closer. "I'll carry you back up."

Mark tried to get near enough to grab Elise, but the heavy thrusts of his wings made it hard to move precisely. Elise lost her grip on one hand and began to slip. Naiyana stood up and pointed both her hands towards the duo, desperately trying to focus.

A small shelf of ice formed beneath Elise. It was attached to the rockface, and was just big enough for her to stand on. Mark moved closer, as Elise's feet found purchase on the shelf. She let go of the rock above her, and her weight pressed down on the ice fully. The surface was too slick. Elise slipped onto her knees, cracking the shelf and tumbling backwards. Mark dove down and caught her wrists. He barely managed to hold their weight, as his wings changed direction and struggled to fly back up.

Naiyana had turned around and covered her eyes in horror when Elise fell. She completely missed Bobby's rapid incoming. Bobby noticed Naiyana turn and block his path. He tried to stop abruptly, but the vine he carried wrapped around his ankle and tripped him violently. Bobby collided into Naiyana, and they both careened over the edge. Mark looked up as he carried Elise, and saw Naiyana and Bobby's entangled bodies hurtle towards him.

"Oh no…" Mark muttered in dread, just before they crashed into each other.

The group fell at an alarming speed, screaming and scrambling. Elise transformed her arms into long serpentine tails and wrapped them around Naiyana's waist and one of Bobby's legs. She pulled them closer, as Mark grabbed Elise's belt with both hands and desperately tried to carry the group's weight. His wings couldn't handle the burden, and they continued to plummet down in contorted arcs and twisted turns.

They passed through a heavy cold spray. Naiyana realized a waterfall was bursting out of an opening in the cliff wall, feeding a surge of water into the lagoon below. She reached out her arm, and tried to freeze a structure out of the torrent that drenched them. But there was too much spray, and it simply transformed into an unstable slush that enveloped everyone.

The chilled sludge did absorb some of the impact, as the children fell into the lagoon. Mark felt cold dread as he heard the familiar dullness of sounds traveling through water. Flashes of Echo Lake filled his mind. He struggled to find the surface, fighting the unruly movements of his wings.

Mark looked down and saw Bobby sinking from the weight of his metallic legs. He kicked them wildly, trying to propel himself upwards. But the vine wrapped around his body hindered his movements. Elise transformed her own legs into two dolphin tails. She dove down and grabbed Bobby's wrists. She attempted to pull his weight to the surface, but they twisted and turned around each other.

Mark felt a tranquility wash over him. He looked down and saw crackling bolts of silver light shimmer off every part of his body. It wasn't the usual luster he had grown accustomed to seeing. Thick cords of energy formed around his limbs and abdomen. He was connected to something powerful; something he could control. Mark understood this without reservations or doubt. He looked to his left, and saw the faint outline of a figure beside him. The figure appeared to be made of coils of light. It stared at Mark with a face that had no eyes.

"Calmly." The now familiar ethereal voice spoke in Mark's mind.

Mark felt an assuring tranquility soothe him. His wings grew still and he hung in the water, unmoving. Slowly, he reached out his hand. A beam of silver jolted forward from his arm, and connected with Elise and Bobby. In their wild panic, they didn't seem to notice the light. Mark instantly felt connected to them. He felt their shape, the movements of their limbs, and their urgent fears.

Mark concentrated. He adjusted Bobby's positioning and straightened out Elise's tails. Their bodies became more aligned. They rose upwards more efficiently, and soon broke through to the surface. Naiyana had formed a large ice raft that was floating in the water. She helped Bobby and Elise in as they climbed aboard.

Just as quickly as it had arrived, the energy faded from Mark's body. He felt the wild fullness of his situation fill his awareness once more. Mark turned and saw the luminous figure was no longer there. He folded his wings neatly behind him and swam to the surface.

Mark realized he had just moved Bobby and Elise's bodies using his mind. Whatever his connection was to this strange place, he now knew the silver light was something he could influence. Mark wanted to know who that whispering figure was. What it wanted. Was it trying to help them? Why did it keep disappearing?

Mark's head breached the water. He took deep calming breaths. He felt different. He was more at ease. Mark swam towards his friends. They peered over the edge of the raft, trying to spot him in the waters below.

"Mark!" Naiyana yelled, relieved when she saw him approach. "I was so worried."

"I'm okay." He replied. "Here, give me that vine. Tie it to the front of the boat and I'll pull us back to land."

Mark gripped the side of the raft, and pulled himself up high enough to free his wings from the water. He spread them wide and shook off the wet residue. Mark gripped one end of the vine, as Naiyana secured the other to an ice hook she formed on the raft. Mark flew towards the shore line, tugging the boat behind him.

The children stumbled onto the sand, and collapsed on their backs. Mark floated down to the ground and took in their surroundings. He could see the end of the blue leaf path, near the tree line of their current sandbank. They had arrived at their intended destination, albeit not by the most desirable route. The lagoon's waters curved around a corner and fed into the river ahead. Mark noticed four elegant wooden boats resting nearby. They looked like large well-polished canoes, with graceful carvings etched into their sides.

"Wow." Elise panted, when she finally caught her breath. "That was close."

"If we ever get out of this place, Elise…" Bobby huffed, rising to a seated position and staring at her coldly. "…I'm actually going to murder you!"

"Relax dingus." Elise replied, rolling her eyes.

"That's the second time we almost drowned." Bobby chastised. "You coulda killed us."

"How is this my fault?" Elise countered indignantly. "I fucking fell, dude."

"We never should have gone exploring, Elise." Mark said, in a disappointed tone. "That's the blue path right there. We could have walked here, and avoided all of that. You don't always have to goof around."

"And you don't always have to have a stick up your ass!" Elise replied, a little hurt and still visibly shaken.

Bobby kicked her side in frustration. He had intended it to be a gentle shove, but the strength of his leg surprised him and sent Elise sliding across the sand.

"Ow!" She yelled. Elise lunged at Bobby and landed on top of him. Both her arms formed large slimy tentacles, and she slapped them across Bobby's face. They were leaving a purple inky residue all over him as he fought to avoid their wet contact. Bobby finally shoved her off, and angrily wiped his face.

"You're such a pain in the ass!" Bobby shouted. "We have no idea where we are, we have one shot at *maybe* making it home, and you just have to try to mess things up."

Elise turned to Naiyana for support. But Naiyana lowered her gaze to the ground. Elise squinted through small hints of tears.

"Guys." Mark intervened, before things escalated further. "There's canoes over there. Let's grab one and get on the river. The sooner we get to Maije, the sooner we get home and leave this all behind us."

Even as Mark said the words, he felt an odd sense of dissatisfaction. He knew he needed to find a way to return home to his father. But a part of him felt increasingly connected to this place. His friends rose to their feet and walked towards the beached boats. They worked together in silence to pull one into the water, and all got in.

Elise sat in the back and stared at the water, while Bobby and Mark took the oars and began to row. Naiyana thought about going to comfort Elise, but she seemed to want to be alone, so Naiyana sat up front and stared ahead. The lagoon's waters took them around a small bend downstream covered in branches, before revealing the wide expanse ahead.

Mark soon understood why Wynn had called it 'The High River'. The winding waterway was nestled on top of what appeared to be a natural stone aqueduct. Elevated far above the valley, the narrow pathway snaked towards a distant horizon drenched in auburn sunsets. The river's surface looked like polished glass, and was framed on either side by thick clusters of bushes. Mark wondered if the plants were stopping the water from pouring over the steep edges. They were essentially gliding along the peak of a very thin mountain. He peered over the brink of one bank as they made a sharp turn, and saw a lush jungle below. There were other rock formations littered throughout forestry, including tall spires and large orbs. Most were covered in their own canopy of bizarre flora.

It reminded Mark of an old elevated train his father had once taken him on, in a city he couldn't quite remember. They had sat together smiling, while the train swam in between giant skyscrapers, and avoided the wild traffic below.

Naiyana was mesmerized by the topography, but when she turned around to share her awe with the group she saw Elise still sulking on the far side of the boat and Bobby clenching his jaw in stubborn irritation as he rowed. Naiyana made eye contact with Mark, and utilizing a series of short head gestures, conveyed her plan. She relieved Mark on the oars, and sat next to Bobby. Mark made his way to the back of the long canoe, and sat by Elise.

"At least we're heading home now." Naiyana offered softly.

She was met by a long silence from Bobby.

"I just...I don't like this place." Bobby said flatly. "We don't belong here."

"I know." Naiyana replied.

She thought that was what Bobby wanted to hear. But if she was being honest, not belonging was a familiar sensation. This place was just prettier than most.

"I'm sorry, Elise." Mark said, seated next to her as she stared into the water. "I didn't mean to make you feel bad. I just want to keep us safe."

Elise furrowed her brow, but repressed her urge to reply. Mark tried a different approach.

"I know you don't want anyone to get hurt either. You're just a lot more adventurous than the rest of us." Mark prodded. "Come on, I know pretending you don't notice this amazing view is killing you."

Elise cracked a frail smile.

"I'm sorry too." She said, turning to face him with glistening eyes. "That shit was scary as hell. And I feel terrible that you guys almost got hurt because of me. I just..." Elise paused. "...I just hate it when people try to tell me what to do."

"I know." Mark nodded, putting an arm around her shoulder. "Just try to remember we're here together. What you do affects all of us. We just want to make it back home safely."

"I know." Elise confessed with a sigh. "But you gotta admit: you guys would be so much more boring without me!" She added, wearing her famous smirk.

Mark grinned and gave her a strong hug.

"Mh apologhee appliehs to yuh too, Buhby." Elise muffled through a plume of feathers.

"Yeah, yeah." Bobby replied, rolling his eyes and shaking his head.

This river looks like it goes on for a while." Elise announced to the group, as she pulled out an elegant silk pillow she found under her seat. "Mind if I take a nap?"

"Yeah actually," Bobby added. "I could use a rest too."

Mark noticed the river's current pick up. It moved them along nicely enough. He stood at the front of the raft and spread his wings. As he curved each wing, Mark found he could steer the canoe to keep it centered in the water and avoid the edges.

"You two sleep." Mark smiled. "Naiy and I will wake you if we see any sky monsters."

"Hey, if this is a dream…" Elise said, ignoring Mark. "Would napping mean we dive into a deeper dream level?"

"Maybe in that level you aren't so batshit crazy." Bobby retorted, his eyes closed.

As Elise and Bobby dozed off, Naiyana moved between the sides of the boat. She created trimaran hulls of ice that she attached with beams to the sides of the raft. She tinkered and adjusted their size and shape, stabilizing the canoe further with a buffer on each side. Mark glanced over his shoulder, and nodded in approval at Naiyana' design.

"I saw it in a book my Dad gave me about sail boats." Naiyana said, squinting at the memory of her father.

She could suddenly smell her Grandmother's cooking. She saw her mother's kind eyes, and remembered the laughter of her family sharing food around their dinner table. She missed them. The thought felt alien in this place.

As they curved around the turns and bends, Mark explored their surroundings. He saw a vast orb of stone in the valley below. It was a massive sphere, dark grey in coloration and rough on the surface. It had an opening that looked like a cave, framed by a beard of long lush white vines. The curtainry of plants draped all the way down to the ground, mixing into the foliage and trees below.

As the boat passed by overhead, Mark saw three large eyes open on the rock's surface. They were shimmering blue, with mirrored pupils that all focused on him. Mark stared back down at the odd stone creature, as it blinked at him. The rock giant smiled, spreading its cavemouth open and shaking several birds out of nests hidden in its beard. The creature closed its two smaller eyes, leaving only the largest one on its forehead open. It bowed its head slightly in a gesture towards Mark. Not knowing what else he should do, Mark also bowed his head and placed a hand on his heart to convey sincerity.

The rock creature smiled once more, and opened its mouth much wider. A vast silver tongue emerged from the cave. The large metallic appendage swept the ground below, hurriedly brushing clusters of plants aside and clearing a smooth surface of flat stone to work upon. The tongue began to drip liquid silver onto the makeshift tablet, feverishly scribbling line after line of exotic looking hieroglyphics.

Mark was so bemused by the entire interaction he didn't notice the river begin to slope. The current picked up speed, and Mark intuitively spread his wings wide to slow the boat down. He saw their elevated platform descend ahead into a gradual downward gradient. The river fed into a beautiful beach; whose white sands spread in a wide embrace of the warm sun kissed sea.

At the center of the shore, Mark saw a complex harbor with the faintest hints of people. They moved across the boardwalks, docked sailboats, and gathered around small fires. Behind the harbor, an immense meadow of golden grass spread inland. Beyond the blond valley, Mark saw a stunning city nestled within a crescent of small blue mountains. Multi-colored pinnacles, domes, and towers alike protruded from behind the city's colossal white walls. The glowing orb of radiant silver light that Mark saw shine off every surface of the city overwhelmed him with awe. It was breathtaking.

The Kingdom of Maije. Mark was certain of it.

8 – TEACHER

A tree of astounding mass sat on a dark hill, utterly alone. Never had another sapling been foolish enough to attempt growth beneath the tree's unrelenting shadows. Its roots slithered into the resistant mud, deeper than the cold soil would have preferred to permit. Giant misshapen branches swelled upwards; forming vast distorted twists which sliced the purple skies above.

Hidden deep within the heart of the tree, a uniquely disquieting creature made his home. In a roughly carved chamber, the creature sat in silence. A towering figure, the creature's lean body was adorned in thick, coiling, ashy branches. The numerous grey twigs crept and protruded off him in curved thorns. The gnarled armor had long ago obscured his putrid flesh. His eyes were green flames, nestled within the branches of his face. The burning embers emitted a mesmerizing radiance, enchanting many who dared to stare into their smoldering ferocity.

The room's walls were adorned with shelves displaying tomes, trinkets, weapons, and numerous treasures. But the creature's gaze inevitably always landed on the same sight: an array of glass containers stacked in perfect symmetry along his favorite wall. Within them, rare captive beings moved helplessly around the confines of their prisons. Their differing emotional states reflected the stark contrasts of their exotic anatomies. Some hammered limbs against the glass in rage, some bowed their heads in despair, a few turned their backs in defiance, one sat reflecting in closed-eyed serenity, and the newcomers uniformly begged for release.

His collection.

The creature reached out a long arm, trailing his course brittle fingertips against each container's surface.

"Such promise." The Creature sighed in a deep granular voice. "Yet, the best of what lies within each of you remains unflourished." A grin of black fangs formed on the creature's face. "Do not be troubled...I will help you unearth those hidden treasures."

The creature wrapped an emerald robe around his body. He prepared a bag with all he would need to hunt the great forest for new captives. The creature moved to seize his iridescent war-cane from the wall, but stopped halfway through his reach. He sensed a presence enter his chambers, and turned to face his guest. The creature stared at the youngling in his doorway.

"Prince Sal'Haf." The Creature greeted his guest. "How long has it been?"

"Karash..." Sal'Haf responded, his voice slithered across the walls in chilling reverberations. "...the Teacher."

"You remember me then?" Karash asked, his gaze unflinching.

Sal'Haf stood unmoving. His crimson hair barely hiding the bottomless pits of his eyes. The pale skin on Sal'Haf's face was the only part of him not encased in formidable dark shards. An unseen force radiated off his stone-covered form, undulating through the room in waves that rattled small objects in their wake.

Karash watched six orbs sail into the room over the prince's shoulder. They were uncommonly black, and rippled with faint hints of consumed light. The spheres moved across the room, and took positions surrounding Karash.

"As it has been an age since a member of your family gifted me with a visit, I must inquire...to what do I owe this pleasure?" Karash asked in a saccharin tone.

"War." Sal'Haf replied, a noticeable clarity in his cold voice. "The final war."

"Aren't they all." Karash grinned. "To my knowledge, the Primals have fought one another for as long as the Raya has

131

been known to exist, young princeling. This isn't even the first time I've witnessed one of them choose..." Karash's eyes scanned Sal'Haf's armor. "...a Reflection as their champion. Our histories are filled with the stories. Perhaps you should have paid more attention during our lessons."

Sal'Haf remained still as Karash continued his mocking lecture. The Teacher squinted.

"I have seen many younglings blinded by the passionate ambitions of their ideology. What makes you so certain of victory, Sal'Haf?"

A darkness spread across the room. The shadows on the wall widened and slipped over every surface. Karash felt a cold fury radiate off the Prince.

"I don't doubt there are many who will cower and kneel before your powers, Princeling." Karash stated calmly. "Do not mistake me for one of them."

After a substantial silence, Karash saw the tension leave Sal'Haf's body and the surrounding shadows recede. He recalled the young prince who had once endured his tutelage. That child had a playfully vicious wit, a disarming charm, and wild aspirations. Now all Karash could see in his eyes was cold loathing.

"What undertaking would you have of me?" Karash asked tactfully.

"Hunt!" Sal'Haf answered, his simmering anger coursing through his voice.

"And who is it you want me to ensnare?" Karash inquired.

Sal'Haf took measured steps towards his former teacher, his gaze unwavering. The thick stones encasing his feet thudded heavily as they strode across the room. He raised an arm, and the black rocks covering his hand morphed into a small figurine. The statuette had wings, and moved in a sluggish simulation.

"A youngling." Sal'Haf hissed. "Travelling with three companions. Kill them all."

"The youngling bears four wings? Most unusual." Karash ruminated. "If you can see him, why can't you catch him?"

"I saw his arrival." The chill of Sal'Haf's voice lingered in the air. "Every light creates a shadow. Many search for him now. Will you?"

"What do you offer in exchange for his...deliverance?" Karash inquired.

"The council." Sal'Haf spoke in entwined voices. "You were banished."

"Indeed, I was." Karash mused. "They did not agree with my particular form of tutelage." He turned to glance at his collection. "But the surest way to make enemies has always been to try to change something. I'm sure you're learning that lesson yourself."

Karash returned his gaze to the boy, smiling broadly.

"You will be the new council." Sal'Haf stated, a rich absorbing density filling his tone. "After we cleanse the broken remnants from the realms. The Raya will be pure."

"That is a most generous offer." Karash replied. "Though, I wonder what will remain for me to council, young prince, after you've devoured every realm in the Raya."

Before Sal'Haf could respond, Karash spun and grabbed his war-cane off the wall with blinding speed. He brought the orb on its crest down onto ground in front of him. A schism of energy vaulted forward, colliding onto Sal'Haf's forehead.

The impact brought Sal'Haf to his knees, as large tendrils of energy wrapped themselves around his limbs and tethered him into immobility. A deafening groan spewed out of him; foul dark vapors rising from his mouth. An explosion of shadow filled the room, as a giant black pillar erupted out of the child.

Sal'Haf remained knelt on the ground; mouth agape, with his pale face staring up in a vacant expression. Towering above his frail form, a monstrous orb of violent darkness swirled with threads of crackling energy. It hovered over Sal'Haf, trying to permeate back into the prince. It was held at bay by the war-cane's struggling power.

Several formidable faces formed within the black shroud. The ghoulish visions were of creatures long lost to time. Their fury was haunting; slithering expressions filled with enraged cruelty. The countless hateful eyes of all focused on Karash.

"**YOU DARE DEFY US.**" A chorus of voices spoke in a deafening cacophony.

Karash felt a cold wave wash over him. He struggled to reclaim his awareness as portions of his mind floated into oblivion. A slow clarity returned to his senses and he raised his gaze towards the towering doom before him.

"Asha's Shadow…" Karash stated with a deep gracious bow of his head. "…Seed of Darkness, First Voices, Old Guard of the Void. It is my sincerest pleasure to face you. I am a loyal servant of the Dark Star, and only wished to speak candidly with your truest form."

Karash raised his staff and dissolved the energy coils. The dark orb exploded throughout the room in a thick plume. It surrounded Karash. The air became dense, cold, and utterly black. The Teacher kept his head bowed low, as various creatures took shape all around him.

He could feel their heavy legs walking across his floors. He heard their thorned tentacles scratching his walls, he sensed their insatiable madness. From every direction, hidden within the unrelenting darkness, monsters of malevolence whispered to one another. Their hatred crawled over every surface. Karash only heard scattered words.

"Insolence…"

"Consume him…"

"Tear him to shreds..."

"What does he want?"

"Make him suffer."

The discord grew still and the room fell silent. Karash noticed a rumbling beneath his feet. It shook the black air around him. He closed his eyes as a formidable presence rose from the ground. Karash's thoughts felt chilled and full of dread. His weakened grip nearly dropped his cane. Something ancient took shape behind him. Its horror was unspeakable. Karash felt it rise from a terrible chasm. It bore a power far darker than anything he had ever felt. The energy radiating off the unseen creature caused the vast tree containing Karash's home to crack under the strained expanse.

With his eyes still closed, Karash heard the creature walk around the room. Each dense footfall shook the branches of Karash's armor. To look upon the creature would mean certain death. He felt the vast form approach him from behind. The air near Karash's face was pulled back in a heavy gust. The creature was smelling him.

"You serve us?" The Creature spoke in a cavernous voice, obscured by immense fangs.

With each word, Karash felt drawn towards his own reckoning. A call in his mind told him to open his eyes and plunge himself into an oblivion that would last forever.

"There is an allure in the darkness which seeks to end us." Karash finally spoke, his voice wavering slightly. "How else can we be free to commence our new beginnings?"

"Pretty words." The Voice seemed simultaneously close and strangely distant; groaningly deep and chillingly precise.

"Have I not been a loyal servant to Asha's dream? I have culled the weakness I found in countless souls." Karash gestured towards the still kneeling Sal'Haf. "Is that twig of a boy truly the Reflection you would choose? The best conduit to unleash the Dark Star?"

"You question us…"

"I merely…"

"Your vanity does not interest us." The Voice was on the far side of the room.

"What must I do to prove myself?"

"HUNT!" The Voice was right by Karash's ear; enormous fangs ground impatiently.

"And if I were to kill the youngling for you?"

"Speak, and whatever trinket you desire will be yours."

Karash took a moment to compose himself. He drew an unhurried breath.

"I want Maije." Karash stated.

Grumbling movements and murmurs rippled across the room. The other shrouded beings emitted cold mocking laughter and whispered suspicions. The large creature growled and the chorus was silenced.

"When we have reclaimed the Raya, Maije will be yours." The Creature spoke.

Karash's brow furrowed. He sensed something beyond the familiar Void he had always known. A new darkness lurked, hidden within the abyss, yet yearning to reveal itself.

"Has the age of Asha truly come? Are the black ocean's tides upon us?" Karash asked.

"Only the noise will perish." The Creature responded in a cloying tone. "We will erase all distortions, and fill the black garden. An era of serenity, that will know no end…"

As the creature spoke, a vision formed in Karash's mind. He saw an endless black expanse. Within this sea of tranquility, countless perfect rows of spheres aligned themselves. They contained furious sparks of light, pulsing and throbbing within the unrelenting walls of shroud that enclosed them. The lights sent desperate ripples of energy outwards, only to be absorbed at the surface of each globe, and harvested back into its depths. The surrounding ocean remained dark, undisturbed, and silent.

"We return to the first harmony." The Creature's cavernous boomed.

"A serene dream." Karash responded. "Contained…and unchanging."

"Do you serve this dream?" The creature asked, menacingly distrustful.

Karash took a restrained moment before responding. He could feel creatures in the room yearning to lunge at him with lustful violence.

"This war will shape the nature of every soul in the Raya." Karash spoke with purpose. "The Primals have always longed to rule unrivaled, each in their own way. Those who preach the necessity of balance fool themselves with our oldest lie. There is no peace to be found in Sawah harmony, only prolonged misery. An absolute victor must prevail, or the conflict will forever ensue." Karash paused, and knelt on the floor. "Koba's chaotic flame is too unruly. She will never reign over the Raya. And Shura's guiding control has not been felt in the realms for far too long, I doubt he has the will left to claim any dominion. Only the Void has the power and determination to bring a final resolve to our disharmony. Asha's time has come. You have my devoted loyalty."

"Find the youngling. Slaughter him, and his companions. We will tolerate no rivals."

Clarity filled Karash's mind. Rivals. Now it made sense.

"After the devastation at Kahltam, when it became clear you had chosen Sal'Haf here as your Reflection, many wondered who the other two Primals would select as their champion. I've heard rumors of a youngling named Payo, who seems to be Koba's choice. The Reflection of Chaos' wild flame. I suppose that means the youngling you'd have me hunt is Shura's Reflection? The wielder of Control." Karash asked with a smile.

He was met with silence.

After a long moment, Karash dared to open his eyes. Sal'Haf stood before him, staring directly at the teacher. The darkness that had filled the room had returned into the prince's form. Sal'Haf's expression was cold, but small currents of unrest struggled in his eyes.

"You've gained a wealth of power, Sal'Haf." Karash said. "And all it cost you was your family."

Sal'Haf narrowed his eyes. He raised a hand and closed his fingers into a fist. All the beings in Karash's collection screamed in agony and burst into dusts of grey powder; drifting to the bottom of their glass enclosures as fine floating wisps.

"Still some of you left in there, after all." Karash continued undeterred. "Withdrawn within the anger."

"The winged youngling…" Sal'Haf gritted, between strained breaths. "…do not fail."

"It will be done." Karash said, bowing his head slightly as Sal'Haf turned to leave. "Though I believe I have the easier task. Shura's power has long been in decline, but Koba is full of newfound fury. This youngling Payo is imbued with the frenzy of Chaos' eternal fire. She will be a formidable foe. Even now she amasses many allies in the wake of your conquests. Warriors from countless realms who all but worship her, perhaps even as much as they fear you. Are you sure you are ready to face her?"

Sal'Haf stood in the doorway, his back to Karash. "The black fire cannot be sated."

"Perhaps." Karash responded playfully. "But the council's wroth is not to be casually dismissed either. They have battled vast armies before."

Sal'Haf turned to face his old teacher. "You don't see what surrounds you, Karash."

Prince Sal'Haf tilted his head, gesturing for Karash to join him outside. The Teacher followed the youngling as they walked through the roughly carved corridors of his home and emerged on the hilltop.

The sight that greeted Karash froze him mid stride. Spread across the valley, in every direction and as far as Karash could see, the Prince's horde stood in perfect stillness. An army of foul creatures, monstrous and deformed, all stared at their young master. It was the largest collection of beasts and warriors Karash had ever seen. The army inhaled and exhaled in unison. The sound felt like a storm as it washed over Karash. An ocean of malice.

"Few remember the truth, *Teacher*." Sal'Haf said, staring at his horde of grotesqueries. "We were all shadow once, swimming together in darkness and peace." He paused to look up at the vibrant fires of Karash's eyes. "Before some of us were stained by the light."

Prince Sal'Haf descended the hilltop. His creatures parted a path for him.

"We will all be united in the stillness again." Sal'Haf spoke over his shoulder.

Karash watched Sal'Haf stride towards the horizon. His countless followers marched behind him. The crashing tremor shook the valley long after they left the Teacher's sights.

9 – GATES

The children docked their canoe on the shore, and
briskly hopped onto the soft sands. They avoided docking at the
crowded harbor; out of caution and because they couldn't fathom
how the boats navigated the imposing, spiraled, multi-leveled
structure.

They watched dozens of exotic looking ships approach
from the open sea, and effortlessly move within the complex
harbor's elegant floating woodwork. Outlandish creatures
walked across the vibrantly colored rope bridges which
connected each platform. They shouted at each other, passed
food parcels, laughed, sang, scolded children for running too
quickly, and even occasionally howled at the three setting suns.

Adjacent to the harbor, a small village bloomed with a
bouquet of shops, large bonfires, bizarre fruit stalls, and other
marketplace treats to welcome weary travelers. Mark noted how
unique the architecture was, from the colorful pyramid shops and
treetop boutiques, to the spiraling eatery towers filled with
feasting customers.

On their secluded corner of the beach, the sand was bone
white and the water was warm. Elise was up to her knees in the
sea, staring at odd aquatic animals that swam between her legs.
A beaming smile consumed her face. She turned to look at her
friends, and saw them eyeing the distant city with determination.

"We can go straight through the field," Mark said,
scanning their surroundings. "aim for the city's main gates."

"Shouldn't we ask one of them first?" Elise suggested,
eyeing the dock's buzz of activity.

"You just can't help yourself, can you?" Bobby scolded.

"It might actually be smart to check." Naiyana
interjected. "Those are big fortress walls. We don't know if it's

definitely Maije or if we'd even be welcome. There might dangers or customs we should learn about!"

Naiyana's practicality won the boys over - begrudgingly. Elise barely suppressed her giddy grin. Her warm eyes landed on Naiyana in gratitude. Naiyana returned a quick smile, then turned away in an awkward blush.

The group strolled cautiously towards the harbor. As they neared the buildings, they tried to seem relaxed and blend into the crowd; but it was hard not be captivated by what they saw. Every person they looked at was strikingly unique.

Mark noticed a group of small children chasing each other and jumping between the platforms of the dock. They looked simian, but had silver scales for skin and glowing indigo eyes. They swung from ropes and wooden edges using six long arms.

Elise spotted two enormous pink slugs, as big as cars, crash into each other and fight. Onlookers cheered and threw flower petals and blue coins on them. A small child with ebony fur all over his body and large pink eyes ran up to Bobby, prodding his metallic legs and laughing. His large mother came and scooped him up.

"I'm sorry." The large furry woman said in a huff. "He's always getting away from me."

"That's alright." Bobby replied, staring up at the giant talking bear-lady.

"Here, have some bislii berries." She said, handing Bobby the fruits. "We picked them today."

Bobby looked at the peculiar fruit. They were turquoise and plump, with yellow dots all over them. They didn't actually look too bad, but Bobby wasn't very hungry. A section on the side of his leg suddenly opened, and slid outwards, revealing a hidden storage compartment.

"I guess I have pockets." Bobby muttered, raising his eyebrows.

He placed the berries inside and the pocket slid back into his upper thigh smoothly.

"Eww!" Elise grimaced. "You just put food *inside* your leg!"

"Will you just go talk to someone already so we can get out of here?" Bobby complained.

Elise grinned and looked for a target. She saw a curious looking creature hanging off the docks by three of its sixteen tentacles. The creature's body was a bulbous orb, rainbow streaked in various leathery colors that shimmered against the waning light. It had a large singular orange eye in the middle of its forehead with four black pupils. Every time someone walked by, the creature whistled or chirped a unique short song from its chunky green beak. Elise strode over to the creature confidently.

"Hello." She smiled, waving her hand. "I was wondering if you could tell me whether that was Maije over there?" Elise pointed to the city behind her.

The creature stared at Elise with its globular eye. After a slow silence passed, the creature opened its mouth and vomited a torrent of colorful foam directly onto Elise. The substance looked like a thick stream of polychromatic glitter. Before Elise could even react to being drenched in the foul liquid, the creature shrieked and cawed at the sky madly.

"Get away from my Dakieu, ya thief." A big portly man screamed, stumbling over to Elise. He had purple skin and three shiny yellow horns on his forehead. His heavy green robe didn't slow his angry stride, as he staggered over to her.

"Gross!" Elise yelled, wiping the warm substance off. "No one's trying to steal your stupid puke monster!" She fumed, then stormed back to her friends.

Bobby fought every muscle in his face to contain a smile.

"Talked to enough people yet?" He mumbled through his teeth.

"Shut the fuck up, Bobby!" Elise scolded, still rubbing the colorful liquid off her body. The foam faded into a mist and floated away. Despite the odor, it left her skin and clothing much cleaner than they were before.

Naiyana noticed an old lady sat behind a stall with dozens of little leather pouches on it. The lady was covered in a thick plume of auburn feathers. She had four large eyes, all mounted on fleshy tubes that protruded from her head. Her mouth was a wrinkly jade-colored snout which swayed slightly in the breeze. Naiyana approached her, offered a short smile, and asked what she was selling.

"Messenger Lizards!" The Lady replied in a squawk.

She lifted a pouch from the counter and shook it violently. The pouch jostled and moved in her hand; the creature inside clearly agitated by the disturbance.

"Got a dispatch you want delivered? Fastest runners in the realm!" The Lady claimed.

"Oh..." Naiyana responded, at a complete loss for words. "...no, that's ok." She snapped back to focus. "I was wondering if you could you tell us if that was Maije over there?"

"Course it is! Where else would it be?" The lady rasped in annoyance. "It's not like it moves, does it?"

Naiyana furrowed her brow and returned to the group.

"Okay, Elise is puke free and Maije is exactly where we already thought it was." Bobby smirked. "Can we go now?"

The children strolled through the valley of high golden grass, brushing their fingertips against the plants. The stalks were tall enough to reach their shoulders, but were light to the touch and swayed in beautiful ebbs and flows in the breeze. Each stem was covered in a fluffy coating of glossy amber fur, which shimmered in the sunlight. A delicate perfume wafted off the plants, and smelled like sweet baked breads.

"This place is fantastic." Elise said, clearly in a better mood.

"Yeah," Mark agreed, breathing in the scented air. "I don't think this is a dream. It just feels so different...and real."

"This is definitely crazier than any dream I've ever had." Bobby agreed.

"What if the only way we can get back home is to drown again?" Naiyana asked sullenly.

"What's wrong with you?" Bobby asked, appalled. "Why would you even think that?"

Naiyana looked surprised by Bobby's judgmental tone. She noticed everyone stare at her. Naiyana was overwhelmed with a sense of being misunderstood. She tried to work backwards through her thoughts, and remember how she had arrived at the notion.

"I was...I'm sorry, I was just very scared at Echo Lake, when we fell in the water." She said in a fluster. "I really don't want that to happen again."

The group kept walking, but a stillness fell over their expressions.

"We were all scared, Naiyana." Mark assured her, placing a hand on her shoulder.

"Well, if it doesn't take nearly dying again, I would love to come back here sometime." Elise said, trying to bring some cheer back to the conversation. "When I'm not getting puked on or falling off cliffs, this place is all kinds of amazing." She raised her arms and transformed them into webbed reptilian limbs. "And having these powers is pretty cool."

"After we get home, and only if we can figure out a safe way to get back here again, I might be down for us to visit. Together." Bobby admitted, semi-reluctantly.

"I wonder if other people from Earth have been here." Mark said, looking around.

"Or if they come back often." Naiyana added.

"How would we even find them? We gonna go around town telling everyone what we saw here? Who's gonna believe us?" Elise rambled. "Maybe we can look online, see if there's a support group or something."

"Oh man, I miss the internet." Bobby said.

"What would we even search for?" Elise asked. "How could you describe this to anyone who hasn't seen it?"

"Or felt it." Mark added softly.

"Just search: has anyone else drowned in a lake and been to the magic kingdom with big flying sky fish." Bobby said, cracking a wry smile.

The group shared a laugh. Their gazes wandered all around them: at the distant forested hills, the beautiful colors spread across the triple sunsets, but most of all – they studied the ever-nearing city of Maije. The city's imposing walls were dwarfed by the impressive towers, domes, and temples that rose from within the kingdom. Maije had clearly been built within a jungle, whose lush plant life still enveloped every crevice unpaved by stone. Tall trees swayed in the wind, and swatted against neighboring towers. Thick blooms of flora burst off every building. The city hosted a playful battle for territory between civilization and nature.

Maije stretched out across rolling hills, from the gated walls at its forefront to the blue mountains that protected its distant rear. Naiyana took note of the bizarre buildings within; ovular homes attached to the cliffsides, and complex bridges connecting spires that stood near the many flowing streams. A formidable looking palace hung above Maije, nestled on a vast shelf of rock. The base of the jagged platform was held in place by a giant silver statue shaped like a tree. The enormous metallic branches intertwined into the stone above, securing the rocky foundations.

"Must be where the King lives." Elise tutted. "Looks like a great view."

Strange birds flew above the city, diving and swirling around each other. The children could hear faint laughter and

145

songs float through the air as they drew closer to the gates. Layered over all the intricate details, Mark's vision was once again awash in a volcanic eruption of silver light. It poured upwards from the city, radiating beautifully as it filled the skies. Mark couldn't help but smile in serenity. It was almost as if the city was calling him home.

The children heard a dreadful roar from their side. They turned to see a dark creature emerge from the tree line of a nearby forest. The beast was a foul mass of grey muscle covered in black slime. It had four legs and two arms all displaying ferocious claws. The creature's wild black eyes stared at them coldly. Its large mouth flashed colossal fangs dripping with bile. The roar it had emitted sent a chill into the children's bellies. They were dizzy with fear.

Mark stared at the monster. He could only see the faintest hints of silver emitted from its body. The slight hue had no directional pull. Even as the creature began to stalk towards them. It was as if the light was being swallowed back into the creature's dark form.

"Guys…" Bobby muttered, his voice cracking in dread. "…I think that's the thing we heard in the forest."

"Should we run?" Elise whispered urgently.

Naiyana looked at the city gates, and then back at the beast. Even if it was a slow mover, it was much closer to them than they were to Maije. They were unlikely to make it to the gates before the creature caught up. And they didn't even know if the city would open their defenses for them. The situation was looking dire.

"I don't think we can make it." Naiyana stammered.

The beast stopped ambling, stared at the children, and broke into a rushed charge.

"NOOO'OOHHMYGOD!" Bobby yelled as he scurried backwards on panicked feet.

The beast's heavy footfalls shuddered the ground. Mark turned to his friends.

"Run!" He yelled in wild fear.

Naiyana, Bobby and Elise sprinted in different directions, as they saw Mark leap into the air and take flight. He hovered a good distance above the monster, while trying to keep himself as the creature's main focus. The beast leapt into the air to claw at Mark, barely missing him. The monster howled in rage, and turned its gaze to the other fleeing children.

"No." Mark muttered fearfully, realizing he had lost the creature's interest.

The children saw the beast pivot to chase Naiyana. Bobby yelled to her in warning, and she turned just in time to see the monster close the distance. Naiyana stood in still panic for a moment, before she shut her eyes and encased her entire body in a thick layer of ice. The monster collided with the frozen hull, and started clawing at it. Substantial chunks of ice came away under the beast's talons, but Naiyana remained safe within her armor.

"We have to help her!" Elise yelled at the boys.

Bobby sprinted straight for the monster, leapt in the air and landed a double kick right against the creature's jaw. He heard some teeth crack under his heel, as the creature was thrown sideways off Naiyana. Bobby scrambled back up, and sprinted in confusing alternating arcs around the dazed creature. Mark swept down and lifted Naiyana from the ground, pulling her body out of the crumbling ice chunks. He carried her towards Elise, as Bobby kept the monster distracted.

"I'm fine." Naiyana said, catching her breath. "Help Bobby!"

Elise and Mark ran towards the monster just as it lunged and tripped Bobby with one of its clawed arms. Bobby was on his back as the monster pounced. He kicked it in the face in rapid successions, scurrying backwards as the strikes collided against the creature's angered features. Naiyana raised her arms and surrounded the monster's limbs in heavy anchors of ice. The beast looked down in surprise as its legs were enclosed in thick frost.

Elise ran up to the immobilized creature as Bobby scurried back. Her arms looked like two bouquets of slithering tentacles. She held them up towards the creature and sprayed its face with a deluge of blinding ink. As she continued to coat its eyes and face, Naiyana worked on covering more of its body in ice.

The creature groaned but seemed to stop moving. The children gathered around each other, hoping they had managed to subdue the threat. The monster growled with amplified fury, and shook wildly within its constraints.

With another deafening roar, the beast erupted from the ice and shook the ink off its face. It locked its eyes on the children, and opened its maw to emit a threating ferocious growl. The children saw multiple layers of cruel black fangs pressed against one another. The monster bolted towards them and an empty feeling of dread filled their hearts.

Despite his frightened state, Mark noticed a figure standing behind the monster. It was the faint outline of the same observer he had seen in the lagoon. The figure of coiled lights stared at Mark with no eyes. Its voice entered Mark's mind, only this time it was no whisper.

"FIGHT." The voice commanded in a boom.

Mark rose to his feet, his mind entranced in clarifying awe. His entire body was engulfed in silver light. The other three children fell backwards as they saw Mark's wings spread wide. The light radiating off his form was almost blinding. Mark pointed his arm towards the charging creature. A bolt of silver energy flew forwards and collided into the monster's bulk. A rancorous crackling filled everyone's ears as the light sank into the monster's flesh and transformed it.

The beast's body rose into the air as various parts of it turned into black crystal. The creature struggled and howled in pain against the forced transformation. Solid flesh morphed into glittering stone as the monster screamed in agony and writhed midair.

Elise looked at Mark. His face was still. The silver light beamed out of his eyes so strongly she couldn't even see them. The hand he held in front of him had an orb of light encasing his fist. The sphere continued to fire a ray at the beast, crystalizing new portions of its body. The monster pulled and tore itself away from the transformation, trying to escape.

"Mark!" Elise shouted in confused fear.

The light suddenly disappeared and Mark collapsed, gasping deeply. He looked around in puzzled alarm as his friends rushed towards him. The creature fell to the ground, and shattered various limbs. The remainder of its mutilated body bore massive sores and wretched wounds. The devasted monster continued its bloody crawl towards the petrified children. They clustered around Mark, hugging each other in fear. There was nothing left they could think to do.

Just as the monster launched its mangled body onto them, a series of powerful energy bolts struck the beast and vaporized it. The children stared in awe as a cadre of guards ran from the city towards them. The Maije sentries carried spears and war rods of intricate design that hummed with the powerful energy they had used to dispel the threat. Their shining blue armor bore glowing runes inscribed in silver markings. The language looked like modest linear patterns, all ending in small ovals.

"Get up, bambas!" One guard said. "You're safe now. Let's get you inside, quickly."

The children were still in a daze, but they didn't need to hear those instructions twice. They rushed towards the city with their new saviors. As they stumbled along, Elise spoke in a solemn voice.

149

"This place isn't fun anymore, I'm ready to go home."

Naiyana looked at Mark, who stared down at the ground in silence.

"What was that thing you did?" She asked softly. "With the light!"

"Yeah!" Elise added, the memory resurfacing through her residual fog of panic.

"I don't know." Mark mumbled hurriedly.

Bobby eyed him suspiciously. Mark was clearly hiding something; his face was strewn in confused doubt. As they neared the city, the guards formed a protective cluster around them. The children listened as the guardians spoke amongst themselves.

"I've never seen anything so vile in all my days."

"And so close to Maije."

"We should send a warning to the harbor, in case there are others."

"You think that was one of the creatures that consumed Rama?"

"We don't know what happened to Rama!"

"I can't believe the foulness that's befallen our realm."

"The Watchers must be weeping."

They arrived at the imposing gates. The children looked up and saw the intricately beautiful carvings on Maije's impressive entrance. Striking symbols were engraved into the dense metalwork in a stunning layered arrangement.

Mounted above the city's walls, circular flags waved in the wind. They were a rich blue in color, and bore a silver tree at their center. A horn sounded from above, and the gates began to open. The children peered through the entryway, and saw a tunnel where additional gates followed in a cascade of opening entrances. Before they huddled inside, Mark turned to a guard.

"Thank you for helping us!" Mark said. "Do you know how we can find the Sacred Eye? Wynn sent us here."

"Speak with an Overseer in any of the city squares." The guard said. "They'll assist your petition for access to the Eye."

Mark nodded his head in gratitude and walked onwards with his friends.

"Guys," Elise said, trembling as she moved. "what happens if we die here?"

10 – HILLTOP

Still shaken from their encounter with the monster, the children hurriedly sought sanctuary in Maije's winding streets. As the alleyways widened into larger avenues, the city's majestic beauty revealed itself. Lush gardens bloomed alongside every pathway, moving mosaics swirled across walls to form exquisite morphing tapestries, and immense trees spewed plumes of colorful mists. Mark saw large petals dance off the branches, hover in the air, and transform into vibrant beetles that fluttered away in the breeze.

Above them, colossal stone towers swayed slightly, as small flocks of birds carved plunging arcs between them. A screeching cluster of minute purple apes swung from colorful banners overhead, and threw remnants of fruit at the pedestrians below.

Of the hundreds of people roaming the city, making purchases in markets, or having conversations – a significant majority seemed to be children. Everyone displayed distinctive physicalities and fantastically unique features, but most appeared to be adolescent in age.

Elise saw a small crowd gathered around a boy with dark wooden skin. He was tall and lean, with braided blue vines swinging from the top of his head. His back was covered in a navy-colored moss. Elise noticed that his orange eyes had two overlapping oval pupils, like a magician's rings.

She made her way to the front of the crowd and observed as the Treeboy held up his hand. Everyone watched as he slowly grew a bouquet of outlandish flowers from his fingertips. The crowd stomped their feet and cheered in amusement. Once the fans had dispersed, Elise approached the performer.

"You're beautiful." She said, with an unabashed look of wonder.

The Treeboy smiled at Elise. He held his hand out, palm facing upwards. Elise noticed the crevices and grooves between his bark begin to shine. Photoluminescent pollen floated out of his hand and lit the air up all around them. Elise's face beamed under the soft glow. She breathed the small particles into her lungs, and felt her whole body grow warm. Elise felt bonded to the boy; an unseen current flowing between them.

Bobby noticed something emerging from the banks of a nearby canal. The man rising out of the river had purple leathery skin and turquoise tusks. Bobby saw that in lieu of legs he had large octopus-like tentacles below his waist. He ambled ashore and mounted a large rock. The way his limbs gripped the stone reminded Bobby of a spider capturing its prey.

Two other cecaelias exited the river, one darkly red and the other vividly yellow. The trio shook the water off their bodies. In their hands, Bobby saw clusters of odd-looking fruit – which they had seemingly pulled out of the depths below. The large berries pulsed in a glowing fuchsia hue. The three men laughed and proudly displayed their hauls to nearby onlookers.

Naiyana beheld the paradise of joys and beauty that surrounded her in complete awe. Every discovery was a delightful new curiosity. She felt soothed into a calm sense of ease; until a movement caught her eye.

"What's that?" Naiyana asked, pointing at a mysterious object heading their way.

The children turned to see a ball of light floating out of an alley. The luminous orb was golden at its core and silver at its thicker edges. The small radiant sphere hovered and glided between people, carving an exploratory path through the city. Everyone seemed to notice and smile as it passed by them.

Naiyana spotted small segments grow out of the golden center. They looked like little limbs wiggling outwards. But they swiftly sank back and disappeared into the yolk. The orb stopped to observe a group of people, then rapidly moved along to its next subject of interest. It stopped in front of the Treeboy, and hovered by the youngling for a while. He reached out one of his wooden hands, and offered an encouraging smile. The orb cautiously moved closer. Pedestrians congregated around the coupling.

The edge of the orb's light pressed against Treeboy's finger. A loud hum radiated from its center. The core formed long streaks of golden light, which pushed through the silver shell. The entire sphere shook and crackled with powerful vibrations as its brightness amplified. In a blinding flash, the orb vanished completely.

Once the light faded, the children saw a small girl standing where the orb had hovered. Her body looked like an imitation of the Treeboy. Her skin was a lilac bark. Her flowing hair was made of lush interwoven locks of white leaves. Her jade-colored eyes looked down at her newly formed hands, and saw they were touching the fingers of the boy in front of her. He smiled, leaned down close, and spoke in a comforting voice:

"Welcome to Maije, Newling."

The crowd around them cheered and stomped their feet. The little girl smiled shyly, and sauntered off to explore the city. Everyone casually returned to their conversations and activities.

"This place just can't stop being weird." Bobby said, turning to his bewildered friends.

"That was the coolest thing I've ever seen." Elise hushed in astonishment.

"Yeah." Naiyana muttered, stupefied. "That light egg became...a girl!"

Mark was just as surprised by the interaction as the rest of them, though he was also comforted in knowing he wasn't the only one seeing things this time.

The group kept exploring streets paved in shimmering stone, until they arrived at a large square. At the center of the plaza, a beautiful fountain displayed a statue of three bizarre animals twisted around each other in a playful brawl. Children and creatures alike frolicked in the gushing water. Three distinct temples rested at the edges of the courtyard. One orange stoned dome had many flame pits and pyres surrounding it. Another building boasted intricately designed constructs of metal, crystal, and stone decorating a perfectly symmetrical entrance. The last was a simple white cube, save for the large black columns and dark sealed door.

Bobby noticed a man standing in the middle of the square. He wore an overstated blue uniform, with a grey cape. His chest emblem was an elegantly stitched silver tree. His arms were folded behind him in a stance of rigid decorum. Strangest of all, his entire head was a featureless smooth white stone: no ears, mouth, or nose. Only a single silver eye was engraved on his forehead. Bobby would have assumed the man was a statue, if his head wasn't turning to scan the surroundings.

As Bobby watched, a small purple lizard scurried towards the stone-faced man. It ran at blinding speeds on six legs, and scampered up his uniform. The man outstretched his arm, and the lizard settled into his palm. The man pulled a small rolled-up scroll out of the lizard's harness. His eye perused the letter. Once he was done, the man rolled the paper into a ball, and fed the morsel to the lizard. The creature squeaked in gratitude, and sprinted off.

Bobby rolled his eyes, annoyed by the constant outlandishness of this place. He stomped over to the stone man.

"Are you an Overseer?" Bobby asked in a huff.

"Yes." The Overseer answered calmly, peering down at Bobby with his unmoving eye. His voice radiated from his head in a soothing tenor.

"Of course." Bobby said, growing numb to the absurdities. "We need to see the King. King Kai, right? Do you know where he is?"

"We were sent here by Wynn." Mark added, catching up to the conversation. "He told us King Kai could help us get home."

"Yeah, we need to use your..." Elise started, hesitating when she noticed the Overseer's face. "...Eye."

"King Kai is currently at the Sacred Eye, preparing to welcome the council for an urgent meeting." The Overseer stated.

His right hand gestured to a distant hill. The children saw the faint hint of a bright blue light at the crest of the hilltop. The Overseer's engraved eye shimmered as it scrutinized the children in front of him.

"The King won't likely be free for quite some time." The Overseer said grandiosely.

"How long man?" Bobby asked petulantly. "We need to get out of here."

"We're really desperate to get home." Mark added. "Our families are very worried."

"Younglings don't customarily meet with the King, unless the matter is truly urgent." The Overseer responded; his tone unwavering. "However, if Wynn did indeed send you, I suppose you could wait in the Palace's grand hall until the council has concluded their meeting. When you hear the bells toll three times, the council's affairs will have ended. You may then join the others seeking an audience with the Ki...YOU THERE! GET DOWN!"

The Overseer broke away from the conversation to chase after some children who were attempting to scale an ivy-covered temple wall.

"Ugh!" Bobby groaned in frustration. "We're never getting out of this place."

"Guys, look up there." Naiyana said, pointing at the hill with the pulsing light. "If that's the Eye, maybe we can find a way up there, and just ask someone if they'll help us get back?"

The group looked at each other. Utterly short of any alternative ideas, they shrugged their shoulders in agreement and started their long march.

As they drew closer, they could see the hill was on the outer edges of Maije, pressed against the vast mountains surrounding the rear half of the city. The hill's crest was obscured by a thick cluster of trees and large boulders. But the distinctly blue light continued to shine from behind the foliage, radiating beautifully into the skies above.

"If that's the Eye up there..." Bobby said, looking around. "...how do we get to it?"

The hill's main entrance was a pathway that rose up a gradual slope. It was gated and defended by a handful of stern looking city guards.

"Well front gate's not gonna be an option." Elise groaned. "Let's check the back side."

The group moved around to the far side of the hill. At this angle, they were safely out of the guard's line of sight. But the hill's rear was a rough looking sheer cliff. The jagged rockface soared upwards, towering at an imposing height no one in their right mind would dare to climb.

"Think you boys can get up there?" Elise probed casually.

"Us?!?" Bobby asked, in shocked disbelief.

"Well Mark can fly, and you can jump super high." Elise replied, feigning a logical tone.

"Not that high!" Bobby snapped.

"You're gonna let Mark to go up there alone?" Elise goaded.

"Bobby..." Naiyana interjected their combative routine. "...look at all the ledges and big chunks of rock that stick out.

There's a few on the hill's cliff, and some on the cliffs of the mountainside right next to it. They're perpendicular to each other. You see? It's like a big L-shaped corner that goes up. Maybe you could jump from one side to the other on all the parts that stick out. Like going up steps. Just…far apart and…very high." Naiyana trailed off, realizing how ambitious her plan sounded.

"*Maybe?*" Bobby asked mockingly. "What happens if I miss?"

He turned to Mark for support. Mark's polite smile suggested he might actually appreciate the company. Bobby rolled his eyes.

"Damn man." Bobby said, looking at his path upwards. "Okay, but Mark you have to hover next to me, and if I slip or something you better dive down real fast and catch me!"

"Deal." Mark grinned reassuringly. "May as well use these powers while we have them!"

"You got this, guys." Elise declared, while taking a few cautious steps back.

"Give us a warning if any guards come." Mark said, turning to Elise. "Like do that thing where your voice imitates an animal noise or something we'll recognize from up there."

Elise nodded and furrowed her brow, trying to think of an animal. She concentrated on morphing her vocal cords. She let out a sudden high-pitched shriek. The children bowed their head in collective embarrassment as a handful of nearby pedestrians turned to look at them.

"Holy shit, Elise." Bobby whispered, after the strangers walked by. "Think you can manage something a little less insane sounding?"

Elise seemed distracted by a flock of winged lizards that flew by them.

"ELISE!" Bobby hissed loudly.

"Yeah, I heard you." Elise snapped, turning to face him. "Less loud, more normal."

"Maybe a bird noise?" Mark said, looking up and noticing many diverse birds in the air.

Elise concentrated again, opened her mouth wide and released a guttural deep bird call.

"That sounds like a drowning ostrich." Bobby said, in mild repulsion.

"Good enough!" Mark said. "Naiy, if any guards come at you guys...I dunno, freeze them in a block of ice or something."

"I can't do that, can I?" Naiyana asked, looking to her friends for guidance.

"We'll find out." Bobby replied, turning to face the cliffs above. "Let's go, I guess."

The others watched as Bobby sank low into his knees and prepared to vault. The whirring noises and lights on Bobby's legs surged in intensity. Mark flew up and hovered near the first landing point, holding out his arms in encouragement.

Bobby took a deep breath, whispered something to himself, held on to the top of his cowboy hat, and launched. He soared in a broad and rapid arc upwards, cresting slightly higher than his intended target. As he came down, he just about managed to get his toes onto the rim of the jutted ledge. Mark swooped in and gave Bobby's back a gentle shove, helping him find his purchase. The boys looked at each other, and exhaled a chest-full of nervous tension.

"One down." Bobby smiled, as he looked up. "About six more to go."

Elise and Naiyana watched Bobby leap from one surface to the next, ascending the cliffs. Mark flew around him in supportive spirals, occasionally intervening to ensure a smooth landing. Bobby seemed to be honing his abilities with each bound.

"Look at them, working like a team." Elise said in faux pride. "Almost gives you hope."

11 – EYE

Mark helped Bobby clamber over the cliff's threshold. Both boys exhaled in heavy relief and smiled broadly at their accomplishment. They high-fived wordlessly. Just ahead of them, a cluster of sapphire trees obscured the hilltop. Arcs of eerie blue light sliced out from between the dense trunks. Mark noticed all the leaves absorb the radiance, shimmering with mirrored brilliance.

Bobby gestured towards the vast pile of boulders adjacent to the tree line. The rockfall had collapsed from the mountainside above, and now offered a vantage point above the treetops. The boys cautiously climbed the moss-covered rocks, careful to stay hidden from whoever might be gathered at the light. They peered over a particularly large rock and saw the splendor below.

Floating atop a polished stone courtyard, the boys saw a beautifully radiant azure star. The shining orb hovered and undulated ever-changing shades of luminescence. The sphere was no bigger than the boulders they stood on, but it pulsed with a power that mesmerized them. Mark noticed a unique iteration of the now familiar silver light manifest out of the blue star. It appeared as a perfectly straight line; originating at the orb's core and pouring skywards in an unwavering current.

"I think that's the Eye." Mark uttered softly.

"Yeah." Bobby murmured, captivated by the marvel.

The forest they had circumvented seemed to only surround the rear half of the courtyard. The other side was a neatly trimmed field, on which various people stood attentively. Some wore robes, some the armor of guards, and a few had distinctly noble attire.

Behind them, Mark saw the downhill path that led back to Maije. He followed it with his gaze, taking in the majestic view of the city his elevated position afforded him. Maije was even more stunning from above.

"Bet you that's the King." Bobby whispered, gesturing at a man.

Mark examined him. He had dark blue skin and long black hair that flowed behind his shoulders. He was dressed in elegant white pants and a sleeveless tunic, which looked surprisingly wrinkled. His exposed arms were patiently folded across his chest. Mark saw silver tattoos on the man's muscular arms. The symbols moved around slowly. A few looked burnt and scarred. The man's expression was weary. Mark saw a deep kindness in his face, but also heavy traces of concern in his indigo eyes. Mark noticed the thin silver coronet around his temple.

"What gave it away, Bobby?" Mark teased quietly. "The crown?"

Most of the guards kept a respectful distance. A remarkably enormous grey-skinned man with three serpent heads stood right next to the King, compulsively adjusting his lavish clothing. His three faces kept moving. They alternated their focus between staring at the glowing Eye, glancing at the King, and searching for creases on his extravagant attire. Everyone in the courtyard seemed to be waiting for something to happen.

Bobby looked at Mark, a squint of suspicion cast over his expression.

"Seriously man, what happened out there with that monster?" Bobby pressed. "It was like some weird-looking lightning shot out of you!"

Mark took a measured pause before responding. He wanted to find the right words.

"I think I have some kind of ability here." Mark said. "I'm not sure how it works exactly, but it's happened a couple of times now."

"That's the first time I saw you blasting silver lasers out your hands." Bobby replied.

"It's more like…I have this connection to things, and can control them a little. There was a cloud, and a tree in the forest." Mark explained, before noticing Bobby's confused eyebrow raise. "When you and Elise were sinking in the lagoon. After we fell off the cliff. I pulled you guys up. Or, I kinda moved her tails and your legs so you could straighten out and get to the surface easier. Even with the monster, it was like I was forcing parts of it to be still while the rest of it struggled to break free."

Bobby took it all in.

"It's connected to this silver stuff I see on everything. Like a soft light glowing on stuff." Mark continued. "People, animals, trees, even that Eye thing down there has silver shining out of it. The light surrounds everything, and moves before the things do. I think it's trying to show me where stuff is gonna go, or maybe what things are about to become. Like predicting the future just before it happens…" Mark struggled. "…or something."

"So, it's like a shadow?" Bobby asked, searching for hints of it on himself.

"More like a silver light all around you, and sometimes parts of the light move, and your arm or leg follow that direction right after." Mark clarified, gesturing with his arm.

"So, it's like the shadow of your future…but silver?" Bobby probed.

"I guess." Mark conceded.

Bobby examined his limbs closely, waving an arm in front of his face.

"Can you see it on me now?" He asked.

"I can turn the sensitivity down, so I don't have to see it all the time." Mark replied.

"Got it." Bobby nodded, in a sullen tone.

"What?" Mark asked, noticing Bobby's dejected expression.

"Why did everyone get way cooler powers than me?" Bobby complained.

"What are you talking about? You run ridiculously fast and jump super high." Mark said.

"And you can fly, shoot energy out of your hands, and see the future!" Bobby countered.

Mark rolled his eyes and returned his focus to the courtyard below. He had neglected to mention the observing figure. He wondered why that felt like a shameful secret he wasn't quite ready to share. Their circumstances were bizarre enough, and Mark didn't want Bobby thinking he was going crazy. Before he could dwell on it any further, Mark noticed the silver light emerging from the Eye expand. It spiraled on a widening axis.

"Bobby…" Mark mumbled, growing aware of a powerful sensation washing over him. "…something's happening. With the Eye."

Mark felt a sharp clarity enter his mind. The swirling silver created increasingly complex formations of light. Multiple arcs fragmented from the main beam, ascending upwards as they rolled and folded atop each other. Curious geometric shapes flurried within the whirlwind of luminescence.

Mark was engulfed by a powerful connection to the Eye. Flowing visions crashed against each other in his mind. He saw the Eye resting on the same hilltop long before the city was built. Lush jungles surrounded the vibrant orb. Mark watched curious animals migrate towards it. He saw tribes of early travelers dance under its radiance. A growing civilization rose up around it. The birth of Maije.

Mark turned to Bobby. His friend gazed at the Eye, but something was wrong. Bobby's breaths seemed sluggish. His fingers nervously drummed on the stone ledge, but moved in incremental gradual taps. Bobby's face looked relaxed and unfazed. Mark felt the roots of time untether from his expanding awareness. He calmly absorbed a storm of details: the rock's diverse texture, Bobby's pace of inhalations, a plumage of clouds, silver cords dancing over the Eye.

His gaze turned to the King. Mark looked at his face, and felt awash in his memories. Waves of visions filled his thoughts. He saw the King standing on a frozen lake, surrounded by bodies. Mark found himself standing on the ice as well. He looked up and saw a young boy shrouded in black clouds staring down at him. The boy's black eyes stared straight through him, emptying him of thought. Mark was on a lavish balcony now. He saw the King with a large woman who had four arms. They looked down at the city of Maije together and laughed cheerfully. Mark saw the King alone in his chambers, weeping softly.

Mark pulled himself out of the churning sea of memories. He noticed the Eye shine brighter and hum loudly. The vibrating radiance rose to a monumental crescendo. The orb flashed in a blinding explosion of brilliance, and shot a beam onto the courtyard stones. The King and his attendees watched the arc of light's focal point. A figure materialized within the blue ray.

Mark saw the silver structures fade away, returning to a single line of light aimed skywards. The Eye's brightness also diminished, reverting to its previously calm glow. Finally, the beam waned completely, revealing the now visible figure.

"Hey, it's that lion looking dude from the forest." Bobby said.

"Wynn." Mark agreed softly.

Mark noticed the speed of things return to normal. The King and his three-headed companion strode to Wynn at a brisk pace.

"I spoke to Fyzo." Wynn said, greeting his King. "He promised to do whatever he could to bring Mokko to the meeting.

Petulant bandits! If these troubles don't merit a gathering of the council, I'm not sure what does."

"And what of the Nekra Kingdom?" Kai asked firmly. "Will anyone come speak on behalf of Leiba?"

"I wasn't permitted beyond the outer gates." Wynn said, raising a suggestive eyebrow. "But Speaker Kulsa came to greet me, and assured me she would join us as an emissary. *If the godling Leiba deems this matter worthy of her attention.*" Wynn flourished an imitation. He turned to face the three-headed man beside him. "Step back, Buhdringa, you ornamental oaf! With three pairs of ears, you should be able to hear me without inhaling my hair."

"Fur-covered fool." Buhdringa huffed, alternating which mouth he spoke with. "It is of the utmost importance I know which guests will arrive, to announce them properly. You'd understand, if you had even the faintest notions of diplomacy."

"It would be diplomatic to eat fewer mud-cherries before breathing on me." Wynn tutted.

"Enough." King Kai barked impatiently. He contemplated the situation while Wynn and Buhdringa glared at each other. "The council has been plagued by far too many of our own conflicts and discords. They'll be suspicious enough about the timing of this war. We need to ensure cohesion between *all* of the attendees."

"Conflicts or not, Prince Sal'Haf and his horde threaten all the realms in equal measure. Even that obscene godling and stubborn marauder will recognize the danger we face, and our shared responsibilities to determine the outcome." Wynn assured.

"How confident are you that Mokko will come?" King Kai asked.

"Moderately certain." Wynn replied candidly.

"Moderate certainty." King Kai repeated with a minor chuckle. "A political ideal."

Wynn noticed Kai's attempts at charm still bore a heavy underlying sorrow. He looked at the faces of the nearby guards. They were all discernably tense. Even Buhdringa's three necks seemed stiff as he sauntered to the courtyard's central oval and prepared to greet the council. Wynn took a measured breath and chose his hushed words carefully.

"Fear has gripped the realms, Your Majesty." Wynn began. "Many know the Primals have chosen their champions. War is on everyone's mind. There are those who want to hide, while others rush to proclaim loyal devotion. But most still yearn for the comfort of your dream. They long to return to Sawah unity."

"I hope you're right." Kai smiled warmly. "What of the second Reflection?"

"Her name is Payo." Wynn said, with a crooked forced smile. "She has agreed to come meet with us, at the very least. Though from what I gather, she is as unruly as her new powers. A passionate bamba, filled with wild imagination. Placating her will be a great exercise in..." Wynn glanced sideways at Buhdringa. "...diplomacy."

"Very well." Kai said, staring at a particularly unremarkable stone in contemplation. "Tell the city guards to double their presence but remain out of sight. Cloak their uniforms. Payo must feel no threat on her arrival. She needs to see us as allies. The council will be weary enough of her inclusion in the meeting without any unnecessary volatility."

Wynn nodded, then noticed a shared absence enter both their minds. King Kai's face fell in blush of sorrow. Wynn placed a heavy hand on his friend's shoulder.

"I miss her too." He said softly.

Kai placed his hand atop of Wynn's and nodded.

"Shura has yet to choose a champion. If the Primals are fighting for dominance of the Raya, a third Reflection is bound

to appear sooner or later. Keep the scouts busy in their search."
Kai instructed.

"Perhaps Shura won't be involved in this particular
battle." Wynn suggested. "The presence and influence of Control
has waned of late, across most of the Raya. This fight could be
just between Koba and Asha."

"That's not how things work, old friend." Kai replied.
"Especially if our hope is to return the realms to Sawah harmony.
Until that can be achieved, we should focus on reducing the
suffering as much as we can."

Mark watched King Kai and Wynn finish their hushed
discussion. They walked to join the three-headed man on the
courtyard facing the Eye. A perfect line of guards formed behind
their King – discretely concealing their weapons under cloaks.

"We need to find a way to talk to the King." Mark said.

"He looks kinda busy." Bobby muttered. "Wait, the Eye
is turning...orange."

Mark saw the change in coloration shift from vibrant
shades of blue to a fiery mix of orange and yellows. The silver
beam once again matched the rising hum of the Eye with
complex shapes and movements. Mark sighed in resignation as
his mind filled with increasingly familiar sensations. The now
fully orange Eye erupted in a flash of light and shot forth another
beam directly in front of King Kai and his welcoming party. As
the beam faded, Mark saw a very strange figure take shape.

"What the hell is that?" Bobby muttered.

At first, Mark thought the man below was burning alive.
He slowly understood the wild moving flames that surrounded
him were actually six arms attached to his back, made entirely of
fire. The fiery limbs danced about gently, their fingers trailing
through the cool evening air.

In addition to his six elemental appendages, the man had
two ordinary arms made of flesh and blood. One was tucked at
the elbow in composed stillness, hand gripped around the handle

167

of his orange sword. The other hand rested at his hip; thumb tucked into the rim of his belt. The old leathered strap held up the only item of clothing the man wore: a modest tan-colored wrap of timeworn fabric, draped over his muscular legs. His chest was bare. His dark tawny skin bore a patchwork of battle scars. His broad shoulders were held open in a poised posture.

Small black stones hovered and floated around his waist and neck. Each stone had a rune carved into it, which glowed with warm orange light. The man's head was encased in a bone white war mask. The surface was completely smooth, save for two holes which revealed his piercing crimson eyes.

"Lord Gohlli," Buhdringa's voice rang out of three mouths simultaneously. "Last of the Ardohr Knights, and Chieftain of the roaming Lykam Tribe."

Buhdringa bowed all his heads. Gohlli returned the courteous gesture, and approached King Kai. Small clusters of blue grass, which had managed to grow between the courtyard stones, were singed underfoot by Gohlli's burning stride. As they came face to face, Kai and Gohlli pressed the palms of their hands against one another.

Mark's mind was pulled powerfully into the golden core of the Eye's light. In an instant, he found himself emerged in front of another Eye in a faraway place. The Eye was orange, and floated on top of a moving stage. The platform was elevated on long rows of colossal stone wheels, and pulled by gargantuan beasts of burden wearing exotic armor. Mark understood this was the world from which Lord Gohlli had just arrived. He felt the active remnants of a connection between the two Sacred Eyes.

Mark realized he wasn't really here. He was swimming in the memories of this place. His thoughts were once again consumed by colliding visions. He saw Gohlli at the helm of a vast army surrounding the orange Eye. The warrior tribe roamed across deserts and jungles, keeping their sacred gateway safe. Mark watched them fight against hordes of raiding creatures and battle-hardened brutes. Gohlli led the charge against the invaders, savaging his enemies in wild displays of swordsmanship and scorching ferocity. Mark saw Gohlli cheer with his people, as many of them danced around giant pyres and drank heartily in celebration. On a more still night, he saw Gohlli seated beneath the Eye meditating in deep contemplation. Gohlli's fourteen children ran up to interrupt their father's reflections, laughing as he joined them in play.

Suddenly, Mark's awareness was back on the boulder beside Bobby. The transitions were becoming increasingly jarring. Bobby noticed his perplexed expression.

"You okay?" Bobby asked.

"Yeah," Mark answered hurriedly. "sorry, it's just whenever they use the Eye, it messes with my head. It's like that silver light I was telling you about, but…different. I think I saw where that fire dude just came from. His world, and maybe even some of his memories."

"For real?" Bobby asked in genuine curiosity. "So maybe the Eye is some kind of portal. If you're connected to it, maybe you can use it to send us home."

"That's a pretty big leap, Bobby." Mark said skeptically. "I have no idea how any of this works. Let's just see if we can get someone who actually knows what they're doing to help us. What if I end up sending us into the middle of outer space or something?"

"Couldn't be weirder than this place." Bobby sighed in resignation.

The boys returned their focus to the crowd below.

"I was very sorry to hear about Rama." Gohlli said, removing his mask.

Thick braids of shimmering golden hair fell over his heavy shoulders. His red eyes were filled with deep kindness.

"She was as fine a warrior as I've ever seen," Gohlli's voice comforted tenderly. "and a remarkably loyal friend."

169

The silver runes on Kai's body grew still for a moment as he sank into his grief.

"Thank you, Gohlli." Kai smiled in gratitude. "I appreciate your words, and even more your presence at this meeting. Please make your way to the palace, the others will arrive soon."

Mark and Bobby watched the fire-armed man walk down the slope to Maije. None of the guards followed to escort him. It seemed he was a welcome and familiar guest.

"I thought your wings were cool." Bobby teased. "But six fire arms is awesome."

Mark ignored Bobby's provocation. Below them, King Kai and his party refocused their attention on the Eye, preparing to welcome another guest.

"Ugh, I hope they're not expecting too many people." Bobby complained quietly.

The Eye hummed loudly again. This time, it took on a deep red coloration. After an all-too-familiar bright flash, the Eye beamed a ray of crimson onto the courtyard.

Bobby and Mark watched a form take shape. The figure seemed to have a feminine slight, but was dressed in a cloak. The material looked like layers of wilted blood-red flowers. The woman held a long golden rod in her right hand, with a black jewel at its crest. At first, the boys thought she was wearing a war mask similar to Gohlli. But they soon realized her entire head was a golden metallic orb. It floated above her shoulders, unsupported by a neck or any other connection to her body.

From their angle, they could just about see the profiled features of her face morphing along the polished metal surface. The woman's eyes were wide and wild. Her nose and jaw hung in a pointed droop, like a viciously sharp snout. Her leer strained in an overly animated stretch.

"Kulsa The Speaker. Emissary of Her Holiness Leiba…" Buhdringa began, in his theatrical timbre. "…Godling Ruler of the Nekra Kingdom."

"Oh no…" Mark muttered, as a tide of formidable sensations flooded his mind again.

A cold dread washed over him, as he was pulled through the Eye. He found himself standing at the edge of a cliff on a dark mountain. The red Eye hummed on the rocks beside him. Down below, Mark saw a vast pristine forest filled with white trees. Strangely, the center of the forest was shrouded in a colossal fog of contained darkness; concealing whatever was hidden within. Mark thought it looked like an enormous black yolk, shimmering under the night's starry sky. At the edges of the forest, small villages warmed themselves with beleaguered fires.

Mark found himself walking among the white trees of the forest. He examined their translucent opal bark. He saw a lost village child wander among the foliage, his purple eyes searching for a way back home. The youngling was lured towards the forest's dark core, beckoned to explore by ghosts of nighttime curiosity. Mark heard whispers saunter in the breeze.

Mark's visions brought him to the dense wall of darkness at the forest's center. It looked like a curtain of glittering shadow. He walked through the divide and revealed a vast city behind it. Black stoned buildings and black metallic mechanisms formed a robust industrialized civilization. Black furred creatures and citizens cloaked in black robes roamed over streets paved with black stone. It was a metropolis of animated darkness.

Suddenly, the people in the streets all stopped moving. They fell to their knees, gripping the sides of their temples as they howled in anguish. The dark fog surrounding the city dispersed, revealing the mountain high above. Mark looked up to the cliffs and saw a foul, terrifying monstrosity his mind could barely fathom.

Crawling across the mountainside, the immense grey creature moved on gargantuan arachnid legs. Its body was a vast globular abdomen, covered in necrotic slime. But the creature's face was its most horrifying aspect. Framed by long slithering tentacles protruding from its scalp, the creature's expression was filled with petrifying madness. Its large white eyes were held wide in shrill lunacy. Its mouth stretched in an unnaturally broad smile, revealing rows of black fangs.

Mark felt the dizzying dread fill the minds of all the shrieking people around him. He drowned in it; his sanity torn asunder. Caught in the monster's expression, Mark felt sunk into madness. The creature's gaze tore through him, ripping and shredding his idea of self. It was furious, cruel, and ravenous. Mark's terror was absolute. He was held captive in the creature's twisted wrath.

Then, there was silence.

Mark stood in the wake of what used to be a city, and a forest, and countless distant villages. Only now there was nothing but an endless expanse of crushed rock. All across this lake of broken stone, thousands of people knelt with foreheads pressed to the coarse flat ground. Their grey-clad bodies all faced the same direction in worship: the black mountain. Mark saw the foul creature roam atop the peak. It stalked the ridges just above the red Eye. Always within striking distance. The creature's countless followers remained folded over and still in the valley below. Their mindless reverence murmured a repeated chant: "Leiba. Leiba. Leiba. Leiba." The collective recitation filled Mark's bones.

He was back beside Bobby again; barely able to breathe through his clutched panic.

"Hey," Bobby said, placing a concerned hand on Mark's shoulder. "you ok?"

Mark couldn't find the words. He sluggishly patched his memories back together.

"The Eye take you somewhere again? Mark? What'd you see?" Bobby pressed.

All Mark could do was raise his trembling hand in a plea for patience, as he laboriously breathed through the tension gripping his body. Down below, the golden headed woman announced her greetings loudly enough for everyone to hear.

"Greetings, King Kai." She said, her voice saccharine and cloying. "I smile blessings upon you at the request of our Queen, the revered Goddess Leiba. She has generously granted me permission to speak on her behalf, in all matters that concern this council."

Kai offered his guest a short bow and a mild smile of gratitude.

"We thank you for joining us, Speaker Kulsa." Kai began, measuring his words carefully. "We are eternally grateful for your Goddess Leiba's grace and wisdom, at this assembly."

As the crowd below navigated formalities, Bobby grew increasingly worried about Mark's inability to speak.

"Hey man, you're really starting to freak me out." Bobby whispered.

Mark steadily found his lucidity; like emerging out of a cold ocean back into the light.

"Sorry, Bobby. That…" Mark spoke in a low hush "…that was really scary. That gold-headed woman comes from a place with a giant monster. I think it conquered the old city that used to be there. It looked like a big spider, but with this crazy face full of moving tentacles. It made everyone in the city go crazy, but then they were all worshipping the monster."

Bobby was troubled by Mark's ramble. Down below, Kulsa descended the hill to Maije. She was accompanied by two large guards.

"Well whoever helps us use the Eye," Bobby muttered. "I hope they don't send us there."

Mark felt the last remnants of fear drift out of his mind.

"I don't think I can do another one of those. That was so creepy." He said softly.

Bobby began to offer Mark some comforting words, when the Eye started to hum again. Bobby's expression filled with pity as Mark closed his eyes in resignation. This time, the Eye shone with an overtly silver light. The vibrations radiating from the orb seemed more harmonious than before. Mark opened his eyes, and felt a serenity unfolding in his thoughts. Everything was clear, and his mind was free of any disquiet.

The Eye shot forth a silver beam. King Kai smiled warmly in anticipation of his guest. The figure that emerged was female, regal in stature, and elegantly lean. She sat on a large golden cube, which hovered over the ground. She wore a jade shimmering cloak, whose silk draped over the back of the cube and stroked the courtyard stones.

The woman's dark purple skin was adorned in lilac markings, painted onto her face and arms in intricate slender patterns. Each rune and line ended in a small perfect oval. A faint lavender hue radiated off her entire body, adding a pleasant luminosity to her form. Her head was completely shaved, and her silver eyes shone with tender kindness. The blue trees near the courtyard swayed in playful arcs of joy at the woman's arrival.

"Imma'Ja!" Buhdringa rang out proudly. "High Priestess of the Ayanakol Temple, Revered Watcher, and Messenger of the Pacham Realm."

Mark felt a profound sense of tranquility as he observed Imma'Ja dismount her cube. As soon as she descended, the metal box vaporized into a glittering mist that floated into the breeze. Her presence untangled the tense roots which had filled the back of Mark's thoughts. He felt more accepting of himself, and even this strange place. Imma'Ja seemed to sense his gaze, and turned her head slightly in his direction with a smile.

"Imma'Ja, you honor us with your presence." King Kai said, rising from his deep bow.

He pressed the palm of his hands against the palms of hers in a welcoming greeting.

"Dark times fall upon our Raya." Imma'Ja's ethereal voice sang soothingly. "We must help each other find our hope."

"Wynn can escort you to the palace." Kai said. "I know you're fond of his absurdities."

"He is my favorite scoundrel." Imma'Ja said, playfully toying with Wynn's hair.

"It is a privilege to be in the presence of someone who appreciates my finer qualities." Wynn grinned craftily.

"How many yet to arrive, Kai?" Imma'Ja asked.

"From the council, only Mokko." Kai replied, unable to hide his apprehension. "And we hope to be joined by the bamba Reflection from Tamat. Koba's champion. I'm told her name is Payo, and that she will be a delightful test of all our patience."

Mark noticed that no silver light shone off the newly arrived woman. Even as she left to walk down the hill. He also realized, with some relief, that his mind wasn't being pulled through the Eye. Whatever she was, Mark wasn't able to see anything beyond her presence here in Maije.

"You still with me?" Bobby asked, noticing Mark's tranquility.

"Yeah." Mark smiled. "I'm here."

They watched as King Kai and his remaining guards stood around waiting. Bobby tilted his head, suggesting this might be a good time to head down and ask the King about using the Eye. Mark looked at the firm expression on the King's face, and shook his head. The Eye began to hum again, and turned brilliantly green.

175

"Here we go." Bobby groaned. A thought occurred to him. "Hey Mark, try to control it this time. If you get sucked into the vision stuff, just try to stay calm and get a feel of how it works. See if you can decide where you go or what you see."

Mark didn't think it was a terrible idea. He nodded his head and prepared himself. The emerald beam that shot onto the courtyard was far wider than those which had manifested before it. Mark and Bobby saw three figures materialize this time, standing in a triangular formation.

The man at the front of the group wore peculiar battle armor. The metalwork looked like dark shiny seaweed, covered in large piercing thorns. Only the man's exposed head peered out of the defensive shell. His skin was a murky turquoise. A heavy white beard draped off his face, woven into three thick braids. Beneath his intimidating armor, Mark and Bobby noticed he had a thick bulk to him. There was a stoic strength in his stance. His four eyes stacked on his forehead. The two larger ones were emerald green; the others fiery auburn.

All four transfixed onto King Kai.

In his left hand, the man held a black war spear. It was adorned in jewels, and had three formidable spikes at its crest. His right hand held onto a heavy chain, which tethered to a thick collar around the neck of the woman beside him.

His prisoner's wrists were bound to opposing elbows across her chest. She had black oily skin, with small streaks of white scars and flecks of glowing white crystals embedded in her flesh. A thick mane of rose-colored tendrils protruded off her head. She was dressed in simple loose pants and a heavy metal chest plate; which clamped firmly to her arm restraints. Her face was covered in a red mask that only revealed her eyes.

Bobby and Mark immediately recognized the third person in the group. It was the man they had met in the forest with Wynn, who had eagerly drawn his swords on them.

"Mokko..." Buhdringa pronounced. "...Commander of the Wohdan Warship, and Master of the Parthos Fleet. Accompanied by his disciple Fyzo the Specter."

"Don't forget my pet." Mokko replied, an oozing charm seeping out from between the bristly hairs of beard. He yanked the chain slightly. "She used to be royalty, after all."

"Ah, yes. Of course." Buhdringa replied in a fluster. "Sebalah, former Empress of Zahg, and current war prisoner of the Parthos Fleet."

Mokko gave Sebalah's chain a firm yank as he approached Kai. She followed behind as Fyzo and Mokko chuckled. Sebalah barely contained her simmering rage.

Mark felt the pull of the Eye again. He remembered Bobby's advice, and resisted. He put a barrier up in his mind, and tried to give the connection shape. Mark saw a silver stream of light materialize from the Eye and float towards him. The current of light flowed in both directions, like adjacent rivers whose waters pulled away from each other. Mark's mind willingly poured itself towards the streak. He felt his destination gradually form in his awareness, anticipating his arrival.

Mark stood on a vast warship. It was anchored off the coast of a burning city. Other ships in the fleet moved towards the scorched harbor. Standing all around the deck, performing various tasks, Mark saw a crew of formidable warriors. The men and women seemed to come from many tribes and races. Their heads were all uniformly drenched in a bright green dye, which gave their skin and hair an aberrant vibrancy.

Mark walked around the ship, glad to be in control of the vision. He examined the details of the vessel, and was impressed by its immense complexity. Mark was in awe of the heavy wooden masts which soared skywards. They were covered in dozens of folded fern-colored sails. Dense plates of armor and vicious spikes encased the ship's exterior. A stone figurehead at the bow depicted ferocious beasts wrapped around each other in violent battle. At the helm, Mark saw the green Eye. It hovered above a thick metal ring, humming angrily. Mark sensed all the memories threaded to the Eye; hundreds of rivers he could send his mind down. He picked one.

Mark found himself stood beside Mokko, as the ship swayed in mammoth waves amid a violent tempest. Mokko laughed wildly, as his crew cheered him on. He steered the ship in pursuit of a colossal sea monster. Mark only saw parts of the creature emerge from the water. The size of its limbs terrified him. The crew howled in mad glory as they threw chained harpoons into the monster to keep it afloat. The spikes sank deep into the creature's flesh. The crew cranked on heavy wheels, pulling the chains and holding the monster back from submerging. The ship groaned under the strain.

Mokko vaulted from the helm and ran across the deck, trident in hand. His crew watched in reverence as he launched himself off the ship and into the air above the monster. Gripping the spear with both hands, Mokko brought the barbs down – lancing the creature's spine. The monster's head broke through the waves to howl in a deafening roar of agony. Its head was shaped like an anvil; armored in hard shell. Mokko raised a hand towards the sky and pulled a bolt of lightning into his war spear. Violent currents shook the dying monstrosity. Mokko's crew cheered loudly as blood filled the churning waters around them.

Mark thought of returning, and found himself beside Bobby again.

"Did it work?" Bobby asked.

"Yeah, thanks man." Mark smiled. "That guy is some kind of…pirate wizard. He has a lot of ships, but his main one is ridiculously huge."

"Good guy or bad guy?" Bobby asked, looking at the man and his prisoner.

"They invaded a city but also killed a giant monster, so I don't know." Mark replied.

The boys watched the tense interactions below to see if they could discern anything else.

"The Wohdan is docked at a less than hospitable port near the Ferukta realm." Mokko announced brashly. "She awaits my return from this *urgent* gathering. You know how much I hate to leave her unattended, Kai." Mokko turned to Fyzo. "But my companion here tells me the Raya is in great peril. Yet again."

"Thank you for coming, Mokko." Kai spoke in a tone drenched in patience. "The coming war is of great concern to us."

"The coming war, the previous war, the not yet imaged wars. They are always upon us, Kai. Let us see if this one is as special as you imagine." Mokko retorted.

Mokko did nothing to hide his contemptuous smirk. Kai ignored the bait, offered a polite nod, and gestured towards the palace.

"My guards can secure your prisoner in our dunge…" Kai began, before being interrupted by Mokko's mocking laughter.

"This foul sorceress will never leave my side." Mokko announced, violently yanking on Sebalah's chain as he marched ahead. "If you're welcoming an unknown youngling to our meeting, I assume you can make room for my prisoner too!" Mokko yelled over his shoulder.

Half of the remaining guards followed Mokko down the hill. Kai and Buhdringa watched them leave with visible tension.

"How many more people can they be expecting?" Bobby asked, palpably annoyed.

"Only four guards left." Mark noticed. "Can't be that many more coming."

The Eye hummed again, and turned bright purple. The boys rolled their eyes at each other, as the orb went through the familiar routine. Bobby mouthed "here we go" silently as the

179

Eye flashed and shot a ray onto the courtyard. The violet beam was the widest they had seen yet.

The large group that materialized in front of Kai was an odd mix of characters. There was an exceptionally tall orange-skinned woman, with wispy blue hair. She wore elaborate clothes, layered in flourishes and decorations. The dynamic fabrics, metal chains, accents, and buttons were all differing shades of purple – save for the large orange fire symbol on her back.

She was flanked by two guards wearing heavy eggplant-colored armor. One of them looked like a centaur, only the lower half of his body was more bear-like than horse. The other guard seemed reptilian, with leathery red skin and six lean arms conjoined at her torso. She held a flagstaff with a large banner. The flag was a circle of rich mauve fabric, emblazoned with a fiery orange flame at its center.

The last person in the group, was a very short old man. He stood meekly behind the others. He was modestly dressed, in a pair of simple pants and a short coat. He removed his hat, and smiled politely at the greeters before him. His caramel skin was heavily wrinkled.

"Ah…" Buhdringa began, before turning one head to King Kai in a whisper. "Your Majesty, I'm afraid I don't know who these guests are, exactly." He raised his voice to a ceremonial tenor again, and faced the new arrivals. "Though they are clearly cherished visitors from the Kingdom of Mount Tamat."

"It's quite alright Buhdringa." King Kai said, offering the newcomers a broad smile. "These fine guests join us on behalf of our special visitor. Who I take it has yet to arri…"

Before Kai could finish his sentence, a deafening crack of energy shattered the air. A large orb of purple fire appeared above them. Surges of potent energy radiated from the sphere and fractured the stones on the courtyard below. The guards got in defensive stances, but Kai raised his hand and assured them they had no cause for concern.

Mark and Bobby were blinded by the sudden arrival of the fiery orb. As his eyes adjusted, Mark watched the giant sphere hover while Kai, the guards, and his new guests stared up at it patiently. Mark noticed the Eye below had returned to its normal shade of blue.

"Can you see that?" Mark asked quietly.

"What, the giant ball of purple fire?" Bobby mocked.

Mark felt a dizzying wave of confusion around the new sphere. He couldn't keep a grip on his thoughts. He could only sense fragments of details around him, which swiftly slipped through his mental grasp. Mark tried to focus his mind.

The purple sphere began to unfold, like a flower opening in bloom. Layers of flame peeled away, revealing new stratums of colored fire beneath it. Lilac, maroon, marigold, mint, and azure fiery petals poured outwards in a beautiful unfurling. The sphere spiraled and descended to the ground; its flames falling to the courtyard in blazing blankets.

Unique forms took shape within the fiery core. At first Mark thought it was two people materializing in the scorching flower. He realized it was a young girl standing still, and the phantom of a larger woman dancing and swaying over her. The phantom was lissome and translucent. Her radiance shifting in coloration. Her long flowing hair tethered to the petals of fire. Once the sphere opened fully, the phantom faded into the young girl's body. She absorbed her floating guardian with a confident smile.

The girl's skin was a beautifully rich dark umber. It had the texture of smooth marble. She had electric blue hair woven in a series of complex knots and heavy braids. Her bright orange eyes radiated wildly. Her clothes appeared to be a meshwork of ribbons and coiled cords, that moved around each other and changed their ever-blending colors as they glided passed one another in transit across her young body.

"You must be Payo!" Buhdringa announced cordially. "Koba's champion, Reflection of Chaos, and our Raya's most sacred new protector."

Mark felt a dizzying headache cluster his thoughts. His mind was filled with a discorded angry irritation in the girl's presence. He focused on the crackling energy around her, and tried to calm it. Payo's body stiffed slightly, as she navigated an uncomfortable shiver. She looked up to King Kai, and squinted at him suspiciously.

"It's very nice to meet you, Payo…" Kai began.

"Wait." Payo replied firmly, maintaining a look of playful mistrust on her face.

Kai paused in curious hesitation. He watched Payo raise her hand and snap her fingers. A spiral of purple smoke manifested on the ground. The vapor dissipated and revealed a little creature bouncing on the courtyard. It ran to a fragment of broken rock and chomped on it.

The creature's skin looked like dark wine, glittering and leathery. It stood on two thick hind legs, and had a broad chest with dense forearms. The creature's head was square, with a crown of crooked blue horns. The claws on its limbs and the fangs in its mouth were a light shade of powder blue, as were its glowing eyes. The creature smiled happily, grunting in glee when it saw Payo. It leapt up her body, and settled on her shoulder.

"That's Dex." Payo announced. "I made him."

"Enjoying your new powers, little one?" Kai inquired, mimicking her playful demeanor.

"My power is more ancient than you are, oldling." Payo replied, a coldness washing over her manner.

Before Kai could react to her scowl, she smiled openly again and looked at the citadel on the opposing distant hill.

"Is that your palace?" She asked.

"Ah, yes. If you'll allow my guards to…"

Kai barely formed the next word before Payo vanished in a storm of purple smoke and rippling violet energy. Dex fell to the ground and looked around in shock for his missing master. Dex shook and split his body into three versions of himself. They all ran around searching for Payo. One of them noticed her purple cloud reappear in the distance. They all leapt into the air, conjoining into one body and traveling to join her in similarly violent bursts of smoke.

The tall woman approached Kai, joined by her guards and the quiet old man.

"I apologize, Your Majesty." The Woman began, bowing before Kai. "Young Payo is new to her powers, and the formalities of political discourse. My name is Ganamahr, newly appointed Emissary to the Kingdom of Tamat. We are very pleased to accompany Payo to this council meeting. We hope to guide her decisions in the interest of our Kingdoms, and the Raya."

Kai graciously bowed his head in gratitude, before making a pressing inquiry.

"She has the ability to travel without an Eye? Across such vast distances?"

"Only one of the many gifts Koba bestowed upon her, when she was chosen as Reflection." Ganamahr replied.

"Truly remarkable." Kai said, in genuine awe.

"And utterly unique, as far as I know." Ganamahr agreed, while turning her head to look at the blue glowing Eye beside them. "The nature of our Raya is ever-changing."

"Indeed." Kai agreed. "If you'll please join my guards, they will escort you to the palace. The long way there, I'm afraid." Kai smiled.

Ganamahr proceeded down the hill with her guards. The old man held back for a moment, and stood before Kai.

"Your Majesty," He began, in a meek tone. "please forgive Payo's brazenness. She wants to do what's best for the Raya, like you, but has many ideas of her own on how to achieve that shared dream. I am sure she will carefully consider the council's opinions."

"You're her father?" Kai inquired, absorbing the pride in the man's eyes.

"Yes," He smiled broadly. "my name is Vikkah."

"What does your daughter know of the coming conflict?" Kai asked.

"When her powers manifested, many of Tamat's leaders and dignitaries from far away realms visited her." Vikkah replied. "They brought advise, warnings of the Prince's conquests, prophetic visions, ancient teachings, and oaths of loyalty. She grew tired of all the...opinions."

"She has a plan of her own?" Kai asked wearily.

"She has always had a strong will, Your Majesty." Vikkah responded. "Even before Koba's gifts, and the sacred voices that sing to her now. She was always special, like her mother. That is why she was chosen. However, she knows I respect the council, and agreed to come here upon my request."

Kai saw a a genuine sweetness in Vikkah's eyes. However severe the situation might be, his heart was filled with love for his only child.

"Does she understand the dangers we all face if she..." Kai began.

"Your Majesty, if I may interrupt." Vikkah said. "We all try to teach our younglings the wisdoms we wish were imparted on us in our youth. But their lives are their own, as much as ours were. Let us all talk, and then see what Payo decides."

Kai was taken aback, but conceded that nothing Vikkah said was unreasonable.

"What else can you tell me about your daughter?" Kai asked.

"We come from humble origins. I'm a blacksmith, her mother was an artist - though she is no longer of this world." Vikkah sighed. "It's fitting Payo was chosen as the Reflection of Chaos. She shares her mother's passion. A wild energy, strong enough to bear the burden."

"Well, you certainly speak with a genuine heart, Vikkah. I will trust that Payo's good nature, and your wise guidance, will lead us to the right path. Allow me to escort you." Kai said.

Mark and Bobby watched the King, old man, and remaining guards walk down the hill.

"Well, there goes our Eye expert." Bobby moaned.

"Let's get back down and tell the girls what we saw." Mark said, leading the way.

As they approached the cliff's edge, Mark shared a plan to glide down in slow gradual arcs while holding Bobby. Both boys peered over the threshold with hesitant caution.

"Just don't drop me!" Bobby said, mustering his confidence. "My legs are heavy."

"I promise." Mark assured.

Bobby lay on his back, and Mark grabbed hold of his wrists. As Mark flapped his wings powerfully, he rose into the air and dragged Bobby to the precipice. Bobby's legs swung free of the ground, and the boys plunged slightly. Mark adjusted his wing beats to keep them afloat. Mark circled down to ground in wide arcs. They took in the magical view of Maije's lights. When they landed, Elise and Naiyana rushed over.

"Well?" Elise asked in exasperation. "What'd you see up there?"

"Let us get our feet on the ground, jeez." Bobby complained, milking the anticipation. "Well, the Eye is like some kind of small blue fire star. It shot a bunch of people out with beams of light, so we think it can probably teleport you places. The King dude was up there greeting his guests, but he's heading back to the palace now. Oh, also Mark is connected to the Eye in

185

a weird magical way and is too chicken to try and use his powers to get us home."

"What?" Elise balked in disbelief. "Is this like that weird shit you did with your hands?"

Mark rolled his eyes. "I'll explain on the way. Let's get to the palace side of the city. King Kai has a meeting with his guests, and then hopefully he'll be free to help us."

"Sounds like a plan hoping for a plan." Bobby mocked skeptically. "But I'm down to explore the city for a bit. Maybe get something to eat."

"If you're hungry don't forget you have those leg berries." Naiyana said, matter-of-factly.

Elise howled in laughter.

12 – COUNCIL

King Kai walked into the meeting with measured steps and focused composure. The council room displayed circular themes throughout every facet of its design. A round table rose from the middle of the floor. On top of its polished wooden surface, a wide bowl cradled several stone orbs. Spherical candle-holders of varying color hung from the domed ceiling. Patterns of intersecting ovals were carved into the marble flooring, filled with gold and silver veins. Heavy pillars surrounded the meeting area, forming a halo of supportive beams. Seven perfectly round windows were spaced out evenly on the walls of the globular room, letting in a pleasant breeze.

Kai watched as each council member picked up a stone orb from the table, and walked to their respective chair – spread apart near their preferred pillar. Each orb began to glow in the corresponding color of their kingdom. Lord Gohlli in blazing orange, Speaker Kulsa in ferocious red, Priestess Imma'Ja in vibrant silver, and Mokko in menacing green.

Kai willed his orb to shine a serene blue. He took a seat and looked at the faces of his fellow Eye-Keepers. In days long past, their chairs had sat closely around the table. Now, after many disputes and rarely forgotten conflicts, they gifted themselves more distance.

"The stones have been lit, Your Majesty." Mokko sighed heavily, falling into his seat. "Shall we begin?"

Mokko smiled. His grip on Sebalah's chain tightened, and he tugged her closer. Fyzo stood behind her, his hand on his sword hilt and eyes locked onto her neck.

"Thank you all for gathering here, there are matters we need to discuss…" Kai began.

"Kai, in times of war the truest courtesy is not to waste time on courtesy. Get to the blood of the matter already." Mokko insisted.

"Where is the little one? Payo?" Kulsa asked, peering her animated golden face around the room theatrically. Her sharp voice resonated out of her metallic mouth unnervingly.

"She awaits us in the other room." Kai replied. "I wanted us to have a moment to discuss the circumstances, before we invited her to join us. This being the, newly named, Kingdom of Nekra's first attendance of a council meeting - I imagined you wished to orient yourself with our traditions, Speaker Kulsa."

"Not in the slightest." Kulsa replied. Beyond her frozen smile, nothing hinted at an imitation of interest or emotion. "But by all means, let us proceed. We shall have to ignore how rude it might be to keep our young guest waiting, as we indulge in decorum and debate."

Kulsa smiled at Mokko, proud of her effort to align with his impatience. Mokko merely glanced back at the gold-headed woman with thinly veiled disdain. He grunted and flipped the heaviest of his beard braids.

"What do we know of the attacks so far?" Gohlli interjected, his tone calmly inquisitive. "Are they indiscriminate? Or do they follow any patterns we can discern?"

Kai studied the faces in the room. They all seemed eager to dive in and understand the situation. Perhaps he could use their shared curiosity to unify them.

"Prince Sal'Haf has been invading kingdoms all over the Raya." Kai began, engaging all his guests in equal measure. "Most of the realms were small; though our pathfinders tell me many of the kingdoms conquered held ancient weapons from the First Wars."

"Any confirmations about the size of his army?" Gohlli asked. "Perhaps he doesn't have the numbers to attack larger kingdoms?"

"His invasions have left no survivors. He arrives, slaughters entire civilizations, and takes any weapons or artifacts of significance." Kai replied. "Those unaccounted for in the rivers of blood and corpses left behind, have most likely been captured as prisoners...or worse."

"So, we can assume some have joined the ranks of his forces – willingly or not." Mokko mused, twirling the orb in his hand.

"Other than their size, what can be said of his targeted kingdoms?" Gohlli inquired.

"None of them appear to be aligned with any one Primal." Kai explained. "He has only attacked civilizations where Sawah harmony prevails. Sanctuaries with gates open to outsiders, tolerant of many faiths, or those where the Primal rituals and traditions are absent entirely."

"Interesting..." Gohlli began, standing to walk around the perimeter of the table.

The six fiery arms trailing behind him swayed with his movements, elegantly closing their fingers around unseen currents in the room.

"Do you think he is purposefully targeting realms who don't adhere to a single Primal faith? Or is that an intended deception to stir mistrust among the more traditionalist kingdoms? Does he wish to isolate us from each other through fear, before he attacks larger prizes?" Gohlli contemplated aloud.

"It's unclear at this stage." Kai responded, watching the flickers of discomfort on Mokko's face as Gohlli confidently strolled around room.

"I've heard disquieting rumors myself, King Kai." Gohlli continued. "Neighboring realms near some of the attacks talk of lingering visions that haunt their people. A tide of dread fills the air. These powers seem beyond our current understanding of Asha's capabilities. Some wonder if Prince

Sal'Haf is more than a mere Reflection. Perhaps a Primal has found a way to truly manifest within the Raya?"

"Those are wild imaginings born of fear." Kai replied calmly.

"I wouldn't dismiss them so swiftly." Gohlli insisted. "We do not know why these champions have been chosen, or what Asha desires from these conquests."

"The Void has only ever had one desire." Mokko blurted out mockingly. "To tear and destroy the changing fabric of the Raya, to devour the broken remnants, and to drown us all in a long-lost lake of pure silence. All souls drifting serenely, for all eternity."

"He can't mean to destroy the entire Raya." Gohlli speculated.

"Why not?" Mokko chuckled curtly.

"What would be left for the Void to consume," Imma'Ja asked, in a soothing refrain. "if all lights in the Raya are snuffed out?"

Mokko rose to respond. He noticed the chain in his grip had more slack than he could tolerate. He yanked it hard, and pulled Sebalah into a forced kneel beside him. Mokko returned his gaze to the council members surrounding him.

"It is not in the Void's nature to question its own hunger. None of you have truly seen what dark desires Asha is capable of possessing! Not all who dwell in the black gardens seek solitude and serenity. Some bear far more malevolent appetites." Mokko seethed.

"We are relinquishing our reason." Kai insisted. "A strategy is at play here, even if we can't see its entirety."

"I don't even know how any of this is relevant." Mokko groaned in frustration. "We will eventually have to face the Prince in battle. Does that not present an obvious choice?"

"What would that be?" Kai asked, genuinely welcoming the discussion.

"To decide when we strike." Mokko stated plainly. "Look at the kingdoms he's attacked. Weak. Small. None purely aligned with any one Primal, and therefore lacking in allies. Though his powers might be terrifying, they are still growing. Still limited in their reach. Attack him now, with everything in our collective power, and we have our most assured path to victory. Otherwise, we merely wait until his horde is vast enough to consume us each individually."

A silence fell across the room as they considered Mokko's strategy.

"There are other paths we can follow." Kai said, hoping to reclaim the debate.

But Mokko found himself in a surge of confidence, and interjected.

"You'll always find cause to ponder, Kai. But the homes of your friends are coming down around you. As you light candles and contemplate, others bleed for your patient caution. Sal'Haf will come for the larger kingdoms soon enough. And he will most assuredly come for our Sacred Eyes too." A stillness chilled the council members. "Nothing will guarantee the spread of his foulness across the Raya quicker, than acquiring one of our Eyes. The longer we gather here, the longer each of our sacred prizes is vulnerable. So, I ask once more: what exactly is the point of this gathering?"

"Apparently to listen to your speeches." Imma'Ja stated.

Mokko bristled in agitation under the critique.

"Despite our differences, I would hope you all trust in my expertise when it comes to creatures afflicted with insatiable lust for power." Mokko glanced at his kneeling prisoner.

"Of course, Mokko." Gohlli replied, turning to face the bearded man. All eight of his arms, fire and flesh alike, tensed uniformly. "Your knowledge is built on experience. After all, your fleet frequently amuses itself by pillaging weaker realms, does it not?"

191

"And killing far more dangerous monsters than your tribe of roamers dares to face." Mokko retorted. He tossed his orb to Fyzo, who caught it deftly with his spare hand. Mokko gripped his trident, and pointed it in Gohlli's direction. "I won't deny that my fleet, on occasion, will relieve some unfortunate souls of powers they don't bear the fortitude to wield. But only because nothing is more unpredictable than a good weapon in unsure hands."

"And yet, the Primals saw fit to gift their greatest weapons to the unsure hands of two younglings." Kulsa's chuckle vibrated through her features. "How curious."

Mokko divided his gaze between his two opponents with equal contempt. Gohlli took a step towards Mokko's spearpoint.

"My tribe roams, and remains hidden, to keep our Sacred Eye safe!" Gohlli barked. "We don't chase the dark delights of battle and bloodshed by bringing its rare power right into the grasp of our enemies." The fists on four of his arms snapped shut in harmonized emphasis.

"No enemy of mine has come close to touching any treasure I possess!" Mokko scoffed. "Though I concede that *other* Eyes have fallen into the wrong hands of late."

Mokko turned to stare at Kulsa disparagingly.

"We can all agree…" Kai entreated. "…that Prince Sal'Haf must be stopped."

"Absolutely." Mokko rejoiced, shifting his mood. "Shall we attack his homeland? I can hardly imagine what he's transformed Kahltam into by now. But I assure you, that is where we will likely find most of his reserve forces. He will surely meet us there in battle if we strike."

"You are too eager for war." Kai sighed.

"And you are too fearful of the inevitable." Mokko replied coldly.

"I believe this goes beyond the old Primal conflicts we've known. The powers that possessed Sal'Haf in Kahltam

192

appeared to consume him. It was more formidable than anything I've ever seen the Void conjure." Kai explained.

"How far have you really traveled from this coddled opulent city, *Your Majesty?*" Mokko asked glibly. "I've seen horrors on the brink of the Raya that would turn your mind on itself."

"And you certainly never fail to remind us of your adventures." Imma'Ja sighed.

"Kai, try to find your own righteous fury for once." Mokko pressed on. "How do you hope to face the Prince's rage, or the Void's dark appetites, if you can't summon a little wrath of your own? Eventually, war will remain our only solution. We may as well embrace it."

"If Kai believes there's another way, let us at least hear what he suggests." Gohlli said.

"There is only one way. There has only ever been one way. Everything else is a dream." Mokko muttered, sitting back down and making a show of looking at Kai with rapt attentiveness.

"We need only target Sal'Haf's power directly to achieve a swift victory, and spare countless souls from perishing in a large-scale war." Kai paced himself.

"An assassination?" Mokko chuckled in surprise. "How unexpectedly delightful."

"No." Kai replied in mild frustration. "I believe Sal'Haf is a prisoner of the Void. Asha's powers have latched onto his despair and devoured him. Turned him into a vessel through which a growing darkness seeps into our realms. But Sal'Haf's role as conduit offers us an opportunity. If we can sever that connection, we can rescue the anguished youngling from the power using him, and spare the Raya further suffering. Sawah must be our ultimate goal. If we close the gateway, we stop the Void's pour into our realms and restore the harmony we all seek."

Kai watched the council members digest his thoughts. Gohlli turned his gaze to the ceiling in rumination. Imma'Ja smiled at Kai in assurance. Kulsa's smirk remained unmoving, as her eyes darted around the room. Mokko shook his head in fatigued disappointment.

"That is your plan?" Mokko finally said.

"How would you achieve this?" Gohlli interjected.

"Koba has presented us with Payo. She wields the forces of Chaos. Payo is powerful, but lacks guidance and support." Kai began, eager to share his strategy. "Rather than amass vast armies from all the realms, which will surely result in immeasurable death and destruction, I suggest we encircle Payo with a small group of our most powerful warriors. Let them hunt out and discover Sal'Haf's location, engage him directly, and use Payo's gifts to separate the youngling from his corrupting powers. The Void's entryway to the Raya will be shattered, and its darkness will return to the ether."

"Let us imagine..." Mokko launched impatiently, his voice drenched in scorn. "...that the youngling in the other room does indeed have enough power to sever a connection between another Primal and their Reflection. And let us assume for the moment, that your small herd of warrior assassins can somehow guide her towards finding her target, before Sal'Haf consumes a hundred more realms. And if by a thousand miracles and the will of the Watchers, they do manage to succeed in their fool's errand...what makes you think Payo won't become our next immediate concern? Do you imagine Koba will release her as chosen Reflection? That her powers will similarly recede so that harmony can restore itself? If Sawah is truly what we're destined for, where is the third Reflection to balance out these two opposing forces? You put much of your faith in a youngling you've only just met. Are you sure she shares your dream?"

Kai bowed his head slightly under Mokko's escalating tone and frustration. The concerns were valid, and Kai needed to find the right words. He had been so consumed with fear of Sal'Haf's growing threat, he had only envisioned Payo's role in the Raya's future with the most optimistic of minds. She could be the perfect ally, and potentially an equally terrifying foe.

"And how does your suggested grand war with Sal'Haf negate any concern of Payo's potential threat to our realms?" Imma'Ja asked sternly.

"One problem at a time, Priestess." Mokko hissed. "And in battle we shall surely see the inner workings of our new youngling ally's mind. If she does indeed, count us as friends."

"You've remained rather quiet, Kulsa." Gohlli said, sparing a glance toward the woman's frozen smile. It smeared unnaturally across her polished golden face. "The council would welcome your thoughts on the matter. This will affect us all, even your distant kingdom."

"Well, this is Nekra's first formal representation at one of these sacred meetings." Kulsa began, pausing to raise her faux eyebrows contemplatively. "My Goddess Leiba instructed me to take this matter very seriously, and convey our most salient wisdoms." Kulsa paused theatrically. "I agree that Payo presents an equal concern, and stands to potentially be as much a tyrant as any other overly-powered Reflection. But we cannot ignore the fact that she only spawned as a reaction to Sal'Haf's rising dominion. So, I would ask us to consider: why Asha chose to exert the Void's cleansing upon us now? Why did the tragic demise of Sal'Haf's family turn into this opportunity?"

Kulsa turned to face Kai. "You preach your desire for Sawah harmony, Your Majesty, and yet you have no appetite for the natural destructions of the Void. Asha's dark tides have a place in the Primal Trinity, do they not? Do rebirths not begin from the endings of old worlds?" Kulsa widened her stance to the whole room again. "Perhaps we should see the rise of Sal'Haf's prominence as a long overdue reckoning for our Raya, and its many rots." Kulsa's sharp gaze turned to Gohlli. "A culling of the weak-hearted." She turned to stare at Mokko's heavy belly. "An end to those lost in bloated indulgences." Kulsa smiled even wider, and then raised her gaze to look directly at Imma'Ja. "A chance to tear out the frail roots which clutter our gardens."

Kulsa spread her arms, opening her dark robe to reveal a lithe body of coiled muscle adorned in darkly jeweled fabrics.

"I believe I speak on behalf of my Goddess Leiba, when I say we musn't trouble ourselves with needless involvement in the Raya's grander mechanisms. Come what may of the Primal's old game, it has shaped the lives and landscapes of our realms since our histories began. We can only hope to embrace whatever new fruitions grow from the ashes of this conflict."

Gohlli and Imma'Ja stood in stunned silence. Mokko snorted in disgust. Kai found his breath, and implored Kulsa to reconsider.

"Think of all the lives that have been given to create these realms, Kulsa. The eons of time, the godlings who stole birthfires from the first unseen light. You'd have all that swept away, out of…curiosity?" Kai asked in appalled disbelief.

"Are we really entertaining the notion that this foul creature deserves a voice in this meeting?" Mokko exploded in rage.

"Mokko!" Kai yelled, hoping to reprimand Mokko away from his worst instincts.

"Bad enough you intend to bring in a youngling - one of the two potential tyrants we must concern ourselves with – to hear her thoughts on our tenuous future. But to listen to this venomous creature spew her filth onto our chamber is too much to bear." Mokko huffed.

"Enough." Kai bellowed.

Kulsa's distorted smile was unwavering. Mokko spun to face Kai.

"Your predecessor banished Karash from this very council for his crimes. And if I recall, you were the one who advocated hiding The Teacher's Eye as part of his punishment! You annihilated any chance of his aberrant realm using their sacred gateway." Mokko exclaimed. "Now you welcome this foulness in here?"

"Karash mutilated every soul under his rule." Kai spoke firmly. "He was mad with unnatural desires. We couldn't just leave his Eye exposed to anyone's claim."

"And what do you think Leiba is doing to her mindless worshipers?" Mokko replied. He turned to face Kulsa, glaring at her cold features. "I hear whispers about what happens behind Nekra's great walls. Your *goddess* and her grotesque cravings."

"Unfounded rumors, I assure you, King Kai." Kulsa responded, her shrill charm reverberating off her face. "Our civilization thrives under the endless grace of Goddess Leiba."

"A civilization of slaves, and you are the unholy whore of a bloodlusting oppressor." Mokko growled. "I know your Queen watches us even now through those empty eyes of yours." Mokko stepped closer to Kulsa, glaring into the narrowing pits of her metallic stare. "Leiba! You turned a flourishing kingdom into an obscene pit of worship for your bottomless vanity. Parasite Godling." Mokko spat. "And these Eye-Keepers honor you with an invitation to speak at our council?" Mokko snorted in contempt. "Perhaps you're right, Kulsa. The Raya has grown complacent. Perhaps blood sacrifices are needed to reinvigorate the fire burning in our souls. Perhaps I'll come visit you one day soon, to ensure rightful tribute!"

"Your fleet would be most welcome in Nekra, Eye-Keeper." Kulsa bowed politely. As her golden head rose again, her gaze lingered on Mokko's belly. "Though your portly ships might struggle to get up our mountain." She offered her widest smile yet; a mouth full of knives.

"You lose yourself, Mokko." Gohlli said sternly, moving between them. "We are honor-bound to respect each council member's sovereignty. Leiba is the lawful ruler of Nekra and its Sacred Eye. Her emissary is a welcome speaker at this council. Conquering a kingdom does not disqualify rightful rule; otherwise you might be asked to return some of your captured treasures."

"How utterly disappointing." Mokko grunted, as he looked over the faces in the room. "You roll out your virtuous tolerance like a carpet, inviting the profanest creatures to crawl into your homes." Mokko looked at Gohlli. "And you...always restraining your wilder nature."

"While you always succumb to yours." Gohlli replied, a fatigued smile on his face. He pivoted to Kulsa. "Know this, Speaker. If these rumors about Nekra turn out to be more than whispers, we will be having a very different discussion altogether."

Kulsa continued to smile as she bowed her head low. "But of course, Lord Gohlli."

"Mokko." Kai's tone betrayed a fraught vulnerability. "I'm entreating you to reconsider. Your skills and wisdom would be invaluable. Payo could benefit from your guidance. You've made compromises before, found paths beyond bloodshed. Your...guest is proof enough."

He looked into Sebalah's eyes, shrouded beneath her red mask. They were pitiless. Mokko also turned to face his chained prisoner.

"This filthy witch?" He burst out in laughter. "I won't allow her name to slither off my tongue. You all know her crimes well. You've seen what her ravenger army did before we captured her."

Mokko and Fyzo both kept keen eyes on Sebalah, despite her numerous restraints.

"Her army worships her. Their possessed little minds twisted in reverence, bound to her by dark magic." Mokko brought his face close to hers. "As long as she lives, they will yearn for her return. They think of nothing else. That is her *only* value to me. If she dies, her hordes scatter like a plague. And I would rather have her once formidable warriors, wither away in her desolate, broken kingdom. Desperately praying for her return. Mindless remnants. Similar to that one." Mokko nodded towards Kulsa. "And all the other insects crawling at the base of Leiba's conquered mountain!"

"You only make a stronger argument for Kai's strategy." Gohlli said. "Instead of facing the Prince's growing army in open battle, we should find a way to strike directly at the heart of his power. Sever him from the force which has consumed him."

Before Mokko could respond, his prisoner Sebalah began to laugh. The cruel cackle bled through her crimson mask.

"The Dark Star is upon us!" Sebalah's hiss crept into the air. "Yours is the heathenous prattle of dying candles. Blights on the night sky. A cleansing is comiiihh…"

Mokko yanked her shackles hard enough for the chains to twist her neck.

"Now we know how those who serve Asha's dark dream feel on the matter." Mokko sighed. "I am no stranger to strategy. I've made more sacrifices than I care to count." He lowered his spear to Sabalah's neck. "Killing this enchantress would bring me immeasurable pleasure. But we would hunt her scattered disciples until our dying days. Do we know the same is true of Sal'Haf? This delicate dance of removing the Prince from the violent tempest surrounding him will most likely result in the loss of our finest fighters, and our most powerful weapon in Payo. We'd sacrifice our greatest advantage and solidify Sal'Haf's rule." Mokko calmed himself with a sigh. "The only certain path to victory, is to annihilate Sal'Haf and his forces."

The council considered Mokko's reasoning.

"There is no hope in this dream of yours, Kai. It is madness." Mokko stated, turning to Kai. "Sal'Haf is lost to us, those he conquers are fallen into darkness. You cannot salvage what the abyss has consumed. Death has come for us, and all we cherish. It surrounds us now. Fight it, or succumb to it."

A heavy silence lingered in the room. Gohlli turned his gaze towards Kai.

"King Kai, you have my support if Payo is agreeable to your plan." Gohlli stated, as he took his seat again. "I should note, that it would be my preference to kill The Prince rather than endeavor to salvage him from Asha's grip. But I cannot deny that by even attempting your path, we have an opportunity to spare countless souls from enduring the horrors of war."

Kai smiled in genuine gratitude. He turned to the High Priestess Imma'Ja.

"The Sisters of the Seven Stars cannot intervene, only advise." Imma'Ja spoke in a tone as comforting as the warm glow which shone off her body. "I believe whichever path you choose to walk; it will ultimately be the Reflections who decide the Raya's fate. I do share your hope Kai, and will make every effort to guide Payo towards a wise decision. But it will still be her decision to make." She placed an assuring hand on Kai's heavy shoulder.

They turned to Kulsa, whose serrated smile sliced across her gold face.

"I've made my position clear." Kulsa stated. "Though I am curious to meet this Payo."

"Well, if it all comes down to the will of a youngling..." Mokko said, shaking his head. "...let's meet the little one."

Kai inhaled in slow patience. Three out of five would have to do. He signaled for Wynn to go fetch their guest of honor. The rest of the council returned to their seats, and awaited her arrival. Sebalah was forced to kneel by Mokko's chair, only a few links of chain tethering her neck to his clenching fist.

13 - TEMPLES

"They all looked different." Bobby explained, as they strolled through Maije's streets. "The coolest one was this lady that floated in on a golden cube. It vaporized when she got off it. There was also this dude who had six fire arms growing out of his back. The last one to get there was this girl, kinda looked our age. But she didn't come through The Eye at all, she just teleported to the top of the hill in this huge ball of fire. It was like a bunch of different colored flames all layered on top of each other. She looked awesome, and kinda pretty actually, but in a really bad ass way. Her hair was like electric blue."

For the first time in their friendship, Bobby had Elise's complete and undivided attention. She was fascinated by his descriptions. Mark noticed Naiyana stare at him, with a scrutinizing expression.

"Mark," she inquired. "what else do you think you can do with your powers?"

"He doesn't know." Elise groaned, teasing Mark with her disappointment.

"And he's too much of a wimp to find out." Bobby added, spotting the signal.

"I could hurt someone!" Mark replied indignantly, falling into the trap. "You want me to just start blasting people with my hands and see what happens?"

"I mean…not no." Bobby smiled.

"Yeah, kinda." Elise added playfully.

"So, you're connected to things here." Naiyana recounted Mark's summary, her face awash in eager resolve. "You can see silver light shining on everything, and you think the light is showing you where things are going to go." She steamrolled ahead in rushed sentences that overlapped each other, as she pieced the puzzle together. "Sometimes, you can shoot the light from your hands, which moves or changes things." Naiyana bounced the summary between the palms of her open hands, feeling the details out in her mind. "And when the Eye was activated, you traveled through it to the places each visitor came from - in your mind - and saw memories of things that happened there?"

Mark nodded silently. Naiyana continued to carry the conversation herself.

"Whenever this power gets very strong, you feel you lose control over it." Naiyana caught Mark's downcast gaze. Her tone became notably sympathetic. "And now you're scared to see what might happen if you try to use it too much?"

Mark looked at her. Any uncertainty in her voice seemed to be aimed at the absurdity of the situation, not the veracity of Mark's claims.

"Pretty much." He replied glumly.

"I dunno guys." Elise said, as she looked around wide-eyed. "Maybe there's a lot more going on here. Don't you think we should stay a little longer and figure it out?"

"Hell no, Elise!" Bobby yelled. "Stop trying to make this an adventure. The sooner we leave this crazy place the better. Did you forget a giant monster tried to eat us?"

"I agree with Bobby." Naiyana said regretfully. "There's too much we don't know about this place. We don't belong here, and it can clearly be dangerous. If we have a chance to go home, we should take it. That's what our families would want us to do."

Mark flinched slightly at the mention of family, but nodded his head silently to vote in their debate. Elise rolled her eyes dramatically.

"Fine, whatever." She said in a huff. "Let's find somewhere closer to the palace. We can chill and wait till the stupid bells ring." Elise looked around. "How about that huge light beam."

"Wait, you can see that too?" Mark asked in genuine surprise.

"Of course, weirdo. It's a giant ray of glittery light in the middle of the city."

Mark hadn't noticed any difference between the distant central beam and all the other variants of silver luminescence he saw swirling around Maije. But now that he looked at it, there was a distinct shimmer infused into its radiance.

Mark noticed the three suns had all but set, and a dark blue tint filled the sky. Maije responded to the encroaching darkness swiftly. Bizarre colorful insects emerged from crevices and cracks, shaking themselves alight in vibrant illuminated displays. Stone faced Overseers carried lanterns and ignited the wicks of large street torches. Temples added kindling, parchment, and logs to pyres, creating monumental blazes at their entrances.

The glowing hints of emerging stars were nearly obscured by the city's newfound brilliance. Mark watched tides and currents of moving energies pour across Maije; tones of auburn, azure, jade, and lilac filling spheres of colorful air above them. They breathed and pulsed around each other in a lustrous garden of light. He felt like he was floating in a warm ocean.

"I wonder if there are names for all these races." Naiyana pondered.

"What do you mean?" Elise asked.

"Well..." Naiyana shied under Elise's excited stare. "...in books you have things like giants, dragons, and trolls. But here, there are so many unique kinds of creatures and people. How could you remember names for all of the different types?"

Bobby looked around at the diverse races and species roaming through Maije's streets. They flowed around one another in shared streams of movement, but wholly in their own stories.

"I like it." He said with an approving grin. "Everyone's different here."

"No problem, Naiy." Elise said cheerfully, as she grabbed Naiyana around her shoulder. "We can come up with names for all of these weirdos." Elise pointed around with her free hand, announcing a series of names loudly. "Silverchimps, Featherblobs, Purple Bears, Megaslugs, Woodwalkers, Lizard Balls..."

Bobby yanked Elise's arm down before she could gesture at another stranger.

"Can you stop being such a fucking idiot?" He said, overwhelmed with embarrassment.

Mark couldn't help but laugh at his friends. He turned to Naiyana with a newfound levity.

"Would you really prefer to see a Dragon right now?" Mark asked lightheartedly.

"I guess not." Naiyana muttered, after giving it some thought.

"If it didn't eat us or anything, seeing a dragon would be bad ass." Elise insisted.

Lost in their conversation, the group didn't realize they had arrived in a square. The plaza was wide, with several roads that led into its courtyard. Aromatic flower bushes bloomed out of large pots scattered around the area. They pulsed colorful perfumed mists into the air.

The people who chose to linger inside the square, appeared to be split between three clustered crowds. Each group surrounded a different speaker, who stood on platformed stages in front of their respective temple. They preached their philosophy aloud to the onlookers, replying to each other's sermons. The attention of the spectators drifted to whoever was speaking. The children strolled towards the nearest crowd.

The first speaker was female, and draped in a fantastical robe of assorted colors. The interwoven fabrics moved and bulged around each other, sliding all over her body. Her bright orange skin glistened with hints of gold flecks. Her lavender eyes scanned the crowd wildly as she spoke, ignoring the errant strands of turquoise hair which fell onto her forehead. Her simple stone stage was framed by two burning pyres, one consumed by a red flame and the other by a blue flame.

"Come closer Bambas, warm yourself on the eternal fire of Koba's love." Her voice was drenched in provocative passion. "The Chaosmaker. Birthmother of the first light. Wildflame, who forges all new wonders in our Raya." She pulled two streams of fire from the opposing pyres, and combined them in her hands. She formed a flaming purple orb which swirled over her palms. "Koba's cosmic love burns within all of you. The most powerful of the Primals."

As she moved around her small stage, she pulled the attention of her onlookers in with elegant gestures and animated expressions. Her voice worked towards a crescendo.

"The more we feed that fire within us, the stronger we all become. Koba is the first awakening, new life, flower Queen. Follow her paths, and you can set yourselves free, fill your minds with endless possibilities, create anything you desire, drink from every stream, defeat your fears, and burn as bright as the stars above." She looked towards the sky for a pause, before gazing at the younglings in front of her. "Only in Chaos do we find our shared power." She whispered in a flourish.

"Younglings, new souls, tender hearts..." The neighboring preacher began, his voice stern with measured precision.

He wore a blue and grey robe, stitched with intricate silver symbols. His skin was beige and weathered, but his silver hair was weaved into a pristine long braid. His six golden eyes were the only thing that seemed to move on his body, honing in sharply on each and every member of his audience. He stood on a cube stage of carved blue marble, covered in smaller engraved designs. He held an elegant metallic rod.

"…listen to how passionate fanatics try to sway you. To pull you to their selfish desires, and rob you of your own council. Observe the fragility and disorder of Chaos' excitable confusion. It burns hot, and hastily!" The speaker leaned down towards the front row of younglings in his audience. His tone took on a calculatedly playful cadence. "Chaos can't build anything that will last, anything that will be remembered. Those of you who have great vision, will only find calm sanctuary from the storm by following Shura."

He rose once more to address everyone.

"Control is the only Primal that gives form to the misshapen, artistry to raw wandering minds, and peace to the conflicts which haunt our souls. In a world of wind and fire, you can build temples! The grace of Control is the most essential of the Primal Forces. Only through Shura's guidance can we achieve Sawah harmony, within ourselves and the realms we cherish. Follow Shura, the wisest creator."

Everyone in the square seemed to intuitively turn to the final preacher, who sat on their stage unmoving. They were dressed in a simple black robe. Their face was covered in a smooth white mask with a single black eye on its forehead. The stage was made of rough black stone, shards of which rose up and ensnared the limbs of the white wooden chair on which the preacher was sat. The preacher's voice croaked out from behind the mask, with a frosty depth.

"Look to your shadows, younglings. They are your only truth. Clear your minds of the endless squabbling these two corrupting siblings force upon you. They disrupt your eternal serenity with their vain ambitions. In your hearts, you know their stories are lies. They seek to deprive you of a lasting peace we all once knew, when we swam together in the perfect silence."

A stillness fell across the crowd as they listened to the speaker's haunting voice.

"Only Asha can restore us to our destined peace. Embrace the Void, the oldest of the Primals. Asha spawned the first voices, and awoke our collective dream. Eat from the fruits of the black garden, and you will walk through the final gateway. Rid yourself of doubts, weakness, and these maddening reveries. The Black Star is our most eternal shared nature. The Void sleeps within the fibers of your soul. Between the wild beams of every light, there is always the Void. Asha awaits you at the petering of all fires, welcoming our return to the infinite and the pure."

"Let's get out of here guys." Elise urged her friends. "Religious people freak me out."

The group followed her onwards, and left the square to head towards the light. Mark looked back over his shoulder one last time. The masked preacher seemed to be focused directly on Mark as their last words seeped out: "The darkness is always with you."

14 – REFLECTION

Wynn returned to the council room swiftly. He tucked himself behind one of the doors to give Payo and her companions a wide entrance. The youngling strolled in confidently, her golden eyes glowing as she examined the room's decorations. Her umber skin rippled with tremors and glitters of pulsing light. In one hand, she twirled the heaviest braid of her shiny indigo hair.

Payo's father and the representatives from Tamat walked in behind her, finding a discrete wall to stand beside. Payo's pet Dex was the last to bound into the chamber. The small creature growled at the strange environment, and vanished into a puff of purple smoke. Kai noticed two Dexes appear on opposite sides of the room. One chewed on a curtain, while the other climbed up Wynn's leg.

"Your creation, Dex...can replicate himself?" Kai asked, hoping to make an opening.

"Among other very impressive abilities." Payo smirked. She had yet to meet anyone's gaze, though she no doubt felt all of them scrutinizing her.

As Payo sauntered around, small transformations bloomed in her wake. Extraordinary plants grew between the crevices of the stone floor. The curtains changed in coloration against the breeze. Payo moved to the central table, and smoothly vaulted herself onto it. She spun into a seated position atop the wooden surface. Despite her small frame, the table groaned under the pressure. The council watched her, as she ignored them and explored the details of the room.

Payo noticed the bowl full of stone orbs beside her and picked one up. She engulfed it in lavender flames. The orb shook slightly, then shattered into fiery fragments which rotated around Payo's lithe arm. Some of the small stones crystalized into jewels, shining with blazing brightness. Payo smiled as the bracelet danced around her wrist.

Kai studied her expression. Her features shifted in flickers of wild emotion. But her eyes had a stillness to them; pure unflinching focus. The calm surface of a chaotic ocean of energy.

"So..." Payo began playfully, not speaking to - or looking at - anyone in particular. "...you wanted to inspect me."

Wynn stood beside one of the pillars, and interjected with an efforted diplomatic tone.

"Payo, if you'll allow me. I could formally introduce the council mem..."

"No need." Payo replied, her voice drenched in boredom. "They are council members. They each represent a kingdom with a Sacred Eye. Old tokens of power that wouldn't really concern someone who can travel across the Raya at will." Payo turned her gaze and met Wynn's surprised stare directly. "Like me."

"Uh, I, well..." Wynn stuttered.

"I, on the other hand, am the Primal Reflection of Chaos. Koba's Flame, and the only hope anyone in this room has of survival. So, are we all adequately acquainted?"

Wynn looked to Kai, unsure of how best to proceed.

"Beyond the large kingdoms we represent," Kai began patiently. "each council member serves the Raya as a whole, ensuring the wellbeing of as many souls within it as we can. We safeguard a lasting harmony in all things. The greatest good for the greatest number of souls. That is the governing philosophy which has united our council since it was first formed."

Kai noticed the other members scrutinize the youngling with glaring expressions. Mokko's face displayed a particularly naked mistrust. His prisoner Sebalah trembled in rage.

"We are here..." Kai resumed. "...to offer our support and guidance, in the hopes you might help us restore the realms to their peaceful..."

"I take it you have a plan then?" Payo interrupted.

She lay down on the table, and casually examined the elaborate designs of the domed ceiling. The council members remained quiet. The only noise came from the two squabbling Dex replications in the corner, viciously nibbling each other's limbs.

"We are somewhat divided." Gohlli stated plainly.

Payo chuckled.

Kai pressed on, gesturing to the respective parties as he explained.

"Lord Gohlli, Priestess Imma'Ja, and I believe we can use your formidable powers to save Prince Sal'Haf; separating him from the dark forces which have consumed him. That would in turn sever the Void's connection to our realms. Our hope is to end the war swiftly, spare countless lives, and perhaps allow Sal'Haf and you…" Kai paused, examining Payo for any indication of a reaction. "…to return to your previous lives, before the Primals felt compelled to transform you into their Reflections."

Payo seemed unamused by the suggestion, but continued to listen.

"Mokko, meanwhile, wishes to face the Prince in open battle, destroy him and his forces while we hold a theoretical advantage in numbers." Kai continued.

Payo tilted her head slightly, and glanced in Mokko's direction.

"And our newest member, Kulsa, who represents the Godling Leiba's Nekra Kingdom, has stipulated that they wish to remain wholly uninvolved in the matter." Kai finished.

Payo vanished from the table in a purple flash, and reappeared by one of the windows. She peered down at Maije, absorbing the view for a long while.

"So many lights." Payo said, eventually. "You won't even allow the night to fully embrace your city. Do you fear the darkness, King Kai?" Payo looked to Kai, and saw him thinking of words to form in response. "So, you are all still debating?" Payo asked in an abrupt sigh. She turned to look at her father across the room, and didn't bother hiding her annoyance.

"Whichever path we end up pursuing." Gohlli said. "We hoped to do it united, with you."

Payo spun to face Gohlli, striding towards him. The radiance of her hair shimmered with a furious luminescence.

"Are you not a fellow creature of Chaos?" Payo asked, absorbing Gohlli's presence. "When did you become such a tepid puddle?"

Mokko stifled a laugh. Gohlli narrowed his gaze down on Payo.

"I have seen what becomes of my power when it burns as wildfire." Gohlli's voice was heavy with derision. "There are scorched realms which still haunt my soul, youngling."

"Sometimes people confess their sins so they can take credit for them." Payo smiled.

She spun to address the room, walking in a broad circle.

"Gohlli is a fool to mistake his gifts for curses. Wildfires are cleansing." Payo stated. "And despite his complete lack of charm or vision in how to accomplish his goals, Mokko certainly has the right idea. We will eradicate the Prince, and with him...the Void."

"We were hoping you would..." Kai began.

"I am here..." Payo interjected, her booming voice filling the room. "...as a courtesy to my beloved father, who respects this council of Eye-Keepers. In addition, the Kingdom of Tamat requested it." Payo said, narrowing her eyes onto the oddly tall Emissary Ganamahr. "And they have on occasion been kind to my village." She pivoted to face the room once more. "But I can see that little has come from your grand discussion. Certainly nothing to alter my intentions."

211

"It seems both Reflections have ambitions of their own, King Kai." Mokko scoffed. "Perhaps we'll have to deal with little Payo here after the Prince."

Payo spared another slight glance over her shoulder in Mokko's direction and smiled.

"You're welcome to try, you old Sagwak!"

"Charming mouth on your youngling." Fyzo said, looking at Vikkah.

"She's trying to save us!" Vikkah replied confidently, smiling at his daughter.

"Is that so?" Mokko mocked, without bothering to look behind him. "Our council grows more crowded with every moment."

"We betray our kingdoms with these squabbles." Kai yelled. "We owe it to our realms to keep their homes safe from the coming storm."

"Stay in your temples." Payo scorned. "Defend your houses. That's all you rulers ever do. I can face the princeling without you." Payo approached King Kai, and a deep hum emanated from her body. "And it certainly won't be to gently cradle him out from of his powers."

Imma'Ja strode towards Payo. Her presence calmed the light radiating off Payo's body. Payo bristled in mild irritation. Imma'Ja stared at the youngling with kind silver eyes.

"Payo," Imma'Ja spoke melodically. "you are undoubtedly the Raya's best hope. But we don't even know if you can defeat Sal'Haf. Should you fail, you doom us all to his reign. Please, allow us to help you."

Payo gazed at the Priestess in silence. The room watched the pair absorb each other. Whatever effect Imma'Ja had hoped to have on Payo vanished with the youngling in a plume of smoke. Payo appeared on the tabletop again to address everyone.

"You can help me…" Payo's voice boomed. Her two pets barked in response, spitting small flames into the air. "…by doing what I say, or staying out of my way. I am here to save what remains of the Raya, and I will do whatever is necessary to achieve that vision."

Payo saw some council members tense in defensive postures. She didn't seem to mind.

"I've heard your debate, now you will listen to my decision." Payo's voice lowered to a more pleasing tenor. "I am not foolish enough to believe I deserve the powers I've been gifted. But I will honor them, by ensuring I stop Sal'Haf in the only way I am certain will work…I will awaken the Children of the Storm."

A stunned silence drowned the room.

"You…you cannot." Kai muttered in dread, finally finding his voice.

"Yes, I can." Payo replied.

She stared down at him; her fiery eyes and small frame radiated a formidable command.

"Payo, their reign nearly shattered the realms." Imma'Ja implored. "They haven't been awoken in…"

"Far too long." Payo replied with a volatile vigor.

She seemed eager to dismiss any challenge. Gohlli approached the table, and kneeled down beneath her.

"Payo…" Gohlli entreated. "…I know the raging fire that burns within you. But the Storm-Born were imprisoned for a reason. They have no loyalty but to their own desires."

Payo chuckled, and looked down at the council member with pity.

"Does your own nature bring you such shame, Lord Gohlli?" Payo asked. "You are too blind to see, but this is the only choice we have. The Children of the Storm were among the first manifestations of Chaos. The seeds of our shared spirit fires."

Payo raised a hand and traced her small fingers through the air. The six arms on Gohlli's back grew in size, changing colors and blazing with more ferocity.

"Half the realms we know were shaped by their hand. They are pure. Force-born from the eldest. What better weapon could we wield against the Prince's growing darkness?"

Payo turned to the room. Her voice radiated from every surface.

"My powers have grown, but Sal'Haf's abilities no doubt significantly exceed my own. We do not know if Shura has yet awoken the gifts of Control in a third Reflection. Even if such a warrior eventually appears, their powers would be even weaker than mine. Reflections enhance the reach and potency of their abilities by spreading them into the Raya. Time is an advantage, and Sal'Haf is winning the race. I must act decisively. The Storm-Born will bridge the divide between Sal'Haf and my capabilities. They will submit to my command. We are warriors of a shared vision; essential to defeat Asha's growing darkness."

"You cannot hope to wield such power!" Kai contended. "Koba's gifts are challenge enough for any being. To add such formidable disharmony...it will be your undoing."

"I am not sure you have a full understanding of the nature of Reflections, King Kai." Payo replied, her expression a strange mix of pity and pride. "We are not simply vessels of a Primal's will. Whatever previous embodiments you've studied in your fables and books, I can assure you I maintain my own mind. The choices I make are mine. Perhaps in the numbness of Sal'Haf's pain he has relinquished his own decisions. But I yield to no commands."

"I found these delightful depictions of the Children of the Storm in Tamat's library." Payo continued, signaling Ganamahr and her two guards to approach.

They revealed three large scrolls, which they rolled onto the floor. Beautiful illustrations and elegant text filled each parchment. Payo looked at the first scroll, and exhaled a graceful swirl of purple fire from her mouth. The spiral collided with the main illustration. The page absorbed the flame, and the drawing rose into the air. Fragments of its previous contoured outline took on a fleshed-out form of color and movement.

"Sarphan the Changeling." Payo announced, her crystalized stare focused solely on the small apparition before her.

Everyone in the room watched as the animated illustration transformed into a figurine of liquid light. It had six legs of formidable strength, a torso with two additional arms, and a spherical head that displayed a crown of eyes. The figure spun around slowly, as it treaded the air and roared silently. In a flash, it transformed into a winged creature with a serrated beak, and then again into a tentacle flailing monstrosity. The luminated representation continued to hover and transform, as Payo moved onto the next scroll and exhaled a new current of spun purple fire.

"Groshk the Destroyer." Payo said, her voice taking on a reverent awe.

The second figure had a serpentine body, slithering against hidden currents as it rose through the air. The torso attached to its long tail had four arms thick with muscle, which protruded in opposing diagonal directions. They formed an X of wildly swinging limbs, each carrying a unique battle axe or war hammer in their grip. The figure's head looked like a curved long horn, sharp at its point and adorned with two parallel rows of eyes.

"Rhispa the Unseen." Payo exhaled her final awakening.

The last figure rose shrouded in a dark cloak, with hands and a face engulfed in flame. In a flash, the figure sliced across the room and appeared behind Payo, only to promptly return to hover above the scroll.

"Sal'Haf feeds on the weakest souls in our realms to give him strength. I will awaken the most ancient of beings, whose fire can outburn the Prince's cold appetites." Payo proclaimed proudly. "We will fill his darkness with enough light to shatter him!" Payo closed her fist. Kai saw a wild craze fill her eyes. "If we meet his calamity with a reckoning of our own, we can hold back the tides of his destruction."

Gohlli tore his gaze away from the three hovering representations, and looked to Payo with a face full of bare fear. He muttered his words.

"You mean to fight one plague by unleashing another?" Gohlli's tone turned bitter. "The misfortunes brought upon the Raya by those godlings can still be felt to this day. Countless souls infected with wild hungers that tore at their minds, left them mad with unnatural desires. Endless conflicts, hatreds, wars, and destructions can be traced back to those creatures. Do not do this!"

Payo stepped to the edge of the table, and peered down at Gohlli. Her voice drank the air out of the room, and rippled out in roaring cascades.

"I am the manifestation of a Primal. I do not need permission from old guards who failed to protect their kingdoms against the very danger we now face." A combative charm returned to her lilt. "Would you rather risk the madness my reign *might* instill in a few weak souls, or the obliteration of our civilizations by Sal'Haf's insatiable cravings?"

The tension in the room made it hard to breathe. Payo noticed her father look at her. With an assuring smile and nod, he encouraged her to find her kindness again.

"Look…" Payo began, addressing the stern faces around her. "…I understand this is all unexpected. I'm sure my words bring you great discomfort. I know the kingdoms, tribes, and traditions you have spent your lives defending are in risk of being dangerously reshaped. And by younglings with powers outside your control. But consider this: Sal'Haf wants to consume the Raya's light. I only wish to flourish it. I won't simply stop his conquests; I will fill our realms with more life than they have ever known. In place of a tyrant, you would have a creator Queen. I am not a slave to my powers as Sal'Haf has become. I am in harmony with Koba's gifts. Listen to my voice. It does not waver. I am not fractured by fickle whim or violent discord. Though my powers are chaotic, my mind has never been clearer. I am full of divine purpose."

"You present your fanaticism as virtue." Gohlli spoke grimly.

Payo ignored him, and addressed King Kai in an assuring cadence.

"You fear the Reflections and the Primals, King Kai. You hope for Sawah to return and avoid any changes to the familiar world you've always known. But change is eternal. Some measure of destruction is always necessary, so that we can renew ourselves and become what our curious souls yearn to discover."

Payo could see Kai's expression fall in crestfallen doubt.

"You have a pretty city, Kai. But there will never be a garden that doesn't one day wilt, decay, or burn. I offer you a chance to embrace the change that's coming, and help shape the eruption of life that will bloom in the wake of this conflict. Change is cleansing, after all. From this destruction we will flourish more powerfully. This precious need of yours to hold onto the familiar, is simply fear." Payo concluded.

Kai raised his head, and met Payo's gaze with steely resolve.

"You will never be able to fully control what you unleash." He said sternly.

"The absence of Control is not my concern." Payo scoffed. "Whichever Reflection wins this fight, will define the future of the Raya. You are welcome to join me in battle, or wait in your temples until your fate is decided for you."

The room was utterly silent, until the hiss of Sebalah's voice seeped from her red mask.

"The Void is our beginning, heathen!" Sebalah mocked from her knelt position. Her cold tones slithered across the room. Mokko gripped her chain, but allowed her to speak. "The Dark Star is our origin. You will never destroy it!"

Mokko and Fyzo pointed their weapon in Sebalah's direction, aimed towards causing pain but not death. Kulsa strode closer to watch the scene unfold, a twisted curiosity swimming across her golden features.

Payo approached the kneeling prisoner without a trace of fear on her young face. A rumbling energy radiated off her body, pushing against the space around her.

"The Void longs only to imprison every soul it can capture." Payo replied, her voice thundered with unnerving reverberations. Something colossal spoke from within the youngling. "It is an old and envious power, lacking in imagination or beauty. Only the strongest lights can reject Asha's dark selfish dream."

Kai noticed others move away from the duo, or take protective postures. A deep tension sank into everyone's flesh.

"There are powers in the darkness you cannot imagine, little one." Sebalah replied, her body coiled despite her shackles.

"Then those who rebel against it are all the braver!" Payo retorted glibly.

She raised her small hand, and engulfed it in an orb of brilliant fire. The flame spiraled and fragmented outwards, creating increasingly complex currents of interwoven forms.

"There is no end to creation, vile parasite." Payo said. "How will you feast on the light which outlasts you?"

Gohlli turned to Mokko, who remained uncharacteristically quiet.

"Now you choose to bind your tongue?" Gohlli barked.

Mokko shrugged, and stared directly at Payo. She had yet to fully look in his direction.

"The Children of the Storm..." Mokko began casually. "...certainly unexpected."

Mokko's grip lessened as his mind contemplated the suggestion. Sebalah sensed the slack. In a sudden shriek, she whipped her mask off and lunged for Payo with fangs bared. Payo merely snapped her fingers. Sebalah's screech stretched in pitch as her body began to splinter. Purple fires erupted from every shattered portion of her form. Within a moment, she was utterly obliterated in an explosion of light. Remnants of her limbs fell to the ground as flower petals and fluttering small creatures that scurried towards the windows in search of freedom.

Mokko jumped from his seat, wild-eyed with outrage.

"What have you done, you stupid Sarkaf!" Mokko yelled in complete disbelief.

"You should have kept your pet tamed." Payo replied, finally meeting his gaze.

"Her armies will unleash themselves upon the realms." Mokko's fury boiled over. "Their cruelty will spread like a flood!"

"Yet another horde I will cleanse..." Payo stated plainly, stepping towards Mokko's looming form. "...as soon as I'm done with Sal'Haf."

Mokko stared down at Payo in shivering rage. He turned to Kai, ferocious contempt burning his features.

"This is Koba's chosen champion?" He seethed, throwing his chain to the ground. "A petulant unthinking youngling, hurling her powers around like a drunken fool."

"I am Koba's Fire!" Payo roared.

Her small body rose into the air and towered above Mokko. A cloak of flames engulfed her. It filled her eyes and mouth.

"The first light moves within me. Who are you to impede my destiny?" Payo boomed.

Mokko grunted in disdain. He turned his back on Payo, and sat in his chair. He slammed the tail of his trident into the floor with a loud crack.

"Two oppressors competing for our misery then." Mokko chuckled coldly. "And it will be the realms who suffer for their whims."

"She was baiting you..." Gohlli muttered, staring at the embers of Sebalah's remains.

"I don't care." Payo replied.

"Payo..." Vikkah said firmly from across the room.

Payo looked to her father and saw the swell of disappointment on his kind face. Her hovering radiance subsided into a slow descent back to ground. She exhaled a deep sigh, and calmed herself.

"I am going to discuss the matter with my father and Emissary Ganamahr." Payo spoke in her plain modest voice. "I hope we will leave here as friends, if not allies in battle. Let us take a moment to compose ourselves. Perhaps an agreement can still be reached."

Kai watched the scene unfold with crushing despair. He felt Imma'Ja's gentle influence enter his awareness. Her voice sounded within his thoughts, moving around the troubled crevices of his mind, soothing and clear.

"Be patient, Kai. This is not over."

Kai turned towards the priestess, who stood near a window. Her soft radiance was bathed in the city lights, blending the glowing swarms of brilliance which embraced her body. Kai focused on his reply, assured it would find its way to her mind.

"Only two Reflections, Imma'Ja. How can this be? Without hope for Sawah, one of these younglings will plunge the Raya into catastrophic disharmony or cruel dominion."

220

Imma'Ja smiled assuredly. She closed her eyes and let her fingertips rise to the window. The lithe digits danced around unseen currents. Imma'Ja tilted her head, as she listened to music beyond understanding. Her eyes flew open, and she looked to Kai with radiant certainty.

"Send Wynn to the fountain, now!" Her command filled Kai's mind.

Everyone else in the room sought tense council with one another. Kai motioned for Wynn to join him. He leaned in and whispered instructions in his ear. Wynn made a hasty exit, as Payo turned to address everyone once more. Vikkah stood behind her, proudly clasping her shoulder.

"My father shares your concerns." Payo began, her tone doused in diplomacy. "He does not wish to see me harmed in battle, or to lose me like we lost my mother. He hopes I can entreat you all to join my cause, and together assure a shared victory. I will stay here, and discuss the matter with you a while longer. Just know, that I only intend to bring the Raya to its full and rightful glory. Prince Sal'Haf is not the dark end of our story. He is an invitation for us to create our brightest light yet. I hope each of you will help me remake our world. Together."

15 – FOUNTAIN

The children walked under the canal archways and bridges connecting the buildings above. The architecture seemed to evolve and shift with every turn, as they worked their way towards the shiny beam. Eventually, they arrived at the source of the light.

"Woah." Bobby muttered, in complete astonishment.

They stood at the edge of a vast garden, filled with hundreds of civilians, unique statues, and exotic foliage. At the center of the park, sat a giant monolith of white jagged stone adorned in beautiful shimmering crystals. The colossal obelisk hummed and pulsed, as it shot out a constant beam of brightness towards the sky.

It bathed everything around it in radiance, soaking the grass, citizens, and buildings alike in an ethereal hue. Some people sat in tree branches, others atop large boulders, small groups huddled down on the lawn, while other onlookers stood on nearby rooftops and balconies. Whether alone or in crowds, sharing hushed conversations or stood in worshipful silence, most people's gaze seemed transfixed on the stone's light.

"What the hell is that thing?" Elise asked, walking onto the garden's lush grounds.

"Is this like The Eye you guys saw?" Naiyana added.

"No…" Mark murmured, his mind reeling and dazed.

"This is much cooler." Bobby said.

The group immersed themselves into the crowd. They watched small children run through the field, saw clusters of friends share seats on floating shelves of moss-covered stone, and noticed two elderly men play a board game with moving stone figures and armored insects.

"Whatever that thing is," Elise said, as she studied the crowd. "people sure like to gather around and stare at it."

The giant rock began to vibrate loudly, and everyone stopped what they were doing to gaze more intently. The rumbling rose in volume, shaking the ground around the monolith. The largest crystal at the obelisk's tip glowed brilliantly, and burst with a flash of brightness. The onlookers all stomped their feet, howled, or cheered.

Naiyana noticed an orb of light float from the top of the stone, and sail down to the crowd. The sphere of light was golden at the core, and silver at the edges. It drifted towards people who all yelled "Reflect me!" or "Choose me!" as it approached them. They moaned in disappointment whenever the light moved on to its next target of curiosity. Seemingly unsatisfied with its options, the orb sauntered off down one of the side streets and continued on its exploratory journey. The monolith returned to its former brightness; the hum which pulsed from its edges now soothing and calm.

"So that's where those things come from." Bobby said.

"What do you think they are?" Elise asked.

"The first one we saw turned into another version of that Treeboy." Naiyana speculated. "Maybe that's how people are made here?"

"Weird." Bobby pouted.

"It's not like giving birth the regular way is any less creepy." Elise grimaced.

"That's exactly what this place was missing: a giant soul-maker rock." Bobby said. "Now everything makes sense."

"Making fun of things doesn't make you smarter than them, Bobby." Elise taunted.

Bobby turned to Mark for support, and immediately saw something was wrong. Mark had a vacant look on his face, and his body was starting to glow again. He was walking towards the monolith, seemingly transfixed.

"Hey." Bobby said, urging the girls to take notice.

They quickly moved close to Mark, attempting to get his attention.

"Uh, Mark." Elise said, trying to get in front of him without raising alarm. "You're doing that glowy thing. People are gonna notice."

Mark was aware his friends were talking to him, but their voices felt like distant echoes. The monolith came alight again. Mark was intoxicated by the connection he felt to it. An overwhelming sense of presence washed over his mind. Memories of his family, home, and Earth alike became faint whispers in his newly clarified awareness. He was fully present. Connected. The obelisk drew him forward with an immersive allure.

The monolith hummed, very loudly. The surrounding crowd looked surprised that it was happening again so soon. Some turned to each other with quizzical expressions. Most were just happy to cheer in eager anticipation. A few noticed the winged youngling walking towards the obelisk, his body reflecting the pillar's brightness in mirrored radiance.

"Mark!" Bobby muttered loudly, moving his face in front of his friend's. "People are starting to stare!"

Mark was entranced. He gazed through Bobby, and continued to march forward. The monolith shuddered visibly, and more powerfully than before. The loud hum grew deafening. More people turned to stare at Mark; some in confusion, some in fear. Naiyana, Bobby, and Elise formed a loose protective barrier around Mark, hesitant and cautious. They hoped they'd be able to control the crowd if things got out of hand.

The obelisk's crescendo of light and sound detonated in an explosion of brightness. Onlookers yelled in surprise and shock. When everyone's eyes adjusted, they looked up and saw several spheres of light floating in a halo around the monument's tip. Dozens of the glowing orbs moved around each other in harmonious interwoven paths.

Gasps of awe and surprise washed over the crowd. Any eyes not focused on the orbs, were transfixed onto Mark – whose body still shone with the same silver brightness. People moved to approach the group, eager to inspect Mark more closely.

"Ugh, guys..." Elise said, concerned about the growing tension.

The orbs spiraled downwards in swirls, sailing directly towards Mark. The onlookers stopped in their tracks, as the spheres danced around Mark's body. They spun in intricate patterns, pulsing bright radiance as they drew nearer to the winged youngling.

The crowd murmured and scrambled over each other to see what was happening. Mark raised one of his hands to touch an orb. All the spheres stopped moving at the same time. As Mark's finger pressed against the nearest orb, all the others shook violently and shone more brightly. Tendrils of golden light seeped out from all of their cores, reaching out to Mark.

In synchronized eruptions, all the orbs burst in a flash and transformed into younglings. Each displayed distinct types of skin, diversities of size and natures, had different numbers of appendages and other physical protrusions, but they all had one thing in common: wings. All of them spread their own sets of wings, whether reptilian, feathered, or elemental.

The crowd gasped in unabashed shock at the newly formed younglings. The mood on several of their expressions darkened with uncomfortable suspicion. The winged newlings looked at their surroundings, and all smiled at Mark. Almost uniformly, they leapt into the air and took flight. The crowd watched as they soared above the city.

The apprehensive mistrust of the crowd escalated and spread. Everyone watched the light stop glowing on Mark's body. Some onlookers cautiously approached, their eyes narrow and limbs tense. Mark shook the fog of confusion from his mind, and turned to his friends with a look of concern.

"Dude, what did you just do?" Bobby asked, as the friends clustered together defensively.

"That wasn't me." Mark replied softly.

"Yo, it really, really was though." Elise said, eyeing the approaching people.

She quietly formed claws on her hands and kept them hidden from sight.

"Maybe we should go..." Naiyana suggested, looking for an exit. "...anywhere else."

Just as the crowd got uncomfortably close, urgent yells filled the gardens.

"Make way!"

"Move."

"City Guards! Clear a path."

The children watched in concern as a formidable cluster of Maije's guards charged through the crowd to create an opening. A figure walked towards them on the newly formed path. It only took them a moment to recognize his friendly furry face.

"Oh..." Wynn said, grinning widely. "...it's you."

#

Wynn led the children up a hill overlooking Maije. Seven guards formed a wide circle around them as they strode onwards. The trail crested onto a flat plateau, which continued to skirt around the city's edge, elevated above the rooftops. The road they were on ended in the distance ahead, at was clearly their intended destination: the Palace.

The vast building sat atop a prolonged rock shelf at the cliff's edge, seemingly teetering on a foundation too slender to hold it. The underside of the stone ledge was upheld by an immense statue of a silver tree. The gargantuan metallic tree was rooted down in the city, but its huge branches rose up and wrapped themselves around the palace's foundations.

"I'm happy to see you bambas making so many friends." Wynn smiled.

"Hey man, we told you in the forest," Bobby huffed indignantly. "we have no idea what's going on here. We're just trying to get home!"

"Yes, I remember. I'm taking you to see King Kai and his guests." Wynn said. "They'll be most interested to meet you. After which, we can discuss getting you home."

The children glanced at each other in unease. They tried to figure out what they could do, while exchanging silent inquisitive gazes. Mark looked at the city below. Churning streams of silver light rushed between the streets. They swirled around Maije's central stone – where Wynn had collected them. It was a galaxy of moving vibrance.

"Guys," Mark spoke softly, so that only his friends would hear him well. "I think we're in another dimension or something. Everything is different, but feels just as real as…home."

"I'd say you're crazy." Bobby said, looking down at his metallic legs. "But nothing about this place makes sense, so you might be right."

"That probably means getting back will be quite difficult." Naiyana considered.

"Wow, now that is a castle!" Elise exclaimed, lost in her own observations.

They were close enough to the palace to see its detailed features. The building was a stunning combination of heavy stone and ornate artistry. It had seven floors, decorated with giant balconies and connective bridges between the towers. Large spherical stone orbs were attached to the walls, like berries hanging from a stem. The spheres had windows that hinted at lavish rooms within.

Lush canopies of outlandish plants draped themselves all over the palace's façade. The ascending garden moved and breathed its way across the building's foundations. The palace's two main strongholds were adorned with silver domes, overlooking the kingdom below. The entire palatial structure appeared to sway slightly in the breeze.

"You sure that thing can hold the whole palace up?" Bobby asked skeptically, gesturing to the tree statue and cliff shelf below the castle.

"It has so far." Wynn replied, with another wry grin.

Elise did a poor job hiding her excitement as they neared the palatial gates. Only when she noticed the sullen concern in Mark's eyes did she feel a pang of guilt and try to console him.

"It'll be ok, Mark." She said, her voice full of compassion.

"I hope so." Mark replied softly.

"I'm gonna be stuck here forever." Bobby moaned, striding onto the lavish grounds.

"Poor Bobby." Elise scolded. "Everything's always happening just to you."

Bobby held his middle finger up over his shoulder.

Mark stopped outside the palace's main doors. He tugged on Wynn's sleeve.

"Wynn, will the King help get us home? Will he allow us to use The Eye?" Mark's tone had a newfound determination in it.

Wynn turned, and knelt to face the youngling.

"Mark, you all seem…" Wynn searched for the right words. "…quite lost. Or at the very least, you seem unaware of your place in the Raya and how you arrived in our realm. Which is certainly a curious mystery. There's much we have to explain to you, and I promise we will. But what you did down there by the fountain…" Wynn stared into Mark's eyes with an intense reverence that made him uncomfortable. "…why didn't you tell me you were Shura's Reflection when we first met? We are in the midst of the greatest conflict between the Primals since The First Wars. The fates of so many souls are bound to yo..."

"Enough, dude!" Bobby yelled angrily, interrupting Wynn. "For the last time, we have no fucking clue what you're talking about, okay? You keep saying these words: Raya, Shura, Primals. How can we get this into your furry ass head man, we aren't from here!"

The guards were visibly confused by Bobby's tirade, both in its audacity and substance. They exchanged puzzled looks, and pretended – quite poorly – not have heard the rant. Wynn sighed and shook his head.

"Then I am just as confused as you are." Wynn said. "You must be from somewhere very far away. But the council needs to see you. Together, I'm sure we can resolve this."

Wynn stood and walked into the palace. The children reluctantly followed.

"We're in another dimension and still getting taken to the principal's office." Bobby groaned as he trudged along.

The group walked through a corridor into the main atrium. The children were awestruck by the sight that greeted them. Soaring marble columns rose up around the enormous oval room, climbing to all the floors above. Each level was marked by a semi-circular balcony ledge, which overlooked the open entrance below. A skylight at the top poured soft moonbeams onto them.

Wynn led them to a herd of bizarre creatures. They looked like massive blue crabs, on which several people could stand. Instead of claws, they had long shimmering tentacles tightly coiled by their resting bodies. The children noticed one of the creatures on the balconies above, carrying other visitors on its back from floor to floor. The creature used its tentacles to grip the beams, climbing up or down as needed – while the travelers sat comfortably on its vast flat shell.

"Hop on." Wynn said, gesturing to one of the creatures.

"Can't we just take the stairs?" Bobby asked, barely hiding his disgust.

"They're perfectly safe, I assure you." Wynn smiled.

"Sure, what could go wrong riding giant elevator crabs." Bobby muttered.

Wynn got onto the creature's back, and took a seat. He dismissed the guards who had accompanied them, and tapped the shell beside him to encourage his young guests to join him. The children climbed on. They tried to ignore the strange moans coming from the creature's hefty beak, as it stretched out its slithering limbs and climbed the building's interior.

The ride was wobbly at first, but for the most part the children couldn't deny it was quite enjoyable. They stopped at the seventh floor, and hopped onto the balcony. Wynn briskly led them down a long corridor, and only slowed his pace as he approached two large wooden doors. They could hear the clamor of heated discussions from within.

"Stay close, bambas." Wynn hushed, before opening the doors and leading them in.

16 – DOORS

The children ambled into the room, warily following Wynn's eager broad strides. Bobby and Mark recognized some of the people gathered in the meeting area. A few took notice of the new guests, while others were lost in hushed conversations.

Naiyana spotted a beautiful girl in the middle of the room with braided electric blue hair; who appeared to be the focus of many people's side-glanced attention. Elise took note of the council members, assigning them nicknames in her mind: *goldyhead, beardyface, blueman, fire arms, purple angel...* she lost track when Wynn addressed the room.

"Council," Wynn strained to evoke a dignified tenor. "please pardon my interruption."

Everyone turned to face Wynn, and his four young companions.

"If you'll allow me to introduce our newcomers. This is Bobby, Naiyana, Elise, and Mark." Wynn rested his gesturing hand on Mark's head.

Kai and Imma'Ja turned their gaze to Mark, understanding Wynn's signal.

Mark noticed the King and the glowing woman stare at him. He sensed an exchange rebounding between them, despite their still expressions. They were connected somehow. It suddenly occurred to him: they were talking to each other. He was inexplicably certain of it, though he couldn't hear their thoughts. He felt the hidden exchange as it transpired.

"You've brought us *more* bambas?" Mokko asked in annoyance. "Why?"

Wynn ignored Mokko, and proceeded with his formalities.

"Younglings, that is King Kai. Ruler of Maije. Next to him..." Wynn began, before Payo cut him off impatiently.

231

"Must we really endure these ceremonial introductions?" She blurted out irritably.

"Yeah, listen we don't mean to offend you or anything." Bobby said, boldly addressing the room. "But we kind of spied on you guys up at The Eye, when we were looking for a way to get home. So, we get it, you guys are the council, right?" Bobby urged the situation along.

"*They* are." Payo replied, her gaze curiously focused on Mark.

Mark matched her stare. He could see hundreds of silver tendrils wildly streaming off her body in various directions. They changed size and occasionally even color. It was dizzying and irritating to observe.

Payo teleported over to Mark, appearing directly in front of him. The light that radiated off her body and the fabric of her moving clothes seemed to grow still in Mark's proximity. Payo leaned in and deeply inhaled Mark's aroma. Dex stalked around the duo, snarling at Mark.

"Who are you?" Payo asked, her tone direct but only mildly adversarial.

Of all the perceptions Mark had navigated since his arrival in this place, his connection to this girl was the most perplexing. She radiated a unique power. It felt like the contorted opposite of the companion dwelling in his mind, which gave him all his heightened awareness. Something about her seemed rare, pure, and alluring – yet also terrifying. Mark felt like they shared something essential, and yet wholly contrasted. It felt like staring into a distorted mirror.

"I'm Mark." he replied calmly.

"Eye-Keepers, Payo, and honored guests," Wynn spoke loudly, trying to recapture the room's attention. "Fyzo and I first met these younglings wandering through Moriae Forest. They claimed to be lost and unable to remember how they arrived in the realm. I guided them to our city to find refuge, hoping our mapmasters or realm scholars might know how to get them back to their homelands."

"And this matter was urgent enough to disturb a council meeting?" Kulsa inquired glibly.

"On instruction from King Kai, I went to the Birthstar Fountain to investigate an anomaly Priestess Imma'Ja sensed within the harmony of our city. After witnessing what occurred down there, I believe this one here – Mark - is Shura's Reflection. Control's chosen champion."

Urgency and intrigue alike spread across the faces of everyone in the room. Most stood to approach Mark for a closer look.

"Is he?" Payo asked, still standing uncomfortably close to Mark. "And what trinkets did Shura deign to gift you? Those pretty feathers?" Payo playfully stroked one of Mark's wings with her fingers. He bristled, and pulled the wing away.

"Hey!" Elise yelled. "We've been trying to tell this Wynn guy here: we have no clue what you guys are talking about. We are very, *very* lost. We don't have any idea how we got here, and we just want to go home."

Wynn struggled to remain undeterred by the constant interruptions, and forged on.

"Mark caused several souls to flood out of the Birthstar in one surge. They all aligned themselves with him – forming reflections in his image. Simultaneously. Those newlings fly in the skies above Maije as we speak. Every one of them a winged youngling." Wynn explained.

"I told you we were going to get in trouble for that." Bobby muttered.

Payo strolled over to the table, and leaned back against it. She smiled, and watched the council members hone in to close ranks around Mark. All the eyes in the room focused on him. Mark felt the weight of their gaze. He was at a loss for words.

"Please," He began, hesitant to say the wrong thing. "you have to understand, I don't know how I did that. These weird things have been happening since we got here."

"You mean since you arrived in Maije?" Kai asked curiously.

"No, to this place. This…" Mark tried to remember the word. "…the Raya."

"What do you mean?" Kulsa asked, her face twisted into a dark suspicion.

"Where were you…" Gohlli added, equally confused. "…before the Raya?"

"Earth." Elise blurted out.

"Never heard of it." Mokko dismissed. "How long have you had your powers, bamba?"

The children shared frustrated sighs.

"My friends and I woke up here. Today." Mark recounted. "We've never been here before, to any of these…realms or Raya. We come from a completely different reality. We don't know what's going on. These aren't even our regular bodies. I don't normally have wings. Bobby's legs aren't made of metal back on Earth."

Mark took a measured breath, trying to slow his exasperated pace.

"I don't know why this is happening to us. But ever since I woke up here, I've been seeing a silver light on everything, and sometimes a weird energy shoots out of me, and it's like this voice is speaking in my head and making me do things. Like with the monster outside the city, and with the fountain light ball things that turned into children." Mark clarified.

"Monster?" Mokko asked, finally interested in the discussion.

"Apparently, they were attacked outside the gates." Wynn explained. "A foul creature set upon the younglings, but the guards destroyed it."

The council members were overcome with further queries.

"You said you woke up here?" Imma'Ja asked Mark.

"You came to Maije, only seeking a way home to hide from the war?" Mokko sneered.

"Where exactly is your Eurth realm located?" Gohlli pressed.

"Earth is our planet." Naiyana clarified. "We're not sure how we got here, or where Earth is relative to this place."

"How could..." Gohlli mumbled in confusion.

"Hey!" Bobby shouted angrily. "We're not answering any more questions! Can you get us back home or not? That's all we care about right now. We told your hippie lion friend here when we met him, we've never heard of your Rayas or your Primals or any of that crap. This entire place..." Bobby gestured in wide arcs. "...the whole thing. We are not from here!" Bobby stressed the last point loudly. "All we want, is to get out of this place and back to our families."

The room was utterly silent as everyone stared at the four younglings.

"These bambas have clearly gone mad." Mokko muttered.

"Perhaps, Payo is truly our only hope." Gohlli said, consumed by the severity of the idea.

Kai stared at Mark throughout the interactions. He spoke with invigorated purpose.

"If this youngling is Shura's chosen champion, then he is our best chance of achieving Sawah between the Primals." Kai stated. "Allow me some time to help him, perhaps gaining his powers distorted his memories."

235

"We are in the midst of a war, and you seek your salvation by playing with younglings." Mokko yelled, his patience finally broken. "Is this the great hope you waited for, Kai? Your weapon of balance?" He turned to Mark, with venomous eyes. "Well little one, are you here to save us? Are you going to defeat the forces eager to feast on our destruction?"

"Uh…look, we're very sorry about all the things you're dealing with." Mark replied. "It sounds like a lot. We don't really know how to explain this any better, but this isn't our home. We can't help in your war, because we don't belong here. We're not a part of this."

"You're here in the Raya, how could you not a be part of it?" Gohlli pleaded, unable to fathom Mark's position. "You can run to your realm if you choose, but this war will find us all."

"The long awaited third Reflection!" Mokko laughed maniacally. "For all your faith in the Primals Kai, gaze upon Shura's choice: a quivering youngling with no understanding. There is your fabled Sawah! The Primals mock us."

"Pitiful." Kulsa added coldly. "He barely has a notion of where he stands. Yet, he wields the gifts of a Primal? He is undeserving of his power."

"There is more to the younglings than we know." Imma'Ja said, studying Mark intently.

"So you claim, Priestess." Mokko yelled dismissively. "Disgraceful. We are leaving! I wish you luck as you meditate on a plan with your new war companions, Kai. I'm going to clean the mess that petulant sarkaf created when she killed Sebalah!"

Mokko pointed a heavy fist at Payo. She barely noticed. Her gaze was locked on Mark, as she leaned on the table and smirked.

"Mokko, we are stronger together." Kai beseeched. "Please be patient, the Primals have a design. We simply haven't seen it yet."

Mokko turned to Kai. A great swell of pity and disdain filled all four of his eyes.

"How seductive it must be to live in the dream of peace." Mokko sighed. "I will protect my people, Kai, any way I can. Enjoy playing with your bambas."

Mokko looked at the devastated fragments of Sebalah littered on the polished floor.

"Today has been a gift." Mokko exhaled. "I have learned what I always suspected to be true. The Primals are vicious, cruel, and utterly indifferent to our suffering. We are playthings to absentminded and destructive godlings. Small insects hurled into uncaring winds. What can we do but enjoy our journeys through the tempest?"

"We have two Reflections." Kai entreated. "The plan to free Sal'Haf is all the stronger."

"I am not as well versed in the self-engrandeure of diplomacy or cautious strategies." Mokko barked. "They are the art forms of preening pandoma fik-umahks!"

"You have no honor, wretched kusashamok!" Gohlli yelled.

"I think we just learned some new curse words." Bobby whispered to Elise.

"Kai, you are a born teacher." Mokko spoke unflinchingly. "Your city is a sanctuary filled with young curious minds, and you see great hope in their endless naivety. But I don't share your patience. I command warriors. I know what it will take to win this war. The Primals chose three bambas, and gifted them powers we can barely fathom. Hurricanes of destruction will follow. Whether we deserve them is a quandary for your philosophers. My fleet will sail on the high tides, where we have always awaited our fate. Farewell!" Mokko turned to Payo and Mark. "*Oja* Bambas, let us see what your little minds are capable of conjuring."

Mokko hurled his orb back onto the pile on the table. Fyzo and him both raised their arm and pressed the glowing jewel on their wristbands. In a flash of green light, they vanished.

"Oja?" Elise asked, a little too loudly.

"It means blessed fortunes." Payo replied through her broad smile. "Though I doubt he meant it sincerely."

Payo saw the disappointment and confusion strewn on the faces around her.

"King Kai," Payo's tone was gentle but unwavering. "my envoys will stay here with you to discuss any strategy you wish to, and how our forces may maintain open correspondence. For now, I intend to go down to your city to enjoy myself before my return to Tamat."

Payo paused for a brief moment, suppressing an impulse and measuring her words.

"I came here because my father requested it, but I see his faith in this council was misplaced. You can try to talk this one into remembering his purpose." Payo gestured at Mark. "As long as it doesn't interfere with mine. I will go to the hidden chamber in Tamat Mountain. Where I *will* awaken the Children of the Storm. Together, we will annihilate Prince Sal'Haf's horde before it grows any larger. Join us, if you ever finally choose to fight for your souls. You can even bring your winged pet here, should you wish."

Payo turned to leave the chambers. Her father and Dex followed.

"Your Majesty," Kulsa cooed in false melody. "I believe the Prince is a threat to us only if we resist him. Have you considered that perhaps this is Asha's era? Goddess Leiba's followers will not be sacrificed in your misguided enterprise. I wish you good fortune in the war ahead, and thank you kindly for allowing me to participate in this *curious* tradition."

Kulsa let her stone orb slip from her fingers, and shatter on the ground. She smiled, raised a hand to touch her bracelet's gemstone, and vanished in a blood red burst.

Mark stood in awkward stillness, turning to his friends for any suggestions. He watched the purple-skinned woman place a gentle hand on King Kai's shoulder, consoling and assuring him in their secret unspoken language.

"Listen, we're really sorry we ruined your party or whatever." Bobby said, pushing his way into the moment. "But we need to go home. Now. We think Mark might have a connection to that Eye thing of yours. So if you don't mind, can we like...borrow it for a while?"

Kai, Imma'Ja, Gohlli, and Wynn turned to each other and discussed the matter in a hush. After a brief debate, they turned to face the children.

"Younglings." Imma'Ja spoke, her voice radiantly calm. "Perhaps you would be amenable to a proposition. Could we have a few moments alone with your friend, Mark? Lord Gohlli here will take you to Maije's finest tavern to wait for him. Perhaps if we discuss the situation, we can figure out how to resolve our crossroads, and hopefully get you all home."

"We're not leaving him alone with you." Elise bristled.

"Just let us use your Eye, please. Or tell us how it works." Bobby added.

"Sacred Eyes are among the rarest and most powerful artifacts in the Raya." Kai stated. "They can send people through gateways that open at other Eyes, or directly to a known location - from which that person can only return if they have a bonded token." Kai raised his wrist to display a silver bracelet adorned with a blue gem. "Unless they prefer to walk back."

Bobby gritted his teeth.

"For us to send the four of you to an *unknown* location, would require much more power and carries far more risk - including the possibility that we send you dangerously in the wrong direction, or even damage the Eye itself." Kai explained. "If Mark is to use his abilities to create a pathway within the Eye, we would be more comfortable if he at least had a better understanding of the nature of the Raya - and the gifts he has been bestowed."

"Guys, it's fine." Mark preempted Elise's next protest. His eyes were locked with Imma'Ja's. "Wait for me down in Maije, I'll talk with them and see what we can learn."

The other three gawked at him skeptically.

"You really think we should split up, man?" Bobby asked. "It's not like you can text us or anything."

"I'll be fine." Mark said. "I'll come find you as soon as I'm done. Then we can all go home." Mark's face radiated absolute composure. "It's the only way."

Before they could object, Gohlli strode towards them. His muscular physique and fiery arms were commandingly imposing, but he wore a warm smile on his face.

"Come, bambas." Gohlli gestured three of his arms towards the door. "I will take you to my favorite place in this beautiful city: The Dancing Slug Tavern. We can dine and share stories, until your friend rejoins us."

Naiyana, Bobby, and Elise hesitated at first, but slowly moved to follow the extraordinary man. They kept a short distance away from his blazing limbs. Naiyana and Elise looked over their shoulders at Mark. He smiled assurances at them, and silently mouthed 'it's okay'.

Imma'Ja approached Mark, outstretched her long arm, and gently took his hand into hers.

"I'll escort you to Kai's chambers." She spoke in her serene ethereal tone. "We can have a discussion there while we wait for the King to bid our guests from Tamat farewell."

Mark watched Kai and Wynn immerse themselves in a discussion with the tall Emissary and her two guards, as he followed Imma'Ja through the doors.

240

Mark explored King Kai's chambers, admiring the room's intricate aesthetics. He recognized the balcony overlooking the city from his visions at the hilltop. The swaying curtains billowed with the ebbs and flows of the warm night winds. Verdant plants draped their flowering vines from within ceramic pots tethered to the ceiling. Their aromas sweetened the air. Diverse art of contrasting styles spoke to a history of treasured travels. Most of all, Mark revered the piles of books littered in columns atop most of the surfaces.

Mark sensed Imma'Ja's gaze watch him. He felt no urgency to engage in conversation. She had a beguilingly calming effect on him. Mark was oddly at ease. He knew she was attempting to pry into his mind. He detected her awareness gently prod against his, trying to gain entry to his thoughts. Mark somehow knew he could remain inoculated from her mystical efforts. Despite his bizarre circumstances, a confident grandeur emerged within him.

"You're not like the others." Mark said, talking over the curve of his wing.

"Neither are you." Imma'Ja smiled. "I must say, I feel the strangest connection to you. And I suspect it goes beyond the gifts you've been given. You seem completely unique within the Raya, yet also deeply rooted in it. And you claim you have no memory of this place. It's delightfully bizarre."

Mark turned to face her. He wasn't sure if he should take comfort in her warm presence, or remain suspicious of her hidden intentions. He honed his wits onto the moment.

"How could I be from here and not remember it?" Mark asked.

"How indeed!" Imma'Ja agreed.

"Could you tell me about this place, the Raya and all the other stuff you guys were talking about?" Mark asked. "Pretend you were talking to someone who didn't know anything."

"Pretend..." Imma'Ja grinned.

"Please." Mark insisted politely.

"Very well." Imma'Ja began. "The Raya is everything the eye can see – every ocean, mountain, forest, and distant star in the endless skies above. The entirety of all that is tangible. To touch one end of it is to find yourself at another point within it."

Imma'Ja's tone encouraged Mark to absorb the underlying meaning behind her words.

"You stand in the city of Maije; one of the oldest civilizations within the Raya. Maije is sanctuary to both a Birthstar Fountain and a Sacred Eye. Very rare artifacts." She continued. "The Primals you've heard us mention are the founding forces which wove the very fabric of the Raya - and most of what exists within it. They are: Chaos, Control, and the Void – known to their worshipers as Koba, Shura, and Asha, respectively. Everything in the Raya, from the living beings to the wind and waters around us, is instilled with the will of the Primals and their differing natures. They are each a part of us, and our collective souls express that connection in distinctive ways. We are all creators, and conduits of the Primals' influence."

Imma'Ja paused, and saw she still had Mark's full attention.

"Though the Primals are often in conflict with each other's desires, the most harmonious state they can achieve is a balance - which we call *Sawah*. However, a Prince named Sal'Haf from the kingdom of Kahltam recently suffered a great tragedy - in which his entire family was slaughtered before his eyes. In the depths of his despair, Sal'Haf became Asha's Reflection: a champion empowered with all the gifts offered in the Void's black garden. He has since conquered many kingdoms and spread his destruction at a terrifying scale. In response, Koba – Birthmother of Chaos – imbued Payo with her powers. You met *her* earlier."

"I remember." Mark replied with a smile.

"Payo stood as our best chance of stopping Sal'Haf's destructive reach – and hopefully restoring Sawah to the realms. That was until you walked into this city, somehow the unknowing Reflection of Shura, wielding the powers of Control. So, if the collective realms have any hope of surviving this war, a balance must be struck between you, Payo, and Sal'Haf. Only then can we rebuild a lasting peace, and avoid the suffering of countless souls."

"So, King Kai is going to ask me to fight in a war?" Mark asked.

"King Kai..." Imma'Ja searched for the words. "...carries a heavy burden. He is, above all else, an idealist. He believes the methods by which we conduct our warfare are as important as the principles we strive to protect. With you and Payo as potential allies, he sees an opportunity to make this war as short-lived and free of cruelty as possible."

Mark took in Imma'Ja's words. She exuded honesty, but he was certain she was veiling a portion of her thoughts from him. So much of her appearance distracted Mark, from her shimmering silver eyes, the soft lilac hue radiating off her body, and even the stunningly intricate designs woven into her jade robe. A mistrusting corner of his mind remembered the colorful animals he had read about, who warned off potential predators with their vibrance; promising a fatal venomous exchange if they came too near.

Mark became increasingly aware of the transition of one moment to the next. He felt the shape of upcoming events call to him from a short distance ahead. A portion of his consciousness fragmented away to observe this new sensation. It was segmented in its own transcendent experience, while the rest of him continued to converse with Imma'Ja. Mark watched himself talk, while still being fully cognizant of the discussion.

"I'm not sure I can help." Mark said honestly.

"Perhaps not." Imma'Ja mused. "But I watched you in the council room. You smile for your friends, despite the sadness that lingers in your heart. That is a nobility of soul that cannot be taught." Curiosity flashed across Imma'Ja's eyes. "What do you see when you look at me?"

"When you arrived through the Eye," Mark began, keeping a measured distance from her. "I couldn't see where you came from. I saw it for the others: The Eyes they used to get to Maije, their home worlds. But not you." It dawned on him swiftly. "You're not from the Raya, are you?" Mark stared at her keenly, willing her to tell him the truth.

Imma'Ja couldn't hide her unabashed surprise. She contemplated the notion that Mark was able to view both sides of a connection between Sacred Eyes. She looked at his young face, something in his expression filled her awareness. He was sincere, and trustworthy. The notion enveloped her mind. It drowned her thoughts. After a prolonged pause in hesitant silence, she felt compelled to open herself fully to this odd youngling.

"I am a Priestess of the Ayanakol Temple, which rests in the Pacham realm." Imma'Ja explained, striding in a wide arc around Mark. "To everyone else in the Raya, including King Kai and the council members, Pacham is merely a secluded holy site where only the ancient priestesses of my order may reside."

Imma'Ja paused in mild hesitation, but soon found herself awash in assurance.

"In truth, Pacham is a gateway. It connects the entire Raya to a place…just beyond." Imma'Ja smiled, pleased to share words she thought were never to be spoken. "Priestesses of Ayanakol do not strictly belong to either reality, though we have a connection to both. We can visit the Raya, in this form…" Imma'Ja raised her arms and gestured to her body. "…but our role here is one of observation and guidance. We help powerful beings of great influence in the Raya, by sharing our insights. Our unique connection to the other world, beyond the Raya, gives us our wisdom - and allows us to act as oracles of powers outside of traditional understanding."

"What do you know about the other place?" Mark pressed eagerly. "The one beyond?"

Imma'Ja was in awe of the effect this youngling had on her, and felt helpless to stop it. Her training faded from her mind. Candor poured from her lips, like the juice of a freshly peeled fruit. His power was overwhelming.

"Our bond to that side is felt solely in our senses and awareness. Celestial whispers we hear in the back of our minds. For a priestess of the Ayanakol to transition fully to that realm, would mean severing our connection to this precious place. Forever." She turned to face Mark. "And I care far too much about this Raya to relinquish my role as its guardian Watcher."

"So, you come from a reality beyond the Raya?" Mark restated. "Or, a place that's stuck between this Raya and another reality? Like a bridge."

Mark thought through the possibilities. If she truly came from somewhere else, it increased the likelihood his friends could leave this reality and return to their own.

"In a way, I suppose." Imma'Ja offered. "I am most whole when I am in my natural *bridge* state. In Pacham. The moving of an awareness across realities is complicated, and not without chaotic surprises. It requires holding an essential part of ourselves, whilst transforming and losing so much of the rest. I can vaguely recall things I know to be true from Pacham, that I cannot fully...*feel* while I am in this form here in the Raya."

Mark felt an emergence of something originating in the back of his awareness. A sense of inevitability permeated his thoughts. Imma'Ja approached a table surrounded by cushions and one wooden chair. She sat on the chair, gesturing elegantly with her fingers as she explained.

"Think about being a wave in an ocean, or a leaf on a tree." Imma'Ja said. "While you are something small, you can forget about the greater body you are connected to - because you are too focused on being one specific thing. Only when that thing ceases to exist, does your energy rejoin the grander awareness. Your truest eternal nature."

"You're definitely a priestess." Mark grinned at the metaphor.

"I take it you don't have much faith?" Imma'Ja asked, detecting his cynical undercurrent.

"I don't know what I believe." Mark answered. "Especially after being in this place."

"A lack of certainty is the best kind of faith to have." Imma'Ja emphasized. "Faith is about being open to the mystery and magnificence which surrounds us; not stringent adherence to rigid doctrines. We are all participants in the magic of creation. The shared existence of reality is awoken through us. We make impressions on each other, shape the thoughts inhabiting our minds, and alter our very natures. Everyone you have ever known resides in the chorus of conflicting voices that haunt your awareness. They live in you."

"What about you?" Mark asked. "What's different about the voices in your head?"

"I carry no adversaries in me." Imma'Ja smiled.

The chamber doors opened brusquely, and Kai and Wynn strode in. Kai walked to join Imma'Ja and Mark, while Wynn went to a table on the far side of the room and began to mix ingredients into a large broth of water.

"Has Imma'Ja helped you orient to your surroundings?" Kai asked with a smile.

"She's been very helpful." Mark replied.

"Then I will be as direct as I can, Mark." Kai stated. "If you tell me how you got here, how you first arrived, I will try to help us both understand what happened to you."

Mark watched Kai sink into a large pillow beside Imma'Ja. He gestured for Mark to do the same. Mark folded his four wings, and dropped into a cushion. He looked at the two bizarre individuals facing him. The flourishing sensations filled Mark's awareness again. He was connected to the people in the room, their movements, and even their words. Everything seeded itself in Mark's mind just before it happened. Mark pondered if he was anticipating or willing events into creation. He tried to ignore the awakening filling the corners of his concentration, and dove into a hurried recounting of his arrival.

"My friends and I came from a different place." Mark explained. "I don't think it's a part of the Raya. We were on a lake with some other children from our city. The lake was frozen." Mark noticed a flinch of fear on Kai's face at the mention of a frozen lake. "We fell through the ice, into the water. I think we blacked out, or…somehow, we all woke up here. This is definitely our first time in this place though. None of us can ever remember being in the Raya before. But we can all remember our home. We're just not sure how to get back."

As he continued to attempt an explanation, Mark's mind drifted to those strange moments between when he first fell through Echo Lake, and when he awoke in this reality. He could vaguely recall the entities and lights of a timeless world that seemed a thousand dreams away. Mark felt a looming understanding approach him in the moments ahead. The ability to clearly sense something which had not yet come to pass distressed him, but also seemed natural.

"Do you remember anything about your transition here?" Imma'Ja asked. "After you fell through the ice, but before you found yourself in the Raya."

Something odd had filled her expression, as if she no longer felt the need to hide anything from him. There was a concealed current moving through everyone in the room, and only Mark appeared to be aware of the tethers between them.

"There were lights and shapes..." Mark tried to recall the fragments of elusive memories. "...I *felt* things. Like energies, or beings, that talked to me using their thoughts. They were watching me. I think they were the ones that pushed me through to this place. To the Raya."

Imma'Ja turned and looked at Kai. His face was still in contemplation.

"Is the Elfsylk ready?" Kai asked aloud.

"Almost." Wynn replied, carefully stirring ingredients in a bowl hung above candles.

Kai looked at Mark, and took a measured breath.

"Mark, I cannot say I fully understand what is happening to you, or why you were chosen to be Shura's Reflection. And I do want to help you." Kai chose his next very words carefully. "But this power growing inside you, it is essential to our collective survival here in the Raya. A means of saving countless souls; including your own and your friends! Now, the choice will ultimately be yours - so I only ask you make it an informed one."

Kai paused, and exhaled as much of the sorrow in his heart as he could.

"Prince Sal'Haf's mother, Queen Siranna, was a dear friend of mine." Kai touched a silver spiral symbol on his upper arm. It rested unmoving, while the other runes glided over his body. "Siranna loved her children more than anything in existence. The spell she cast to warn me of their massacre, was taught to her as a young priestess – during a ritual that most likely involved bringing her to the brink of death. She was undoubtedly terrified and heartbroken, yet with the last of her will she asked me to save what remained of her family. I know Sal'Haf has been chosen by a force bigger than most of us can conceive. But I believe he can be saved from the storm that consumes him. Perhaps even control it. I have to believe that. I owe it to Siranna."

Wynn approached with the bowl, and set it on the small table. An unusual aroma wafted up from the container. It smelled like warm honey, crushed herbs, exotic petals, and wet leather. Mark peered into the ceramic vessel and saw the tea was milky white, with iridescent streaks of inky silver syrup gliding across the surface.

"In a moment, I will ask you to drink a small portion of that tea." Kai said. His face was resolute, kind, and calm. "Imma'Ja and I will drink some first, and guide you through the experience that follows. We believe this will help you understand your role here, and hopefully clarify how to get you back home."

Mark felt a swirl of apprehension drift through his mind, but it was drowned out by a rising curiosity and the allure of undiscovered wonder.

"This is Elfsylk tea." Imma'Ja explained. "It is infused with an exceptionally rare elixir. A potent syrup extracted from the only Jalahsyd tree known to exist. The tea is...*mind revealing*. Elfsylk has been used in awakening rituals to guide many great leaders and help them walk the paths of their vastest decisions. It will show you yourself, fully. Open doors otherwise locked in your awareness." Imma'Ja looked at Mark's young face with reverent awe. "It is usually reserved for the most significant moments and special guests. You will be the first youngling in Maije's history to consume it."

"I believe this will help you connect to the Raya, understand your powers, and reveal your true path." Kai added. "Afterwards, if you still choose to return home with your friends, I only ask that you please consider using your powers to strengthen our forces. So we may fight to save the only home we've ever known."

Mark felt like he was standing on the precipice of infinity. He was frozen in this moment, and aware that a great transformative emergence awaited him just beyond it. Something powerful called to him on the other side of this decision. He knew he would drink the tea. He must.

Mark looked up to Kai, and nodded his head. Kai placed a hand across his heart, and bowed his head in gratitude. He reached out to lift the bowl to his lips, and took a small sip. Wynn stood nearby, leaning against the wall. He watched them with a protective countenance.

"You need only drink a little, Mark." Kai said, as he handed the bowl to Imma'Ja. "One small mouthful should be fine. Then lean back and close your eyes."

Mark bristled a little at the stringent guidelines. The moment before him and the people in front of him began to feel small. Beneath his concerns. King Kai's instructions formed faint emotional echoes in Mark's mind. Reverberated memories of children urging him to light the wick on a cluster of fireworks, his father chastising him, and other fragments of long-lost moments swirled in the winds of his wakefulness.

"Don't search for it, embrace whatever comes." Imma'Ja said, taking her sip.

Her silver eyes locked onto Mark's gaze. He allowed her voice to enter his thoughts.

"Let it all happen. The beautiful, and the terrifying. Take everything in. There is no end."

She handed Mark the bowl. He looked down at the tea. There was still more than enough for ten people. Mark watched the silver streaks dance through the warm white ocean surrounding them. Ethereal serpents searching for something unfamiliar to connect with. Mark raised the cup to his lips, and tilted it slightly to take in the smallest amount.

The taste of it washed over his senses, filling his nostrils with a dense fragrance and coating his tongue in a heavy sweetness. Before he could swallow, a singular decision filled his mind. Its absoluteness was pure. The whispers in the back of his thoughts rushed forward, shrieking their command. Mark leaned his head back, opened his mouth wide, and poured the entirety of the bowl's contents into his belly.

17 - AWAKENING

Mark was engulfed in silence.

As soon as he consumed the potent elixir, he felt its amplifying power course through him. In an instant, all the noise was sucked out of the room. Mark placed the empty bowl down in front of him. He looked at the horrified faces of Kai and Imma'Ja. They stared at him, motionless...untethered from time.

Mark saw everything in the room captured in shared stillness. The curved dance of candleflames halted on their wicks, in graceful postures that longed for pulses of energy to flow through them. Lights from the city no longer throbbed into the dark skies, but held themselves aglow in vibrant gasps - yearning to exhale potent brilliance outwards once more.

Everything awaited what was to come.

Mark rose. He stretched out his wings, limbs, and mind. A growing portion of his awareness drifted out of his physical form - plucked from his sinews, and blooming into his surroundings. A silver current emerged from his chest and snaked ahead, gliding a path toward the balcony. Mark realized this was the first occasion the light had materialized from his body.

Mark followed it towards the terrace. He felt no desire to resist its suggested path. He was fulfilling a dream conceived long before he ever found himself awake within it. This was always going to happen, one way or another. In that certainty, Mark found himself shed of any fears.

He reached the edge, and peered at the city below. Maije was a splendor of still beauty. Layers of reality infused with cosmic light. The stones of the buildings, the vines of the plants, and the clusters of creatures. Radiance made solid. Mark saw the hidden wonder in each person. Souls longing to bond with one another through masks of flesh, spoken words, and the conventions containing their minds. Mark saw all the details, from the miniscule to the grand. Bright ethereal strings bound everything in a web of unfulfilled potential.

He felt connected to all of it.

From this view, Maije looked like a dense unmoving solar system. Complex celestial bodies, explosions of energy, vibrant stars, and intricate compressions, all bathed in the same rich radiance. The dizzying complexity and scale illustrated in one perfect moment; its absolute uniqueness never to be repeated. This striking singular instance, laid out for Mark to savor. Endless possibilities could unfold from this splendor. But for now, it was seized into one particular perfection.

It occurred to Mark that seen through this lens, any moment plucked from the span of time could offer similar magnificence. The countless mechanisms of movement that yearned to explode, shrink, expand, collide, fuse…Mark's mind could barely grasp the infinite majesty.

The silver stream emerged from Mark's chest, and curved to his right. He followed it with his gaze, and saw the beam stop at a central point on the balcony. It was swallowed into a small vortex. The hovering sphere of shimmering darkness, was surrounded by a halo of omni-colored lights. At the center of the black jewel, Mark saw the expanse of a celestial vista. A stunning cosmos filled with systems of spiraling brilliance, scattered across the black vastness.

It was a gateway. Mark knew he must walk through it.

Mark's mind was at peace. He strode forward. As he drew closer, the silver river grew in size and surge. It urgently yearned for his advance. A discovery called for him from the other side, with thunderous power and a peculiar familiarity. His face pressed against the sphere, and he was pulled through in an instant.

A cataclysmic awakening filled Mark's mind. He was shed of everything, except truth. Mark returned to a state he had always known. He was a force of creation, remembering itself as it relinquished a fading dream that grew ever distant. He rejoined the eternal ocean of awareness. Individual souls expressed thoughts in minor waves, yet remained united by the shared depths of their origin. The overwhelming absoluteness of it filled him entirely. Open, endless possibility. Everything. Forever.

Mark only had the faintest recollection of where he had come from. He felt tethered to all ideas, and none at all. He could float down every imagined path, and those not yet conceived, encompassing all possibilities. He felt the absence of time. He was trapped in a world beyond variance. All potential swam within its waters, and sank back into the depths of its embrace.

Every thought seemed to manifest by unchangeable design: his awareness, his yearning to understand, his resistance to the unfolding realizations, and even his reluctant acceptance that such defiance was futile. The patterns were predetermined. A journey he had no choice but to experience. He was wholly possessed by an ethereal rhythm which marched him onwards. Unyieldingly inevitable possibilities opened from within him, like petals of an infinite flower.

A rising infuriation swelled inside him. Mark wanted to reject the endless construct, despite the impossibility of escape. Even that desire felt like a routine of preordained rebellion. He was both creator, and slave to the creation. Every variable of thought played itself out. In the comprehensive completeness of it all, it allowed for no true originality. It would end up contained in the same transforming foundations. Anything new, was swallowed into the whole. Born from it, desperate to reject it, then ultimately succumbing to the realization it only ever had this one destined place within it.

For where else was there to go?

Mark felt helpless. He was only calmed by the realization that this reality was everlasting, absolute, and no fault of his own. A controlling knowledge pressured him to succumb.

The command to sacrifice any semblance of self bled into his awareness. It urged Mark to give up any remnants of independent will, and rejoin the grander immanence. Graceful wisdoms sought to appease him with soothing assurances.

But they only enraged him.

An interconnected path of memories flooded Mark's mind. For every moment of his existence, he could only recall being swayed, pushed, and forced in directions he never chose. Mark's outrage crystalized and rumbled. His explosive wrath fragmented the design enshrouding him. Mark sensed the fissures in the enveloping shell of certainty. He pushed against them. His need to break free was unrelenting.

Everything shattered, and in that shattering Mark was free. He formed a spear point with his mind, piercing through every layer that tried to contain him. He surged onwards as fast as he could, escaping into the unknown. Mark was serene, singular, and entirely himself. The tensions and doubts washed off his consciousness. Mark salvaged a familiar perception: vision.

Mark beheld an awe-inspiring marvel revealed before him. An astonishingly vast sphere. Swirling within this lustrous bubble, was a galaxy of spiraling stars. Long streaks of light formed luminous arms of resplendence, cycling and twisting over each other. They danced around a shared core at the heart of the sphere. Nestled at the very center, a blinding vibrance of light shone proudly. A pupil of unflinching purity staring back at Mark. The glistening outer surface of this enormous marble was a translucent membrane, containing the flower of radiant creation at its bosom.

Mark examined the barrier encapsulating the maelstrom of light. In realizing he was floating outside the barrier, Mark perceived the endless expanse that surrounded the orb.

As he looked into the beyond, Mark saw countless other orbs scattered into the distance. They littered an infinite black canvas. Each one a distinct glimmering marble of contained magnificence. They glinted with their own unique light, held afloat in nothingness, proclaiming their one proud corner of the immeasurable. Elegant individual parts of a boundless and monumental beauty.

The Raya had been bizarre enough, but floating within a cosmic ocean drowned Mark in the crashing realization he understood nothing at all about the nature of reality.

Mark wished to give himself form, and chose a memory of the boy he once was. He looked down and saw his hands, legs, and other nearly forgotten familiarities. Light made solid. He knew it was only a projection of self, a relic of a long-lost dream still lingering within him. But it brought him great comfort.

"Welcome." A voice unfolded in Mark's mind.

Mark turned to his left, and saw something colossal take shape beside him. The Entity's form was composed entirely of coils of light. They weaved themselves together, intricately creating the appearance of a large body. The figure took on familiar qualities: two eyes, a substantial beard, imitations of limbs, and a bald head – all formed from the same radiant twines of luminescence.

The lights throbbed in spellbinding flows of transformation. The Entity examined its newly formed hands, and watched small cracklings of lighting shatter away from its fingertips. Each splintering of electricity decelerated quite suddenly, drifting outwards into the darkness like tree branches searching the unknown for hope.

The Entity turned to face Mark; their shared gaze an exchange of sentience.

"Quite a view." The Entity projected into Mark's mind, its face unmoving.

Mark looked at the Entity. He felt a connection to its presence, but also a great difference dividing them. Not only in the distinction of their forms, but one of minds. The Entity's eyes were filled with promise and keen attention. Yet they also carried the heaviness of lingering memories. Mark recognized his hidden observer from moments in the Raya.

"You're Shura." Mark stated.

"Yes."

Mark sensed the bond between them come alive. It felt rich with conflicting emotions: familiarity, suspicion, curiosity, and tranquility. Mark's arrival at this moment felt long-awaited, but the details were shrouded in the depths of his mind. Unreachable by his current perception. Mark scrutinized Shura.

"What were you expecting?"

"More of a...moment." Mark said candidly. "For it to make more sense."

"Anything you ask, I will answer."

Mark's gaze returned to the immense orb before them.

"What is that?" He asked.

"Gahan Shelohr. All that is. Every form of creation, held within a perfect sphere."

"What about those?" Mark gestured at the other orbs in the vast distance.

"Unreachable variations, beyond our concern."

Mark saw several graceful expressions move in the orb, suspended in celestial harmony.

"Do you recognize it?"

"It's the Milky Way." Mark said, marveling the splendor.

Shura smiled at the name.

"Yes, the *galaxy* you call home. At least, a depiction you are most ready to understand."

Shura paused.

"Until you arrived here, I had the singular privilege of seeing it from this view. That is, outside the encapsulation. This is a sanctuary I seek when I wish to escape the tempest within."

Shura turned to Mark.

"It is wonderful to have a visitor."

Mark felt questions pour out of him before he had time to consider them.

"What's the bubble holding it all?" Mark asked. "That layer around it?"

"What do you think is it?"

Mark examined the outer layer. It wasn't light, or a form of energy. It seemed translucent, but its presence had a significant potency which gave it structure.

"Is it the galaxy's awareness of itself?" Mark asked, as the idea materialized in his mind.

"Yes. A shared border of thought. The stars and light and matter, like your body on Earth, are only one layer of a unified ocean of existence. That...*bubble* is the outer most layer. Within the core of it all, lies the seed of our creation and imagination. The first awareness. The soul."

"The galaxy has a soul?" Mark asked.

"Of course, and we are all small parts of it."

Mark watched as most of the stars in the sphere dimmed and faded away, until only a unique radiance remained at the core. Thought come alive. Boundless possibilities waiting within an ethereal yolk of potential.

"*That* was the first awakening. Existence in purest form. That seedling birthed everything in the garden of life that followed, filling light and darkness alike with countless creations."

Mark absorbed this new knowledge, his peculiar companion, and the bewildering view. The sphere returned to its fully illuminated form, and displayed a striking hurricane of stars within once more. Mark was aware of the outlandish novelty of it all, yet his mind felt still.

"If that's everything that is, how are we outside of it?" Mark asked.

"Think of this place as...self-reflection."

Mark sensed parts of himself still seeded deep within the galactic orb. Concealed connections that clung to him, and whispered for his return.

"The place I just came from...the Raya. What was that?" Mark asked.

Shura radiated a distinct warmth; seemingly satisfied with the direction of their exchange. Mark suddenly found himself back in the Raya. He soared above a vast landscape of mountains. He had no body. It was only his awareness that flew through the colorful clouds and balmy skies. Shura was with him, their minds formed an ether of thought.

"The Raya is a plane of consciousness shared by all energy and living beings. Our dreamscape. It connects and collides us into a storm of unified awareness. What you see before you, is the cumulative expression of every soul in existence; manifesting their imaginings, desires, influences, and conflicts across one common experience."

Mark saw new ideas take shape as expressions of life below. The thoughts of countless souls came alive and evolved into the vastly complex and the imperceivably miniscule.

"This is all a dream?"

"In a way."

Mark saw hints of three distinct forces flowing through everything. A ferocity of light, surging within every being and rippling ahead in search of the unformed. A common darkness filling the gaps of creation, and pulling the fragments into its hungry depths. And finally, a thin layer of delicate awareness, giving all matter shape and understanding. He recognized the three Primals at work. Mark noticed a lingering desire to find a way back home grow in his mind.

"How's this connected to where I came from? Earth?"

"All the layers of reality are bound to each other."

Mark sensed a purposeful evasion in Shura's response. Hints of hesitation. Shura was contemplating how best to explain things. Mark searched for a way to guide the conversation towards his friends and their home.

"Was my life on Earth..." Mark adjusted his thoughts. "...was my body on Earth more real than what I was in the Raya...soul dream...reality?"

Shura held them afloat above a particularly stunning lush valley. It was bathed in the sunshine of a fresh morning. Strange flowers poured pollens and petals into the serene air above.

"If a beam of light hits a mote of dust floating in the wind, and warms that speck of matter with its energy...what part of that connection would you consider most real?"

Mark tried to process the concept being conveyed, but he couldn't hide a slight agitation at Shura's elusiveness. He tried to think of all the memories of his life on Earth, nearly tangible in his recollections. Shura's voice interjected into Mark's reminiscences.

"You want to understand the differences between the mortal plane and the Raya, in terms of reality. However, it is our minds and souls that make it all real. The experiences we endure change our fundamental natures, across all branches of one shared tree."

"Why did no one in the Raya know about Earth?"

"Most only exist where they are. We share portions of ourselves across planes of reality. Transfer certain qualities. But we are ultimately wherever we find ourselves. Always where we most choose to be."

Shura sensed Mark's dissatisfaction. In an instant, they found themselves floating back in the black vastness overlooking the galaxy. Mark looked over Shura's luminous form beside him, then back at the spherical jewel of creation. A growing understanding flourished in Mark's mind. He not only saw it, but felt the various parts of it unfold in his awareness.

"Everything came from one thing." Mark stated, constructing his understanding. "All existence started from the same core idea. Which was…the desire to exist. Souls were created over time. But they're all just individual parts of that same first idea. They have their own thoughts. They can imagine, create, and affect each other. They're separate, and connected. It's a shared dream, but it's also the only thing that's real."

Shura smiled in silent encouragement. Mark became aware he was being led down a path. He shook away the daze of alluring wonder, and clarified his mind.

"How does this affect my life on Earth?" Mark asked, fortifying his resolve.

Shura responded, unvexed by Mark's fluctuations.

"Souls are prisms through which existence forms new possibilities. The material plane, the reality you left behind on Earth, is only one variation of that potential. A fleeting layer, in which the eternal forces of creation imbue themselves for a moment. Souls are shaped most potently in the Raya. They, in turn, feed into your nature in the material reality. The actions you take in your mortal existence then flow back into our shared awareness. Your pains, joys, sorrows, and hopes. Your love, and your fear. The realities are mirrored expressions of each other. The flesh you remember with such familiarity, is simply light and thought brought to a slower tremor, given a brief form, and expressed as another dream within a dream."

Shura's mildly dismissive view tickled a distant part of Mark's memory.

"You and the other Primals. Are you gods?" Mark asked, his gaze fixed on the mesmerizingly complex arrangement of Shura's light.

Another smile spread across the tethers of Shura's face.

"We are creators. But we did not create the Raya itself, nor the awakening which first spawned it. The Primals were among the first expressions. Ancient foundational forces that shaped many of the creations within the Raya, and by extension the material galaxy you know. We live within the light, and form, and darkness of reality – and much of what followed. Yet we are still children of the same pure splendor, like you. Just...older."

"So, the Primals don't control everyone? We have choices?" Mark pressed.

"We influence your souls. The way a planet is warmed by a sun's light. We affect aspects of your nature or the landscape around you. We attempt to draw you towards paths we believe will bring you fulfillment, and in turn hopefully reflect our own aspirations. Some souls are highly susceptible to our effects, some more resilient. But your lives are ultimately your own creations. The connection flows both ways. If you didn't leave room for us to flourish within you, the bond is severed."

Mark felt a faint but familiar sense of mistrust surface.

"What do you Primals want?" He asked.

Shura sighed.

"That is no easy question. Asha was one of the first expressions to emerge from the seed of our awareness. The souls spawned within the silent vastness of Asha's Void knew only one truth. One way of being. Simple serenity in a shared abyss. It was Koba who first fractured the tranquility with her explosion of light and new imaginations. She pulled souls from their slumber in the black gardens, awoke them to infinite possibilities. Some felt liberated, others felt corrupted. In that first schism, I was born. Surrounded by conflict, I gave form and understanding to every divergence. In turn, I had to endure the pain of experiencing each one. Koba and Asha are urged by their desires. They wish only to render reality to their wishes. However, I am moved to act by my observations. It is a curse, to see the eventualities of things. The dangers lurking and yet to come. I act to ensure all souls know a harmonious existence. Free of the destructions we so often unleash on ourselves."

"Is that why you're all fighting this war? For control of the Raya?" Mark pressed.

"No. Conflicts are infused into the fabric of existence. It is unavoidable. Curiosity, exploration, evolution, the hunger for new possibilities...will always lead to opposing desires. Change pitted against what is treasured. Hope defying fear. Conflicts are inevitable. My sole intention is to ensure we are not destroyed by them. That our most precious essence endures."

Despite the whispers of doubt and mistrust Mark harbored, he felt the weight of Shura's words and knew the burden he carried was sincere. He thought of the scale of the war as it played out across the Raya. Countless souls swept up in the carnage.

"The Void...is it killing the souls it conquers?" Mark asked.

"Prior to this war, I would have said such a thing was impossible. Souls can be morphed, fragmented, and certainly transformed through conflict. Those experiences could be agonizing. But it was not an end. There are wise and ancient souls who swim in the shadows of the Void. Swallowed into the abyss with all their understandings."

For the first time, Mark sensed dread in Shura.

"You said before this war." Mark probed. "What's different now?"

"Asha and Prince Sal'Haf are not transforming those they capture. I do not sense them dwelling in the Void's vastness. Those souls seem to be vanishing from the Raya entirely. Every aspect of them gone from existence, never to be imagined again. Sal'Haf's power and presence in the Raya grows, but the number of souls diminishes with each conquest. I cannot fathom what Asha is transforming those souls into. Hideous new creations born from the shattered remnants. And I dread the destructive fury Koba will unleash in her response."

Mark contemplated the situation. His desire to get his friends back home safely remained undiminished. He missed his heartbroken father. But he was increasingly struck by how natural his presence in this situation felt. His mind floated above the galaxy, discussing the nature of reality and cosmic wars, with a deity whose existence Mark had never thought possible. He thought the best chance he had of getting back to Earth, was to make an earnest effort to bond with Shura. Show a thoughtful understanding.

"Maybe Asha found a way to kill souls." Mark suggested. "Completely."

Shura tensed visibly. Clearly the thought had crossed his mind.

"Perhaps. A new ocean of darkness, everything within it shrouded by its cold hunger."

Mark's attention was drawn back to the immense orb below. He studied the galaxy's swirling arms, simultaneously moving away and towards each other. An expression of outward thought and internal reflection. Light yearning to explode onward, and dark forces pulling them into conformed contours.

"What can Payo do?" Mark asked. "With the powers Koba gave her?"

"Payo's gifts are fueled by her own imagination. She is, above all else, a Creator. She will be able to forge new forms, even alter the designs of reality as they unfold. She can divide things into variations of their internal selves, including the thoughts of others. She could cause deranged madness in some. Split a mind into fragments of itself. She can also swell the hidden potentials in all of us. She is connected to the fire that burns in every soul. She is a wildfire. A creature of boundless light."

Mark heard a loneliness in Shura's words. He was tired.

"I'm your Reflection, aren't I?" Mark asked.

Shura seemed to lighten with an air of anticipation.

"Yes, you are."

"You gave me your power. Control." Mark said.

"I did."

"That light I see on everything in the Raya, what is that?" Mark probed.

"The Silver River." Shura smiled. "It is the unfolding path of our shared fates. The flow of the Raya's dream. You are seeing the destined moments that we were created to face, that can define our existence. Those faint silver hints, are all we will ever know of the Raya's soul, the dream seed which nurtures our collective story. Our choices shape us, and in turn the River."

"So, it's not guaranteed?" Mark asked. "We can change it? Affect it?"

"Yes," Shura said. "and none more than you! All those countless threads weaving towards a shared end. If you can see them you can change them. You see what will become of people, their natures. With that power, you can alter their destinies. And your own."

Mark saw excitement in Shura's expression; keenly encouraging his curiosity.

"I don't want to..." Mark said. "...I'm sorry."

"I know." Shura replied. "Creating a force of control means relinquishing control."

Mark sensed a swirl of emotions radiate from Shura. Regret, sadness, and frustration.

"What could I do with your power?" Mark inquired cautiously. "In the Raya?"

"Your abilities would increase as you honed your perception. As your understanding of how things are connected grows, you will be able to alter the forms, foundations, and awareness of other souls. Solidifying them, or even shattering them. If your will is strong, you could even imbed your mind within the mind of others. Though powerful souls might be able to resist. Your powers are bound to the other two Primals. You draw from their strengths. The complexities of your capabilities are tied to how open you are to that bond."

Mark was torn. He could see Shura had hoped this newfound understanding of the Raya would move Mark to protect it. That he would freely embrace these heavy responsibilities. Mark did want to understand why, of all people, he was even chosen as a Reflection. What did Shura expect him to do? But he could no longer ignore the lingering fears that he would soon lose his only chance of getting his friends back to their families.

"You are of two minds." Shura's accepting tone spread throughout Mark's thoughts. "Mystics on your world train for years to see but a glimmer of the true nature of creation. The hidden language of our shared union. You have it laid out before you in all its magnificence. Yet, your thoughts still linger on Earth."

Mark hesitated to respond. Shura seemed to accept something he had hoped to avoid.

"Let us go there. Perhaps it will help you understand."

Mark found himself hovering in space. A giant fiery orb shone at him from the distance. The Sun. Mark watched two hurtling celestial bodies collide in a powerful explosion in front of him. The cataclysm sent burning fragments into the blackness around them. Two new vast arrangements of matter formed from the collision: one large, one smaller. Morphed confluences of colossal stone, burning magma, and orbiting rubble.

Shura appeared beside Mark, his form of similar scale to Mark's this time.

They watched in silence as time accelerated. The two jagged orbs of rough matter continued to orbit the sun. They condensed under their own gravity, their uneven extremities collapsed and folded into the formation of perfect spheres. Ferocious churning cores of liquid metal pulled layers on top of them, forcing lighter elements through the cracks and onto the surface above. The larger of the two spheres was coated in a thin layer of shimmering blue water. Bathed in the unending warmth of the Sun, Mark's planetary home took shape. Earth, orbited by a companion moon, reflected their shared cosmic light onto each other.

Shura and Mark beheld the planet's unique beauty.

"I didn't know that's how Earth was made." Mark said, in awe of the view. "Two big meteors colliding into each other."

"Beautiful expressions of existence are quite often born from violent convergences of opposing forces. That is where new life must sometimes thrive. The origins may be long forgotten, but that hidden history always lingers within us. Echoed in our souls."

They appeared above the churning waters of an endless blue ocean. Mark watched fleeting expressions of waves form, shatter against one another, and sink into nothingness. It looked like angry gods were hammering their fists against the watery surface of the planet. Communities of waves swelled into great tribes. Pairs of waves entwined into swirls of beauty. Most often, waves stood alone in magnificent cascades of crashing fury. But ultimately, they were all pulled down to the same darkness below. Mark found himself hoping the bravest, wildest formations would struggle against all the odds, hold their ephemeral shape for as long as they could, and defy the fate awaiting them in the cold depths. But they all eventually joined their ancestors, in the graveyard of forgotten memories.

Mark sensed what Shura was trying to show him. The hidden expressions of celestial mechanics moving throughout the material plane. The unseen physical forces giving it shape. The reactive chemical creations of every particle. The intricate biological constructs that would eventually evolve a growing sense of awareness. It was all influenced by the Primals.

Mark saw continents rise from the vast shelves of converging stone below. He observed the earliest clouds of life float within the ocean's waters; flecks of minuscule movement that would one day give birth to giants. He saw microscopic

267

organisms absorb the sun's radiance, and spew oxygen into the air above; setting in motion a heritage of ever-evolving life that would dance across the planet for millions of years.

Mark watched droplets of water pulled into the sky, rising to the heavens on radiant beams of warm sunlight. They carried within them minute travelers, unaware of the worlds they were being carried towards. Storms of these converged condensations rained down on the mud below, burying small specks of life deep into the soil.

The seeds of potential slept in unfamiliar darkness. They dreamed of clawing out, yearned to ascend, battling against their confines. Their hardships spread across eons, strengthening them, pushing their roots of will into the earth, and surging upwards with the strength of their ancestors' struggles. They grew tall and vast, the wisdoms and magic of their history meshed into the fabric of their being. Earth's first forest.

Mark stood in the massive jungle, clustered trees and a surging river beside him. The foliage looked large and prehistoric. Shura stood beside him, he admired the lush bounty of life surrounding them. For the first time, Shura's mouth opened when he spoke. His voice was precise, compelling, and deeply soothing.

"Of all the variations of creation, there are few interwoven pairings I admire more than a river and a forest." Shura said. "The flowing exchange of life, the nurturing of possibility, the expressions of interconnected imagination. If one of these giant trees should fall, thousands of smaller plants will fill the void of its absence. Truly a harmonious beauty."

Mark sensed the contingent exception lingering in the words Shura kept unspoken. Before long, the forest around them began to grow overrun. Roots, branches, trunk, and vine alike, condensed upon each other in a clambering competition for light. Trees and plants suffocated under the endless coils, and sank below the continued war above. Their dried-up remnants turned to brittle husks and petrified corpses, forming a foundation for new life to reach even higher.

"What you are witnessing occurred before any organism had evolved to break down plant matter." Shura announced, watching the violent saturation of life play out in front of them. "The dead trees just lay there, forming an increasingly heavy platform for their descendants to grow upon. Filling the skies with more oxygen than Earth had ever known. All until..."

Shura looked up, and watched a horrifically powerful lighting strike cut a crooked white smile across the dark winds. A frenzy of fire rained down onto the vast compressed forest, turning it into a terrifying inferno. Mark was overwhelmed by the catastrophe; the ravenous heat shredding, burning, and vaporizing the bounty that had once stood there. The timeless struggle of organisms that defied so many obstacles, and manifested in beautiful expressions of colorful life. All swallowed into the hellscape of an insatiable firestorm.

"This fire lasted for hundreds of years." Shura said, observing the same destruction.

Mark willed the vision to end. He saw the scorched black remnants of the forest. Trunks burned to a crisp, charred and lifeless. Mark felt hollowed by the enormous loss of life.

"This dead forest was eventually buried under the tides of wind-blown soils." Shura continued. "Swallowed under the formations of mountains and valleys, over great stretches of time. The dance of new landmasses above cooked and ground the corpses below. An unending pressure that solidified them into brittle black coals. Eons later, they would be unearthed by barely evolved apes. Pulled from their graves, only to be burned again. Filling the sky with the smoke of their twice scorched souls."

"Why are you showing me this?" Mark asked in frustration.

"A tree's roots know only the darkness of the soil." Shura persisted. "They are connected to the world above, of course, but to them sunshine and light are myths. Completely counter to the dark reality they reside in. Both sides of the same living organism, nurturing each other, from across different planes of reality."

Shura turned to face Mark, radiating his words into Mark's mind.

"That is what I'm trying to show you. This tragic loss of life was certainly devastating, but even the trees that survived couldn't change their nature. They continued to produce the very oxygen that nearly destroyed them. The same river still flowed through the haunted remnants of this forest, nurturing whatever life it could find. Hoping that a new harmony would randomly be achieved. But hope is not enough. Every facet of existence must be guided and cultivated towards harmony, or it will be swallowed into eventual devastation. That, is our purpose."

They had finally arrived. Mark understood what outcome Shura wanted out of the war in the Raya: for there to be no war at all. Shura was an observer of life, and wished to preserve it above all else.

Mark was back floating above the familiar heavenly sphere. Shura spoke beside him.

"I know you miss your life on Earth, but the events unfolding in the Raya could create an all-consuming destruction. I understand you don't feel you belong to this fight. I am trying to help you remember, that you are the only one who can decide its outcome."

A cautious shadow in the back of Mark's mind clawed to the forefront of his awareness.

"Most souls within the Raya never even experience life in a material plane. It is a rare and fleeting gift to live a mortal life. Yet, it can also be a terrible captivity. Some choose it, some avoid it entirely. Whichever layer of reality we find ourselves in, a part of our souls always remains in the Raya. Seeded in the dreamscape. That is the plane that matters most. What occurs there affects everything else."

Mark considered the notion that a part of him had always been in the Raya. Shura spoke.

"Sometimes, we are so immersed in the story we find ourselves in or the forms we've taken, that it becomes difficult to remember anything else. Even when we return to our true home. It can seem...*unfamiliar.*"

"I didn't forget Earth." Mark realized. "When I moved between the layers."

"No, you didn't."

Mark could feel Shura's anticipation. There was a difficult revelation ahead of them.

"You are divided, present in two realities. Not fully in either. That is where your doubts come from. To be witness to the wonders of two possibilities, makes it hard to choose either."

"That's why we need to forget, when we move between the layers." Mark understood.

"Yes."

"Then why did you choose me? If I didn't forget?" Mark asked.

"...Choose?"

"As your Reflection. To be your Champion." Mark struggled to understand.

"I didn't choose you..." Shura responded. "...I created you."

A door suddenly opened in Mark's mind. A flood of realizations poured through him. This was a moment he had dreaded and run from his entire existence. He was born here. Created within the Raya. *Mark* was a story he clung to, an armor he used to hide from haunted memories.

Shura. His loathed creator.

Mark's thoughts felt like they were on fire. He remembered being carved into existence by Shura's will. Formed

271

and shaped by his intricate designs. He remembered the early
bonds of their shared awareness, the power flowing through both
their souls. He remembered a blinding rage when he discovered
why Shura had made him. He remembered a terrible conflict
between them. He remembered fleeing.

"I ran..." Mark could barely process it. "...I escaped
you."

Shame washed over Shura's face.

"You left, yes. You were angry, and you hurled yourself
to the outskirts of the galaxy. To that small blue planet. You
rooted yourself in that world. Severed your connection to the
Raya. You erased your memories. Forgot who you were."

Mark's mind raced as Shura's words flooded his
confused thoughts with lost memories.

"I don't remember." Mark struggled to cling to tethers of
clarity. "I can't remember why you made me."

Shura's face was crestfallen. He had dreaded this
reunion as much as he had longed for it.

"A long time ago, a cataclysm shook the foundations of
the Raya. A terrible explosion surged from the center of the
galaxy. The shockwave rippled through all planes of reality. It
transformed the nature of countless souls, twisted them in
conflicts and despair. The Primals all suspected each other. We
formed new weapons and infused many champions with our
power. Those were the First Wars. They nearly destroyed us."

Shura paused, giving Mark time to absorb it all.

"We never discovered the origin of the calamity. Never
knew which Primal was to blame. But Sawah harmony had been
restored, and the remaining souls yearned for peace. The Primals
remained suspicious, worried such a devastation could someday
be brought upon the Raya again. That one of us would seek
dominion over the others in terrible new ways. Instead of waiting
for that time to come to choose our champions – we made a
terrible decision. We created our own."

Mark had no words. It slowly came back to him.

"Each Primal forged a new soul, born of their power and crafted from their will. Unique creations, nurtured into their evolving powers. The three new Reflections were more than chosen conduits of our power, they were...our children. Extensions of ourselves that could one day..."

"Weapons." Mark said coldly.

He felt empty. Everything he had known torn asunder in a storm of forgotten memories.

"You are more than a weapon. You are my finest creation. I knew that when disharmony struck the Raya again, you would herald hope. But when you discovered my intentions, you resented me. Cursed me. Feared the fate I burdened you with. That is why you have always felt lost. You deny your true nature..."

"No." Mark's fury engulfed him. "I left you! I abandoned the war you created me to fight. I found a small lonely planet. Away from everything. I chose to live, and forget you!" He faced Shura accusingly. "But you followed me, didn't you? Watched me!"

Mark could barely process the outrage of it. Shura's expression was downcast.

"You've been fighting your nature since I first made you. A creation of control, who sought control by avoiding it. I only wanted to prepare you..."

"By making my choices for me? Forcing me onto a path you designed? Payo and Sal'Haf were created to serve their Primals too. We're the bastard children of selfish fucking gods!"

Mark couldn't recall ever feeling so much anger. Shura radiated sorrowful shame.

"I lost you. I tried to shape you from afar, show you your true nature. But even then, you resisted. I had given up hope you would ever be a bringer of peace in the coming conflict, when

Prince Sal'Haf suddenly brought a new darkness to the realms. And you fell through a lake…"

"Stop lying!" Mark yelled. "Losing me made you weak! It broke your power. It gave the other Primals the space they needed to grow stronger. To wake up their own…slave soldiers. Asha was just the first to act!"

Mark stopped abruptly, piecing fragments together. *Tried to shape you from afar.*

"The lake…the fight with Sebastian. How much of that was you? To get me back here?" Mark's mind spun. "My mother…" Mark glared at Shura, eyes soaked in cold fury. "Did you kill my mother? My sister?"

"I would never…"

"Liar!" Mark roared. A devastating explosion of energy burst out of his form. He could never recall feeling this much rage. "I don't believe you! How could I ever believe you?"

A clarity washed over him. His power came alive. It coursed in the fibers of his being.

"This is the weapon you made me to be." Mark seethed. "You're trying to control me."

"Please…try to stay calm."

A heavy concern swam within Shura's features.

"Why would I ever trust you?" Mark asked frostily.

"You are me. A version of me. The difference between a creator and what they create, is where all life occurs. I understand your time on Earth was precious to you, that you think I stole something from you. But can't you see how important your role in the Raya is? Your purpose…"

"It mattered to me." Mark interrupted. "You couldn't let me have my small little life."

"I didn't take them. Believe me, or don't. It doesn't change anything. They don't exist in that reality anymore, and you will never save your father from his grief. Not as his son, not in that world! But there are countless souls here you m…"

274

"You couldn't just let me go." Mark continued.

"This is your purpose."

"YOUR PURPOSE!" Mark yelled.

"I..." Shura began.

"Shut up." Mark spoke with a decisive chill. "Shura, I'm going to take my friends home. I am going to take care of my father, and rebuild the life you tried to steal from me. I am getting rid of these powers. I am going to give them to someone who will make better choices than either of us ever would. And then I never want to see you again! Do you understand?"

Shura was at a complete loss. No words he could offer would regain Mark's trust, yet he felt compelled to share them anyway.

"I only ever wanted to prepare you for your fate. That's why I named you..."

"My name is Mark." An icy certainty gripped Mark's tone.

"Please..."

Mark's power radiated in equal potency to Shura's. Clarity awoke him to the possibilities of his abilities. He understood how to take his friends home.

"You are running away from your destiny."

"It was never my destiny. It's yours." Mark said. "You just wanted me to do it for you."

Shura looked at Mark, and lost all hope. There was no conjuring of thought or will that would change the outcome unfolding before his eyes. This was the end. Shura closed his eyes in shame. Mark raised his arm, and watched the brilliance of silver light living within him glow around his clenched fist. In an instant, he was pulled back into the Raya.

18 – RAYA

Mark restored his form, like sand grains leaping up the slender neck of an hourglass. The reality around him took shape. He was on King Kai's terrace, overlooking Maije. Time returned to the moment; noise and light crashing into fulfillment. Mark knew this was only a layer of perception, coating the pure state of awareness he had just abandoned. But as he examined his body, smelled the air, felt his muscles and wings move...it felt as real as anything ever had.

Mark heard voices filled with alarm. He saw Kai and Imma'Ja panic as they searched the ceremonial table where he had sat moments ago. A lifetime, and a fracture of a second, ago. Wynn joined their search of the room.

Mark's mind was still adjusting. He couldn't make out any clear words in the fog of noise. He moved to observe them from a hidden corner. Mark realized how much of what he had just experienced would be unimaginable to them. The Raya was their only reality. Even Imma'Ja and her temple priestesses had only gleaned hints of the origins of existence. He would not deprive them of their certainties.

Mark heard them clearly now. Kai ordered Wynn to find as many city guards as he could and search for Mark. Guilt and worry washed over the King's features. Mark studied Kai, and saw the qualities of his soul radiate through him. Kindness, wisdom, and heartfelt love for his fellow beings. There was courage there, and fear too. But Kai's dread was a trusted companion, guiding his decisions rather than tormenting him like a malevolent specter.

Mark wondered if Kai existed in any form on the material plane. Probably an ancient tree, standing stoically in the middle of an exotic jungle on some distant alien world. In a wave of absolute certainty, Mark realized there was no better choice.

Mark envisioned his return to Earth, bringing his friends back to their homes. He thought of his father, the bond between them that had suffered so much. Would he be able to mend their relationship? Would their lives flourish if liberated from the machinations of Mark's tormenting creator? Mark considered whether he would truly be able to appreciate and cherish the fleeting wonder of a mortal existence, knowing that a portion of his awareness would always linger here. He hoped he could forget the weight of his history here once he returned. Anything to savor his connection to Earth with a full heart and genuine gratitude. He decided to spare his friends this doubt. Ensure the joy they felt when they made it back was unsullied.

Earth. His favored reality existed within a thin layer of air on the outer most crust of a stone sphere. The entire material plane itself was only one particular coating over a large layered series of perceived realities. Why did he want to return so badly? All the suffering he had endured there. Wasn't this place the grander truer *world*? He'd end up back here eventually, when his time on Earth came to an end.

"Mark!" Kai exclaimed, rushing over with Imma'Ja.

"How did you…" Imma'Ja began, her confusion overwhelming her. "…you were…"

"I'm fine, I promise." Mark assured. "I was with…Shura."

Kai and Imma'Ja exchanged looks of complete shock. But they both saw the firm certainty now emanating from Mark. His presence and tone lacked any previous hesitations. The newfound depth in his eyes was haunting. Wynn burst back into the room. He saw the trio stroll back into Kai's chambers from the balcony.

"How are you alive?" Wynn bellowed through a wide beam of awe. "I've never seen anyone gulp so much Elfsylk in my life!"

"Do you feel well, Mark?" Imma'Ja asked, concern radiating from her kind eyes.

"What did you learn?" Kai added with urgency.

Mark gained control over the situation, and instilled a calming attentiveness in everyone. His powers felt more natural, their expressions mere reflexes of will. Yet he still resented them.

"There's too much to explain." Mark said. "I know how to use my powers now. I'm going to take my friends home. If you'll permit me to use the Eye."

Mark saw the disappointment on all their faces.

"I'm going to give you my powers." Mark added directly to Kai. "Once I activate the Eye, I will give you all of my abilities. I believe you will do the most good with them, and I think you deserve them more than I did."

Kai's sapphire eyes were filled with stunned confusion.

"The war between the Primals and their Reflections. I don't want any part of it." Mark continued. "I know that seems selfish to you, but there's a lot about this I can't describe. I just hope, we can trust each other."

King Kai, Imma'Ja, and Wynn shared looks of hesitant bewilderment. None of them were sure how to proceed.

"You truly are a wonderfully strange youngling, Mark." Kai said. "If your wish is to give me the responsibility to wield Shura's power, then I accept on behalf of my people and all the souls that dwell in our Raya. I hope I can live up to your judgement of my character."

Imma'Ja studied Mark with a squint of suspicion.

"Is that what Shura told you to do?" She asked. "Is that what is best for the Raya?"

"It's my choice to make." Mark said, facing her with an unflinchingly tranquil gaze.

"Your Majesty," Wynn infused himself into the moment enthusiastically. "with your permission, allow me to take Mark down to his friends at the Slug. Let them enjoy a night in our city before they leave us. We can meet at the Eye as the suns rise. You two will do your little exchange, and send them home with happier memories."

For the first time since Mark had seen him, King Kai had a hopeful smile.

"You would be an honored guest of Maije, Mark." Kai said graciously. "If you don't mind, I would like a few of my guards to keep watch over you. At a reasonable distance, of course. But you are most welcome to enjoy the city's many delights. I hope that in more peaceful times, you will come visit us again. As a cherished friend."

"It would be my pleasure." Mark smiled genuinely.

"Come!" Wynn burst cheerfully, placing a paw on Mark's shoulder and pulling him to the door. "You must tell me how you drank that entire bowl. That was the most pao thing I have ever seen!"

#

Mark followed Wynn through the winding streets of Maije. He noticed a new array of perceptions afforded to him by his powers. He could see the inner workings of reality come alive, celestial lights hidden just below the surface of everything around him. Small mechanisms and exchanges of energy, bringing about creation, change, and destruction at every scale.

Mark watched a blacksmith hammer a bar of heated metal atop a dense anvil. He heard the shriek of the small sailing sparks carving a path through the air. They created wafting currents of warmth, which existed for only fractions of a moment. Mark saw the sweet aromas of baked breads invade the nostrils of a passersby, igniting joy within the slumbering coils of their memories and tugging on their smile.

Mark increasingly noticed the flaws in the details. The countless cracks and broken paths of potential. The dizzying chaos of small colliding destinies. Mark was overwhelmed with the temptation to affect those currents. He wanted to merge everything into a serene flow of shared harmony. The thought disturbed him. This power was a sickness. It connected Mark to all the aspects of reality, but inherently separated him from the world due to his inability to let things simply exist as they were. The wonderous unfolding of natural paths was a faint secondary concern, compared to Mark's surging compulsion to correct all the perceived imperfections.

Mark thought about the curse Shura had placed on his existence. He buried his powers as deep as he could in his mind. Wynn's voice brought Mark back to the moment, as he tried to teach him the local vernacular.

"Do you understand?" Wynn asked jovially, bouncing around the crowd.

"Yeah, we have different words for *Bamba* where I come from though." Mark replied, trying to match the pace of Wynn's dancing strides. "*Kid* might be the closest. And on Earth, I think *cool* is our equivalent of *pao*."

"Teaching you our phrases gives me hope you may return someday to visit." Wynn smiled over his shoulder.

"I'll try." Mark replied, wondering if there was any truth to his words.

"What else do you want to know?" Wynn asked.

Mark thought about what his friends might enjoy learning.

"What's your favorite curse word?" Mark grinned.

"Curse? Like a spell?" Wynn inquired.

"No, like a bad word. Something you say when you're angry or mean." Mark clarified.

"Oh…we don't really value words in terms of good or bad." Wynn furrowed his brow. "Though, I suppose some words have a darker music to them. There are certainly words I wouldn't say in the palace, if that's what you mean? Like *Sagwak*."

Mark's eyebrows rose in perplexed curiosity.

"Sagwak is a blend of a fool and the droppings of a sick animal." Wynn explained.

"That's definitely a new one." Mark chuckled.

"It isn't known in all realms, but careful who you say it to in Maije!" Wynn emphasized.

As Wynn spoke, a small bird fluttered out of his heavy beard, and flew into the night sky with a happy chirp.

"Was that living in there?" Mark chuckled.

"Just visiting for a while." Wynn said.

"They really seem to like you." Mark added.

"It's very mutual." Wynn smiled, glancing at Mark's wings.

"If I could give them to you, I would." Mark said playfully.

"Well how can I know what your powers are capable of?" Wynn groaned.

Mark felt the weight of something unsaid lingering in Wynn's mind.

"Do you think I made the right decision?" He asked.

Wynn kept walking, but his bearing tensed with caution. He was choosing his words.

"We alone have to live with our decisions, Mark." Wynn said. "I'll offer you this advice: I trust those who encourage me to ask questions and find my own path, more than those who feed me their certainties. If someone tells you their way is the only truth, it's usually because they *need* it to be true."

"Thank you, Wynn." Mark nodded. "I think Kai will do good things with these powers."

"King Kai is one of the greatest souls I've ever known." Wynn said. "He gave me a home in this city when I thought I'd never find one. I can't pretend to fully understand the designs at work here, but personally...I trust you to make this decision. My new favorite weird bamba."

Wynn smirked, and pointed ahead of them.

"That's the Slug Tavern right there." Wynn began. He stopped when he noticed Imma'Ja and Payo standing near the entrance. "How did that beautiful sorceress get here before us?" Wynn admired in astonishment.

They watched Payo and Imma'Ja exchange a heartfelt conversation. There seemed to be a strong connection being fostered between them. After a few moments, they embraced and Payo turned to enter the tavern. Imma'Ja saw Mark and Wynn, and smiled at them warmly.

"I'll leave you here, Mark." Wynn mussed Mark's hair. "Your friends are in the Slug. I recommend you spend all of your evening in there! Few places in Maije can compare to the fun of Lady Doseya's tavern of mischiefs." Wynn gestured at a trio of city guards in the distance. "I'll tell them to keep back and not bother you. You don't seem like you're in any danger."

"Thank you, Wynn." Mark said. "It's nice to have a friend here. Even if he is a Sagwak!"

Wynn burst out in a roar of laughter.

"Fast learner." Wynn chuckled, as he walked away.

Mark approached Imma'Ja, who waited patiently by the tavern's entrance. Whatever flickers of hesitations Mark had, he felt them reflected in her silver gaze. He considered unburdening himself, and maybe finding a sanctuary of guidance in her wisdom.

"You can speak freely, Mark." Imma'Ja encouraged. "You'll find no judgements in me."

Mark saw that she was being honest. She genuinely only wished to help.

"I feel…divided." Mark admitted; his composure melting slightly under her radiant compassion. "I know I was chosen to do this. I have a responsibility to this place. But I really think Kai would be a better choice. I just want to get my friends home before things get any worse. I don't know how anyone can make decisions this big."

Imma'Ja placed a hand on Mark's shoulder, and exhaled both their tensions.

"Big decisions or small decisions, you simply choose, Mark." Imma'Ja said. "You walk, and see where the path takes you. There is no wisdom that can safeguard us from our fates. It is only by living that you provide an answer. Every moment and every choice, is an opportunity to recreate yourself. To act towards beauty, towards good, to be braver, more open, and truer to your innermost self. Run from this opportunity, and you may be haunted by regret for the rest of your days. Dive into it, and you may experience great suffering beyond all imagining. No one can make that decision for you, and no one can judge it either."

"I do feel connected to this place." Mark said. "Even if I don't want to be."

"We are all linked to this place, and its shared antiquity." Imma'Ja smiled kindly. "In my realm, we have a word: *Kinotarra*. When loving souls reconnect powerfully, after a long time apart. You have history here, more than you know. But our lives are always about the now. You don't have to be defined by your past. What is the point of time, if not to offer us an opportunity to change?"

"Do you think Kai will use my powers well?" Mark asked hopefully.

"For life to flourish, it needs diversity, change, and evolution." Imma'Ja reflected. "The Void wants there to only be one thing, and Chaos wants everything to change constantly. Control must always mediate between them. Give things their structure, understanding, opportunity to exist, and even help them find their optimal paths. It's terribly *exhausting*."

Mark smiled at her sudden levity.

"Luckily, Kai is experienced with the tiring work of creating balance." Imma'Ja said. "Look at the harmonious beauty of this city. It is largely in thanks to King Kai's designs."

Mark was comforted by her assurances. But a lingering conflict clouded his thoughts.

"Are you afraid of the powers you carry?" Imma'Ja asked.

"Yes." Mark replied honestly.

"Good!" Imma'Ja exclaimed. "In my experience, the fearless tend to also be thoughtless. I see the grace of your decision to give Kai your gifts, and I hope it will mean a more prosperous outcome for us all. But may I offer a suggestion?"

"Of course." Mark said.

"Whatever path you choose to take, do it with your friends." Imma'Ja affirmed. "They will lighten your burdens, and sweeten your victories. The priestesses and I have an expression we abide by: *Together in laughter, alone in reflection.* Solitude may be fitting for deep thoughts or big decisions. But once we walk down our chosen paths, our journeys are always made brighter by the joys of cherished friendships."

Mark thought of the other two Reflections. He didn't know them, but the three of them were bonded to each other in a shared burden and uniquely cursed heritage.

"Imma'Ja…" Mark began, choosing the right words. "…Sal'Haf, Payo, and I. We weren't chosen. We were made by the Primals. To fight this war."

Imma'Ja couldn't hide her surprise at the revelation. She felt a pained sympathy for the plight of the Reflections; and a stern anger for the entities she had revered, knowing they were capable of such cruelty.

"You poor, precious things." Imma'Ja sighed. "There are no words."

"I do hope King Kai can save Sal'Haf rather than destroy him." Mark added.

"Me too." Imma'Ja smiled softly. "I hope there is enough of Sal'Haf left in there to save. It's no easy thing to destroy, Mark. It takes a toll. There is a language of transference. Destroying something ensures a portion of it becomes a part of you. A stain on your soul. I am glad you will be spared that affliction."

"I'm glad you're not mad at me for leaving." Mark said.

"If I'm completely honest, I think you have it within you to do this, Mark." Imma'Ja confessed. "But we must all conquer our own fears. I can sense tremendous change coming to the Raya, and an uncertainty I've never felt before. Any hope I had for you to have a role in the shaping of our future, was based on the kindness in your eyes. I like the way you look at people, and the world around you. There is a beautiful hope in you, undiminished by your ability to see the nature of others."

Imma'Ja paused and focused her tone.

"But to face life's biggest challenges, you must leave behind the doubts which fragment your mind." Imma'Ja asserted. "Fear clouds the soul. You must unleash what lives in the deepest parts of you, and become its master. Fully. To know others is certainly a wisdom…but to know yourself is true enlightenment."

#

A few buildings away, on the terrace of an abandoned temple, a trio of creatures watched Mark and Imma'Ja's exchange. They remained hidden from perception by the whisper shrouds they wore; enchanted cloaks perfectly imitating the surface they leaned upon.

As Mark embraced the Priestess and entered the tavern, the group's leader stepped forward and removed his concealment. The creature's skin was grey and covered in pulsating dark wounds. Its six eyes were glossy black orbs scattered across a bulbous head. It wheezed as it dragged the evening air across its fangs.

It watched.

The creature raised one of its arms, and whispered into a particularly large sore. The wound throbbed with glistening necrotic slime. Slowly, a jagged insect pushed its way through the scab and out into the world. It shook the goop off its body and unfurled a set of wings. With a screech, it took to the skies to carry its message across the night.

19 – TAVERN

Mark was stunned as he entered the tavern's vibrant mayhem. A faint fog of changing colors filled the air. Unusual music coated the space with stretched chords and overlapping harmonies. The crowd swam around each other, dancing, swaying, drinking, cheering, or exploring the room's unique trappings.

Mark saw the ceiling was wholly formed by the giant body of a slithering serpent. It coiled into heavy folds and moving portions, while inexplicably never falling to the ground. The magical creature, which Mark assumed gave the tavern its namesake, was colored in a variety of details. An azure body, with long magenta strikes, vivid shimmers of lilac, and oddly shaped turquoise spots. Those arrangements shifted, and it became apparent the ceiling slug was constantly changing the radiance of its scales. It gave the room an evolving cascade of blooms and pigmentations, which the crowd enjoyed immensely.

Mark spotted Payo's pet Dex, running around the floor between people's feet and barking up at the giant serpent. He saw Naiyana seated at the bar, drinking strange elixirs with a handful of new friends. Bobby emerged from a cluster of people on the dancefloor, impressing the onlookers with the smoothness of his metallic legs. He basked in the attention.

Mark noticed Payo and Elise in the far corner of the room. Mark observed a potent exchange of energy flow between them. Payo was enthusiastically describing something, while Elise stared at her in reverent awe. The limbs and skin on Elise's body transformed into various animal features throughout the conversation.

Mark saw a large bowl filled with peculiar looking fruits on a nearby table. He picked up a bulbous fuchsia orb, flecked with golden dots and jade streaks. The berry felt firm in his hand.

He brought it to his nose and inhaled the syrupy aroma of its succulent skin. Mark took a bite, and felt the surge of rich flavor drown his senses.

As he chewed, he considered how real it all seemed. He supposed that, in some way, it was. All the flesh and fruit of the material plane he longed to return to, was formed of fibers of energy which had slowed enough to form solid matter. Those solidifying bonds were born of the same wavelengths as the light that swam through them; even if they had entwined themselves away from the origins of their celestial ancestors.

Was the shared awareness of the Raya any different?

Mark wondered where these enraptured contemplations came from. He saw that Payo was radiating an aura onto the crowd, enhancing their euphoric daze. Apparently, he had fallen victim to the same cloud of influence.

Mark also noticed she was pushing a few people to the point of mindless exhaustion. He raised a hand, and allowed his fingers to realign the unseen currents floating around him. The room gradually found a calmer pulse. The potency of color and sound reduced, and the frenetic vigor which had filled the tavern's ambiance quelled into a more harmonious atmosphere

Many members of the crowd achieved a sudden clarity that had eluded them. Some whined in disappointment; while others seemed bewildered at the state they had been in, and shuffled to the exit in embarrassment.

Payo noticed Mark's effect, and saw him stood by the door. She smiled, and gestured towards an empty booth. Elise had missed Mark's arrival, and joined Bobby on the dancefloor. Mark joined Payo in the booth, folding his wings to sit on the soft cushioned chairs.

"Must be awkward to move around with those things." Payo offered.

Mark smiled, but the heaviness of his thoughts radiated from his eyes. Payo saw.

"Shura finally found you then." Payo said, her vibrant orange gaze filled with sympathy. "How was it?"

Mark looked Payo over. Her marble skin, braided electric hair, and humming form all exuded power. She seemed unreasonably calm.

"You mean finding out that you, Sal'Haf, and me were created by the Primals to fight in a war we never asked to be a part of?" Mark asked glibly. "That our lives before were all lies?"

"They weren't lies. What a foolish thing to say." Payo scoffed. She looked around, ensuring no one could hear them. "Whenever people ask me how Koba *came to me*, I always tell them different things. I walked into a great fire and my powers awoke, Koba appeared in the sky and struck me with lighting, or some other nonsense. They don't really want to know. They just want to channel their excited imagination onto a story. I couldn't tell anyone else the truth. But between you and me...Koba came to me in a dream."

Mark couldn't help but laugh. "A dream within a dream..."

"...within a dream!" Payo added petulantly. "What does it matter? Each layer is just as real as any other, and I am choosing to be here."

Mark saw she was being sincere, and passionately so. "Aren't you mad at them? For making us this way?" He asked.

"Why would I be mad?" Payo responded. "I always wondered if the Raya was really all there was, especially after my mother died. Now I know I have a deeper history. That my soul comes from somewhere special. It doesn't lessen the love I feel for my parents, or stop me from cherishing this existence."

"But we were made to be weapons." Mark implored, seeking a companion in indignation.

"Who cares?" Payo dismissed. "Creators always think what they make will come out a certain way. But the act of creating means giving life to something else. You can't control what happens after that. And Koba probably understood that better than the other two."

"Did she?" Mark asked, oozing doubt.

"You seem suspicious." Payo tutted. "But after Koba showed me my origins, and awoke my gifts, she told me she trusted me to do whatever I wanted with them. The Primals were born from the same seed as the rest of us. They make mistakes just like anyone. They probably made mistakes when they chose to make us! So, we decide what we do with that power now."

Payo looked around the room, at the intoxicated levity and good cheer.

"I like taverns more than temples." Payo said. "All those worshippers always telling you that the Primals rule over everything, that there's a grand design...now I know why I was always so annoyed by them. They're just coddling their own fear. Hiding in false comfort so they never have to choose a path of their own. They decorate their uncertainty with words like *destiny* and *fate*. But it's all Fik-Umahk. Terrifying doubts they can't bear."

Mark enjoyed the zeal with which she spoke.

"All the mysteries of existence live in every beam of light and in every shadow, Mark." Payo resumed. "Even if we can only see small slivers of it at a time. That's what I'm going to do with my powers after the war: awaken everyone to a full understanding of our shared fire."

Mark couldn't help but admire her. Payo yearned for what lay ahead with such a thirst. He wondered what his ideal outcome would be for the Raya if he were to take part in the conflict. Then his thoughts drifted to the third Reflection.

"What Sal'Haf went through...watching his family die." Mark contemplated. "Only to find this out. That he was created just to suffer. To be a champion in a war between powers that use us like puppets. He could be drowning in an ocean full of monsters we can't even imagine right now. I feel sorry for him."

"I feel sorry for the souls who have to endure his anguish!" Payo replied sternly. "Asha has him trapped in a cocoon of despair. Grasped him in his most painful moment, and coddled him in a dream that tells him none of this is real." Payo gestured all around. "That's how Asha gets him to destroy it. To kill the nightmare that gave him his pain. If Sal'Haf is in there, he is buried deep. With Asha wrapped around him tightly. I can admit, I admire Kai's plan to save him. But I don't think that's how this is going to end."

Mark considered Payo and Sal'Haf's opposing desires. Despite his hatred of Shura, he saw that he was the only Primal seeking a harmonious resolve.

"Why is Shura the only one that wants Sawah?" Mark asked.

"HA!" Payo burst out dismissively. "Don't be naïve. That might be what he told you he wants, but Control can be just as terrible a force of oppression as the careless winds of Chaos, or the cold destruction of the Void." Payo leaned across the table for emphasis. "Imagine a world that never evolves, Mark. Holds onto the familiar with a clutched fear that mistrusts any change. A hatred for new ideas because only the old ones have established history, and can be *relied upon*. Shura is just as much of a slave to his desires as Koba or Asha. He wants the entire Raya carved in images of a lasting peace that he can understand. He beautifies that obsession by calling it Sawah." Payo shook her head in disdain. "A balance born of suffocated stagnation? What kind of victory is that? Control is an expression of the other two Primals and their conflict. It has the best of their qualities, and the worst of their potentials. I don't envy you wielding it."

Mark felt an urge to play with Payo a little before he revealed his intended plan.

"Well of course you'd tell me not to trust the Primal I'm reflecting, you're Koba's loyal warrior." Mark mocked.

"I don't trust Koba." Payo stated plainly, cutting through Mark's coyness. "I'm thankful to her for my gifts, but I will do what I believe is best with them."

There was a cautious pause between them, as they considered each other's role. Payo ran out of patience first.

"So, what you plan to do with it? Control?" Payo tensed. "You joining the fight?"

Mark smiled as he held a moment of silent suspense.

"I'm giving it to someone else." He finally said.

"Giving your powers away?" Payo's eyes filled with astonishment. "I didn't even think that was possible. And I'm supposed to be the one who thinks of new ideas."

They shared a smile of camaraderie, before concern fluttered into Payo's mind.

"Who? You don't know anyone here you can trust, do you?" Payo inquired.

"King Kai." Mark smirked proudly.

"You're not serious?" Payo paled, rambling in annoyance. "Kusashamok, you really want to gift your powers to that old rule worshiper? Aghka, I was just starting to like you. Tachahtom winged bamba duparnok." Payo expelled a frustrated groan. "I really hope that old King doesn't nag me to death before I have a chance to save us all."

Payo slammed her fists onto the table in jest annoyance. She raised one of them in front of Mark, and opened her palm to reveal a swirling fireball raging in her hand. Mark stared at it and, with a few adjustments in his mind, transformed it into a glass statuette of a flower. Payo smiled at him, then dropped the delicate construct onto the table - shattering it.

"You see intricate beauty; I see a suffocating prison." Payo said, looking at the shards of Mark's correction.

"You see the fire of life; I see a burned down tavern!" Mark retorted playfully. "I think King Kai is going to be a good ally for you. You're gonna need his help, and these powers."

"Mark…you don't pay tribute to fire by making art out of its ashes." Payo said, leaning back in her chair. "But don't worry about the Raya. I'll make sure everyone is taken care of here. My mother was a great artist before she died, and my father has an irrational love for all these stupid old kingdoms. So, in tribute to their wonderful, foolish, adorable souls, I promise to spread beauty, love, and life throughout the realms."

"I hope you do." Mark encouraged.

"You know, there's a game where I'm from called *Shinnaro*." Payo grinned wryly. "It's a maze that changes and adapts, trying to prevent you from getting the gemstone in the middle. Nearly impossible to beat. It's meant to teach you not to focus on your competitors in the race, and concentrate instead on improving yourself when faced with increasingly difficult odds. A lesson in grace and composure under pressure, or something stupid. When I got my powers, the Tamat Kingdom asked me to play a big version. *To assess my mind.*"

"How'd you do?" Mark asked.

"I burned the whole thing to the ground and took the gem." Payo smiled.

They both burst into laughter together.

"Of course you did." Mark nodded at his new friend.

"I'm genuinely surprised you're giving up this much power, Mark. We could be godlings here, together…" Payo announced proudly. "…assuming you know your place, of course."

"You really think you have your powers under control?" He asked.

"Controlling Chaos is different than controlling Control. But you do what you believe is best, Mark. Get your friends home safe. I'll take care of the big shadow bamba." Payo assured.

"I'm sure you will, Payo." Mark said.

"Travel well, Mark. It's been...interesting to know you." Payo declared.

Payo got up gracefully, and blew onto the fragments of glass on the table. They soared into the air and transformed into strikingly beautiful insects, that fluttered in escapes out the nearest windows. Payo walked to the bar and ordered something to drink.

Elise and Bobby spotted Mark in the booth, and ran over. They grabbed Naiyana by her arm on the way. She seemed wobbly on her feet, and wore a delirious smirk.

"Mark! Holy crap how awesome is this place?" Elise yammered.

The three friends squeezed into the booth around Mark.

"Move your wings, stupid." Naiyana burped, shuffling up next to Mark.

"Is she ok?" Mark asked.

"I think she's drunk." Elise beamed proudly. "It kinda suits her."

"Dude, what happened up there? Did you guys figure it out? Can we go home?" Bobby stampeded through his questions.

"It's a lot to explain. This place, it isn't another dimension, or maybe in a way it is." Mark began, before hesitating. He wanted to ensure his friends wouldn't feel detached from their lives back on Earth. "This place is kind of like a dream, for everyone in the galaxy. All of our minds, or souls, are connected to it. Not just people. Stars, animals, and other stuff too. Any kind of energy really. It all shares a common imagination here. Where we can affect each other."

"Oh my god, so Elise's mom was right about all that yoga spirit crap?" Bobby uttered.

"This place is like a shared experience of what's happening to all the energy in the galaxy." Mark tried to simplify. "It's like the hidden dream of everything, if that makes sense."

"Woah." All three of them muttered.

"I'll try to explain everything better when we get back." Mark offered, hoping the distance from the Raya would blur the details in their memory. "But the good news is I can get us home. I can use my powers to open the Eye and..."

"Told you!" Bobby blurted out.

"Shut up." The girls yelled.

"After I open the Eye, I'll give my powers to King Kai so he can use them. It's the right thing to do." Mark announced. "But we'll just walk into the Eye, and be right back on Earth."

"We'll be alive?" Naiyana asked bluntly. "What if you bring our...souls back or whatever, from this galaxy dream, but our bodies are dead from falling in Echo lake? Are we gonna be zombies? I don't wanna be a zombie."

"Please drink some water." Bobby rolled his eyes.

"I think if our bodies were dead, we wouldn't be here resembling ourselves so much." Mark tried to formulate an assurance he wasn't certain he believed. "Or maybe we'll just get sent right back here, so it's still worth a try. Before I fell under the ice, I saw people running towards the lake. They could have pulled us out in time!"

"Oh shit." Elise said in sudden realization. "Sebastian and his asshole friends."

The group winced in collective shame at having forgotten.

"I don't think they could make it back, Elise." Mark said candidly. "You remember their skin? They looked like they were rotting, and they never woke up...I think they're gone."

The group sat in still silence for a moment.

"Well, I'm voting we go home as soon as we can." Bobby said. "Whatever's waiting for us there, it's gotta be safer than a dreamworld full of monsters and war."

"Yeah," Naiyana said, wiping her mouth with her sleeve. "But this place is pretty magic."

Mark noticed Elise being uncharacteristically quiet. "What were you and Payo talking about?" He asked her. Elise snapped out of her daze and smiled at Mark.

"She said there's a great power in me, and that others will fear it. But I shouldn't let that stop me from growing its potential." Elise boasted. "She said I was a goddess."

Elise's eyes were filled with swooning admiration as she stared at Payo across the room. Naiyana wore a perturbed grimace, and let out another burp.

"Can you two get it together?" Bobby groaned.

"When we get back to Earth, are we gonna remember this place?" Naiyana asked.

"How could we ever forget it?" Elise said. "Not that anyone's gonna believe us."

"I think we'll remember." Mark assured. "But it'll seem less real. Like a regular dream."

"Think we can ever come back?" Elise asked excitedly.

"Maybe." Mark smiled. "But for now, let's just enjoy tonight."

A server arrived carrying a tray of elixir concoctions in bizarrely shaped glass vessels. He used his eight thin arms to place them all over the table's surface. Naiyana's eyes lit up.

"Ohhh, you guys should try the blue one that looks like a three-headed piglet." She said.

"Courtesy of your friend." The server added, gesturing to the door.

The group saw Payo standing by the exit. She took a bow, and blew them a kiss goodbye, before strolling outside. Dex soon noticed her absence, and began to angrily yap and bark around the tavern searching for Payo. He heard a loud whistle outside, and vanished in a puff of purple smoke.

20 – PASSAGE

The children followed Wynn up the hill, bathed in the soft warmth of three rising suns. They were still radiating happiness from their festivities the night before, supplemented by the knowledge they would soon be returning home. The buildings across Maije looked stunning, their stones awash in overlapping sunbeams.

Bobby looked ahead in eager anticipation, Elise stared down at the city in a reluctant gaze of fond farewell, and Naiyana buzzed with an easy feeling of closeness to her friends she had never felt. She leaned into Mark, who embraced her with an arm and a wing around her shoulder. As they arrived at the crest of the hill, they saw King Kai surrounded by a large crowd of at least one hundred citizens clustered around the outer rim of the courtyard.

"Woah." Bobby muttered, surprised by the crowd.

"It seems the rumors have already flown." Wynn said, with an assuring smile.

The crowd stomped their feet and cheered as the children approached. King Kai raised a hand for quiet.

"Citizens of Maije, please welcome Elise, Bobby, Naiyana, and Mark!" Kai announced.

A louder roar of cheers and foot stomps filled the air. The children smiled shyly under all the attention, and awkwardly meandered towards the Eye at the center of the crowd. King Kai stood beside it, and knelt down to greet them. He placed a hand on his heart, and bowed his head in deep gratitude. The children all imitated the gesture. Mark sensed something disturbing flutter through the crowd, but was distracted from it when he realized everyone was staring at him.

He took a couple of breaths, and composed himself as he faced the large orb of blue fire. Mark's four wings spread in wide curves as he raised both hands and aimed them at the Eye. The crowd grew intensely quiet as they watched Mark close his eyes in concentration.

Mark opened his mind fully, and allowed the powers he wielded to flow through him. He cultivated a strong bond with the Eye, and began to conjure a complex arrangement of sacred runes that manifested throughout the sphere's blue radiance. The symbols interlocked and swirled around each other, as the Eye took on a blended silver-blue coloration. Turning something hidden within the large orb's nature, Mark unlocked a solidified connection. The Eye pulsated a powerful wave of sound. Everyone gasped in awe, as the energy washed over them.

"It's ready." Mark said, turning to his friends.

"Dude." Bobby muttered. "This is the coolest you have ever been!"

Bobby, Elise, and Naiyana shuffled towards the Eye's radiance, and stopped just beside it waiting for Mark to join them. Mark approached King Kai's kneeling form, and tried to ignore the wide-eyed crowd staring at them in a trance of anticipation. He reached out and placed one of his fingers on the weathered blue skin of Kai's forehead.

"This might hurt a little." Mark said.

"A small price to pay." Kai replied, encouraging him to proceed.

Mark took a deep breath, and closed his eyes. He took hold of the powers resting within him, uprooting their entanglement around his soul. The rips and tears of the countless bonds caused his mind great discomfort. But the pain was subdued by a strong desire to proceed. Mark poured the power towards Kai, layering it over the shape of the King's soul. Allowing it to tether itself to his spirit and awareness. Mark heard Kai groan in great pain, but it seemed distant. The process was just beginning to take on a harmonious flow, when Mark sensed a terrible shift.

"No..." He managed to mutter, as the fear of a cold dread sank into him.

A massive explosion roared from the city below. Mark's transfer was interrupted as everyone turned to gaze down at Maije. A ferocious monstrosity was attacking Maije's gates, ramming its vast body onto and clawing the large stone walls. It looked three times bigger than the beast that had attacked them. Mark saw a large moving pool of black smoke sail across the golden field facing Maije. With another thunderous clap, the dark fog spewed out another enormous creature. The second monster charged to join the attack.

King Kai rose to his feet in shock. Before he could command his guards to take action, three cloaked figures pushed through the surrounding crowd and began screeching as they hurled small black spheres all over the courtyard. The orbs rapidly exploded in violent powerful bursts of black shards. Onlookers were sent hurtling backwards in the detonations, and suffered deep laceration from the sharp fragments.

Mark saw his friends standing by the Eye. It had turned a dark grey color, as its fires schismed under the ongoing assault of violent blasts. Bobby braced against the discharges, trying to block any flying fragments with his metallic legs. Elise created huge bear claws with thick fur which she used to shield her friends, while Naiyana formed a shield wall of ice that kept shattering. Mark rushed over to help them, and saw a black orb hurled at their feet. He raised his hand to try to contain it, but the force of the detonation sent all four of them flying into the Eye.

Mark watched a tunnel of grey energy envelop him as he was pulled into a cold vortex. Maije's hilltop disappeared into a faint pinpoint above him, as he fell backwards into a violent torrent. He saw his friends screaming in fear as they plummeted beside him, but he couldn't hear their yells over the deafening surge of ferocious roaring winds.

It sounded like the tunnel itself was shrieking in a rumbling rage. Mark felt a suffocating pressure grow around him. In an instant, Mark knew he was sensing Prince Sal'Haf's unique presence in the tide that pulled them. The Void watched them hurtle to their despair, terror emptying them of any hope.

Mark reached out his hands, and tried to create an insulation to envelope his friends. An oval of light formed around them, pulling them together into the sanctuary. It encapsulated them in a shared sphere that continued to fall rapidly towards a bottomless doom. A furious bolt of dark energy crashed into the sphere and shattered it. It sent all four friends flying away from each other against the walls of the vortex.

Mark watched each of them collide against the dark grey prism, get absorbed in a crash of colorful lights, and disappear down their own branch of oblivion. He had lost sight of all of them. Just as he felt the last shred of hope leave his mind, Mark was devoured by the storm, swallowed into darkness, and spat out into the beyond.

CONTINUED IN PART II...

AUTHOR'S NOTE & ACKNOWLEDGEMENTS

Countless friends and family members helped me along this journey to complete my first novel.

There's a unique affliction that many writers suffer from, where the moment they put a thought down on paper it takes on a strange outer-body quality to it. The idea becomes almost unrecognizable as the writer's own thoughts. Reading old words you've written can oftentimes sound like a stranger reciting their poetry.

I've been writing this book, in one form or another, for years. It's been with me as an idea throughout countless moments of my own growth. I can barely begin to describe what it feels like, emotionally, to put it to page and part with it by sending it off into the world - after having kept it safeguarded within me all this time.

It's like ripping a band-aid off, but in this particular case pulling from the oldest and deepest parts of me, and at an agonizingly slow pace. This world that I've created was something that for so long was a secret sanctuary utterly familiar only to me, but now to some degree can no longer be a part of me, because it's been exorcized from my mind. It needs to exist out there...meeting other people, having conversations. Living a life altogether on its own.

This process is akin to birthing a portion of yourself into a new form. There is a loss, a hope, a farewell and a future, but more than anything a legacy of things your soul used to feel...things your mind used to wonder.

Everyone should write their own bible. This is mine.

I would also like to thank the following talented artists for their contributions to the completion of this novel:

Alexandra Rubinstein – Cover Art
Gille Klabin – Cover Effects
Robin Scheines - Illustrations